INTO THE JAWS OF A SAVAGE GOD

Gray was sliding down a gravity well, as though he were being funneled straight toward the wildly rotating cylinder ahead.

Somehow, he realized, the Sh'daar had compressed a medium-sized star into a hollow cylinder a kilometer across and twenty long. Something didn't add up. Beings that could create this thing weren't merely good magicians. They were *gods*, or the closest thing to gods mere humans could imagine.

Gray's fighter, falling free, was accelerating, moving faster and faster as the maw of the cylinder yawned ahead, the opening empty and utterly lightless.

Fifty more seconds, at this rate, and he would be drawn inside.

If the Sh'daar possessed such power, they didn't need to rely on the Turusch or their other subject species.

Why fight this protracted war for almost forty years, when such technology could wipe Humankind out of existence with scarcely a thought?

By Ian Douglas

SINGULARITY

STAR CARRIER

BOOK THREE

IAN DOUGLAS

HARPER Voyager

An Imprint of HarperCollinsPublishers

This is a work of fiction. Names, characters, places, and incidents are products of the author's imagination or are used fictitiously and are not to be construed as real. Any resemblance to actual events, locales, organizations, or persons, living or dead, is entirely coincidental.

HARPER Voyager

An Imprint of HarperCollins*Publishers*
10 East 53rd Street
New York, New York 10022-5299

Copyright © 2012 by William H. Keith, Jr.
Cover art by Gregory Bridges
ISBN 978-0-06-184027-2
www.harpervoyagerbooks.com

First Harper Voyager mass market printing: March 2012

Harper Voyager and ⟩ is a trademark of HCP LLC.

Printed in the U.S.A.

10 9 8 7 6 5 4 3 2 1

For Deb,
whose science is about as hard as it comes

SINGULARITY

Prologue

5 April 2405

Ad Astra Confederation Government Complex
Geneva, European Union
1450 hours, local time

It's not possible to torture a piece of software. Not even an intelligent one.

Not that artificial intelligences possess anything like the civil rights of humans. With no rights to violate, the Internal Affairs interrogators could take the AI apart almost literally line by coded line, searching for hidden files or withheld memories.

The software avatar's *prototype*, as its human object was known in the electronic intelligence business, had recorded a sizable amount of his own character, thoughts, and motivation within his AI counterparts. It was always possible that thoughts, memories—even entire histories—had slipped through from the fuzzy logic and holographic analog perceptions of the organic brain to a far simpler silicon-based digital format. This particular prototype was Admiral Alexander Koenig, and he worked closely with his AI personal assistant.

He had, in fact, developed what amounted to an emotional relationship with it, deliberately programming it with

the personal characteristics—voice, thought patterns, judg-
ment, the simulacra appearance, and so on—of his lover,
Karyn Mendelson, killed during the battle to save Earth's
solar system just over six months earlier.

The primary software resided inside Koenig's head,
within the nanochelated implants in the twisting folds and
furrows of the sulci of his brain. It served as his PA, or personal assistant, a kind of electronic secretary that could
handle routine calls and virtual meetings, could so perfectly mimic Koenig's appearance, voice, and mannerisms
that callers could not tell whether they were speaking to
the human or to the human-mimicking software. However,
more than a month before, shortly after the Battle of Alphekka, Rear Admiral Koenig had copied his PA software,
uploading it into one of the HAMP-20 Sleipnir-class mail
packets carried as auxiliaries on board most of the ships of
the fleet. Almost three times faster than the best possible
speed for a capital ship under Alcubierre FTL Drive, they
were used to carry high-velocity express communications
across interstellar distances.

It had been this copied software that had piloted the most
recent mail packet from Alphekka back to Earth.

And multiple copies of this copy were running inside
the computers of the Naval Department of Internal Affairs, completely isolated from the outside world, electronic
iterations that could be taken apart, tested to destruction,
electronically shredded and pulled through a metaphorical
sieve, in search of possible traces of Koenig's thoughts.

Karyn Mendelson possessed within her coded matrix
a very great deal of both the original Mendelson and of
Koenig himself. And it was the Koenig analog in which the
Internal Affairs officers were most interested.

"Anything?" one shadowy figure asked the other. They
were deep in the nuke-shielded lower levels beneath the
ConGov pyramid, perhaps three kilometers down and well
out under the placid-mirrored waters of Lake Geneva itself.

"No," the other said. He gestured vaguely at a wallscreen,

which showed a graphic representing progress so far. There'd been very little. "This is going to take a while."

"What are you trying?"

"Incoming call iterations. It's cycling through at almost a million per second now."

The first IA programmer gave a low whistle. "He's got the top-of-the-line model, huh?"

"He's a freakin' rear admiral, fer Chrissakes. What did you expect?"

Within the computer in the console in front of them, a subroutine was emulating real life for the admiral—but at a vastly accelerated rate. A copy of his PA software was fielding incoming vid calls as Koenig, very quickly indeed. Eventually, the orderly presentation of the program would begin to break down, and other watchdog routines would snatch at what amounted to electronic shrapnel, saving it for later analyses.

They'd already destroyed a dozen copies of the PA software . . . but there were plenty more, and more could be created easily enough if these ran out.

And abruptly, the emulation stopped.

"What the hell happened?"

"Dunno. And what's *that*?"

On the large screen, a woman in a black Confederation naval uniform looked down at them. "Who are you?" she demanded. "What are you doing to me?"

One of the interrogators gave her a cool appraisal. "You're Mendelson?" he asked.

The screen image morphed into Koenig, also in naval uniform, and looking angry. "This is the personal assistant of Rear Admiral Alexander Koenig," it said. "And attempting to hack private PA software *is* illegal."

"Department of Internal Affairs," the interrogator replied. "We have authorization."

"To do what? And by *whose* authority?"

The interrogator showed the AI behind the screen image his security code level. Possibly they could get what they needed by asking directly, *if* they could enlist the AI's co-operation.

"We are trying to get a lead on where Admiral Koenig is taking CBG-18," he said. "It is vital that we get in touch with him, and we'd hoped you might be able to help."

"I was . . . *he* was at Alphekka when I was downloaded into a *Sleipnir*-class packet," Koenig's face said. "I have no idea what has happened with the fleet since I left it for Earth."

A copy of a copy, its memories had been copied as well. It would think that it was the original electronic duplicate placed in the mail packet.

"You brought with you a list of over two hundred possible targets," the interrogator said. "We think he must be headed for one of those. Can you tell us which one that might be?"

"No," the electronic image on the screen said. "If Admiral Koenig had wanted you to know, I feel sure he would have told you in his final report."

And as suddenly as Koenig's image had appeared, it was gone, dissolving into a shrill hiss of white noise.

"Damn."

"What happened?"

"The software . . . killed itself," the interrogator said. "Electronic suicide."

"It can't kill itself if it's not alive to begin with."

But the interrogator wasn't certain of that. Other iterations of Koenig's software had switched themselves off when they'd discovered that he was tampering with them.

He loaded another copy.

"We'll try again," he said. "But I have a feeling it's going to be a long night. . . ."

Koenig's electronic persona seemed determined not to cooperate, and he could not figure out how to get past the program's guardian aspect.

The interrogator was very good at what he did.

There *had* to be a way to break the thing. . . .

Chapter One

In Alcubierre Space
Approaching HD 157950
98 light years from Earth
0840 hours, TFT

The star carrier *America* fell through darkness absolute.

Intense, artificially generated gravitational fields warped space tightly around the *America*, and no light could enter from the universe outside. While material objects like a spacecraft could not travel faster than light, there was no such prohibition about space. Indeed, in the earliest moments of the big bang, over 13 billion years before, newly born space had expanded with that initial burst of energy from two colliding branes considerably in excess of *c*.

And a ship embedded within that swiftly moving space could be carried along inside the gravitationally closed bubble at a pseudovelocity of nearly two light years per day.

America and her battlegroup had been traveling through the darkness within their separate bubbles for sixty-three days, now. And they were very nearly at the end of the first leg of their voyage.

Rear Admiral Alexander Koenig, the battlegroup's CO, was seated in *America*'s command lounge. The room, broad and circular, projected the surrounding vista across the gently curved overhead when the ship was in normal space, showing the unmoving panorama of stars outside. Within the confines of metaspace, however, the interior of the fast-moving bubble of enclosed space-time, the lightless Void was at arm's length. Currently, it was displaying the blue, cloud-scattered skies of Earth.

Two men appeared in the lounge entryway. "You wanted to see us, Admiral?"

Captain Randolph Buchanan was *America*'s commanding officer, tall, long-faced, with perpetual worry lines. Captain Barry Wizewski was the CO of the star carrier's space-fighter wing commander, her CAG—an ancient acronym derived from "Commander, Air Group."

"I did. C'mon in."

"Staying off the record, sir?" Wizewski said, smiling.

"Yes, actually. I don't expect to salvage my career after this, but I'll be damned if I'll give them the rope to hang me . . . or anything on the record to drag *you* into this."

Anything discussed on either *America*'s main bridge or her flag bridge was recorded, as were conversations in the Admiral's Office and all other working compartments on board ship. Virtual meetings held in-head were recorded as well by the ship AIs responsible for moderating all electronic communications.

"You're doing the right thing, Admiral," Buchanan told him, taking one of the low, round seats opposite Koenig.

"Thanks, Randy. But we both know the Senate's never going to stand for this kind of insubordination. They can't, not without looking like they're not in control."

"The *Confederation* Senate, no," Buchanan replied. "Things may be different in Columbus, D.C."

"Maybe. But it's Geneva that's calling the shots, and Columbus will have to go along."

Koenig had never been entirely comfortable with his position as commanding officer of a Confederation Star Navy battlegroup. The star carrier *America* and her crew were

USNA—the United States of North America—but they'd been reassigned along with most of the other ships of CBG-18 to the service of the Terran Confederation.

The problem, Koenig thought wryly, was that while the majority of Confederation naval officers—including the Joint Chiefs of Staff—were USNA citizens, the majority of the Confederation's politicians were not. It was the Pan-Europeans, the Empire of Brazil, the South American EAS, the North India Federation, and others who were determining Confed policy in Geneva. Those nation-states that tended to support the USNA's initiatives in the war with the Sh'daar were badly outnumbered—Russia, the off-world colonies, and Japan.

There were times when he was forced to walk an extremely narrow path between his oath to the Confederation . . . and his allegiance to the USNA.

"We're . . . what?" he said. "Ten hours out from Emergence?"

"Yes, sir," Buchanan replied.

"We don't know if Giraurd followed us."

"We don't need him," Wizewski said. "The USNA reinforcements are solidly with us. I think the Chinese are too."

"I'm not worried about that," Koenig said. "If the Pan-Europeans followed us from Alphekka, they might try to force the issue when we emerge."

Buchanan nodded. "Giraurd didn't seem all that happy when you told him off."

"No. And his orders are to bring us back. But . . . I'm not ready to do that yet. We haven't finished what we've started."

"Do you expect a fight, Admiral?" Wizewski asked.

"It's at least a possibility. And we need to be ready, just in case. No matter what Giraurd decides to do."

"If he was smart," Buchanan said, "he turned around and headed back to Earth to report. Tell them that we weren't playing nice."

"His orders might not allow that," Koenig replied. "In fact, he may be under orders to take us under fire if we refuse to go back. He was certainly threatening as much when we started accelerating out-system from Alphekka."

"Threats," Wizewski said. "Blusters and bluff."

"Maybe. But, as I said, I want to be prepared for anything. CAG, I'm going to have you put everything we have into space as soon as we emerge. We'll pass the word to the other carriers to do the same as soon as we've re-established contact. Randy? I want you to make sure *America* stays well clear of the Pan-Europeans if and when they emerge. Don't let them sidle up close for a conference. Don't allow them to send over small craft to discuss things. And be ready to put out a warning shot if they do try to force their way inside our primary defensive zone."

"Yes, sir."

Koenig looked at Wizewski. "CAG? How are the reorganized squadrons shaping up?"

"Not as good as I'd like, Admiral. The new recruits have been training hard on the sims, but that won't haul much mass when they hit the real thing."

Koenig nodded. *America*'s squadrons had taken fearsome losses at Alphekka; one had been reduced to just three fighters.

"I hope to God they don't get their baptism of fire against humans," he said. "But if it's a matter of guaranteeing the safety of this carrier . . ."

"They'll do what they have to, Admiral. They all will. I don't think *any* of them care all that much for the Confederation, when it comes to that. Their loyalty is to the USNA, to America, to you and me, to their buddies. . . . Hell, I think Geneva comes in somewhere *way* down on the list. Fiftieth or sixtieth, maybe."

"I want you to impress on the squadron leaders, CAG, that their squadrons will not open fire on human ships unless they receive a direct and confirmed order from you. Understand?"

"Yes, sir."

"If there's a diplomatic way to resolve this, I'm going to

take it. The last thing I want is to add a *civil* war to the war we already have."

"I understand, Admiral."

"I know you do. See to it that they understand as well."

There was little more that could be said.

Koenig dismissed the two of them, and returned to his brooding thoughts.

Star Chamber
Ad Astra Confederation Government Complex
Geneva, European Union
0950 hours, TFT

President Regis DuPont hated the place. It felt so exposed . . . so *empty*.

Well . . . it was filled with stars, of course, but somehow that made it even worse.

The star chamber was a planetarium and more, *much more*—an immense sphere a hundred meters across, the inner surface designed to project imagery relayed from the big astrogational complex at Bern. Near stars were shown scattered across the interior space, scattered through three dimensions; more distant stars and the glowing, ragged lacework of the Milky Way were projected against the curving inner surfaces.

Followed closely by a small knot of people, his personal security detachment and presidential aides, DuPont walked out onto the narrow catwalk leading to the viewing platform suspended at the sphere's center. The others were waiting for him there already, a dozen Confederation senators in civilian dress, their shoulders and sleeves heavy with the gold and silver brocade, aiguillettes, medals, and intertwining decorations that declared their importance.

There were no military officers present, though, and DuPont wondered why.

For that matter, he didn't see any senators with military

experience—or any representing outworld colonies, like Andrews or Kristofferson.

Sometimes it was possible to judge which way the political winds were blowing by noting who was present . . . or absent.

"Mr. President," Senator Eunice Noyer said, nodding. "Thank you for coming."

"Why *here*?" he asked. "Why not at ConGov?"

"Because," Noyer said, "the *America* Battlegroup could pose a problem. We're trying to determine just where Koenig is going now."

"Surely that's something the Confederation Military Directorate could advise you on," DuPont said. "The Joint Chiefs, I gather, have been following Koenig's campaign with great interest."

Noyer made a face. "*They're* no help. Not to us."

"They may well be in collusion with one another," Senator Sheehan added. "Carruthers wasn't supposed to send Koenig reinforcements. He was *supposed* to order Koenig to return to Earth."

"The military," Senator Galkin pointed out, "is no longer trustworthy. Carruthers and his cronies need to be reined in, reined in hard. Too much is riding on this. The safety of Earth, of all of Humankind, is at stake."

"So?" DuPont said with a Gallic shrug. "Where is the battlegroup now?"

"We don't know for sure." Noyer told him. "CBG-18 has left Alphekka . . . but it's not returning to Earth. According to Giraud's report, the CBG is heading for a nondescript star called HD 157950." The red line drew itself from Alphekka across the sky to the right, touching another star, a dim one. "Ninety-eight light years from Earth. One hundred fourteen light years from Alphekka."

"That's not on the Directory," DuPont said. "What's there?"

"Nothing, so far as we know. It may be that he intends to take on reaction mass there. Likely it is a waypoint, with the final destination somewhere . . . farther out."

Senator Lloyd gestured, and a red beam of light drew

itself out from the observation platform, connecting with
one of the near stars—a golden-orange sun gleaming at the
base of the constellation of Boötis. "On January seventh," he
said in a lecture-hall monotone, "the battlegroup leaves Fleet
Rendezvous Percival—Pluto orbit—and does so apparently
after learning from an incoming mail packet that the Sh'daar
had taken Osiris, at Seventy Ophiuchi." A fainter star well
off to the group's left flashed bright white. "The battlegroup
proceeds to Arcturus, thirty-six light years from Earth,
where it engages the ships of several of the Sh'daar client
races and rescues a number of human prisoners of war, at
Arcturus Station."

"The plan," DuPont said, "was to raid deep into Sh'daar
space, perhaps forcing the Sh'daar to pull back, at least to
delay them."

"Indeed," Senator Suvarov said. "There was talk of raid-
ing Eta Boötis after Arcturus. The two are only a few light
years apart."

"Instead," Noyer said, "Koenig leads his fleet all the way
across to *here*." Another star, somewhat above and to the left
of Arcturus and twice as far away, lit up as the red line connected them. "Alphekka. Seventy-two light years away. If the
report is to be believed, he engaged a much larger Sh'daar
client force and destroyed a moon-sized construction facility.
At this point, he has a large percentage of our defensive fleet
engaged seventy-two light years away . . . while the Sh'daar
remain at Osiris, just sixteen light years from Sol. *Sixteen
light years!* The enemy could be here at any moment!"

"Well . . . it's been . . . what? Six weeks since the Battle
of Alphekka?" DuPont said. "And the Sh'daar have not ma-
terialized in Earth orbit yet. Perhaps Koenig's plan to draw
them off is working."

"Perhaps," Noyer said. She gestured, and the star map
around them vanished. "But this is what Admiral Koenig
has been doing in the meantime. . . ."

DuPont squeezed his eyes shut, then slowly opened them
again. The three-dimensional representation was worse than

an in-head download, because the brain accepted it as being *out there*, not within the visual cortex. Vertigo tugged at the president's sense of balance, and he put a hand out to steady himself on the viewing platform's safety railing.

A brilliant double spark of a sun hung at the center of a vast and somewhat hazy disk with an interior void—a disk of protoplanetary debris orbiting the A0V/G5V double star of Alphekka. With a disconcertingly swift motion, the view shifted down and in, rushing toward a pinpoint that appeared near the inner edge of the debris field.

Confederation Navy warships were passing a large alien structure—the roughly egg-shaped facility designated A1-01. DuPont watched an immense black mushroom shape with a slender, elongated stem drift past the far larger alien structure, beams of intolerably brilliant blue-white light stabbing out, striking the moon-sized artificial planetoid and plowing deep molten furrows into its outer shell. Thermonuclear explosions strobed and flashed and blossomed across the structure, dazzling multi-megaton pulses sparkling against and within A1-01 as fusion warheads homed and detonated in eerie and absolute silence.

An alien warship, minute against the artificial planetoid, was struck by a beam and began to crumple and spin, its mass folding up unevenly into the black hole that powered it. A flash of hard radiation, and it was gone. . . .

DuPont was sweating as the simulation played itself out. It *was* a simulation, of course, and not an actual visual record. He'd read transcripts of Koenig's after-action report, and downloaded some of the visuals. The human fleet, in reality, had flashed past A1-01 in the blink of an eye, the weapons served entirely by AIs that could process incoming data far more rapidly than organic systems. The images Noyer was projecting had been concocted from the original after-action data by the AIs in Bern.

But the realism and sharpness of the projection's detail left DuPont's heart pounding, his head swimming.

He tightened his grip on the railing.

"The battle at Alphekka," Noyer said, "was a splendid success. Our intelligence services—the ONI in particular—are convinced that we have sent a *powerful* message to the Sh'daar. One that cannot possibly be misinterpreted. It is now time to bring the task force home."

"We dispatched Grand Admiral Giraurd to Alphekka with reinforcements," Senator Lloyd said, "with orders that the fleet immediately return to Earth. Evidently he arrived shortly after . . . all of *this*." Lloyd waved a hand, taking in the chaos of thermonuclear fury and high-energy-charged particle beams surrounding the group of senators and aides standing on the observation platform.

"Seventy-two light years is a forty-day journey for our ships," DuPont pointed out. "They would only now be approaching Sol, even if Koenig turned back immediately after the Battle of Alphekka. And he would have needed time to effect repairs on his fleet."

"But a mail packet can make the same voyage in two weeks," Senator Galkin reminded him. "And one arrived in Earth orbit four weeks ago, delivering Koenig's report on the Battle of Alphekka. A message from Giraurd announces that Koenig is continuing his original mission, that he is headed for HD 157950. No word of Giraurd's plans. He may not have known himself at the time. No word of where Koenig is planning on taking the fleet beyond HD 157950. Mr. President, we are completely in the dark. A quarter of Earth's fleet is somewhere out well beyond the farthest limits of human space, and we have no idea where it is or where it is going!"

DuPont couldn't help smiling at that. "That *does* sound like Alexander Koenig."

Months ago, before the battlegroup had left Earth, members of the Senate Military Directorate had approached DuPont with the suggestion—the *order*, actually—that he retire from the presidency of the Confederation Senate so that Koenig, the Hero of the Defense of Earth, could be voted into the office instead.

The political union known as the Terran Confederation was not a simple or straightforward democracy, despite what the media and the history downloads would have you believe. More than six hundred senators represented much of Humankind—though the Chinese Hegemony, the Muslim Theocracy, the Peripheries, and a few other smaller groups were not yet represented out of the turbulent, squalling billions of Earth's population. Perhaps two hundred represented off-world colonies, near worlds like Luna and Mars, more distant out-solar ones like Chiron and Osiris. The president of the Confederation Senate generally was chosen from among the Senate proper by his or her peers, and held the position for six years . . . but a constitutional crisis, a vote of no confidence, even just the *threat* of impeachment could recall a Senate president and have him replaced by another. Beneath the democratic exterior, the Confederation government was a dense and labyrinthine tangle of alliances, promises, secret agreements, mutual back scratchings, and outright vote buying, to the point where very few bills actually reached the Senate floor without the vote's outcome already being known.

DuPont was nearing the end of his term, and frankly, he was going to be happy to step down.

He'd long been aware that certain power blocks within the Senate were planning on replacing him with Koenig. The only question had been whether it would be at the end of the year . . . or immediately.

The idea, he'd been told, was to put Koenig where the man could be watched and controlled. Koenig was dangerous politically, a loose cannon who could do untold damage to that labyrinth of political entanglements. His leadership at the Defense of Earth had saved the Earth from annihilation and the people loved him, which might make him ambitious. More problematic, there were also logistical considerations. The farther out from Earth Koenig voyaged, the tougher it was to maintain even a semblance of control over him and his force. Better to bring him home and make him president—a position where he could be effectively managed.

Koenig, however, seemed to be playing by an entirely different set of rules. He'd turned down the presidency, pushing instead his extended operations plan, which he called Crown Arrow, an extended carrier battlegroup raid deep into enemy space. Koenig, DuPont thought, just might be one of those utter rarities—a man of absolute integrity who simply could not be bought.

No wonder the Conciliationists within the Senate were in a state of panic.

"So why have you brought me down here?" DuPont asked. "*I* don't know what Koenig is doing. No more than you do."

"You can," Noyer told him, "sign an executive order directing Koenig to *immediately* relinquish command to Giraurd, and to return home. CBG-18 is under the direct control of the Senate, not the Navy. When he disobeys the Senate Military Directorate, he's guilty of dereliction of duty. If he disobeys you, your direct order, it's treason."

"And how do we get the order to him?" DuPont asked. "If we don't know where the fleet is, or where it is going?"

"Through a small fleet of mail packets," Suvarov told him. As he spoke, the 3-D star map returned, this time with bright blue points of light scattered among the stars. "AI piloted. We have the Alphekkan Directory, after all, as well as copies of his avatar. And we can guess what targets might be of particular interest to him."

"Ah."

The Alphekkan Directory had been included with Koenig's after-action report. It was a list taken from the wreckage of the immense alien space-going factory designated A1-01, including more than two hundred star systems in the general vicinity of Sol that were of interest, in one way or another, to the Turusch, a major Sh'daar client race. Those systems were pinpointed now in blue on the map. A few were relatively close—the nearest perhaps a hundred light years from Earth.

The rest . . .

The trouble was that the term "general vicinity of Sol" was misleading, at least from the human perspective. Until Koenig had taken CBG-18 beyond the boundaries of human space, no human, no human ship, had ever ventured farther than sixty-some light years from Earth.

And one of the places listed in the recovered directory was almost certainly the Lagoon Nebula . . . some five thousand light years away.

Five *thousand* light years. A battle fleet leaving Earth at the best possible interstellar velocity would take more than seven years to get there. DuPont shook his head. If Noyer and the other Conciliationists were unhappy at the problems of command and control of a fleet at Alphekka, a mere seventy-two light years out, how would they deal with a distance seventy times greater?

Such inconceivable gulfs of space.

That, DuPont thought, was what he disliked most about this place, this simulation of nearby interstellar space in a presentation guaranteed to put Humankind in its place. The Terran Confederation was a wood chip adrift on the galactic sea . . . a few hundred populated worlds against . . . how many within the Sh'daar alliance? A million? A *hundred* million?

No one knew. What *was* known was that the Sh'daar dominated such a vast swath of the galaxy, that they controlled so many technic civilizations, that the Terran Confederation's chance of victory in this lopsided war were exactly zero. For the past decade there'd been pervasive rumors that human states not yet members of the Confederation—the Chinese or the Islamic Theocracy in particular—might be hoping to cut a separate peace with the Sh'daar.

Hence the political grouping within the Confederation Senate unofficially known as the Conciliationists. Defeat by the Sh'daar Empire and its allies meant utter destruction, quite possibly extinction for the human species. If a face-saving means could be found to agree to Sh'daar demands, Earth would be saved and, quite possibly, the power structure of the Terran Senate could be saved as well, with those states that weren't full members folded into the Confederation with a minimum of popular unrest.

That, at least, was Noyer's hope, and the hope of the senators who routinely voted with her. The problem with the Conciliationist program, though, was a few of the old democracies—the United States of North America in particular, with its outdated traditions of independence and individual liberty.

And Koenig and the heart of his battlegroup were USNA. No wonder Koenig was mistrusted, even feared, by Noyer and her followers. The North American Union had never been comfortable with its role as one of the founders of the Confederation; too many of its citizens still longed for their old glory days . . . as independent Canadians, Mexicans, Guatemalans, or as citizens of the United States of America.

He wondered what had happened to Giraurd. Had he followed Koenig into deep space? Had there been a fight between loyalist and mutinous fleet elements?

DuPont didn't think Koenig was capable of actually killing the man in order to avoid relinquishing his command . . . but he *had* once thrown a Senate political liaison off his bridge. He was a superb military leader . . . and a very poor subordinate.

"I'll sign the order," DuPont said. "But . . . you're going to have to find the man to pass them on, and I have a feeling that you're going to have some trouble there. There are a lot of stars out there, and he has a very long head start."

"We will find him," Noyer said. There was bitterness behind the words. "We will find Koenig if we have to mobilize half of the remaining fleet to do so! He *will* be brought to heel!"

The myriad stars scattered across the interior of the planetarium dome seemed to mock them all.

TC/USNA CVS America
Kuiper Belt, HD 157950
98 light years from Earth
1320 hours, TFT

The star carrier *America* dropped out of the grav-twisted dimensions of Alcubierre space in a characteristically intense burst of photons, a dazzling flash of energy crawling outward in all directions at the speed of light. If there were technically accomplished residents of this star system, they would soon know of the arrival of the fleet.

In fact, it was unlikely that anyone else was here. Koenig and his advisors had chosen the system carefully. They weren't looking for combat, but for a chance to refuel.

The star was a close double, the brighter member of the pair a yellow-white F3V sun listed in the star catalogues as HD 157950. From Earth, it had a visual magnitude of 4.5—a faint and unremarkable star in the constellation of Ophiuchus. It possessed a planetary system that was young and still chaotic; a gas giant the size of Neptune circled in close, a so-called hot Jupiter, with a plume like the tail of a comet streaming out behind it away from the sun. Farther out, chunks of ice drifted in an extended, ragged disk, invisible to the naked eye, but glowing faintly at infrared wavelengths.

"Fifteen other ships have emerged so far, Admiral," Commander Benton Sinclair, *America*'s tactical officer, told him. "Now sixteen. The *Abraham Lincoln* just came through."

"Very well."

The wait this time was particularly agonizing. How many more would be coming through?

The original battlegroup, CBG-18, had lost five of its thirty-one capital ships at the Battle of Alphekka, plus two more so badly damaged that they'd been left behind to await the arrival of support and repair ships from Earth. Shortly after the battle, forty-one more warships had arrived, reinforcements dispatched by the Confederation's Joint Chiefs

of Staff. Of those forty-one, twelve were USNA ships, a battlegroup formed around the star carrier *Abraham Lincoln*.
Nine were Chinese, the Eastern Dawn expeditionary force,
led by the carrier *Zheng He*.

The remaining twenty vessels were a Pan-European task
force commanded by Grand Admiral Francois Giraurd on
board the star carrier *Jeanne d'Arc*.

Technically, all of the ships except for the Chinese vessels were Confederation Navy, but . . . there was a problem,
a *big* problem. Koenig wasn't sure yet how it was going to
play out.

"The *Cheng Hua* and the *Haiping* have both just materi-
alized," Sinclair announced. "Range twelve light minutes.
And there's the *Zheng He*. . . ."

He'd been expecting the Chinese and the North Americans to follow the battlegroup into the Abyss. The question
remained: What would the Pan-Europeans do?

After the Battle of Alphekka, CBG-18 had remained in
the system, refitting, re-arming, and consolidating. Grand
Admiral Giraurd had brought his flagship alongside the
America and told Koenig that he was taking command of the
entire fleet, and that the fleet would be returning to Earth.

And Koenig had refused the order.

Giraurd had threatened to open fire as the fleet elements
loyal to Koenig had begun accelerating out-system, and for
a nerve-wracking few hours, the Pan-Europeans had pur-
sued the rest of the battlegroup. They'd never quite pulled
into range, however, and, once the rest of the battlegroup
had begun dropping into Alcubierre Drive, there was a good
chance that Giraurd had ordered his contingent to break off
the pursuit.

But Giraurd knew Koenig's plan, knew the coordinates
where they would be emerging. If he *wanted* to, he could be
moments away from Emergence . . . and Koenig would be
looking at the very real possibility of either capitalization
or mutiny.

Which would it be?

"Admiral!" Sinclair called. "Another star carrier emerging, range fifteen light minutes! Sir, it's the *Jeanne d'Arc*!"

Giraurd had followed them after all.

"More ships emerging from the horizon," Sinclair added. "*De Gaul. Illustrious. Frederick der Grosse.* Looks like the Pan-European main body."

Now they would learn whether or not Koenig's mutiny had just precipitated a civil war.

Chapter Two

VFA-44
Kuiper Belt, HD 157950
98 light years from Earth
1342 hours, TFT

Please, God, don't let me screw up, don't let me screw up, don't let me screw up . . .

"And acceleration in four . . . three . . . two . . . one . . . *launch!*"

Acceleration slammed Lieutenant Trevor Gray back in the cockpit as his SG-92 Starhawk hurtled down the spinal launch tube and into space. At seven gravities, he traversed the two-hundred-meter length of the tube in a fraction over two and a third seconds, emerging at just under 170 meters per second relative to the carrier. The vast, black, circular dome of *America*'s forward cap receded swiftly behind him, the ship's name in faded letters meters high, the word sandblasted to a faded and ragged gray by long voyaging through the interstellar medium. He switched to view forward. Ahead, the local sun showed as a close-set pair of intensely brilliant sparks.

"Blue Dragon One clear," he called over the communications net. "CIC, handing off from Pryfly."

"Blue Dragon One, CIC. We have you."

"Imaging," he told his ship's AI. "Show the squadron, please."

"Blue Two, clear," a second voice said. Lieutenant Shay Ryan's Starhawk had launched in tandem with his. Computer imagining showed her ship as a blue diamond, high and forty meters to port. He switched to his in-head display. With his cerebral implants receiving feeds from external sensors all over the craft's fuselage, his Starhawk seemed invisible now, at least to his eyes, as though he'd merged with his fighter and become a part of it. Ryan's Starhawk sharpened into high-res magnification, a long and slender black needle with a central bulge, her ship, like his, still in launch configuration.

With a thoughtclicked command, Gray flipped his fighter end for end and began decelerating, his maneuver matched closely by Shay. Other SG-92s were appearing now, spilling two by two from *America*'s forward launch tubes.

"Blue Dragon Three, clear."

"Blue Four, in the clear."

Fighters from other squadrons were dropping laterally from the carrier, propelled by the centrifugal force of the rotating hab modules behind the forward cap, and slowly, a cloud of fighters was beginning to surround her. *America*, he knew, was just one of many warships in the newly reinforced CBG-18, with several other carriers out there, but, from this vantage point, he couldn't see any of them save as colored icons painted into his visual cortex by his fighter's AI.

"Dragonfires," Gray said over the tac channel. "Go to combat configuration and form up on me."

"Copy, Skipper," the voice of Ben Donovan said. "We're coming in."

And the other ships of VFA-44 began closing with him.

Skipper . . .

The title still didn't fit. The Dragonfires' skipper, their CO, was Commander Marissa Allyn . . . but CDR Allyn had gone streaker during the Battle of Alphekka, her fighter badly damaged and hurtling out of control into emptiness. The SAR ships had found her three days later and brought her back, still alive but in a coma. She was still in *America*'s sick bay ICU, unconscious and unresponsive.

And CAG had told Gray that now *he* was the squadron commander.

The assignment was strictly temporary and provisional. VFA-44 had come out of the furnace of Alphekka with just three pilots left—Gray, Shay Ryan, and Ben Donovan. And of the three of them, Gray held seniority; Donovan's date of commission was two years younger than Gray's, while Ryan was a relative newbie, fresh from a training squadron at Oceana.

Over the past month, the three of them had worked together training a batch of replacement pilots, men and women recruited from other shipboard divisions to fill the squadron's missing ranks. How well the new squadron performed, how they pulled together as a team, likely, would determine whether Gray would keep his new billet—and perhaps receive an early promotion to lieutenant commander to go with it.

The trouble was that Gray had no desire for either the promotion or the responsibility. He and his wife had been Prims—primitives—squatters in the unorganized and half-drowned ruins of coastal cities around the peripheries of the old United States. As such, they'd not been full citizens, and when Angela had had a stroke, he'd been forced to join the military as a trade-off to get her medical treatment.

Gray's plan had been to put in the mandatory minimum— ten years—and get out. His time would be up in another six years. Damn it, he was *not* going to hang around one second longer than he had to.

Other Starhawk pilots began dropping into formation with him as they continued to exit the carrier. Jamis Natham and Calli Loman, both formerly of *America*'s food services department. Miguel Zapeta, admin. Rissa Schiff, avionics. Will Rostenkowski, personnel. Tammi Mallory, medical department. There were nine newbies in all, not counting Shay, who *had* been through the fight at Alphekka.

"Stay tight," Gray told the formation. "Close perimeter defense."

"Who the hell's going to attack us out here?" Carlos Esteban—until recently an AI systems analyst—asked. "This star system is supposed to be empty!"

"Just do it, Lieutenant," Gray said. "You can analyze the tacsit later."

"Scuttlebutt had it we might be fighting the Europeans," Mallory said. "Giraurd wants Koenig to go back to Earth."

"Quiet, Dragonfires," Gray snapped. "No scuttlebutt, no talking. Line of duty only."

"Uh . . . permission to ask a question?" That was Schiff.

"Granted."

"Is that true, Skipper? We might be facing off against Confederation forces?"

"They haven't told me, Lieutenant," Gray told her. "When they do, I'll pass it along. For right now . . . follow orders, stay in tight formation, and maintain radio silence."

But Gray had heard the same scuttlebutt. Everyone in the fleet must have heard it by now. Fleet Admiral Giraurd outranked a mere rear admiral, and the word was that Koenig had been ordered home—presumably with the rest of the battlegroup. For the past two months there'd been intensive speculation on the topic in the squadron ready rooms and lounges. Koenig had figuratively thumbed his nose at the Pan-Europeans and departed from Alphekka, destination . . . unknown. Had Giraurd followed them?

His tactical display had been partially blocked by *America*'s Combat Information Center. He could see *America* and those of *America*'s fighters that were already deployed, but not the rest of the battlegroup. Unless something had gone horribly wrong, there should be at least another twenty-five warships out there, the rest of the original CBG-18. And there were the forty-one Confederation vessels that had arrived as reinforcements at Alphekka; some of them should have come over to Koenig as well. If they'd emerged too far from *America*, the light from their collapsing Alcubierre fields might not yet have reached them, but it had been almost half an hour since *America* had emerged. They all *ought* to be out there by now. . . .

"Blue Dragon One, CIC, command channel."

"CIC, Blue One. Go ahead."

"This is the CAG. I, ah, heard the chatter just now."

"Yes, sir." He wondered if Wizewski was about to chew him a new one for his people's poor communications security.

"We're getting the same from every squadron out there. Don't sweat it. They have a right to know."

Gray relaxed slightly. "I agree, sir."

"But not just yet. We're releasing the tacsit data to squadron leaders, but not to the general fleet. I want you to see this."

A separate window opened in his mind as new data streamed into his implant. It showed *America* near the center of a scattering of ships, each tagged with name and hull number.

"It looks like they all did follow us," Gray said.

"They did. We're still missing eight ships. They're probably still outside of our light-speed horizon, and we'll see them in a few more minutes. Green are ships we know we can trust. Red are probably hostile. Amber are unknowns."

The twenty-six ships of the original battlegroup were green, Gray noted. So too were twelve more ships—*Abraham Lincoln*'s battlegroup—which meant they were North American.

Twelve were red . . . the Pan-European contingent, minus eight stragglers. The remaining nine—the Chinese—were unknowns.

"Sir," Gray said, "we're not going to *fight* them, are we?"

"I don't know, son. Possibly they don't know either. They're probably going to try to bluff us, and the old man is going to call them on it."

It seemed like utter lunacy. The North Americans comfortably outnumbered the European warships, but an exchange of fire would cause a lot of damage on both sides, something the human fleet simply couldn't afford this far from home. Damn it, the Sh'daar and the Turusch and the H'rulka were the enemies . . . not the damned Europeans!

"We expect the French carrier *Jeanne d'Arc* to attempt to close alongside of the *America*," Wizewski continued. "The fighters are going to block her, because we can't afford to let a ship with her firepower get close enough to fire a broadside. One hundred thousand kilometers. That's the minimum stand-off distance. Understand?"

"I think so, sir. Are . . . are we authorized to fire?"

"*Only* on my command, or on the command of Admiral Koenig himself."

"Yes, sir."

"We're going to try our damnedest to talk our way out of this. If we can't . . ."

He left the thought unfinished.

"I understand, sir."

On the tactical display, the *Jeanne d'Arc* and her consorts were still almost a full astronomical unit away, but they were on a convergent course, closing with the *America*. The American ships were positioning themselves in a tight globe around the carrier, with the heavy cruisers *Valley Forge* and *Ma'at Mons*, along with a number of frigates and destroyers squarely between the approaching French flotilla and the USNA carriers. The *Ma'at Mons*, particularly, was a heavy bombardment ship . . . but she'd expended a lot of her warload against the A1-01 orbital factory. Gray wondered if she had enough munitions on board to keep the Europeans at a healthy distance.

Civil war.

Gray had little use for the Terran Confederation. Hell, as a Prim living out on the USNA Periphery, in the ruins of Old Manhattan, he'd had little use for the United States of North America, either. So far as he could tell, the argument between them involved a difference of strategy. The

Confederation wanted to talk with the Sh'daar, and perhaps accept terms, while Koenig wanted to draw the enemy off into deep space, away from Earth and her colonies. Gray didn't understand how the two could be mutually exclusive, or how Koenig could get away with setting Confederation military policy.

If forced to choose between the two, though, Gray would go with Koenig, if only because he was doing what he thought was right, and to hell with the politicians and rear-echelon second-guessers in Geneva *or* in Columbus.

Koenig was a fighter, and that was enough for Trevor Gray.

CIC
TC/USNA CVS America
Kuiper Belt, HD 157950
98 light years from Earth
1358 hours, TFT

"Do you think they'll fight, Admiral?" Captain Buchanan asked.

The voice spoke inside Koenig's head, since *America*'s commanding officer was on the ship's bridge, forward from the Combat Information Center, which was the central brain for the entire battlegroup. Koenig was looking down into the tactical display tank, where a cloud of green, amber, and red icons drifted toward a seemingly inevitable collision.

"I don't know, Randy," Koenig said. "I don't know Giraud. Can't get a handle on him."

He'd called up every bit of biographical data on Francois Giraud that he could find in the Fleetnet database, but found little that was useful. Giraud was only fifty years old, remarkably young for a grand admiral. Born in 2344, he'd been twenty-three, an engineering major at the Sorbonne, when the Sh'daar Ultimatum had come down through their Agletsch proxies. He'd entered the French *Acádemie d'Astre* as a midshipman cadet in 2368, the year of the disaster at Beta Pictoris, the opening round in the Sh'daar-Confederation War.

His first command had been the gunship *Pégase* in 2374, and on his promotion to *capitaine de frégate* five years later he'd been given the command of the *De Grasse*, serving with the Terran Confederation's Pan-European contingent.

He'd never commanded a ship in battle, however, for either Pan-Europe or the Confederation. He'd made *contre-amiral* in 2389, at age 40, then *vice-amiral* in 2394, and *vice-amiral d'escadre* in 2397, a spectacularly swift rise up the hierarchy of flag rank. His final promotion to *grand-amiral* had been conferred in 2403. He'd been in command of a joint Franco-German-Russian fleet in Earth Synchorbit, Koenig noted, during the Defense of Earth, but that fleet had not seen combat.

An uncle of Giraurd's had been the French prime minister from 2385 through 2397, which just might explain his lightning rise through the ranks. He also had a cousin, General Daubresse, currently on the Confederation Joint Chiefs of Staff, and the Giraurd family was one of the wealthiest in Pan-Europe. Family, political, and financial connections weren't supposed to have any influence on promotions within the Confederation military, but everyone was all too aware of the reality. Both Pan-Europe and the UNSA had families who'd rotated between politics and the military going back for generations.

"I think he's more bluff and bluster than anything else," Buchanan said. "The real problem is going to be DuPont and the politicos back in Geneva. I'd like to know exactly what Giraurd's orders are right now."

Koenig had been thinking the same thing. Clearly, the Confederation government had hoped that Girard's arrival would overawe Koenig enough that he would meekly return to Earth—coupled, carrot and stick, with the promise of being made president of the Confederation Senate.

"Admiral? This is fleet communications," Lieutenant Julio Ramirez said, interrupting electronically.

"Excuse me, Randy. Go ahead, comm."

"Incoming transmission from *Jeanne d'Arc*. Time lag . . . seven minutes, twenty seconds."

"Very well." Koenig opened the channel to include Buchanan. "Captain? You might want to listen in on this."

"Of course, sir."

A window opened in Koenig's mind, static-blasted, then clearing. Giraurd's face peered out at him. "Admiral Koenig, this is Grand Admiral Giraurd, on board the Confederation star carrier *Jeanne d'Arc*. I must inform you that I have the authority of the Terran Confederation Senate to place you under arrest if you do not comply with their orders."

"He followed us for a hundred and fourteen light years to tell us that?" Buchanan asked.

"He probably can't go back empty-handed," Koenig replied, as Giraurd continued talking in the background. The transmission was strictly one-sided, a monologue. It would take another seven and a half minutes, nearly, for any response to get back to the approaching *Jeanne d'Arc*.

"My orders," Giraurd was saying, "are to take command of CBG-18 and organize its immediate return to Earth. . . ."

"So what are we going to do about it?" Buchanan asked.

"What am *I* going to do about it," Koenig replied. "No sense in your career getting fried too."

"Admiral, we're long past that point. If they hang you, they're going to hang every senior officer in the battlegroup."

Giraurd kept speaking. "You are hereby directed to shut down your maneuvering drive and your weapons systems and prepare to receive the *Jeanne d'Arc* alongside. I am awaiting your immediate reply. Giraurd, *Jeanne d'Arc*, out."

"Well," Koenig said. "Short and to the point."

"We're going to have to make a fight-or-flight decision in another . . . call it three hours, sir."

"I know. Ramirez?"

"Yes, Admiral."

"Can you patch through a high-focus laser on *Illustrious*?"

There was a brief delay. "Yes, sir. No problem. We have a clear shot. The time lag is . . . make it seven thirty-five."

"Do so. I want Captain Harrison on the link, personal and private."

"Aye, aye, Admiral."

Koenig knew Captain Ronald Fitzhugh Harrison, the skipper of the British assault carrier *Illustrious*. If Giraud was bluff and bluster, Harrison was the real deal. He was a veteran of a number of actions, including both Sturgis's World and Everdawn against the Turusch; Cinco de Mayo, against EAS; and the Chinese Hegemony and Spanish rebels, and he included among his service medals both the Conspicuous Gallantry Cross and the Distinguished Service Cross.

"*Jeanne d'Arc* has tagged their transmission with an immediate response requested, Admiral."

"Ignore them."

"Aye, aye, sir."

Koenig thought for a moment, then began recording his transmission to Harrison.

"Hello, Ron. This is Alex, on the *America*. I'm sure you're under orders not to receive transmissions from us, but before you cut me off you'd better have a look at the attached intel. They might not have told you everything.

"If you'd care to chat, tag me back. Koenig, awaiting your reply. Out."

He attached a file with the name "Operation Crown Arrow" and uploaded it to Fleet Communications. It would be on its way down a laser beam aimed at the Pan-European carrier *Illustrious* within seconds.

It would be more than fifteen minutes before he could expect a reply.

For almost four decades, since the Sh'daar Ultimatum, the Terran Confederation had been shrinking, its borders on several fronts relentlessly pushed back by the encroaching Sh'daar Alliance. They'd taken Rasalhague, forty-seven light years from Sol, in 2374. Twenty-three years later, they'd hit Sturgis's World, at Zeta Herculis, thirty-five light years out.

And a few months ago, just before CBG-18 had left the Sol System, they'd taken the colony at Osiris, 70 Ophiuchi AII. That was just sixteen and a half light years away, practically on Earth's doorstep, astronomically speaking.

The Sh'daar and their subject races were closing in.

Operation Crown Arrow had been devised to buy the Confederation time, a raid deep, deep into Sh'daar-controlled space, striking at fleet assembly points, manufactory centers, and staging areas. WHISPERS, the Weak Heterodyned Interstellar Signal Passband-Emission Radio Search, had detected a number of sources of faint, intelligently directed radio signals and identified them as probable sites of Sh'daar or Turusch activity. The immense manufactory at Alphekka, sucking in debris from the star's protoplanetary disk and building Turusch warships, had been one of the loudest of these, but there was a list of more distant sites as well.

And with the capture of the Alphekkan manufactory had come the Alphekkan Directory, a Turusch list of other military bases within about five thousand light years of Sol.

That list proved one important thing. The Sh'daar and their Turusch proxies were stretched *thin*. It couldn't really be otherwise, not in a galaxy of 400 billion stars. The enemy *couldn't* maintain a guardian fleet within every star system. They couldn't even put guards within every inhabited system.

Koenig was certain now that the Alphekkan base had been designed for nothing less than building a fleet intended to subjugate—possibly to destroy—Earth. A huge number of ships, empty and waiting, had been captured there. The Sh'daar *might* be planning on using the newly captured base at 70 Ophiuchi, but that was across 42 degrees of Earth's sky, a straight-line distance of 62.5 light years from Alphekka. The almost overwhelming likelihood was that the enemy had hit 70 Ophiuchi as a diversion, to pull human fleet resources away from Sol. The main strike, Koenig thought, would come from the direction of the constellation of Corona Borealis, from Alphekka.

Operation Crown Arrow called for an initial strike at Alphekka in order to cripple the Sh'daar assets there . . . and that strike had been an unprecedented success. But the follow-on had called for CBG-18 to continue deeper into Sh'daar space, ideally drawing off the enemy forces now pressing so hard on Sol, getting them to follow *America* and her consorts.

Exhaustive analyses had gone into the planning. Step by step, Koenig, using a small army of artificial intelligences, had shown conclusively that running from point to point to meet individual Sh'daar advances—like the taking of Osiris—would inevitably leave Earth vulnerable to a final, overwhelming attack. The Confederation did not have the capacity in personnel, in equipment, or in industrial strength to meet the Sh'daar on anything like an equal basis long term.

That, Koenig, thought, should have been self-evident. According to the alien Agletsch, the Sh'daar dominated something like a third of the galaxy, which meant more than 100 billion suns, billions of habitable worlds, and an estimated 5 million technic civilizations. The Confederation had Sol and a handful of colonized star systems—twenty-five, at last count, plus a couple of hundred outposts and research stations. Twenty-five worlds against an unknown number of billions . . . a flea against some giant, enormous extinct beast, a tyrannosaur, a titanothere, or an elephant. It was impossible. . . .

But Koenig had an idea that might work. Alphekka had been a spectacular victory; now, CBG-18 needed to hit the next target, and the next one after that. The Alphekkan Directory had pointed him to a likely candidate, a star system not listed on any human catalogues, but known to the Agletsch as Texaghu Resch.

Hit that, and Koenig believed that every Sh'daar fleet within a thousand light years would be chasing him. After that . . .

"Admiral? Incoming . . . from Captain Harrison, on the *Illustrious*."

Koenig checked his internal clock. What the hell? Only five minutes had passed since he'd sent the message to Harrison; he hadn't even had time to receive it yet. This must be one of those "great minds" moments; Harrison had tried to reach him within moments of his trying to communicate with Harrison.

"Put it through. Randy? Listen in, please."

Within his mind, a communications window opened, and Harrison's face appeared. "Alex! This is Ron Harrison. Remember me? The academy speech, two years ago."

Koenig remembered. The two of them had together addressed the 2403 graduating class at the Naval academy. It wasn't the last time he'd seen the man, but it was the last time he'd had more than a few minutes to talk with him.

"What the hell is going down, Alex?" Harrison continued. "Giraurd is about to bust a gut. He's calling you a traitor and worse, and he's told us that he intends to attack your squadron if you don't do exactly what he says.

"This mess is a put-up hatchet job, I'm certain of that. This isn't the Senate speaking. It's a small clique inside the Senate—the damned Conciliationists. They haven't figured out yet that appeasement *never* works.

"Now, I notice the other USNA ships in our flotilla broke off and followed you. That was to be expected. *Illustrious* and two others, *Warspite* and *Conqueror*, are under my direct command . . . and I'll be damned if I'm going to see them fire the opening shots of a civil war. Give the word, and I'll slide the three of us over to your side of the line.

"Harrison, awaiting your reply. Out."

"Well, well," Buchanan said. "Division within the enemy's ranks?"

"They're not our enemies," Koenig said.

He was thinking furiously. How well did he trust Harrison? Was this a genuine offer to change sides . . . or was it a covert move directed by Giraurd, an attempt to get three major warships in close to the *America*? Koenig hated the paranoid thought, but he had to consider every possibility.

What, he wondered, had been the speech at the academy? When the topic didn't come immediately to mind, he downloaded it from his personal database. Koenig's speech had been about the need to be vigilant and develop a unity of purpose and strategy in the war against the Sh'daar. Harrison's speech had been titled "The Worm Within: Covert Penetration of the Enemy's Infrastructure." He'd been telling the graduating midshipmen that they needed to think outside the box, to think not only in terms of classical fleet strategies, but to use high-tech infiltration techniques to tap into alien command and control systems. Koenig had done exactly that three months before, when he'd deployed a small SEALs team to covertly breach and enter a giant H'rulka warship moving into the Sol System in order to establish contact with the beings inside.

And now, Koenig thought, Harrison was using the title as a warning. This *was* a covert attempt to get his forces in close to the *America*.

"Ramirez," Koenig said. "Reply to Captain Harrison, personal and confidential. Message begins.

"Hey, Ron, you Limey bastard. Got your message, *all* of it." He thought for a moment. Chances were good that Giraud was tapped in to *Illustrious*'s comm suite and reading the mail. He decided not to mention his previous message, which Giraud may or may not have seen.

"The thing about a civil war," Koenig went on, "is that it is *never* civil. We can't afford to bloody each other, and I refuse to become the bone of contention that splits open the Terran Confederation. The enemy is *out there*, not within our own ranks.

"I appreciate your offer, but for now, I'd prefer that *Illustrious*, *Warspite*, and *Conqueror* remain with the Pan-European fleet. We are establishing a no-cross line one hundred thousand kilometers from the *America*, and we ask that you respect that.

"I hope that when this is over, you and I can sit down in a wardroom, your ship or mine, and have a cold one and a good laugh about this. For now, please stay clear.

"Koenig, *America*, out."

In the tactical tank, the two fleets continued to draw closer together.

Chapter Three

VFA-44
Kuiper Belt, HD 157950
98 light years from Earth
1715 hours, TFT

"Things are about to go supercritical," Gray said over the squadron tac channel. "Reconfigure to sperm mode."

The SG-92 Starhawk's outer hull consisted of a matrix of conventional metals and ceramics blended with nano-molecules controlled by an electrical field projected by his ship's AI. Launch configuration was a slender needle with a swollen central area housing the cockpit, designed for magnetic acceleration down the launch tube. Combat configuration looked a bit like a headless bird with down-canted wings, providing widely separated weapons and sensor platforms useful in a fight.

Sperm mode was fighter-slang for high-velocity configuration—a blunt-nosed egg shape with a long, tapering tail. The old, conventional wisdom that said that spacecraft didn't need to be streamlined in the vacuum of space broke down when the vessel could approach the speed of light. At those speeds every little bit helped.

Gray didn't know what was going to happen in the next

few moments, but he did know that their survival would depend upon their speed and their maneuverability.

The twelve Starhawks had been patrolling in combat mode, but now their wings began folding in toward their bodies, their black surfaces turning cold-molten and flowing like thick water. They were drifting along the no-cross line, an empty region of space defined by its distance, 100,000 kilometers, from the *America*.

The heavy cruiser *Valley Forge* was only five kilometers off his starboard side at the moment, three quarters of a kilometer long, a slender stem behind an outsized forward cap shaped like a flattened dome. To the naked eye, she appeared slightly blurred and indistinct. Shield technology involved bending space sharply above and around a ship's hull, and that bending caused light to twist. When an incoming projectile or thermonuclear detonation struck the field projected across a warship's outer hull, that spatial warping momentarily became much stronger, deflecting the threat. Gravitic shielding was costly in terms of energy, however, and was generally switched on only when combat was imminent. Koenig, clearly, was taking no chances; high-velocity kinetic rounds could come slamming out of the darkness with little to no warning at all, and all ships in the battlegroup were at the highest possible alert status.

According to the tactical display, *Jeanne d'Arc* and the eleven other capital ships of the Pan-European contingent were a scant half million kilometers away, drawing ever closer.

"Hey . . . Skipper?" It was Shay Ryan, on a private channel.

"Yeah?"

"I don't like the idea of shooting at our own guys, y'know?"

"Neither do I, Lieutenant."

"If we get shot up way out here, it's going to make fighting the Sh'daar, or getting home, a hell of a lot harder."

"The brass'll figure something out," he told her. "They know a lot more about what's happening than we do."

He wished he felt that confident, though. Koenig was a

good officer and a brilliant strategist, Gray thought, but he shared with most fighter pilots a measure of distrust for the men and women who made the tough choices in the relative safety of the CIC. Sure, their lives were on the line if the capital ships came under attack, but they weren't out here, crammed inside a gravfighter with nothing but speed, maneuverability, and skill between you and the enemy's incoming rounds.

He found himself wondering just what the battlegroup could do if Giraud tried to push things. A traditional shot across their bows? And what if they called the bluff and kept coming? He called up a battlespace view, imagery transmitted from one of the thousands of robotic drones now dispersed throughout this region of space, for a closer look at the enemy.

There she was . . . the *Jeanne d'Arc*, a light star carrier, perhaps three quarters of the mass of *America*. Like all Alcubierre Drive ships, she had the same general design—slender spine aft, large, flattened dome forward. The shield cap had been painted blue and white, a sharp contrast with the sandblasted gray-black of *America*'s prow. Her name and number appeared pristine, newly painted. According to the warbook, the *Jeanne d'Arc* didn't have *America*'s twin launch tubes running through the center of the shield cap. Instead, she possessed a single high-energy particle cannon, which gave her a formidable long-range bombardment capability above and beyond the punch carried by her fighters.

A whale swimming with minnows, the *Jeanne d'Arc* was accompanied by a cloud of fighters, tiny blue motes moving in her shadow.

Gray didn't immediately recognize the Pan-European fighters, and had to pull an ID up on his warbook: Franco-German KRG-17 Raschadler fighters. He felt himself relax slightly. The Raschadler was roughly equivalent to the USNA SG-55 War Eagle, a design about twenty years old. They didn't have the delta-V of Starhawks, the endurance, or the warload capability, and they didn't possess the Starhawk's high-tech ability to change its configuration for launch, for high-velocity travel, or for combat. In head-to-head knife fights with the Pan-Europeans, the Dragonfire Starhawks would come out on top every time. The problem was that no one wanted such a confrontation in the first place, least of all, Gray was certain, Koenig.

How could CBG-18 stop the Pan-Europeans without destroying their ships or risking the destruction of their own?

He zoomed in closer, magnifying the image. The Raschadler fighters were obviously positioned to prevent CBG-18's fighters from getting close to the carrier's central spine—the weapons sponsons and rotating hab modules and drop bays tucked away just aft of the shield cap.

Just ahead of the *Jeanne d'Arc* was a tiny, blurred tumble of distortion—the projected drive singularity that was pulling the giant through space.

The ship's gravitic shields would be down on the forward cap, to enable the field projectors to create the singularity, a tightly knotted distortion of space.

And Gray thought he saw a way. . . .

CIC
TC/USNA CVS America
Kuiper Belt, HD 157950
98 light years from Earth
1732 hours, TFT

"Admiral?"

"Yes, CAG?"

"One of our people came up with something. Thought you should see it."

Koenig read the downloaded text, transcribed from a pilot's laser-com transmission. "Lieutenant Gray?" Koenig asked.

"Yes, sir. Acting CO of VFA-44."

"I remember. Hero at the Defense of Earth . . . and again at Alphekka. He knows his shit."

"Yes, sir. And his idea might work. Gives us something to go on, anyway."

"We've got nothing better," Koenig said. "Okay. Mr. Sinclair? Pass the word to all ships, tight beam and quantum encoded. *Jeanne d'Arc* will be the first target. We won't hit the others unless this doesn't work and they keep coming."

"Aye, aye, Admiral."

Koenig, an avid military historian, smiled. Lieutenant Gray, he thought, knew a secret first uncovered by an aviator back in the days of fabric-winged biplanes and oceangoing navies, a man named General Billy Mitchell.

"It appears," Koenig said, "that our fighters are going to earn their pay today, David-and-Goliath style."

"David and who, sir?" Sinclair sounded puzzled.

"Never mind."

Since the passage of the White Covenant, in the late twenty-first century, the religious beliefs or training of others—or the lack of such—was no one's business. Technically, it was only against the law to try to convert someone else, but in practice it was considered bad manners even to make a casual religious comment, or to make a reference to religious mythology.

"Our boys and girls out there are going to need something more than a sling," Wizewski said quietly. The CAG, Koenig recalled, *was* religious, a member of some small and semi-fundamentalist Christian sect. There were so many nowadays it was impossible to keep track.

"Amen to that, CAG," Koenig said quietly, so no one else would hear. "Amen to that. . . ."

CIC
TC/PE CVS Jeanne d'Arc
Kuiper Belt, HD 157950
98 light years from Earth
1739 hours, TFT

Grand Admiral Francois Giraud studied the pattern of colored icons unfolding in the tactical display tank. Koenig would *have* to capitulate. He had no other sane option.

"Sir," his tactical officer said. "We cross their line in twelve minutes."

"Very well."

"Sir . . . do you intend to attack?"

"It won't come to that, Lieutenant. We will cross their line, they will scatter and refuse to confront us, and we will put our boarding party across. And then . . ."

"Sir?"

"And then we go home."

They were ninety-eight light years from Earth, farther than any human had ever before voyaged. The emptiness, the darkness scattered with myriad unknown suns and civilizations, filled him with foreboding and a brooding sense of agitation, even fear. Humans didn't *belong* out here, not in a galaxy already staked out and claimed by millions of other technic cultures.

He magnified the image in the tank. "What ship is that?"

"The *Valley Forge*," the tactical officer told him. "One hundred fifty thousand tons."

"Target to disable her," Giraurd said. "Power systems and weapons. We will push past her, then, and engage the *America*."

"The cruiser is accompanied by a number of fighters."

"Those are of no consequence. If they get too close, destroy them."

"Our orders, sir, are to effect Koenig's surrender *without* causing damage to their ships, or causing casualties."

"We will damage them as little as possible, cause as few casualties as possible. But I see no other way of reaching the *America*, do you?"

"No, Grand Admiral."

"Direct our fighter escort to move out ahead of us," Giraurd said. "They will be our wedge to sweep the enemy aside. Order them to fire only if they are fired upon."

"Yes, sir."

"And accelerate to combat speed."

"Yes, Grand Admiral."

Giraurd smiled. They would end this standoff soon

enough. Koenig was a fool if he thought he could make military policy for the Confederation. The *Jeanne d'Arc* would push through Koenig's outer screen, close with *America*, and put boarding parties across to capture Koenig and take command of his fleet.

And then they could all go home.

VFA-44
Kuiper Belt, HD 157950
98 light years from Earth
1748 hours, TFT

"Here they come!" Gray called. "Their fighters are deploying ahead of the carrier, and they're accelerating!"

"Hold position, Dragonfires," Wizewski's voice said in his head. "We're doing it by the book."

"Holding, aye, sir. . . ."

By the book meant a warning shot, a formal nicety in which modern naval vessels rarely engaged. Generally, the idea was to launch an attack, all-out, complete and devastating, zorching in before the enemy was even aware that your forces were in the area, with missiles and kinetic kill impactors coming in just behind the light announcing their arrival.

He switched to the tactical channel. "All ships! Engage squadron taclink."

Gray and the other pilots each focused their thoughts, connecting with their fighters' artificial intelligences. The twelve fighter craft were interconnected now by laser-optic feeds linking their onboard computers into a single electronic organism.

The *Valley Forge* was pivoting slightly now, bringing her main battery, a spinal-mount CPG, to bear. A moment later, she fired—a burst of tightly focused high-energy-charged particles invisible to the unaided eye but showing clearly on Gray's instruments and on his visual display. The beam burned past the shield cap of the *Jeanne d'Arc*, missing the carrier by less than a hundred meters.

"*Jeanne d'Arc*," Koenig's voice said over the fleet channel. "That was a warning. Change course immediately, or we will take you under fire."

"You're not going to fire on Confederation vessels," Giraud's voice came back. "Surrender and save your people, and your reputation."

"Dragonfires!" Wizewski's voice snapped. "You are weapons free. *Go!*"

"That's it, Dragons!" Gray called. "Maximum acceleration in three . . . two . . . one . . . *now!*"

Twelve Starhawk fighters leaped past the challenge line, hurtling toward the oncoming Pan-European warships. The range was just under 480,000 kilometers. At fifty thousand gravities they closed the gap in just forty seconds.

A typical strike fighter mission had the fighters zorching through an enemy formation at high velocity after a long period of acceleration. This was different, however, with only a relatively short distance for acceleration before the fighters reached the target. The squadron's newbies hadn't practiced this sort of tight, close-quarters maneuvering in training sims, and they were going to be making mistakes.

Gray just hoped none of those mistakes would be fatal.

"Jink!" he yelled over the tactical channel. "All Dragonfires, *jink!*"

By throwing drive singularities to left, right, above, and below at random, they could jerk their fighters around enough to fox enemy targeting AIs as they continued to close the range.

On the tactical display, the Pan-European fighters had leaped forward, seeking to head the Starhawks off.

"Ignore the fighters," Gray told the squadron. "Stay on the carrier!"

"They're firing! Missiles incoming!"

Missiles streaked out from the incoming fighters, curving to meet the fast-moving Starhawks.

"Don't let it rattle you," Gray said, suppressing the trembling surge of fear he was feeling. "Stay on course. Stay on the carrier. . . ."

White light flared, dazzling and silent in the darkness. The Dragonfires flashed through expanding clouds of plasma, emerging . . . and then the two clouds of fighters interpenetrated, passing through each other in an instant.

The *Jeanne d'Arc* and her consorts lay just ahead. . . .

CIC
TC/PE CVS Jeanne d'Arc
Kuiper Belt, HD 157950
98 light years from Earth
1748 hours, TFT

"Harrison has betrayed us," Hans Westerwelle said, bitterly. "He warned Koenig, somehow."

"We don't know that," Giraurd replied. "I . . . agree that he was less than eager to open the dialogue with Koenig."

" 'Less than eager'? The Englander swine fought the idea tooth and nail. Koenig was his friend. We should investigate Harrison when this is over, and see where his *true* loyalties lie."

The plan to have the three British ships pretend to join Koenig's squadron had been Westerwelle's. He was the European fleet's political officer, a civilian appointed by Geneva to maintain loyalty and an acceptable level of enthusiasm within the Federation's ranks.

The first nuclear-tipped missiles were detonating in brilliant, savage silence across the CIC's forward view screens. They were unlikely to cause more than superficial damage to the incoming fighters, but they might deter, might force the enemy squadron commander to break off.

"Enemy fighters are still approaching from dead ahead!" the tactical officer called. "They're at seventy percent of *c* and accelerating!"

"Engage point defense!" the *Jeanne d'Arc*'s captain ordered. "Fight them off!"

Giraurd sat back in his command chair, watching the CIC and bridge crews carry out their routines. It had been months since the *Jeanne d'Arc* had been in combat, and many in her crew were new to the ship, having come aboard just before the flotilla had left for Alphekka. It would be interesting to see how well they did in this, their first exercise that was *not* a drill. Her captain, Charles Michel, had seen action during the Defense of Earth, but he was Belgian rather than French, and Giraurd wasn't sure he trusted the man.

Unfortunately, there were a lot of officers on board he didn't entirely trust. Sawicki, the tactical officer, was a Pole. Mytnyk, the fighter wing commander, was Ukrainian, while the political officer, Westerwelle, was a German. And then there were the British, *always* a problem in European Federation politics.

The Pan-European Federation had been a superb idea on paper, but even now, more than 270 years after the *Pax Confeoderata* and more than 400 years after the Treaty of Maastricht, the idea of a union of European states sounded better than it worked. The Terran Confederation, it was said, was only as strong as its weakest members, and for all their public bravado, the Pan-Europeans rarely were able to show a solid or united front.

Of course, the North Americans had the same trouble— descendents of the old United States trying to show a common front with Canadians, Mexicans, and a clutter of tiny Central American states. Political unions simply didn't work when the member states had more differences than similarities.

The odd thing about the situation was that threats from outside generally forced such unions to put aside internal differences and pull together; but if anything, the war with the Sh'daar had reawakened old animosities, infighting, and name-calling. The ancient cracks in the painted façade were showing, not only within the European Federation, but all throughout the realm of Humankind.

What was needed was a stronger government, a government with the resolve to *force* the disparate fragments of humanity into line. Politically, Giraurd was a Federationialist, a neosocialist political party calling for the final abolition of the old nationalist states and the creation of a genuine United Terra.

And that day *was* coming. Humankind had no choice but to unite in the face of the threat from outside. The first step was to crush the so-called independence movements in the USNA, and that meant bringing mavericks like Alexander Koenig into line. A united Humankind couldn't afford individualists like Koenig or the right-wing political reactionaries remaining within the USNA's government.

And so, in a way, the unification of mankind began here. "Hit them with everything we have, Mr. Sawicki," he said.

Nuclear fire continued blossoming in stark and dazzling silence against the forward view screens.

VFA-44
Kuiper Belt, HD 157950
98 light years from Earth
1749 hours, TFT

A European Federation Raschadler flashed past on Gray's port side, a thousand kilometers distant, practically at point-blank range, though too distant and far too fast relative to him for him to pick it up optically. Their name meant "Swift Eagle," but in space combat, it was how many gravities a drive could pull that counted, not the actual velocity. Where the USNA Starhawks could pull up to fifty thousand gravities—an incredible performance—the Raschadlers could manage only about two thousand Gs. Where Starhawks could be pushing the speed of light after ten minutes of acceleration, it took the older Swift Eagles over four hours to reach near-*c*.

Gray needed to use that superior acceleration now to outperform the European fighters.

Twenty seconds passed swiftly, and Gray gave the order to decelerate. The Starhawks, still in their acceleration configurations—teardrop-shaped with slender spikes astern to bleed off excess gravitic energy—began slowing at fifty thousand Gs.

Another twenty seconds passed, with the SG-92s jinking wildly to throw off the European anti-fighter defenses. In such a tight formation, there would have been a danger of some nasty high-velocity collisions if the twelve fighters hadn't been electronically tied together.

The enemy fighters were trying to slow and reverse course, but it would take them a long time to come around. *Too* long . . .

"Let your AIs handle the rendezvous," Gray told the others. "Going on automatic for final deceleration and maneuvering. . . ."

At ten thousand kilometers per second, there'd been no evidence to human eyes that the fighters had been moving at all. The stars hung motionless in space, a cold testament to their distance and the gulfs between them. But under that searing, AI-controlled deceleration, the *Jeanne d'Arc*, suddenly, magically, was *there*, hanging in the black sky directly ahead, and Gray could see with his own eyes the gleaming blue-and-white curve of her shield cap, the neat letters and numerals picking out her name and registry number.

She was five kilometers away, and the linked fighters were closing now at a relative velocity of a half a kilometer per second.

"Combat mode!" Gray called. "Target the shield cap!"

The *Jeanne d'Arc* was still accelerating, so her forward shields were down. Gray thoughtclicked an icon within his virtual in-head display, and opened up with a long burst from his Gatling RFK-90 kinetic-kill cannon. Firing with a cyclic rate of twelve per second, the Gatling loosed a stream of magnetic-ceramic jacketed slugs, each with a depleted uranium core massing half a kilo and traveling at 175 meters per second *plus* the 500 meters per second of the fighter's relative closing velocity. That much mass traveling that fast possessed a kinetic-energy punch powerful enough to shred hardened steel and ceramic laminate; bright flashes of light walked across the shield, and almost instantly a dense, white mist appeared above the impacts—water gushing out into vacuum and freezing almost instantly, creating a glittering cloud of ice particles.

"Watch his drag!" Gray shouted over the squadron link. "Stay clear of his drive field!"

Gravitic drive ships moved by projecting an artificial gravitational singularity ahead of their bows, creating an intense and tightly focused black hole that flickered on and off thousands of times per second, allowing the ship to fall forward into an ever-receding gravitational well. A fighter getting too close to the singularity would be drawn in and crushed out of existence in an instant, a process called "spaghettification" because of the effect on ships and personnel as they were torn by close-in tidal effects. The Dragonfires whipped past the projected drive field, feeling the hard tug but applying acceleration of their own to counter it. The other fighters were firing their Gatlings now as well, ripping the *Jeanne d'Arc*'s shield cap into ragged fragments and geysering sprays of fast-freezing water.

Like the *America*, the *Jeanne d'Arc* carried some billions of liters of liquid water inside its shield cap, water that served both as radiation shielding when the carrier was moving close to *c*, and as a reserve of reaction mass for the ship's maneuvering thrusters. As the shield cap's double hull was shredded, that water poured into space. Within seconds, most of it was falling in gleaming streamers into a tight spiral around the flickering drive singularity.

Gray's fighter fell past the shield cap now, and he could see the turning hab modules in the cap's shadow; where *America* had three hab modules mounted on the end of rotating spokes, the smaller European carrier had two. He also spotted the bridge tower, a building-sized structure rising from the ship's spine between the shield cap and the hab module collar.

Laser and particle-beam fire snapped out toward his fighter, invisible to the eye but painted on Gray's tactical display by his AI. He jinked, then pressed in closer, matching the carrier's acceleration so that he seemed to be hanging just above her spine.

"*Jeanne d'Arc!*" he called using the general fleet frequency. "This is Dragon One, off the USNA *America*! Unless you want to lose your bridge and CIC, I suggest that you break off your attack run."

There was silence for a long handful of seconds. The carrier's hab modules and bridge tower were shielded, of course; he could see the faint blurring of edges where the gravitic shielding twisted light. But a nuke or a determined particle-beam attack could overload those shields or destroy their projection wave guides, and then the carrier's vital nerve centers would be defenseless.

On the other hand, the *Jeanne d'Arc* had point-defense turrets that were doing their best to hit him. This close to the carrier's spine, they were having trouble reaching him, but they were trying to hit the other fighters in the squadron as they moved in closer. A stream of KK rounds reached out and caught Dragon Eight—Lieutenant Will Rostenkowski's ship—sending it into a helpless tumble.

"*Jeanne d'Arc!*" Gray barked again. "Cease fire and cease acceleration or I'm going to put a hundred megatons right on your bridge tower!"

"Don't shoot, Dragon One," a voice said over the fleet channel. "We will comply."

He had to back out of his safe pocket, then, or risk hurtling into the underside of the carrier's shield cap when the *Jeanne d'Arc* cut her acceleration. It could have been a trick, a ruse designed to pull him out of his pocket . . . but the other Dragonfires were in close now, and the Pan-Europeans evidently had no desire for a stand-up fight.

Gray's threat to use nukes had been pure bluff, of course. A Krait missile going off at such close range would probably have burned through the carrier's bridge shielding, but definitely would have vaporized Gray's fighter.

"*America* CIC," he called, "Dragon One. Hostile carrier has ceased acceleration."

"Well done, Dragonfires," Wizewski's voice called back. "Keep them in your sights. *California* and *Saskatchewan* are on the way to take over."

"Copy that. He hesitated. "We also need a rescue SAR. One casualty."

Rostenkowski was no longer transmitting. His ship had been smashed; he *might* have survived the impact, but a search-and-rescue tug would have to match courses with him and drag him back to be sure.

He watched as *Jeanne d'Arc* continued to bleed water into space.

How, he wondered, was Koenig going to handle *this* one? . . .

Chapter Four

CIC
TC/USNA CVS America
Kuiper Belt, HD 157950
98 light years from Earth
0940 hours, TFT

"Admiral Giraurd," Koenig said, standing. "Welcome aboard." He kept his voice and his expression pleasant, even mild. It was important at this point to avoid any sense of drama.

Testosterone-laced posturing would not help at all at this point.

"Koenig," Giraurd replied with a curt nod. "You *still* have the option of surrendering."

"I think, sir, that I will decline that privilege."

They were meeting physically instead of through virtual communications, within the spacious officers lounge in *America*'s hab modules. Present were Captain Buchanan and most of Koenig's command staff and, just in case, several Marine guards flanking the doors as unobtrusively as they could considering that they were in full combat armor. Koenig and the other USNA officers wore full dress; Giraurd wore his command utilities, a blue jumper with the gold emblems of his rank on the shoulders and down the left sleeve.

"You are making an enormous mistake," Giraurd said, taking an offered seat.

"Perhaps." Koenig sat down as well, watching Giraurd across a low table grown from the deck. "But if so, I risk losing my command and, possibly, my fleet. If you and the Conciliationists are wrong, however, we could lose all of humanity. Our species could become extinct. Can you understand my point of view?"

Giraurd hesitated, then gave another nod. "I suppose so. But it is not for the military to make political decisions of this magnitude. You, of all people, should know *that*."

Giraurd, Koenig knew, was referring to the peculiar political baggage the USNA derived from two of its predecessors—Canada and the United States of America. In those nation-states, the military had been expressly forbidden to participate in political decisions. While military coups had not been unthinkable, certainly, they'd been extremely unlikely when the military's commander-in-chief had been the civilian president.

It was a tradition not all members of the Terran Confederation shared. Giraurd was chiding him for breaking that tradition, for making what was essentially a political decision without going through a democratic process.

"Out here," Koenig said quietly, "we have to make our own decisions. They don't see what *we* see, not from a hundred light years away."

"And suppose your little raid behind the enemy lines backfires, Koenig? Suppose it brings down upon us the full weight of the Sh'daar?"

"In other words," Koenig replied gently, "what if we make them angry? Earth lost sixty million souls during their last foray into the Sol System. It's hard to see how they could be any madder."

During the Defense of Earth, in October of 2404, a twelve-kilo mass traveling at a significant fraction of c had skimmed past the sun and slammed into the Atlantic Ocean, 3,500 kilometers off the North American seaboard. The resultant tidal waves had scoured the coastlines of North and South America, Africa, and of Europe, killing an estimated 60 million people.

"Perhaps," Giraurd said. "We might not be so lucky with another direct attack on Earth. That impactor might have simply been a demonstration of their power. We would not survive a *determined* attack."

"I agree," Koenig said. "And that's why we're out here. Even the Sh'daar don't have unlimited resources. If we pose a threat to their worlds, to their star systems and the systems of their allies, we'll draw them away from the Confederation."

"You are a fly attacking an elephant, Koenig."

"Perhaps. But elephants, I will remind you, are extinct. Earth still has *lots* of flies."

"Listen to what I am saying! My point is that the Sh'daar and their allies, the Turusch, the H'rulka, the Nungiirtok, and others, are too big, too powerful, for Earth to face alone!"

"I hear what you're saying, Grand Admiral. *My* point is that Earth needs time, and I'm attempting to buy that time. I'm not against negotiating. I'm just hoping we can negotiate with the Sh'daar when they're not holding a gun to our head!"

"And if we give in to the Sh'daar demands . . . what is the worst that will happen? We give up our insane gallop into a world of ever higher and higher technology! We become content with what we have! We avoid the Vinge Singularity! And what would be so bad about that?"

Giraurd was referring to a long-expected exponentiation of human technology, sometimes called the Technological Singularity, when human life, blending with human technology, would pass out of all recognition. It was named for a late-twentieth-century math professor, computer scientist, and writer who'd pointed out that the rate of increase in human technology had fast been approaching a vertical line on the graph, and *that* had been in 1993. When the Sh'daar had delivered their ultimatum almost four centuries later, they'd demanded that Humankind stop all technological development and research, especially in the fields of genetics, robotics, information systems and computers, and nanotechnology. These so-called GRIN technologies were seen as the principal drivers in the coming Technological Singularity; arrest them, and human life might not evolve into something unrecognizably alien.

"I don't know," Koenig admitted. "But I *do* think we deserve to make our own mistakes."

"The Sh'daar seem terrified of the Singularity," Giraud said. "Perhaps it is with good cause."

"Terrified of the Singularity itself?" Koenig asked. "Or of what happens if another technic species like us reaches it?" He shrugged. "In any case, if it's a mistake, it's our mistake. We should not allow ourselves to be protected from it by the Sh'daar or anyone else. And more than that . . . don't you think we should make our own decisions about our future and about who we're going to play with as we move out into the galaxy? If the Sh'daar fold us into their little empire, they'll use us like they use the Turusch and the others, right? As frontline warriors? Damn it, Admiral, the Confederation military will end up working for *them*, puttering around the galaxy putting down upstart technic species . . . species like we are now. That is, unless they decide to just turn us all into slaves and be done with it!"

"I hadn't realized, Admiral Koenig, that you were a xenophobe."

"I am *not*, Admiral Giraud. But I *do* believe in self-determination for my species!"

The two men glared at each other for a moment across the table. Gradually, Koenig relaxed. He'd hoped to get the Pan-European admiral to see reason—as, no doubt, Giraud had hoped for him—but the argument was going nowhere. Giraud would not change his mind, and neither would Koenig.

"I see no reason to continue this discussion, Admiral," he said. "How badly was the *Jeanne d'Arc* damaged?"

"Our water reserves are gone," he said with a Gallic shrug. "Repair robots are working on the breached tanks now."

"I've given order that the battlegroup's repair and fabrication ships be deployed to lend you a hand. There were no casualties?"

"No. Your fighters were . . . surgically precise."

In 1921, General William Lendrum "Billy" Mitchell had argued, then demonstrated, that aircraft, only recently emerged as military weapons, could sink battleships. Within another twenty years, air attacks against naval fleets at Taranto and Pearl Harbor would completely change the way wars were fought at sea, but in 1921 the idea was not merely revolutionary, but heretical.

Young Lieutenant Gray had demonstrated a similar principle, one now well known within the military and political hierarchies back home but frequently ignored: a twenty-two-ton fighter could disable a capital ship a kilometer long and massing millions of tons. The trick was in slipping it in exactly where it would be most effective, with enough firepower to overcome the target's gravitic shielding. *Surgical precision*, as Giraurd had put it, made possible by advanced technology, was the only means by which a lone gravfighter could take down a far larger foe.

Something of the sort would be necessary if the Terran Confederation was going to win over the Sh'daar.

"The intent was to stop you, Admiral," Koenig said. "Not hurt you."

"I could wish, sir, that you had destroyed the *Jeanne d'Arc* . . . and me with her."

Giraurd's emotional pain showed for a moment, but Koenig ignored it. The man would have to explain his failure later, in front of the Senate Military Directorate. It might even mean the end of his career.

Welcome to the club, Koenig thought.

"Do you anticipate any problem getting the *Jeanne d'Arc* ready for Alcubierre Drive?"

"No. The damage is superficial. But we will need to take on water."

"Of course. And this is the place for it."

Fleet tugs were already jockeying iceteroids in so that the ships of CBG-18 could drink their fill. The Kuiper Belt of any star was the storage freezer for leftovers from that star system's creation. Asteroids, comet nuclei, icy Kuiper objects like Pluto and Eris back in the home solar system . . . they drifted out here in centuries-long orbits and at temperatures a few degrees above zero absolute, with the local sun merely the brightest star in a sky filled with stars. Chunks of ice were nuzzled in close to resupply ships, which injected them with self-replicating nanodisassemblers. These, in turn, broke the ice down into fragments a few microns across, separated out the frozen methane, ammonia, and other contaminants, and transported pure water into the shield-cap tanks of the waiting ships. As quickly as one hundred-meter iceteroid had dwindled away, another was moved in to take its place; a quarter of CBG-18's ships had already been topped off, and the rest would be refueled within four more days.

"As soon as the European contingent has been watered," Koenig continued, "you can take them back to Sol. It's a fifty-four-day flight under Alcubierre Drive back to Sol, so you'll be home by early June. I've already spoken with the commanding officers of the other ships. The USNA flotilla will be joining me."

"And the Chinese?"

Koenig smiled. "They're still considering the question. Their orders were to support your operations against me . . . but I suspect they also have orders to keep an eye on what we're doing out here."

Beijing, Koenig thought, might well be interested in a separate peace with the Sh'daar, and if so, they needed to keep track of what Koenig's expeditionary force was doing. The nine-ship Eastern Dawn Hegemon fleet might still decide to accompany the *America* battlegroup.

How well he could trust them when they did encounter Sh'daar forces was another matter, and one he would address when it came up. The *Zheng He* and her fighters would be welcome additions to the fleet, however, the next time they met the enemy.

"And where will you be going?" Giraurd asked. "If you're willing to tell me, of course."

Koenig considered the question. He didn't want the politicians on Earth to be too up to date on his plans. He didn't want CBG-18 to emerge at a target star system and find a Confederation fleet—one larger, better prepared, and more determined than Giraurd's squadron—waiting for him there.

On the other hand, the next stop on his agenda, taken from the Turusch Directory, was a star called Texaghu Resch, located 133 light years ahead, and some 210 light years from Sol. Even if Giraurd shot the news of Koenig's planned destination back to Sol on a Sleipnir packet, it would be eighteen days for that leg of the trip, and another 116 days for a fleet to get to Texaghu Resch, not counting the time it would take to assemble such a fleet if the Confederation Senate decided to send one. It would be more than four and a half months before Earth could reach Koenig's next destination.

CBG-18, on the other hand, would be at Texaghu Resch in another seventy-four days. Whatever they found there, it would be another two months *at least* before the Confederation Military Directorate could catch up with them.

And by that time, Koenig expected that they would be long, long gone.

"Would the information, do you think, be of help to you personally when you face the Directorate?" Koenig asked.

Giraurd's eyes widened. "Why should you care?"

"Because I know what it's like to face losing it all, while doing what *I* think is my duty."

Giraurd nodded slowly. "It would help, yes. I wouldn't be going back . . . empty-handed."

"We're heading for Texaghu Resch. The Agletsch know of it . . . and it's listed in the Turusch Directory."

"Texaghu Resch? Strange name . . ."

"It's a G-class star that's not even visible from Earth, which is why the alien name. According to the Directory, there's something there the Agletsch call a 'Sh'daar Node,' and it appears to have something to do with the Sh'daar communications and control net across the galaxy."

"Interesting. Is it inhabited?"

"Not according to the Agletsch. Not anymore."

The two Agletsch guides on board the star carrier *America* had translated the name *Texaghu Resch* as something like "the Eye of Resch," Resch being the name of a mythological being in the folklore of a race called the Chelk.

Nothing was known about the Chelk now, save that, like humans, they'd once voyaged among the stars, and like humans, they'd seen pictures of their deities and heroes in the night skies of their homeworld. Exactly who or what Resch had been—god, demigod, hero, or sky monster—was unknown. Its image had been seen in the night sky of the Chelk, who'd held a modest interstellar empire in this region of the galaxy perhaps twelve thousand years earlier.

According to the Agletsch, the Chelk had refused to yield to the Sh'daar demands that they freeze all technological development.

The Chelk were now extinct.

"And after that?" Giraurd asked. "Where will you go after Texaghu Resch?"

Koenig grinned. "Even if I knew, I wouldn't tell you. *You* know that. But I can tell you truthfully, Admiral, I just don't know. It'll depend entirely on what happens at the Sh'daar Node, and what we learn there."

"I understand."

"I will suggest that Earth send a follow-up, though. If we can, we'll leave word of where we're going next. They can keep track of us that way."

"Yes . . . months too late to do any good."

"Depends on what you mean by 'good.' I don't intend to let them stop us, if that's what you mean. But at the same time, we're learning a lot out here about the Sh'daar, about who and what they are, about their client races, about how they see the universe. Geneva will need to know this stuff, no matter what they decide to do back there . . . negotiations, or a military offensive."

Giraurd studied Koenig carefully for a moment. "You really believe that what you're doing is for the good of Earth, don't you?"

"Of course. I wouldn't be out here if I didn't."

Giraurd shook his head. "I truly hope you know what you're doing. I hope—"

"What?"

"I actually hope you are right, Admiral, and that the Confederation Senate and Military Directorate are wrong."

"So do I, Admiral."

"Because if *you're* wrong, Admiral Koenig, God help us all."

Officers Mess
TC/USNA CVS America
Kuiper Belt, HD 157950
98 light years from Earth
1215 hours, TFT

"Hey, Sandy. Mind if I join you?"

Trevor Gray looked up from his food, startled. Only a few of his friends called him that—*Sandy Gray*, a memento of the tactic he'd suggested at the Defense of Earth. It was a hell of a lot better than the hated nickname "Prim."

"Schiffie! Please! Grab a seat."

Lieutenant Rissa Schiff set her tray down and sat, smiling. "I'd grab *yours* if I could, Trev. But I think you've been avoiding me."

"Just busy, Schiffie. You know how it is."

He wondered if the young woman was going to be a problem.

Nine months ago, Gray and Schiff had had a little something going between them—nothing *physical*, quite. They'd dated, they'd flirted, and they'd talked about taking things further—she'd been a cute and enthusiastic little armful, and Gray had been trying out the idea of casual sexual relationships after a lifetime of monogie self-control. When his wife had divorced him, he'd had no one. For two years afterward, he'd had little interest in filling that aching emptiness Angela had left in him, but then he'd met Rissa, and she was cute and sweet and fun, and she'd indicated a willingness to play.

It had damned near gotten him court-martialed.

Not because he'd considered having sex with her. At the time, he'd been a lieutenant and she'd been an ensign, and officially, physical relationships between people of different ranks were discouraged. An officer handing out special favors or status in exchange for sex from a subordinate was *very* bad form, though it did happen, of course. But Gray and Schiff had kept their playtimes secret and, in any case, he'd been a pilot while she worked in the avionics department. He might outrank her, but he was not her boss.

But a couple of other pilots in Gray's squadron, Howie Spaas and Jen Collins, had run into them while they'd been at a place called the Worldview, a bar-restaurant next to the spaceport at the SupraQuito space elevator. They'd started hassling him about being a Prim and a monogie in front of Rissa and he'd lost it, had decked Howie Spaas. Commander Allyn, the Dragonfires' skipper, had come that close to sending him up for a court martial, closer still to kicking him out of the squadron.

He still liked to imagine that the extra duty, the anger-management therapy, and the ass-chewing he'd gotten from the skipper had all been worth it.

Lieutenant Spaas was dead, now—killed trying to bring his damaged Starhawk down on *America*'s flight deck at Eta Boötis. Collins was still in *America*'s sick bay, broken physically and emotionally at Alphekka. Commander Allyn was still in the sick bay as well, her brain damaged by oxygen starvation after her fighter drifted for three days through the Alphekkan debris field.

Riss had more than once indicated that she was still interested in Gray . . . and when her promotion to lieutenant came through on Earth four months earlier, even the technical barrier of their respective ranks had been removed. Gray had come very close to taking her to bed then . . . but he'd run into Angela at a big political function at the Eudaimonium in New New York and that had raised once more all of the doubts and self-searchings. Damn it, he'd thought Angela was dead after that Turusch impactor had sent a tidal wave thundering up the Hudson Valley.

Somehow, it had never happened.

And then Commander Allyn had been injured at Alphekka, the Dragonfires had suffered 75 percent casualties, Gray had been given temporary command of VFA-44 . . . and Schiffie had volunteered to transfer from Avionics to a replacement slot in the squadron. Now he *was* her boss, *and* he was responsible for her training.

The situation, clearly, had changed.

"I was wondering, Trev, when you were going to have some downtime. I'd still like to see you. Like we talked about, y'know?"

Gray leaned back in his chair, his lunch, half-eaten, forgotten now. Their table was near one of the compartment's viewall bulkheads, which curved all the way around to create a 270-degree panorama of the starscape outside. The cameras transmitting the image were mounted on *America*'s nonrotating spine or shield cap, so that the star field didn't move with the turning hab modules—which included the mess deck—through a full circle.

In the distance, several of the battlegroup's members were taking on water—the *United States of North America* and the *Abraham Lincoln*, both Lincoln-class fleet carriers slightly smaller than the *America*. They looked like toys at this distance, gleaming in the hard white glow of the distant HD 157950. The supply ships *Mare Orientalis, Salt Lake,* and *Lacus Solis* drifted close by the carriers, each tucked in close against its own kilometer-wide floating iceberg, converting them to reaction mass and organic volatiles for the fleet's nanufactories.

"Riss," Gray said, "it *can't* be like that. Not now. I'm your CO now."

She laughed. "Geez, get over yourself, Trev! I'm not talking about monogie, here! Who's going to know?"

"Me, for one," Gray said. He'd not intended his voice to sound so cold.

Her voice turned cold as well. "Very well, Lieutenant," she said. She stood and picked up her tray. "I apologize for bothering you."

"Aw, sit down and eat your chow, Riss!"

But she was gone.

Monogie . . .

After three years, he was still having trouble fitting in.

Trevor Gray was still a Prim, raised in the cast-off wreckage of the USNA's Periphery, specifically in the Manhattan Ruins. Squatties in the Periphery didn't have access to the high-tech toys of full citizens, like cerebral implants and Net access, and they didn't have the social entitlements—like medical care—of citizens either. That had been why he'd agreed to join the service: to pay for the med service when Angela had had her stroke.

Cut off from the social mainstream, Prims also had a completely different take on society. The garbage that passed for art and music, the truly bizarre fashions both in clothing and in body, the spoiled and pampered decadence of ordinary citizens, all of those were so far beyond the ken of Prims struggling just to survive within the old and flooded coastal city ruins that there seemed to be no point to social contact at all.

One major difference had been the mainstream's attitude toward sex—casual, recreational, and often with little or no emotional commitment. In the Ruins it was different. Couples paired for life, a survival strategy in an environment where one hunter-gatherer partner watched the other's back.

Throughout much of the human population, now, the mainstream view held that monogamous pairings—"monogies"—represented an archaic and flawed twist in human behavior. A few religious sects still required monogamous sexual relationships, while a few—the NeoMorms and fundamentalist Muslims, especially—allowed polygamy, but not the reverse, polyandry.

Damn. He'd not wanted to make Rissa angry.

Maybe when the Skipper came back and took over the squadron again. Or maybe someone else would be transferred in. Squadron CO was a commander's billet; Gray wouldn't even be looking at a promotion to lieutenant commander for another four years or so, and commander was a good four or five years after that, generally.

And maybe he should just forget about having a private life at all. There were always sex feeds, downloaded through your implants. Virtual sex was as good nowadays as the real thing. . . .

What Gray missed, he knew, was not the physical release so much as the companionship, the closeness, the *belonging*. When you were a part of a closely bonded pair . . .

Damn it all to hell. . . .

Standing, he took his tray to the mess deck entrance and tossed it and his half-eaten lunch into the converter. The Dragonfires were due to go on duty in another six hours, flying CAP just in case the Europeans went back on the hastily organized truce.

He wondered if the problem with Rissa was going to screw the flight scheds.

CIC
TC/USNA CVS America
Kuiper Belt, HD 157950
98 light years from Earth
1530 hours, TFT

"Message in from the *Illustrious*, Admiral."
"Thank you."
Koenig opened the channel, and Harrison's face ap-

peared, grinning. "Good afternoon, Admiral," he said. "Thought you'd like to hear the news."

"What news is that, Ron?"

"Some of us have finished up with our council of war. Looks like Admiral Giraurd is going to be going home by his lonesome."

"Really?"

Harrison nodded. "*Illustrious*, *Warspite*, and *Conqueror* were with you from the get-go. You knew that."

"I did. And thank you."

"Don't mention it. I'm just glad to get that weasel Coleman off my ship. She smells a lot better now that he's gone."

Willard Coleman had been the Confederation political officer on board the *Illustrious*, a civilian reporting to Hans Westerwelle on the *Jeanne d'Arc*, and tasked with keeping an eye on the loyalties of Confederation officers in the British squadron.

"In any case, we've been talking with the other commanders in the Pan-European squadron," Harrison continued. "Except for the *Jeanne d'Arc*, they're with us. Captain Michel, on the *Arc*, would have been too . . . but old Giraurd *does* need a way to get back home."

"Good God. . . ."

"Don't know about the Chinese, yet," he went on. "But you can count on the rest of us. Nineteen ships, including two light carriers."

"And that," Koenig replied, "is the best news I've heard all day. Welcome aboard."

He didn't bring up the problems this decision would make for the various ship captains. They *knew*.

That they were willing to join Koenig's career suicide, however, spoke volumes about how other naval officers viewed the Confederation . . .

. . . and what to do about the alien Sh'daar.

Chapter Five

Admiral's Office
TC/USNA CVS America
Approaching Texaghu Resch System
112 light years from Earth
1002 hours, TFT

Seventy-four days after departing the refueling rendezvous within the Kuiper Belt of HD 157950, a total of fifty-eight ships tunneled through the Void within their Alcubierre bubbles, their AIs holding them on course for a star invisible from Earth. Admiral Koenig sat in his office, reviewing again the electronic files of the ships and crews that had joined CBG-18.

In fact, only seventeen of the Pan-European Federation ships had joined the battlegroup, not the nineteen Harrison had promised. As it turned out, Captain Michel and the *Jeanne d'Arc* had voted to join the squadron, a surprise last-moment mutiny that had thrown the European contingent into considerable disarray. The crews of three European ships—the destroyers *Karlsruhe* and *Audace*, and the heavy cruiser *De Grasse*—had voted not to join CBG-18, and returned to Sol. Admiral Giraurd had left on board the *De Grasse*, along with the political officers and a number of other men and women who'd chosen to adhere to Confederation Navy orders. Those three ships were crowded. A number of the officers and crew of the remaining Federation ships had elected to return to Earth as well, while some on board the three had transferred to vessels remaining with the battlegroup.

Four of the nine Chinese ships had returned to Earth as well. Five, however, under the command of Admiral Liu Zhu, had elected to join *America* and CBG-18. Koenig wasn't sure, yet, if that represented Hegemon approval of his strategy . . . or if Beijing, independent of the Confederation, was simply determined to keep an eye on him.

Fifty-eight ships, then—more than twice the number surviving after Alphekka—were about to emerge at Texaghu Resch, and Koenig needed to have a long-anticipated conversation with the two nonhuman beings on board the star carrier *America*.

"Admiral," Koenig's personal electronic secretary said, "the two Agletsch are here to see you, as you requested."

"Thank you. Send them in."

The office door opened, and the aliens walked in, followed by a Marine guard.

Humans called them "bugs" or "spiders," though they were, of course, unrelated to anything that had ever lived on Earth. Flattened and slightly elongated disk-shapes on sixteen slender, jointed legs, each stood as tall as a short human but took up considerably more space. Instead of chitin, their integuments were red-brown, soft, almost velvety, with blue and yellow markings like the reticulated patterns of some snakes. Legs and what passed for faces were black; four eyes on stalks emerged from each face, and Koenig was only now beginning to realize that the movements of the eye stalks added emphasis to their speech. Silver markings on their bodies were decoration of some sort, while each had a metallic device below its face that served as a translator.

Both Agletsch—their names were Gru'mulkisch and Dra'ethde—were, technically, female; their nonsentient males hung like grotesque, gelatinous leeches from their faces.

Koenig stood as they entered. "Thank you for coming," he told them.

"We appreciate you seeing us, Admiral," Dra'ethde told him. "We have been . . . concerned. We have not been allowed into your CIC or bridge since leaving Arcturus."

Even now, Koenig had trouble telling the two apart, though there were subtle differences in the decorative silver inlays on their skins. A subroutine programmed into his cerebral implant had learned to recognize those patterns, however, and threw the name of the individual up against his visual field when one spoke. Dra'ethde appeared to be the senior of the two, though the niceties of Agletsch social structures were not yet well understood.

Koenig nodded to the Marine. "You can leave us, Staff Sergeant," he said. "Wait in the office outside."

"Aye, aye, sir." The Marine turned and left, the door sliding shut behind her.

"I do understand you concern," Koenig told the aliens when they were alone. "You were excluded from the bridge and CIC on my orders." He thoughtclicked an icon in his in-head display, and a three-dimensional image winked on in the air above his desk. It looked, Koenig thought, like a tangled mat of hair a meter tall, slowly rotating in space. "When we found these. Can you blame me?"

"No, Admiral Koenig. But we regret that you still do not . . . understand. Yes-no?"

The fact was that the two aliens were *bugged*—a humorous-enough statement given what Agletsch looked like to humans. Each being contained, hidden away within her brain, something called a Sh'daar Seed. The image of one, magnified several million times, hung in the air between them now.

The implants had only been discovered at Arcturus, when information concerning the destination of CBG-18, Alphekka, had been relayed from the Agletsch to a Sh'daar data web within a H'rulka community in the atmosphere of Al-chameth, a gas giant circling the star Arcturus. The H'rulka were another species within the Sh'daar galactic web, and that intelligence had been transmitted to the Sh'daar forces stationed at Alphekka. The things were tiny, the metal in them masked by the silver inlays on their carapaces. Only after the transmission had been detected had close internal scans picked the things up, microscopic tangles of artifi-cially grown components that apparently served as minute electronic nodes of an extended Sh'daar intelligence.

They allowed the Agletsch to serve as far-traveling eyes and ears for the absent Sh'daar, rulers of an extended galac-tic empire that had never been seen by humans . . . or by the members of any other species with which Humankind had communicated thus far. It was assumed that the Turusch and other nonhuman species aligned with the Sh'daar also had the implants. There were, Koenig knew, a number of Turusch now living in a base on Earth's moon run by the Office of Naval Intelligence.

He wondered if they were broadcasting details of their life there to the Sh'daar net.

"And what is it that we don't understand?" Koenig asked.

"That the Sh'daar Seed only becomes active when an-other node is close by."

"And what do you mean by 'close by'?"

"A few thousand of your kilometers."

Their translators, Koenig thought, were doing a good job of turning Agletsch measures and numbers into human units. At least he *hoped* that was the case. A misunderstand-ing here—or a deliberate lie—could make for a serious in-telligence leak to the enemy. That was why he'd ordered that the Agletsch be restricted in their freedom of movement on board the *America*—and why they now had a Marine guard following them everywhere except within the shielded suite of compartments designated as their quarters.

Because they *were* alien, with alien ways of thinking and of expression far more extreme than any mere outward differences in appearance and biology, Koenig was careful when talking with them. They were here as guides; the Agletsch were interstellar traders whose homeworld lay somewhere within Sh'daar space, but who also ventured far beyond those boarders into other regions not claimed by the Sh'daar. When the Sh'daar had issued their ultimatum and the war had begun thirty-eight years ago, numerous Agletsch had been trapped inside Confederation territory. Some had left; many had stayed. The possibility that those who had stayed were acting as enemy agents—as *spies*—was worrisome to the Office of Naval Intelligence . . . but there'd never been any indication that the Agletsch were in contact with either the stay-at-home Agletsch or their Sh'daar masters.

When the Turusch defenders of the manufactory complex at Alphekka redeployed their fleets to trap the incoming Confederation battlegroup, Koenig had suspected an electronic hand-off of data at the H'rulka colony on Alchameth. Microscopic medical scans had turned up the implants; the Agletsch themselves had admitted that they were Sh'daar Seeds, a term that seemed to mean quasi-sentient computers that acquired, stored, and eventually uploaded data to a Sh'daar equivalent of the e-Net.

The question, so far as Koenig was concerned, was just what the range of the Sh'daar Seeds might be. If it truly was a few thousand kilometers, there was no chance of the Agletcsh passengers alerting Sh'daar forces in the target system upon Emergence.

But what if *America* engaged with enemy ships later on, within the target system's core? If *America* passed within a thousand klicks or so of a Turusch battle cruiser, what information might be transmitted to the enemy?

That was why Koenig had ordered them to stay off the bridge and out of CIC, the nerve centers for both the carrier and the battlegroup. What they couldn't see and hear, the Sh'daar Seed couldn't store.

Unless there were other twists to the alien technology

Koenig didn't understand, or which the Agletsch were concealing.

How the hell could you tell if an alien was lying?

Another fleet commander might have ordered the two aliens thrown in the brig and surrounded by a Faraday cage . . . or even killed. Koenig didn't want to take a step that drastic, not yet. The Agletsch so far had been most helpful in their general information about the Turusch Directory, and about the nature of the worlds listed there.

"A few thousand kilometers?" Koenig said after a long and thoughtful pause. "I'll accept that." He thoughtclicked an in-head icon, and the holographic image above his desk winked out. "I still don't want you in certain sensitive areas of the ship, though. I don't know if these Seeds you've described can probe our electronic systems, or if they're just eavesdropping on what we say."

"This we do understand, Admiral."

The information transmitted to the Sh'daar at Alchameth had actually consisted of a speech Koenig himself had made over the shipboard intercom. He'd mentioned that their designation was Alphekka, and the Sh'daar Seeds, evidently, had been smart and autonomous enough to figure out which star system that was—the Sh'daar didn't call it "Alphekka," certainly—and pass on the warning.

If he understood what the Agletsch were describing, billions, perhaps *trillions* of separate Sh'daar Seeds were planted inside individual members of various subject species: Turusch, H'rulka, Nungiirtok, and some tens of thousands of other species. Each individual then, became a free-moving and independent computer node within an incredibly vast and far-flung network.

No one had yet intercepted a Seed transmission, however. How powerful they might be, what their range was, how easily shielded such signals might be, their duration, all of that was as yet unknown.

Koenig wondered if Gru'mulkisch and Dra'ethde knew how many high-tech sensors were focused on their bodies at every hour of shipboard day and night, using *America*'s own internal electronic Net, with the intent of capturing and recording a transmission in order to learn more about its capabilities.

"There remains much that we do not understand about the Seeds' capabilities ourselves," Dra'ethde told him. "We know simply that they are."

"And that they are what you would call a fact of life," Gru'mulkisch added. "Yes-no?"

"We would very much like to know," Koenig said carefully, "if we can use access to the Sh'daar Seeds—meaning through *you* two—to communicate with the Sh'daar directly. Since you delivered their ultimatum thirty-some years ago, we've not been in direct contact. Being able to talk to them might help us avoid needless bloodshed."

Not to mention, Koenig added to himself, the extinction of the humans species.

"It is possible," Dra'ethde told him, "though it would take time to pass communications from node to node all the way to the old galactic core. We would need to be in contact with another transmission node, however."

"Hold up, there," Koenig said. "What did you just say? 'Old galactic core'? I've not heard that term."

"Indeed? We don't know anything about it either, save that it is what the Sh'daar call their . . . not homeworld. But the region where their homeworld lies."

"Is that the core of this galaxy? What we call the Milky Way?"

The aliens exchanged a momentary glance of weaving eyestalks. "We don't know," Gru'mulkisch said. "It is simply a name. *Gu reheh'mek chaash.* You would say 'old galactic core' or perhaps 'center of the old galaxy,' yes-no?"

The galactic core, Koenig thought, that teeming mass of billions of close-packed stars residing at the heart of the Milky Way, lay roughly 25,000 light years away in the direction of the constellation Sagittarius. It was old, yes—as old as the galaxy, which by best estimates had formed about

12 billion years ago. But why distinguish it as the *old* core? Or the old galaxy . . .

Was Gru'mulkisch suggesting that the Sh'daar had come from a *different* galaxy?

That set the hairs at the back of his neck prickling. No one knew quite how large the Sh'daar expanse of space actually was, though intelligence estimates based on interviews with the Agletsch suggested that it embraced something like half of the galaxy—perhaps as much as two thirds, perhaps as little as a quarter. That was big enough . . . but if they had the technology to travel between galaxies, to come to *this* one from some other galaxy hundreds of thousands or even millions of light years away . . .

What the hell did they mean by "old galactic core"?

He flagged the term with a mental note. He would forward it to the ONI boys down in Intel and see what they could make of it.

Koenig considered the two aliens for a moment. First Contact with the Agletsch had occurred in 2312, nearly a century ago, but humans still knew remarkably little about them. The Agletsch as a species were interstellar traders, star-faring merchants, of a sort. Not traders of *material* goods, of course. One solar system contained much the same in the way of natural resources—water ice, organic volatiles, metals, energy—as the next. Even cultural artifacts— artwork, say, or textiles or gemstones or commercial items of technology—could be carried between the stars far more efficiently as stored patterns of information rather than the original bulk items.

So the Agletsch traded in information, a kind of universal medium of exchange. And for ninety-three years they'd shared very little about themselves, or about their galactic masters, the Sh'daar. As Koenig understood it, merchants like Dra'ethde and Gru'mulkisch traveled far beyond the borders of their own stellar polities and lived for decades as visitors to other cultures, other civilizations, where they recorded what they could, and determined what, if anything, the new civilization had to trade. One observer had likened them to alien Marco Polos in the courts of alien Khans. Another had once suggested that they were a kind of living *Encyclopedia Galactica*, slowly accumulating information on all sentient life throughout the galaxy . . . which they would trade to others in exchange for *more* such information.

Had they accidentally let slip that tidbit about the old galaxy? Koenig tried the direct approach. "So tell me . . . where *are* the Sh'daar from?"

Gru'mulkisch twisted her eyestalks in what Koenig had been told was an expression indicating humor—the equivalent of a human smile. "We can't tell you that, Admiral," she said. "That data would be extremely valuable, yes-no?"

"There must be an exchange," Dra'ethde told him. "We have been asked about this before by your intelligence people. . . ."

"And what would you accept in exchange for that information?" Koenig asked.

"We are not aware of anything you possess worth such an exchange, Admiral," Gru'mulkisch said. "We regret this . . . but what you ask is *mish'a'ghru*. Of first importance, you might say, yes-no?"

"In fact," Dra'ethde added, "I regret having mentioned *gu reheh'mek chaash* at all, and perhaps I was irresponsible in doing so. But since the words will not help you, no harm has been done, yes-no?"

The phrase translated as "yes-no," Koenig knew, was what the xenolinguists referred to as an *agreement manipulator*, a way to get others to agree with you, to be on your side in a conversation, and to disarm any potential hostility. Individually, the Agletsch were more agreeable to talk with than many humans Koenig knew.

But talking with them tended to lead in unsatisfying circles. Even if the Agletsch translator units perfectly shifted between the English and Agletsch languages, there was a hell of a lot missing on both sides simply because of differences in culture, attitude, and worldview.

Koenig wondered how much of their professional reticence was due to business considerations, and how much to the fact that both of them carried Sh'daar Seeds that, no doubt, were listening in on this conversation and recording it.

"We are about to emerge from Alcubierre Drive," he told them. "I can't allow you on the bridge or in the CIC, but I've given orders to dress the crew's lounge for external view, and you can watch from there."

"Thank you, Admiral."

"My senior aide, Lieutenant Commander Nahan Cleary, will be with you. If I have questions of you two, I'll pass them to him. Okay?"

"Quite acceptable, Admiral."

"And if either of you have insights about what's happening, I'd appreciate it if you could share them with him. Such information will be considered to be under the terms of your contract."

"Of course, Admiral."

The two Agletsch had volunteered to accompany *America* and her battlegroup on this mission as guides—which meant that they were expected to share data with Koenig and his officers without the need to haggle over the informational price of each item. His understanding was that the Agletsch mission on Earth had been "paid" for their services with several exabytes of information drawn from the New Library of Congress in Columbus, and from the British Library in High London. He wondered what, specifically, the Agletsch had learned in exchange for the services of these two.

No matter. He expected them to deliver.

"You're certain," Koenig said, "that you have nothing to add to your report about this system we're about to enter?"

"Quite certain, Admiral," Gru'mulkisch said. "We know that the system is of importance within the Sh'daar network, but we've not been here before. We do not believe it to be inhabited, but cannot tell you if it is defended, or if there is a military base or outpost."

"In fact, we hope to acquire profit here ourselves," Dra'ethde added. "Yes-no?"

By *profit*, Koenig assumed the Agletsch was referring to new information, something even the Agletsch did not know.

"What happened to the Chelk," Koenig told them, "might well happen to *my* species. If you two learn anything new, I'll expect you to share it with us. I *will* invoke the contract if I must."

"We understand this, Admiral." Gru'mulkisch sounded almost contrite . . . or possibly cautious, as though she were picking her sixteen-legged way across thin ice.

"And we appreciate you including us in the investigation," Dra'ethde said.

"We will be emerging from metaspace in another hour," Koenig said. "I suggest you get down to the crew's lounge and make yourselves ready. Mr. Cleary will join you there."

"Thank you, Admiral," Gru'mulkisch said. "We expect that this will be of great profit to both our peoples, yes-no? A place neither human nor Agletsch has yet ventured."

But Koenig still wondered if the many-legged beings could be trusted.

VFA-44
Approaching Texaghu Resch System
112 light years from Earth
1058 hours, TFT

Lieutenant Gray tried to relax within the close embrace of his fighter. Always it was the waiting that was hardest. He checked his in-head time. Five minutes.

The Dragonfires were doing a drop-launch this time, free-falling with the centrifugal force of *America*'s rotating hab modules. When it was time to launch, Gray's fighter would pivot ninety degrees, pointing out and down relative to the turning bay, the magnetic clamps would release, and the hab module's rotation would fling him into space with a half-G of acceleration—about five meters per second. Once clear of *America*'s immense forward shield cap, the squadron would orient on the local system's sun and then boost; fifty thousand gravities would bring them close to the speed of light in just a whisker under ten minutes.

"Hey, Skipper?" It was Miguel Zapeta, on the squadron channel. "Any word yet on who we're gonna be fighting? Or *if* we're going to be fighting?"

"Nothing yet, Zap," Gray replied. "We'll be the first to know, right?"

"Yeah. Except the scuttlebutt I heard was that the bugs know, and they're leading us into a trap."

"So, you're believing scuttlebutt, now? Who told you that shit?"

"Uh . . . a gal I know in S-2."

S-2 was the designation for *America*'s intelligence department. "Ah, well if Naval Intelligence said it, it *must* be true, right?"

He heard several chuckles over the squadron channel. *Good. Loosen them up a bit. You don't want them thinking too hard before a drop.*

"We'll be emerging far enough out-system that we'll have plenty of time for a look around, okay? The entire Sh'daar galactic fleet could be in there, and they'd never even see us if we dropped in, took a look, and then jumped back into Alcubierre Space." He hesitated, then grinned as he added, "Yes-no?"

That raised laughter from the waiting Dragonfires. The odd patterns of Agletsch speech and their constant use of the phrase "yes-no" was well known to everyone on board *America* by now.

"Sounds like we have an Agletsch loose in the squadron," Rostenkowski said, laughing. "Since when did *they* start driving Dragonfires?"

"Dragonfires, PriFly," Wizewski's voice broke in. "Is there a problem?"

"Negative, CAG," Gray replied. "No problem."

"Can the chatter in there and focus on your finals. Emergence in three minutes. Drop in sixty seconds after that."

"Aye, aye, sir."

No sense of humor, that one.

He was glad the newbies in the squadron *could* laugh, though. They'd been training hard in sim, but the real deal was *never* like electronic simulations, no matter how bad-assed realistic the downloads.

If they could enjoy a joke *now*, they ought to be okay.

He hoped. . . .

CIC
TC/USNA CVS America
Outer System, Texaghu Resch System
112 light years from Earth
1103 hours, TFT

Emergence.

The star carrier *America* dropped into normal space as her Alcubierre bubble collapsed. Since she'd been motionless relative to the volume of space wrapped up inside the Alcubierre field, she emerged traveling at a velocity of only a few kilometers per second—the difference in relative velocities between *this* patch of space, and the space within the Kuiper Belt of HD 157950. The transition released a great deal of potential energy as light and hard radiation, a flaring burst spreading into and through the new star system at the speed of light.

Koenig studied the new system, both represented by icons within the tactical tank, and as revealed by optical sensors across the bulkhead viewalls of the Combat Information Center. They'd emerged ten astronomical units from the local star—a little farther than Saturn was from Sol. There were planets—five visible immediately, and there likely would be others as the ship's navigational AIs scanned local space.

"Admiral?" a familiar voice asked. "This is CAG. So you still want to launch fighters?"

"Wait one," Koenig told him. "We need to see what we're launching *to*."

Data continued to cascade in from the AIs scanning the system. Two inner rocky planets, small enough and close enough to their primary that they likely were too hot for Earth-type life. Planet III, 1.5 AUs from the star, was a small gas giant, about the size of Neptune. Beyond that, at 3 and 5 AUs, were two more rocky planets, both dazzlingly bright and probably encased pole to pole in planet-wide sheets of ice.

"Astrogation," Koenig called. "Give that gas giant a close look. Maybe it has Earthlike moons."

He was thinking of Alchameth, circling the star Arcturus, and its moon Jasper.

"We've been looking, Admiral. We've spotted several small moons—rocks, really—but nothing like a *real* planet."

"Carry on, then."

He felt a small bite of disappointment. Because of this system's listing in the Turusch Directory, he'd assumed there would be an inhabited planet here—if not one with an oxygen-nitrogen atmosphere and temperate climes comfortable for humans, than one with the reducing atmosphere and hot, sulfur-laden conditions enjoyed by the Turusch.

The truth of the matter, though, was that habitable worlds of either type were painfully few and far between within that sliver of the galaxy explored so far by Humankind. The chances that a world of near-Earth mass would just happen to lie within the band of liquid-water temperatures around a star were slim; the fact that the Confederation had discovered as many as twenty where humans could walk unprotected—Chiron and Circe and Osiris and the others—spoke more to how many stars were out here, not to how common other Earths might be.

Texaghu Resch was a G2-type star almost identical to Sol . . . but it simply hadn't won the planetological crapshoot that would have led to its possessing a planet humans could call home.

Something was flashing red in the tactical tank. Koenig looked . . . then blinked. There was something there. *America*'s instrumentation was picking up a gravitational anomaly. In essence, the ship was feeling about twice the force of gravity it should be feeling at this distance from a G-class star. It was *exactly* as though there were two stars in there—a close binary—each of about one solar mass . . . but one of the stars was invisible.

Either that, or the single visible star was twice as massive as it should be, and that simply wasn't possible, not within the rules governing stellar classification as humans now understood them.

"Admiral?" another voice said. "This is Lieutenant Del Rey, in Astrogation."

"Go ahead."

"Have you seen the GA alert, sir?"

"Yes, I have. What do you make of it?"

"We didn't know what the hell it was at first. We still don't. But . . . take a look at this, sir."

A visual feed came through, opening as a new window within Koenig's in-head display. It appeared to be a highly magnified image of a portion of the star itself, with the light drastically stepped down by the AI controlling it. Koenig could see the curving limb of the star, the mottling of the surface granulation, the sweep and arch of stellar prominences. At first, he saw nothing out of the ordinary.

And then . . .

"Good God!" he said, expanding the image for a closer look. "What the hell is that?"

"We have no idea, sir," Del Rey replied. "But we thought it might be important."

And that, Koenig thought, was a hell of an understatement.

Chapter Six

VFA-44
Outer System, Texaghu Resch System
112 light years from Earth
1106 hours, TFT

"PriFly, this is Dragon One," Gray called. "What's the hang-up?" They were supposed to have dropped two minutes before, but Primary Flight Control had called for a hold.

"Wait one, Dragon One," a voice replied—one of the traffic control personnel in PriFly. "There's been a hitch. The Space Boss is talking to the admiral now."

The "Space Boss" was Commander Avery, *America*'s primary flight controller.

Gray scowled. His cockpit was projecting a view of surrounding space, overlaid with icons representing the ships of CBG-18 as they continued to emerge from metaspace. A dozen Confederation vessels were out there, now, with more popping in every moment as the light from their Emergence reached the *America*'s sensors.

There were no icons representing enemy or unknown vessels. It appeared that this system might be clean.

Possibly the drop was going to be scrubbed.

Well, that was the battle cry of the Navy: *hurry up and wait.*

"Dragonfire Squadron, this is PriFly," Commander Avery said. "The drop is scrubbed. Repeat, the drop is scrubbed. VFA-51 will remain on Ready Five. All others will stand down."

VFA-51, the Black Lightnings, was one of the Dragonfires' sister Starhawk squadrons on board the *America*. Commander Alton Crane was their new skipper, and like the Dragonfires, they'd taken heavy losses at Alphekka, and a good half of the pilots were newbies.

Gray felt a jolt as his Starhawk began rising within its magnetic cradle. A moment later, it passed through the drop-tube vacuum seal, allotropic composites within a nanomatrix that made solid metal flow like a thick, viscous liquid, allowing the fighter to be drawn into the carrier's flight deck while maintaining the compartment's atmospheric pressure. His cockpit melted open and swung away as a rating outside triggered steps that grew out of the deck.

"Short flight, huh?" the guy said, grinning.

"The best kind," Gray replied with considerable feeling. *"Uneventful."*

An hour later, Gray entered the crew's lounge, located at the third-G level of *America*'s number-two hab-module stack. The compartment was large and furnished more like a civilian social center Earthside, with numerous entertainment pits, food bars, and low couches grown from the deck and turned soft. The overhead was an enormous dome, and at the moment, it was displaying the view outside. The local star, yellow, bright, and showing a tiny disk, gleamed halfway up the gently curving bulkhead.

Shay Ryan spotted him and walked over. "Hey, Skipper," she called. "Looks like they don't want us here, either."

Like Gray, Ryan was a Prim, formerly of the Periphery areas that once had been Washington, D.C., until rising sea levels had reclaimed the lowland areas as a ruin-littered salt marsh. Like Gray, she'd joined the service because she'd had few decent options. Like him, she mistrusted both government authority and technology, but she'd tested well on her inborn spatial and coordination skills, and they'd made her a fighter pilot.

"Hello, Shay," he said. He walked over to a food bar and placed his palm on the contact. He ordered a cola, which rose from within the black surface a moment later in a sealed cup with a built-in straw. "Looks like we lucked out, huh?"

"Shit. I don't like going through all of that, getting ready to drop into hard-V, and then suddenly get pulled back. They're just jerking us around, y'know?"

"Any day they pull us back," Gray replied, "is a day we don't get into a knife fight with toads." *Toads* was pilot slang for the blunt, heavy, hard-to-kill fighters used by the Turusch. "And that suits me just fine."

"I guess. Hey . . . did you see? A couple of our old friends are on deck."

Gray turned and glanced in the direction she was pointing, his eyes widening a bit. "So! They're allowing the spiders out to play?"

"Maybe the brass trusts them now."

Gray glanced at the Marine staff sergeant standing behind the two Agletsch. "More likely they figure they can't do any harm here. Let's go say hi."

Gray and Ryan both had met the two Agletsch three months earlier, just before the battlegroup had departed from Earth's SupraQuito synchorbital complex. They'd been at a restaurant called the Overlook, and an officious headwaiter had been trying to expel the two many-legged aliens for no other reason than, as far as Gray could tell, that they didn't happen to be human. Gray, Ryan, and several other service personnel had lodged a protest by leaving en masse, taking the Agletsch with them to another restaurant, one without so narrow a definition of acceptable patrons.

And they'd gotten to know the two pretty well, Gray thought, as well as it was possible to know beings with both physiologies and psychologies utterly different from anything from Earth.

A small crowd had gathered around the two Agletsch, who

were standing with a lieutenant commander in a full dress uniform. Gray thought he recognized the guy—someone on Admiral Koenig's staff. When he pinged the man's id, he got back a name and rank: LCDR N. Cleary.

He wasn't sure which alien was which, but he had their names stored in his implant memory. "Hey, Dra'ethde," he said. "What brings you down here?"

The Agletsch on the right twisted two of its eye stalks around for a look, identifying itself for Gray as the one he'd named. "Ah! You are the fighter pilot Trevor Gray, yes-no?"

"Yes. We met at SupraQuito, remember?"

"We do. We are delighted to see you again. And Shay Ryan as well! We remember you, too."

"Stay clear of this, Lieutenant," Cleary said. "We're on duty."

"Doing what?" Ryan asked. "Watching vids?"

A three-meter-high portion of the viewall dome directly in front of the small group had been turned into a display window, showing, it appeared, a portion of the local star.

"We're looking at what scrubbed your drop, Lieutenant," Cleary said. "And we would appreciate it if you would stand back and not crowd."

Gray and Ryan did move back, but only one step. Gray was intensely curious. So far as he could see, they were studying one quarter of the system's G2 star. Nothing remarkable there at all.

"We have heard of this sort of thing, Commander," Gru'mulkisch said, apparently continuing an interrupted discussion with Cleary. "But only in whispers. The Sh'daar masters do not speak of them."

"Is it Sh'daar?" Cleary asked. "Did they build it?"

"Perhaps," Dra'ethde said. "But it would have been in the *Schjaa Krah*. You would say the 'Old Time,' or possibly the '*First* Time,' yes-no? A time a very, very long time ago, perhaps before they *were* the Sh'daar."

"What the hell are you talking about?" Gray asked, then added, "Sir."

For a moment, he thought Cleary was going to tell him to get lost, but the staff officer just shrugged and shook his head. "Have a look."

A small square outlined in black appeared just below the limb of the star, then expanded, magnifying the image sharply. The image now showed the uneven granulations of the star's surface: twisting, linear patterns of lesser light against the greater. And there was something else. . . .

To Gray, it looked like a fuzzy shadow, but one made out of light—bright light, but still dimmer than the glare from the star behind it. The thing, whatever it was, had a definite shape—elongated, considerably longer than it was wide— but it was masked in a hazy, twisted blur that made it look fuzzy and indistinct.

It was moving across the face of the star, and as it moved, the granulations appeared to pucker and twist behind it.

"It's bending light," Gray said.

"It looks like a dustball," Ryan added.

Dustballs were tiny clots of matter scooped up by the flickering, artificial singularity projected ahead of a fighter or larger vessel using its gravitic drive to move through normal space. Though the drive singularity switched on and off thousands of times per second, it dragged hydrogen atoms, dust and debris swept up from the space ahead just as it did the fighter falling along behind it. In space where the local density of hydrogen and flecks of dust was relatively high—within the inner reaches of a star system, for instance—the dust could collect faster than the microscopic singularity could swallow it, creating tiny, light-bending patches of fuzz the fighter pilots called dustballs.

"What we're looking at," Cleary explained, "has a mass of about one point nine times ten to the thirty-third grams . . . or about the same as Earth's sun."

"A black hole?" Gray said.

Take a star as large as Sol and crush it down until it's just six kilometers wide. What you get is a gravitational singularity with the same mass and the same gravitational field as the original star . . . but in close, *very* close, the gravitational field becomes so strong that not even light can escape it—hence the name: *black* hole.

"Wait a minute," Ryan said. "I thought stars like Sol were too small to become black holes."

"Exactly," Cleary said. "If a star of about three solar masses collapses, it becomes a black hole. A smaller sun becomes a neutron star . . . and if it's smaller still, like our sun, it becomes a white dwarf."

"The object we are observing," Dra'ethde pointed out, "is clearly artificial. A natural stellar collapse would result in a sphere . . . or, rather, a spherical ergosphere, with the singularity within."

"The thing," Cleary said, "is roughly twelve kilometers long and about one wide, and it appears to be rotating around its long axis at close to the speed of light. Whoever built it can do tricks with mass and gravity that we can't even imagine yet."

"Okay," Gray said. "It's super-tech. But what does it do?"

"That's what we're trying to decide," Cleary said. "Our best guess so far is that it's a kind of Tipler machine . . . but we know that *that* is absolutely impossible."

"Perhaps," Gru'mulkisch said quietly, "the builders do not agree with you as to what is or is not possible."

Gray had to access the ship's library and download information on Tipler and the machine named after him. Frank Tipler had been a mathematical physicist and cosmologist in the twentieth century who'd written a paper based on the van Stockum-Lanczos solutions to the equations of general relativity. That paper, "Rotating cylinders and the possibility of global causality violation," had presented the possibility of what were called closed timelike curves appearing in the vicinity of a very long, very massive, rapidly rotating cylinder. According to Tipler, if you could stretch a black hole into a rigid length of spaghetti and spin it up to something like 60 percent of the speed of light, some billions of rotations per second, the thing warped surrounding space in such a way that it would open portals not through space, but through *spacetime*, the two being inextricably linked within Einstein's equations.

The Tipler machine, in other words, was a time machine.

Toward the end of the same century, however, another physicist, the legendary Stephen Hawking, had proven that it simply couldn't be done. In order to open a doorway into the past, you would need a rotating cylinder that was infinitely long.

The Tipler time machine became a footnote in the physics textbooks, and was eventually almost forgotten.

Perhaps, as Gru'mulkisch had just suggested, the beings who'd built that thing out there hadn't read the same textbooks.

Gray felt a rising tingle at the back of his scalp.

"Who," he said quietly, "could possibly have built such a thing?"

"That is what we would like to know," Cleary replied.

Shadow Probe 1, Drop Bay 1
TC/USNA CVS America
Outer System, Texaghu Resch System
1224 hours, TFT

"Shadow Probe One ready for launch," Lieutenant Christopher Schiere reported.

"Copy that, One. You are clear for launch," Commander Avery replied. "Good luck!"

"Let's just hope it's better luck than last time," Schiere muttered.

"What was that, Probe One?"

"Nothing, Boss. Let's get this show going."

"And launch in three . . . two . . . one . . . *launch*!"

The CP-240 Shadowstar hurtled down the two-hundred-meter launch tube at seven gravities, emerging from the center of *America*'s shield cap 2.39 seconds later and traveling at 167 meters per second. The CP-240 was a near twin to the conventional SG-92 Starhawk strike fighter but was designed for just one task: *reconnaissance*. One of the ships assigned to *America*'s VQ-7 recon squadron, the Sneaky Peaks, Schiere's craft carried no weapons other than a collection of VR-5 recon drones. Slightly more massive than a Starhawk, it possessed a Gödel 2500 artificial intelligence, a self-aware system far more powerful and flexible than the Starhawk AIs.

And it could bend light around itself in a way that gave it near invisibility.

Lieutenant Christopher Schiere was an old hand with the Sneaky Peaks—named for their CO, Commander James Peak. *Sneak and peek* was their squadron motto, and they were an effective means of exploring ahead of the battle-group to see what might be lurking up ahead.

Schiere's last mission had been a high-velocity flyby of the manufactory orbiting Alphekka, and it had nearly been his last. Attacked by dozens of Turusch fighters, all he'd been able to do was tuck himself into a tight little invisible ball and hurtle on into emptiness. A day later, he'd risked decelerating and sending out a questing signal, a rescue beacon. One of *America*'s SAR tugs had picked him up forty hours later.

It had been a near thing. Finding an all-but-invisible sliver of a spacecraft many AUs from the battlespace was far worse than looking for the proverbial needle in a haystack. *Needles* you could see. . . .

Despite the near miss, Schiere had put up his hand when the skipper had asked for a volunteer. "What, are you nuts, Chris?" Peak had asked him.

"It's that damned horse, Skipper," Schiere had replied. "I need to get back on."

His post-mission psych check had flagged him as marginal, a downgrudge that normally would have taken him off of active flight status for at least six weeks, followed by re-evaluation. Schiere had fought the listing. Dr. Fifer and his damned psychtechs were *not* going to ground him.

Amazingly, the psych department had relented—no

doubt, as Schiere had told his buddies in the squadron, because they *knew* recon flight officers were nuts. Three days locked up inside a Shadowstar cockpit had been rough, yeah, and the thought that he might drift for eternity through the emptiness had preyed on him.

But he'd *made* it. They'd *found* him. He was good to go!

And he wanted to go, to go *now*, before he lost his nerve.

"*America* CIC, this is Shadow Probe One, handing off from PriFly and ready for acceleration. Shifting to sperm mode."

"Copy that, Shadow Probe One," a new voice said. "You are clear to accelerate at your discretion."

"Roger, *America*," he replied. "Bye-bye!"

He accelerated at fifty thousand gravities, and *America* vanished astern so swiftly it might have been whisked out of the sky.

And Christopher Schiere once again was as utterly alone as it was possible for a person to be.

The objective lay some eighty light minutes from *America*'s emergence point. At fifty thousand gravities, Schiere's Shadowstar was pushing 99.9 percent of *c* in ten minutes, and the universe around him had grown strange.

CIC
TC/USNA CVS America
Outer System, Texaghu Resch System
1225 hours, TFT

"Shadow Probe One is away, Admiral," the tactical officer reported. "Time to objective is ninety-three minutes, our reckoning."

"Thank you, Commander," Koenig told him. He noted the time. An hour and a half for the probe to reach the mysterious object, plus eighty minutes for the returning comm signal to reach the *America*—they could expect to receive a transmission in another 173 minutes, at around 1517 hours, or so.

Assuming the pilot didn't encounter hostiles.

He opened a channel. "Commander Peak? Koenig. Who's the VQ-7 pilot who just launched?"

"Lieutenant Christopher Schiere, sir."

He knew the name. "He was our advance scout at Alphekka, wasn't he?"

"Yes, sir. He's a brave man."

"Indeed. Thank you."

Koenig wanted to know who it was who was putting his life on the line for the battlegroup. He deserved to be remembered.

CBG-18 was still engaged in the tedious process of forming up around *America*. All fifty-seven of the other capital ships had reported in after Emergence, and all were now showing on *America*'s tactical displays.

And so far, not a single enemy target had appeared—no bases, no fighters, no capital ships, no sensor drones, no heat or energy signatures on or around any of the planets, nothing except for that enigmatic and utterly impossible object orbiting the local sun.

It was amusing, Koenig thought. The small army of artificial intelligences operating within *America*'s electronic network had first identified the thing, now called TRGA, for the Texaghu Resch gravitational anomaly, but not one had been able to hazard a guess at what it might be. Dr. Karen Schuman, a civilian physicist in *America*'s astrogation department, had been the one to make the connection with Frank Tipler. AIs tended to have extremely focused and somewhat narrow ways of looking at the universe, and would have had no reason to be aware of Tipler's long-forgotten theory.

Schuman, however, had a packrat mind and a fascination for the history of physics. Koenig had once spent a pleasant evening in the officers mess discussing Einstein over dinner with the woman.

Of course, traveling through time was still impossible. Stephen Hawking and others had proven that centuries ago.

Unless the Tipler cylinder was infinite in length, there would be no time travel.

There might well, however, be *space* travel, without a temporal component. That much mass rotating that quickly, according to the physicists and the AIs in Schuman's department, might well warp space in unusual ways, opening up a passage—the technical term was a wormhòle—allowing instantaneous travel across unimaginably vast distances. That was still strictly theoretical, however. They would need Schiere's report from an up-close examination of the artifact before they could refine their initial guesses.

Koenig considered ordering the fleet to begin moving in closer to the star, then decided against it.

There were simply too many unknowns to allow him to risk the fleet that way.

They would wait.

Shadow Probe 1
Approaching Texaghu Resch System
1357 hours, TFT

For Chris Schiere, only about twenty-five minutes had passed since he'd boosted clear of the *America*. His seventy-three-minute drift between his flight's acceleration and deceleration phases had been carried out at 99.7 percent of *c*, and time dilation had squeezed the subjective passage of that time down to just over five and a half minutes. He was now fifty kilometers from his objective and approaching it at a relative velocity of two hundred meters per second.

Close. Very close. And still no sign that the thing was occupied or guarded.

He stared ahead into bright-lit distance, adjusted the incoming levels of radiation, and stared again. He'd never been this close to a star before—fifteen million kilometers, a tenth of an AU, or roughly one quarter of the distance from Sol to Mercury. At this distance, the expanse of the local star covered over five degrees of the sky ahead—ten times wider than Sol appeared from Earth. Its brilliance would have blinded him instantly had the Shadowstar's AI not been stopping down the optical sensors. With the light reduced so much that he could look into it with his naked eyes, it was difficult to make out detail.

But the AI had bracketed the TRGA object, marking it for him.

And he was beginning to see it more clearly.

From *America*, ten AUs out, the artifact had appeared to be tiny, almost lost against the vastly enlarged backdrop of Texaghu Resch's photosphere, but that had been an illusion of distance and magnification. Here, the artifact seemed far larger in relationship to the star, and had drifted off to one side. It was still damned tough to make out the details, though. It looked like nothing so much as a long, slender knot made out of golden, glowing fuzz.

"This is Lieutenant Schiere, Shadow Probe One," he said, opening a laser-com channel back to the fleet. "Beginning reconnaissance report."

It would take eighty minutes for his words to reach them, but it was important that he begin transmitting immediately, sending them not only the data now being acquired by his ship's sensors, but his words, thoughts, and impressions from moment to moment . . . just in case.

"The near-*c* passage was completed without incident. I'm currently fifteen million kilometers from the outer regions of the stellar photosphere—what passes for the star's visible surface. It's hot. My hull is cycling most of the incident radiation around me, of course, but if it wasn't for that, I'd be basking at about six hundred degrees right now. My nano-matrix is still operating within acceptable tolerances, and I'm missing most of the rough stuff. If you decide to bring the fleet in this close, you'll have to do so with shields up full.

"I'm now forty-nine point seven kilometers from the target. Its mass is equivalent to that of a G-class star—call it one point nine-eight-eight times ten to the thirty-third grams. Intense gravitational folding in the object's immediate vicinity. I'd call the thing a black hole, except that it obviously is not. It's between twelve and thirteen kilometers long, roughly one kilometer wide or a little less. Still very hard to get precise measurements, because the volume of space immediately surrounding the object is extremely twisted. Light from the star is falling into that twisted space and emerging at odd angles, from constantly changing directions. Magnetic flux, too. It's like the thing is tying knots in space.

"Judging from the way the thing is twisting the local magnetic field, I'd have to say it is spinning. Can't even guess at how many rotations per second, though. It would have to be billions. Can something rotate at the speed of light?

"I'm accelerating slightly, moving closer. I've got the hull invisibility switched on. Still no sign there's anyone home. I'm going to arm three of my VR-5s and release them at intervals. That'll give us a closer look . . . and might get their attention if there's anyone in there."

The VR-5 was a remote-scan probe, a mass of sensory, transmission, and drive components imbedded within a nanomatrix that could shape itself as a slender needle a meter long for launch, or collapse into a black sphere twenty centimeters in diameter for reconnaissance. Schiere spent a moment linked with the Shadowstar's AI, programming the probes.

"Okay," he said. "We're good to go. Launching Probe One in three . . . two . . . one . . . *launch*!"

The first ebon needle slid from the CP-240's belly and vanished into space.

"And Probe Two in three . . . two . . . one . . . *launch*. And Number Three in three . . . two . . . one . . . *launch*."

Within his in-head display, he watched as the twist of clotted space around the objective grew rapidly larger.

"Okay . . . you should be seeing the imagery from the probes, now. My AI is linking it back on the primary data channel. I'm still not entirely sure what I'm seeing. The area of twisted space appears to extend out from the central object by a kilometer or two. The object itself . . . looks like a dark gray cylinder buried inside a thick fog of hazy light. I can't get radar or lidar reflections back, nothing coherent, anyway. The warp effect around the object is scattering everything I send.

"First probe is starting to enter the warped area. I . . . wait a sec . . . wait a sec . . ."

The VR-5 was penetrating the clotted light close to the near end of the object, and the shape inside was growing clear.

"My God!" Schiere said. "It's *hollow*!"

The image transmitted from the first probe suddenly seemed to leap forward, as though something had reached out, snatched the probe, and jerked it into that rapidly spinning maw.

Schiere and his recording instrumentation caught just a glimpse down a long, black tunnel—to a blaze of light at the far end.

And then the probe was gone.

"*America*, Probe One," Shield said. "It looks like my first drone got caught in an intense field of focused gravity and was pulled into the cylinder. Contact with the drone is lost.

"But if I had to guess, I'd say we're looking at a star gate."

Chapter Seven

CIC
TC/USNA CVS America
Outer System, Texaghu Resch System
112 light years from Earth
1518 hours, TFT

Technically, the objective appeared to be a stable artificial wormhole.

In fiction, such things had been called star gates, jump gates, jump portals, and a dozen other names. In physics, they were termed Lorentzian wormholes, Schwarzchilde wormholes, or Einstein-Rosen bridges, but all of the names meant the same thing: a means of warping local space so tightly that a tunnel or doorway was opened between two points in spacetime quite possibly *very* far removed from each other. Albert Einstein and Nathan Rosen had first postulated the idea of the Einstein-Rosen bridge as early as 1935, though the structure they'd proposed mathematically would have collapsed. Other physicists, much later, had proposed theoretical constructs called wormholes. The idea was that a worm crawling over the curved surface of an apple might take a long time to reach the other side; the trip would be shortened if he bored through the middle. The concept depended on three spatial dimensions being curved through a fourth.

For four centuries, wormholes had remain strictly theoretical, a possible outgrowth of certain equations within Einstein's field equations. Whether they existed in nature was still unknown. Whether some advanced technical civilization could create wormholes, and keep them open, permitting shortcuts not through but *past* enormous stretches of space was likewise unknown . . . or it had been until now. There could be no thought that the TRGA object was natural; someone had built the thing.

But to do so required a degree of control over the laws of physics that was nothing short of godlike.

Koenig had frozen the image transmitted from Schiere's remote drone at the eye-blink instant when the solid sheet of brilliant light had appeared on the other side. To human perceptions, the glimpse had been so brief that all that could be perceived was white light; at first, the people studying the images on board *America* had assumed that the probe was looking all the way through the hollow tube at the glaring surface of Texaghu Resch beyond.

With the image frozen and cleaned up by the AIs, however, the solid wall of white had been resolved. It wasn't a picture of the surface of one star, but of many tens of thousands together. Beyond the wormhole, stars were swarming within a dense-packed cluster where individual suns were separated from one another, on average, by only about a tenth of a light year.

According to *America*'s astrogation department, there were only two possibilities. Either the wormhole opened within the heart of a globular star cluster . . . or it opened within the core of a fair-sized galaxy, either the Milky Way or some other, distant, galaxy. Which was it? The answer was important, and the stargazers were hard at work on the problem now.

And Koenig now had to make some important strategic decisions.

"*America,*" he said, addressing the primary artificial intelligence that ran the ship.

"Yes, Admiral."

"Link through to the other ships in the battlegroup. Inform all ship captains and their staffs that we will hold a strategic virtual conference in . . . make it twenty minutes."

"Very well, Admiral."

Koenig continued studying the image transmitted by the recon probe. Tipler's original theory had suggested that doorways between widely separated regions of space as well as of time might be opened around a dense, rotating cylinder. A ship would have accessed those doorways by following pathways just above the cylinder's surface; he'd said nothing about what happened if the cylinder was *hollow*, however. That wall of stars clearly existed a long way away from this region of space—tens of thousands of light years at the very least, millions or even hundreds of millions of light years at worst. The question was whether it also was reaching through time, either into the past or into the remote future.

"*America,*" he said.

"Yes, Admiral."

"Pass the word to all ships. We're going to move closer to the TRGA."

"Very well, Admiral."

Shadow Probe 1
TRGA
Texaghu Resch System
1540 hours, TFT

By now, Schiere thought, his running commentary and the accompanying images had reached the battlegroup, and were causing all sorts of consternation. Within another hour and a half, he should have heard a response—stay put or come home. It would take that long for the transmission to reach him.

He hoped it would be a recall. For the past one hundred

minutes, he'd been cautiously moving about the artifact, using VR-5 probes to get in close while keeping himself well outside the zone where the thing's deadly gravitational grip might tear his ship to pieces—or send him somewhere else. Two of his probes had been destroyed within that dangerous region close to the cylinder; another had vanished down the cylinder's maw. He'd launched two more VR-5s and maneuvered them in carefully, until they were stationed off the opening of the tube.

Through these proxies he continued watching, but there wasn't a lot more he could do from here. He'd measured what there was to measure and transmitted the data back to *America.* Now all he could do was wait.

Movement . . .

One of his drones picked it up, a flash of movement emerging from the kilometer-wide opening of the rotating cylinder. He ordered the drone to pivot and track the object, to follow it . . . but too late. The drone was gone, vaporized. Before he could connect with the other drone, it too had been wiped from the sky.

By this time, Schiere realized that he was under attack, and that the situation was *not* good. His remote eyes had been swatted out of space, and he still hadn't had a good look at the attacker.

Attackers. There were more than one.

A *lot* more . . .

Virtuality
CBG-18
Outer System, Texaghu Resch System
1548 hours, TFT

Koenig had returned to his office for the staff meeting, and technically, that's where he—or at least his body—was now. Within his mind, however, he was in an artificial space generated by the fleet net, the interlinked network of communications and information systems spread throughout all fifty-eight capital ships of the battlegroup. "I suggest," Admiral Liu Zhu of the Chinese Hegemony light assault carrier *Zheng He*, was saying, "that we not enter the local star's gravity well to such depth. Better that we remain in the outer system, against the possibility of ambush."

"With respect, Admiral Liu," Captain Harrison said, "we haven't seen any sign of enemy ships in this system. *What* ambush?"

"As has been pointed out, the . . . the artifact, TRGA, may well be a means of creating a wormhole passage between two widely separated regions of space. The other end may open at a Sh'daar base. If so, large numbers of enemy ships could come through from unseen bases on the other side. We would have no way of knowing that we were in fact badly outnumbered."

Koenig listened impassively to the debate as it unfolded. Within the minds of the ship captains and staff officers linked into the simulation, they were seated around a large conference table, within a room digitally re-created from one in the Hexagon basement in Columbus, where the USNA Joint Chiefs held their briefing sessions. In deference to the other Confederation members, the USNA flag and the 3-D portrait of American Senate president Carolyn Saunders had been edited. Now it was the Terran Confederation flag and a portrait of Regis DuPont.

Politics . . .

Admiral Liu, of course, wasn't interested in Confederation politics other than in how they affected the Chinese Hegemony. Koenig didn't know him personally, but he appeared to be a hardheaded sort with a keen eye for the long-term advantage.

And Koenig had to admit that he had a good point.

As if to underscore the unknowns, one bulkhead of the virtual conference room showed vid transmitted from the CP-240 reconnaissance probe—the enigmatic cylinder suspended in a golden glow of twisted light.

"We don't have to close with the Triggah," Colonel Murcheson pointed out, using the newly arisen slang for the TRGA. Murcheson was the commander of the USNA Marine contingent on board the *Nassau*, a Marine expeditionary force numbering some nine hundred infantry and a close-support group of SG-86 Rattlesnake fighters. "Our recon units can camp out close to the thing, while we take up a station that will let us pace it within fighter range. If anything does come through, we'd be able to catch them while they're bottlenecked."

"What is this term, 'bottlenecked'?" one of Liu's aides asked.

"He means any enemy ships coming through the TRGA would have to do so one at a time," Koenig replied. "They'd be bunched up when they emerged, and relatively easy to pick off."

"We could bloody well nail 'em one at a time," Harrison said.

"This might also be our chance to steal a march on the Sh'daar," Captain Jossel of the railgun cruiser *Kinkaid* said. "Can we assume that the Triggah is a Sh'daar artifact? That it leads to an important Sh'daar system . . . perhaps even their homeworld? For sixty years, now, we've been on the defensive. This is our chance to take the war to them for a change!"

"Right," Captain Grunmeyer added. He was the CO of the heavy missile carrier *Ma'at Mons*. "Kick them where it hurts!"

"Except that if we traverse that tube," Kapitän zur Weltraum Roesller of the Pan-European battleship *Frederick der Grosse* said, pointing at the image of the cylinder on the bulkhead, "it will be us who are bottlenecked at the far end."

"If the other end of that thing does open in the Sh'daar home system," Captain Blaine of the cruiser *Independence* pointed out, "it's going to be protected. Heavy monitors, maybe. Or fortresses of some sort."

"Good points," Koenig put in. "But Captain Jossel is

right. The chance to strike back at the Sh'daar is why we're out here. If the TRGA offers us a shortcut to get at them, we're going to take it."

"Jesus," Captain Samantha Adams of the cruiser *Bainbridge* said with considerable feeling, "We're going to jump down a rabbit hole with no idea of what's at the bottom?"

"The dangers—" Liu began.

"Can be met and matched," Koenig said, interrupting. "We will, of course, use AI probes to investigate the cylinder, as well as any other technology we can bring to bear on the problem. We will *not* go through blind."

"Probes will alert the enemy on the other side, Admiral," Captain Buchanan said.

"We'll address that when we get there," Koenig said. "I want each of you to put your tactical teams to work on this . . . how to put our fleet through that wormhole with a good chance of breaking through on the other side. I want to see contingency plans assuming a large Turusch fleet on the other side . . . and for the possibility that they have the far end covered by some sort of fort or heavy orbital base. We *must* assume they'll have that end well protected.

"Once we reach the artifact—that will be in another nine hours, give or take—we will assemble the fleet a hundred thousand kilometers from the opening and begin sending sneak-probes through."

"Unless we get there and find the enemy has already emerged," Captain Charles Whitlow of the star carrier *United States of North America* said. "I suggest we send in fighters ahead of us, just in case."

"Sounds good," Koenig said. He'd been about to suggest the same thing. "I suggest one Starhawk squadron apiece from the *United States*, the *Lincoln*, and the *America*.

"We'll take it one step at a time. Okay . . . questions? Comments? Very well, ladies and gentlemen. Dismissed."

And the figures gathered around the virtual table began winking out.

VFA-44
On board TC/USNA CVS America
Outer System, Texaghu Resch System
1622 hours, TFT

Gray was lying in his bunk downloading Dolinar's *Cultural Technologies* as the battlegroup continued forging deeper into the Texaghu Resch system.

As squadron commander, Gray, theoretically, rated quarters of his own, but like so much else within the Navy hierarchy, theory gave way to practicality. Lieutenants rated four-to-a-compartment living space on board a carrier, which consisted of a small room with desk and lockers, a single-stall fresher, plus four occutubes set into the bulkhead opposite the door. Occutubes served as bunks—which common Navy usage still referred to as "racks" even though they now were completely enclosed.

The two-meter-long enclosure provided privacy and soundproofing for sleep, but also contained a full electronic hookup for various electronic services, including virtual rec and library access. He could link in with a movie, either passively or as a major character, or he could, as now, download text, lectures, and interactive question-and-answer sessions with an AI simulating a book's author.

The tube was large enough for two, and was one of the few places on board where people could find the privacy for *that* type of activity as well, deliberately so, though the Navy and the ship's command structure never admitted to that. Sexual activity was a normal aspect of human behavior and flight officers *were* human, despite persistent jokes to the contrary. Though physical relationships weren't officially condoned or encouraged, they were usually ignored so long as they were kept quietly out of sight.

Gray had given that fact considerable thought lately, especially since Schiffie was one of the other three officers sharing this compartment.

It wasn't even the sex he was missing so much, now, as

the fact that Gray was lonely. Angela had left such a raw and gaping hole. Schiffie wasn't interested in anything long term, but for a night or two . . .

Who would know? Where was the harm?

But he'd been making do with selections from the ship's erotic interactives instead. It was a whole lot less complicated.

And at the moment he wasn't even immersing in an erotiactive. *Cultural Technologies* had been recommended by the CAG as a must-down for all pilots. Frank Dolinar was a nanotech specialist with sharply focused insights into the high tech of a wide range of sentient species, including Humankind, with an emphasis on GRIN tech—genetics, robotics, information systems, and nanotechnology.

The driver technologies that the enigmatic Sh'daar seemed determined to suppress throughout the galaxy. Captain Wizewski believed that understanding the enemy, understanding why he did the things he did, was vital in fighting him, a basic combat dictum first written down by Sun Tse a good 2,900 years before. According to Dolinar, GRIN was on the point of transforming Humankind into gods, with power over mass, energy, gravitation, and even reality itself. The Technological Singularity . . .

If the Sh'daar wanted to suppress human technological development, it could only mean that they *feared* what humans might soon achieve.

And that meant that the Sh'daar might not be the invulnerable and unconquerable super-beings people assumed them to be.

At the moment, Gray was immersed in a docuinteractive, with an AI sim of Dolinar leading him along the edge of an oddly patterned cliff face on Heimdall. The landscape around him was barren and broken, cloaked in ice, with red light glinting from the crest of a kilometer-high glacier on the horizon. Bifrost, the world's gas-giant primary, arced from north to south, showing a slim bow of red and orange. Above, the system's star, an M1.5 red dwarf, catalogued as

Kapteyn's Star, shone as a bright red point of light some 3.5 AUs away. Aurorae fired by Bifrost's radiation belts interacting with Heimdall's magnetic field shimmered across a deep violet sky.

Dolinar and Gray both stood on the icy desert unprotected, the writer in civvies, Gray in his undress Navy blacks, despite the fact that the temperature hovered around ten below Celsius and the atmosphere was a thin mix of carbon dioxide and methane. That was the beauty of visiting a place in sim: you didn't need special protection in hostile environments.

Despite this, there was life, masses of ropy, orange polyps in sprawling patches on the ground, and methane-breathing floaters like wisps of wind-blown cellophane adrift in the thin and poisonous air. More, though, there was evidence of past life, *technic* life, imbedded in the rock. A cliff face nearby showed geometric patterns resembling the straight-line traceries of a huge circuit board, apparently etched into basalt with nanotechnic tools.

Exposed by the retreat of a glacier only a few years before, the tracings were crisp, sharp, and enigmatic. They were huge, spanning an ice-polished wall of rock eighty meters long and fifteen high. Who had made them? Not the wispy cellophane creatures, surely, which were as insubstantial as soap bubbles and showed roughly as much promise of tool-use or industry as the terrestrial jellyfish that they resembled.

"The problem, clearly," Dolinar was saying, "is whether Heimdall evolved its own native life, life that in time developed sentience and a technology of high order, or whether these patterns were created by . . . visitors, representatives of a space-faring technic species from someplace else."

"The Sh'daar?" Gray asked.

"Unlikely," was the sim's reply. "Based on radiometric dating, these pattern are at least a billion years old. Given what we think we know about technically oriented sentience, it is unlikely that any culture could survive for anything nearly that long. They either pass into decay and ultimate extinction, or their technology evolves to the point where they no longer interact with or even occupy what we think of as normal reality. They go . . . someplace else."

Gray reached out and touched one part of the structure—something like a flattened bagel or donut imbedded in the pattern of straight lines. The surface was cool to his touch, gritty, and flaked a bit, like rusty iron. Grasping its edges, he was able to pull it free, but the shape crumbled into dust and fragments as soon as it came free. "It's like rust," Gray observed. "But there's no oxygen in the atmosphere."

"The atmosphere may have contained an appreciable level of oxygen in the remote past. We're still puzzling out the geochemical history of this world. We know that a billion years ago there were oceans of liquid water, thanks to the warming effects of tidal interaction with Bifrost. But planets age, change, and die. Like the civilizations that occasionally inhabit them.

"The Heimdall artifacts are important, though, because Kapteyn's Star is only twelve light years from Sol. That wasn't the case a billion years ago, of course. Both Sol and Kapteyn's Star pursue separate orbits around the galactic center, and a billion years ago—that's four times around for Sol—they were probably on opposite sides of the galaxy from each other. But the fact that, by chance, this system is here *now*, so close to the Sol System, still means that technic civilizations must arise on a fairly common basis throughout the galaxy and across at *least* a billion years."

"So you're saying that intelligent life will become technic life, given half a chance."

"Precisely. We know several sentient species that do not make tools or create technological infrastructures. The Hasturs of Beta Hydri. The Gnomen of Thoth. The Troads of Barnard IIc. The Hasturs and the Troads never discovered fire, of course, so they're at something of a disadvantage to begin with, the Hasturs being deep-sea dwellers, and the Troads living in a methane-carbon dioxide atmosphere . . .

a lot like this one, in fact. The Gnomen . . . we don't know. They seem content to contemplate their equivalent of navels and act like terrestrial trees. But as near as we can tell, these are the exceptions, not the rule."

"The Turusch couldn't have had fire," Gray pointed out. "They evolved in a CO_2 atmosphere too. And the H'rulka are floaters in the atmospheres of gas giants."

"Which proves my point. We think someone gave the H'rulka their technology before they met the Sh'daar, but they may have learned to filter metals out of the gas-giant atmospheres and developed a working knowledge of exotic chemistry. The Turusch probably learned to refine metals around volcanic fumaroles or lava flows. Planets with oxygen-nitrogen atmospheres are in the distinct minority, remember. And yet intelligence continues to evolve, sentient species continue to develop tool-using technology, and technic species continue to reach for the stars."

"Which must mean the Sh'daar have their hands full," Gray mused. "If they *have* hands."

"Indeed. In fact—"

The simulation froze. Gray had time to think, *What the hell? . . .* and then a voice came through his cerebral link. "Now hear this, now hear this. VFA-44 Dragonfires, scramble, scramble, scramble. Launch in ten minutes, repeat, launch in ten minutes."

Gray bookmarked the sim and killed it, returning in a blink to the softly lit interior of his occutube. He palmed a contact and the end cap dilated open. He grabbed the hand holds to either side of the opening and hauled himself out.

Schiffie, Nathum, and Mallory, the other pilots in this compartment, were clambering out of their tubes as well, in various states of undress, reaching for their uniforms and letting them flow into place. A touch and a thoughtclick could tailor the nanomatrix as anything from full-dress blacks to utility grays. The flight-utility format—the slang term was *jackies*—served as flight suits, with connections for flight control, life support, and waste recycling.

Mallory was first out the door and Gray was close behind her. The descent tubes were just down the passageway outside.

It was hours too early for the fleet to have reached their objective, the thing labeled TRGA in close orbit around its sun. A scramble meant either that the fleet was under attack—unlikely this far out—or that the brass had decided to put a fighter force in close to the TRGA and that this needed to be done *now*.

Gray slid down the tube pulled by the hab module's half G of acceleration, emerging on the flight deck one level out/ down. Twelve Starhawk fighters awaited them on the drop line, as flight crews completed final inspections and equipment checks. Gray vaulted up the steps beside his ship, snatched up his helmet, and stepped into the cockpit, which smoothly closed in around him. As the helmet sealed itself to his jackies, the squadron channel opened in his implant, bringing his in-head display on-line.

Three squadrons, the Dragonfires, plus the Hellstreaks off the *Lincoln* and the Meteors off the *United States* were launching together. The CBG had been traveling toward Texaghu Resch for just over an hour at five hundred gravities; currently, they were 9.4 AUs from the star and traveling at eighteen thousand kilometers per second.

Pushing fifty thousand gravities, it would take the fighters almost seventy-two minutes objective to cross that remaining distance and come to a relative halt near the TRGA.

There was still no sign, the data feed from CIC told him, of enemy forces in the system. The fighters were being deployed as insurance against the possibility that enemy units might come through the TRGA before the battlegroup reached it.

Gray's cockpit sealed itself above his head, and he felt the movement as the fighter dropped through the nanoseal decking beneath and into hard vacuum. The fighter rotated within its magnetic grapples, facing down, now, as the hab module around him continued its stately, twice-per-minute rotation.

"This is Dragonfire One," Gray said. "On line." Red lights flickered to green within his inner display, as other fighters in the squadron linked in.

"Dragon One, PriFly," a voice said. "Stand by for drop."

"PriFly, Dragon One. Twelve Dragons are lit and ready for drop. At your discretion."

"Wait one," the voice of PriFly told him. "The ship is cutting acceleration."

When the fighters dropped clear of the carrier, they would do so with the carrier's current forward velocity. It could be *very* bad if the carrier was changing that velocity—accelerating or decelerating—at the same time the fighters were being released.

"Acceleration suspended, Dragonfires. Drop in three . . . and two . . . and one . . . release!"

Gray felt his stomach jump as he went into free fall.

And the stars exploded into view around him.

Chapter Eight

CIC
TC/USNA CVS America
Outer System, Texaghu Resch System
1645 hours, TFT

"The fighters are away, Admiral," Wizewski told him. "The Dragonfires just handed off to CIC."

"I heard them, CAG. Thank you."

He looked into the tactical tank. Over the past hours, the battlegroup had formed up for its passage to the TRGA, adopting one of several standard fleet formations—carriers grouped together in an elongated cluster behind the battleships and railgun cruisers. The destroyers out in front and in a protective cloud around the big boys, and with the support and logistical vessels to the rear. The frigates and gunships, the smallest of the capital ships, held the outermost perimeter, ahead, on all flanks, and astern. The idea was to focus firepower forward, while providing detection and defense in-depth in all directions.

Of course, no fleet formation could adequately protect against enemy vessels or kinetic-kill projectiles zorching in at near-*c* velocities, but this one, dubbed "spearhead," provided a fair balance between focused offense and general defense.

And there was still no sign of enemy forces within the

Texagu Resch system. Unmanned recon drones were on the way to each of the planets for a close look, but so far, nothing had turned up, not even the power signatures of zero-point energy emissions. The system appeared to be undefended.

And why not? Even the Sh'daar couldn't be everywhere, covering every system with defensive fleets or bases, not in a galaxy of 400 billion suns.

It *couldn't* be that easy, could it?

In Koenig's estimation, it never was.

If it was impossible to base crewed naval forces in every system, it *was* possible to leave behind detector satellites and drones. They could be powered by batteries or local sunlight, and didn't need quantum power taps, at least not until they had to accelerate to high velocity. They could be completely static, orbiting the local star and transmitting a signal when anything unusual—like the arrival of a carrier battlegroup—took place. Like the low-power signals used by the Sh'daar Seeds implanted in the Agletsch, the signals might not be detectable at all if you didn't know where to listen, or what to look for.

Koenig had to assume that the enemy knew they were coming.

Assuming, of course, that the TRGA artifact was indeed a part of some sort of interstellar Sh'daar transport system—the likeliest explanation for the thing, he thought. It *could* belong to someone else, of course . . . and might even be left over from some other star-faring civilization now long extinct.

But according to the Agletsch, this region of space was known to and traversed by the Sh'daar. The vanished Chelk had been here twelve thousand years ago, defied the Sh'daar ban on advanced GRIN technologies, and been exterminated.

Koenig had questioned Gru'mulkisch and Dra'ethde closely about the Chelk, wondering if perhaps they had created the TRGA object. According to them, the Chelk home-world was somewhere close by, but not *here*. "The Eye of Resch"—evidently, their name for this star—was visible in their night sky, a part of one of their constellations. The star was similar in most respects to Sol . . . and to human eyes a G2 star was only visible for a distance of about ten parsecs—roughly 32 light years. The Chelk might have had more efficient light-gathering organs than did humans, true, but the likelihood was that the Chelk homeworld had been relatively close by—say within ten or fifteen light years.

It would be interesting to survey the nearby star systems in an attempt to find the Chelk homeworld. It should be easy enough to locate. Gru'mulkisch had told him that the planet had been glassed over by the Sh'daar. That meant most of the evidence of their technology had been erased, but surely *something* had survived, on a moon or another planet, if not on the homeworld itself.

He suppressed a shudder. The Chelk and their fate had been preying on his mind now for some days, ever since he'd learned about them from the Agletsch.

What, Koenig wondered, had been the sin of the Chelk, a sin so grievous that billions of living souls had been extinguished?

And was that what the Sh'daar had planned for Humankind?

In any case, the two Agletsch had been certain that the Chelk had not been responsible for the Texaghu Resch gravitational anomaly. The physics boys had gone over the data transmitted back from *America*'s recon probe and suggested that the object, obviously artificial, had been created by taking a star of the same mass as Earth's sun—Texaghu Resch must once have been a double star—and somehow crushing it down into a rotating, hollow cylinder.

Worse, a star was composed mostly of hydrogen. The TRGA appeared to be . . . well, not solid, but not a gas, either. A black hole wasn't comprised of anything recognizable as one of the traditional states of matter, since, technically, the mass had collapsed into a singularity. Was the TRGA a singularity—by definition a dimensionless point—somehow unfolded, stretched into a hollow needle twelve kilometers long?

That was advanced technology, a technology so advanced as to seem literally godlike.

"Any sufficiently advanced technology is indistinguishable from magic," ran the old aphorism.

Was *that* what the Sh'daar feared?

Was that why the Chelk had been exterminated . . . because they had been exercising such magic? Or perhaps they'd simply been about to reach this system and perhaps the Sh'daar had feared they would learn something they weren't supposed to know?

Surely, if the Chelk had possessed such technology, the Sh'daar would not have been able to wipe them out.

"Karyn?" he said.

"Yes, Admiral?" The voice was that of his electronic personal assistant, a simulation of his dead lover. *God, I miss her. . . .*

"Take over for me here. I need to grab something to eat, then crash for a couple of hours."

He'd skipped lunch, as he often did, and was just realizing that he was hungry. And the battlegroup would be arriving at the gravitational anomaly at around 0100 hours, ship's time, so he wasn't going to be getting a full night's sleep. He'd already told Commander Jones, *America*'s exec, to pass the word to all hands on the day watch to get their sleep ahead of time. He needed to do likewise.

"Very good, Admiral. I'll alert you if anything comes up."

Karyn's simulation would keep a practiced electronic eye on things in CIC. Koenig released himself from his seat and floated toward the hatchway leading to hab module access and his quarters.

VFA-44
En route to TRGA
Texaghu Resch System
1650 hours, TFT

For Gray, only seconds had passed since the fighters had stopped their high-G boost. For just less than ten minutes, the Dragonfires had boosted at fifty thousand gravities.

Coasting, now, at 99.7 percent of the speed of light, they hurtled in-system as subjective time, squeezed down to nearly nothing by the effects of relativistic time dilation, flashed past. For them, the coast phase of their flight would last just less than six minutes instead of more than seventy-one.

With acceleration, the universe around them had grown strange, with all incoming light compressed into a glowing band encircling the heavens forward, the light itself sorted by wavelength from blue on the band's leading edge to red on the trailing, the gorgeous starbow that traditional physics said should not be, but was.

But they were just beginning their c run. In another five minutes and some seconds, as the fighters were measuring the quickly passing time, they would flip end for end and throw out the drive singularities in their wakes for the ten-minute deceleration in to the objective.

"Lieutenant?" his fighter said to him. "I'm parsing out some anomalous signals from directly ahead."

Gray felt a cold chill prickle at the back of his neck. "What kind of signals?"

"They appear to be drive signatures. I am also detecting what may be power-plant signatures."

The starbow was an artifact of Gray's near-c velocity. Just as a flier moving through a rainstorm on Earth creates the illusion that the raindrops are coming from ahead, not above, incoming electromagnetic radiation—light, among others—appeared to be compressed forward until even light from directly astern seemed to be coming from ahead, although even visible wavelengths were stretched into the radio portion of the spectrum, just as visible light from dead ahead was compressed into ultraviolet and X-ray frequencies.

Because of this distortion, it was extremely difficult to pick out individual signals and make sense of them. The AI running Gray's Starhawk, however, was tasked with doing just that, sampling thousands of discrete frequencies, teasing them out of the compressed mash of stretched and squeezed wavelengths, and converting them back to their originals.

The distortion was too severe for ships traveling at near-*c* to pick up radio or laser-com transmissions and make sense of them—fighters traveling at a hairsbreadth beneath *c* were all but cut off from the rest of the universe—but *some* data could be discerned.

Drive signatures were ripples in space caused by relativistic moving objects—like high-velocity fighters or kinetic-kill rounds moving at a fair percentage of *c*.

Power-plant signatures were different. Mere fusion or antimatter power was insignificant when it came to the energy needed to boost a spacecraft to near-*c* velocities. That sort of speed required vacuum energy, the all-but-infinite energy fluctuations occurring in the quantum foam of what was laughingly known as "empty space." Quantum power taps—and the enemy appeared to use an identical technology here—used paired artificial microsingularities to pull a fraction of this energy out of hard vacuum. Inevitably, there was some leakage—and distinct ripples in spacetime created by the fast-orbiting black-hole pairs that could be detected across vast distances.

Despite his fighter's velocity, Gray's AI was picking up those ripples from directly ahead, and reading them as evidence of ships using quantum power taps and traveling at high speeds.

The only things Gray could think of that would explain those signals were either ships or, more likely, KK warheads coming straight for the fighters head-on, and doing so at close to light speed. Two objects, each traveling at near-*c* and hitting each other did *not* do so at twice the speed of light; *c* was always *c*, no matter what the circumstances.

What they *did* do was release one hell of a lot of energy.

As squadron commander, Gray had to make sure the other Dragonfires had picked up on this. Possibly, their AIs had detected the same signatures—not at all a sure bet—but the squadron would have to react as a unit, damned tough when no one could talk to anyone else.

But there was one thing he could do.

"Okay," he told his AI. "Stand by for near-*c* maneuvering. . . .

Admiral's Quarters
TC/USNA CVS America
Inbound, Texaghu Resch System
1659 hours, TFT

"Admiral!" Karyn's voice called suddenly. "We have an emergency incoming transmission!"

Koenig had only just reached his quarters, had not even opened his occutube yet. He stood in the middle of the spacious compartment, looking up at the softly lit overhead with an expression mingling exasperation and wry amusement. "You're kidding me."

"I would not do that, Admiral, as you well know."

He knew. "What do you have?"

"Our reconnaissance probe sent an emergency transmission at 1540 hours. Something has emerged from the wormhole."

"On my way."

Technically, he could view the data here, but he preferred to be in CIC, the fleet's nerve center. He had more options there.

He'd already decided to skip dinner until after he'd grabbed some tubetime, or at least defer it until later. But now, even sleep would have to wait.

VFA-44
En route to TRGA
Texaghu Resch System
1704 hours, TFT

The worst part about fighter combat at near-*c* was the fact that you were experiencing events so slowly. Traveling at 99.7 percent of *c*, the passing of one second for Gray was almost thirteen seconds for the universe outside, the time dilation predicted by Einstein's general theory of relativity and calculated by the equation known as the Lorentz-FitzGerald transformation. The problem was one of reaction time. At those speeds it took Gray thirteen times longer to notice a threat, thirteen times longer to react . . . and if those drive signatures he'd detected were of ships or missiles themselves traveling at close to the speed of light, they would be zorching in just behind the wavefront that had alerted him to their presence.

It might already be too late.

He told his AI to begin jinking.

He couldn't use laser com to warn the others, of course, not at that speed. At near-c velocities, communication within the squadron—or with other squadrons or with the *America*—was tenuous at best. All incoming signals, even from other ships with perfectly matched vectors, were smeared by relativistic spacetime distortion into that circle of light ahead. The individual fighter AIs could tease some low-level bandwidth data out of that hash, but not enough for voice or implant communications. His Starhawk could sense the other spacecraft in the formation by the dimples their power-tap singularities left on the fabric of space, but little else.

Since his instrumentation could only approximate the positions of the other fighters in the squadron by their mass effects, any change in vector at this velocity was potentially deadly. By having his AI calculate those positions, however, using fuzzy logic to calculate probable locations, he minimized the chances of a collision. The rapid, jittery movements as his fighter threw out gravitational singularities, first in one direction, then another, then a third, did two things. They reduced the chances that an aimed projectile coming in from dead ahead would strike him, and they guaranteed that the AIs of the other Dragonfires would notice his fighter's erratic behavior. That by itself would alert the rest of the squadron that something was wrong, that they were being tracked . . . and that they had to start jinking themselves to avoid disaster.

Side-to-side jinking could be carried out within a relatively narrow area—Gray was changing lateral vectors within a cross-section a hundred meters or so across—and Gray was trusting his AI to keep from colliding with the nearest other Dragonfire Starhawks. A tactical display window opened in his mind, showing the probable relative locations of the other eleven fighters. As he watched, four of the other Starhawks began moving back and forth in erratic and random patterns as well. Then a fifth joined in . . . a sixth, and within a few seconds all of them were moving unpredictably within the display. Gray's AI was estimating the nearest fighter to be five kilometers away. *Plenty* of space . . . assuming that all twelve AIs were guessing accurately.

The question was, what was it that was hurtling toward the fighters head-on, and how much time did they have?

As the seconds crawled past, the Dragonfires' formation began to spread out slightly. The AIs at the outer edge of the flight tended to move out more than in, which left more space in the middle for the interior Starhawks to begin dispersing. If they were being targeted, the dispersal should help by making individual ships harder to hit, and a high-speed impact would be less likely to destroy more than one or two fighters at a time.

Gray extended his tactical display's field of view to take in the other two squadrons, the Hellstreaks and the Meteors. One by one, the individual Starhawks in those formations began jinking back and forth as well. Good. Someone in those squadrons had been paying attention, and had either spotted the oncoming threat or noticed when the Dragonfires began carrying out evasive maneuvers.

Then the starbow ahead of Gray's fighter turned as bright as the face of the sun, and the shock wave of hot plasma struck him an instant later, sending him into a wild and catastrophic tumble.

CIC
TC/USNA CVS America
Inbound, Texaghu Resch System
1707 hours, TFT

Koenig watched the view unfolding on the CIC's display screens, and realized that the fleet was now in serious trouble. The three tightly interwoven questions facing him now were, what could be done to retrieve the tactical situation, what could be salvaged, what would be lost?

The scenes showed the recon mission's point of view, and so was now more than eighty minutes out of date thanks to the slow-crawling speed of light. According to the time line imbedded in the data stream, something—correction, a lot of *somethings*—had emerged from the artificial wormhole at 1540 hours.

Were they missiles or small spacecraft? Koenig couldn't tell at first, though as minutes passed, be began to get the distinct impression that they *were* crewed—spacecraft slightly smaller than a Starhawk, and apparently far more maneuverable. Each was different in detail, lozenge shaped, flattened side to side like leaves or the scales of a fish, with whorls and blisters and smoothly curving lines etched into mirror-bright surfaces. Their hulls were decorated in sinuous swirls of dark blue and gray-silver, but gleamed brilliantly, reflecting the glare of the nearby sun.

They were coming through in hundreds, a cloud of the things. One, Koenig saw, was larger than the others, a fat cigar shape with five knobs like thick antennae projecting from its leading end, its hull hidden beneath clusters of slender objects like black, double-pointed pencils. Lightning flared between the antennae, encircling the craft, and the pencils began coming off in unraveling sheets and accelerating.

"What are those?" Sinclair said in Koenig's head. "Missiles?"

"Crowbars," Koenig replied.

And an instant later the feed from Recon One went dead.

VFA-44
En route to TRGA
Texaghu Resch System
1715 hours, TFT

Gray tumbled through the Void at the speed of light.

G-forces tore at him. Where his gravitic drive acted on every atom of his body uniformly, allowing him to fall toward the singularity in zero-G, his Starhawk's spin exerted centrifugal force that simulated gravity—about eight Gs, he estimated. He was perilously close to blacking out.

He was able to thoughtclick on icons showing in his in-head display, however, directing his AI to use the gravitic drive to slow the spin. The G-force lessened . . . then, in a series of fits and starts, dropped gradually away to nothing. He was in free fall once more.

As soon as he could bring up his tactical display, he checked to see what had happened. Two fighters from the formation were missing—Preisler and Natham, both hit, evidently, by high-grav impactors passing through the formation. Though hard vacuum could not transmit a shock wave, the shattering collision of two bodies each moving at close to *c* had released a *great* deal of kinetic energy, and that energy had driven an expanding shell of plasma—the vaporized mass of both fighter and projectile—outward with force enough to tip Gray into an end-for-end tumble.

He was under control, now, however—shaken, but still on course. That was a given; an expanding bubble of plasma with energy enough to deflect him onto a new vector at this speed would have reduced him and his Starhawk to individual free-flying atoms.

His AI completed a full systems check. There was minor damage, both in attitude control and in life support, but the fighter was already repairing itself. The nanomatrix of the hull could reconfigure itself, filling in gaps, bypassing burned-out zones, and even literally rewiring itself. The one system that could not be repaired under way, the oscillating micro-singularities at the heart of the Starhawk's quantum power tap, were still in place and functioning at optimum, and the energy flow was steady.

He checked the stats on the other pilots. Gray couldn't tell from the tactical display if any of the other Dragonfire pilots had been affected by impact with the fast-expanding plasma shells. His equipment could detect a nearby mass by the impression it made in spacetime, but not whether that mass was spinning or even fragmented. Preisler and Natham, though, were definitely gone, their fighters' mass smeared outward into low-density clouds of star-hot plasma. There was some possibility of losses within the Meteors and the Hellstreaks as well, though the data was fuzzy and would remain so until they decelerated to saner velocities.

What the hell had happened? Clearly, something up ahead had detected the incoming squadrons of fighters and launched a cloud of near-c kinetic-kill impactors, a type of weapon generically known as crowbars. They had no guidance, no onboard AI; they were simply slivers of ultra-dense metal launched in clouds against incoming targets.

The slivers that had missed the individual fighters would be traveling on, now, headed out-system toward the far fatter and slower targets of the carrier battlegroup.

And Gray had no way of warning them that the impactors were on the way.

CIC
TC/USNA CVS America
Inbound, Texaghu Resch System
1720 hours, TFT

It was sheer luck that Koenig and his combat team in CIC had seen the crowbar launch . . . luck, and the fact that they *did* have intelligence resources watching the TRGA tube. That single bit of advance planning might have just saved the fleet in the relatively short term.

In the long-term, they were still in deep trouble.

According to the time stamp on Recon One's data, those high-velocity projectiles had been launched at 1540 . . . more than forty minutes before the fighter squadrons had been deployed. That meant they were targeting the fleet, which they would have been able to pick up on long-range gravitational mass sensors, and not the fighters, which should by now be two thirds of the way to their objective.

Kinetic-kill projectiles could not be precisely aimed across more than 9 AUs. They would be coming in blind, a cloud of the things dispersing in such a way that something might be hit simply by chance. Their actual speed was unknown; they would arrive at relativistic speeds, but anything above, say, 70 percent of the speed of light was possible. The battlegroup's only possible defense was to disperse even more to reduce the chance of a lucky hit.

Koenig thought the matter through further. It might also help to put out some additional fighters .5 AU or so ahead of the fleet. They might detect the incoming projectile cloud, and be able to give the fleet some advance warning, anything from seconds to a few minutes, depending on the velocities involved.

He began giving the necessary orders.

More serious was the long-term problem. The fleet was scheduled to arrive at the TRGA at around one in the morning. They would arrive to find several hundred hostile spacecraft, however—spacecraft of unknown design but obviously hostile.

No fleet commander cares to take his ships into a fight with a totally unknown but numerically superior enemy. The odds are too long, the threat unguessable, the potential consequences terrifying . . . and it was a hell of a long way home.

But Koenig now had an unsavory choice to make. He could stick with the original plan and engage the unknown foe, or he could order the fleet to begin immediate deceleration with an eye to changing course and re-entering Alcubierre space. The fleet *could* escape, and that was almost certainly the safest and sanest call right now.

But if he did that, the thirty-six fighters of three Starhawk squadrons already en route to the TRGA would be abandoned and lost.

The math was simple enough; he could save fifty-eight ships and nearly fifty thousand men and women by sacrificing the lives of thirty-six pilots.

The math was always simple. It was living with the results that was a problem.

Chapter Nine

29 June 2405

VFA-44
En route to TRGA
Texaghu Resch System
1745 hours, TFT

The fighters had hit their decell points and were slowing now at fifty thousand gravities. As their velocity dropped, the rings of colored light representing the entire outside universe smeared and expanded, breaking up into discrete stars as it stretched out to once more envelope the fighters. Radio and laser communications signals once again emerged from the background hash of relativistically distorted spacetime, and Gray again could talk to the other pilots.

The first thing he did was check the status of each ship. Each Starhawk constantly transmitted a data stream giving its condition and flight status, the health of its pilot, and other critical data, but at near-*c*, his navigational AI could pick up the presence of nearby mass and little else; it could not read whether the mass of another fighter was traveling normally or in a headlong tumble.

Two fighters had been vaporized. Priesler and Natham were gone, their Starhawks' masses spread out across such a large volume of space that they could no longer be detected, and the paired, microscopic singularities of their power plants had radiated away into nothingness.

Gray could now see that three other fighters besides his own—Donovan's, Zapeta's, and Kuhn's—had been put into tumbles by the blasts. All three had recovered, their pilots uninjured, thank God, and all were coming back fully on-line as their systems repaired themselves.

"Everyone okay?" Gray asked, more for the reassurance of human contact than anything else. The readouts had already answered the question.

"Okay now," came Donovan's voice, faint and static-blasted despite AI enhancement. They were still moving quickly enough that the transmissions between ships were almost lost in the relativistic distortions of space.

"That was quite a ride," Lawrence Kuhn added. "I hit five Gs."

"What the hell happened?" Shay Ryan asked.

"A spread of crowbars passed through the formation," Gray told them. "My AI is guessing that they came through at about ninety percent of light speed."

"What the hell is a crowbar?" Rostenkowski asked.

"Kinetic-kill projectiles, null brain," Calli Loman replied. "Bullets, very *heavy* bullets, traveling very fast. It's in your training downloads."

"Oh, yeah . . ."

"Jesus, the bastards are *shooting* at us!" Zapeta's voice called.

"Not necessarily," Gray replied. He was studying the available data, letting it scroll through his in-head display as he absorbed it. After the enforced isolation of the near-c leg of the flight, he was starving for data. "We're on a direct line between the fleet and the Triggah. It's possible that they were shooting at the big boys, and we just happened to be caught in the line of fire."

Aiming anything across more than 9 AUs, whether solid projectile or a beam of coherent light, was a complex task, one dependent on luck as much as upon precise measurements of the target's course and speed. The enemy was very rarely where you expected him to be.

It was impossible to know just yet exactly when those deadly slivers of ultra-dense metal had been launched, or at what range they'd been fired from. Gray's AI was picking targets up now in the vicinity of the alien artifact ahead, lots of targets. They'd emerged from the spinning, high-mass cylinder sometime within the past couple of hours, and loosed that cloud of projectiles either at the fleet or directly at the fighters.

Probably the fleet, Gray decided, examining the AI's vector analysis. The cloud of KK projectiles had been widely dispersed; if the bad guys had been shooting at the fighters, they would have kept the cloud tighter, more compact, in order to hit more than just two.

Correction, *five*. The Meteors had lost two fighters as well . . . and the Hellstreaks one, and that suggested the cloud of high-velocity slivers had been huge, spread throughout a volume of space fifty thousand kilometers across or more.

Okay, the bad guys were taking potshots at the fleet. Gray's AI had automatically transmitted an update that should arrive at *America* a few moments before the cloud did, and there was nothing more he could do in that department. The CBG would have to deal with the attack on its own.

"Hellstreak One, this is Dragonfire One," Gray called. "Do you copy?"

"Copy, Dragon One," the voice of Commander Gregory Claiborne answered. "Go ahead."

Claiborne was the skipper of the Hellstreaks off the *Abraham Lincoln*, and the senior-ranked officer among the three squadrons. As such, he was in command of the overall mission, though, in fact, the Hellstreaks, the Meteors, and the Dragonfires were flying independently on this op. Except for a few short training flights back at Alphekka, the three squadrons had had little practice working together. Hell, most of the newbies in the Dragon fighter pilots were so raw, Gray wasn't sure they would be able to stay in single-squadron formation, much less mesh with all three.

"Five minutes to intercept, sir," Gray said. "What kind of closing velocity did you have in mind?"

If they continued pulling fifty-K Gs, they would arrive at the objective motionless relative to the TRGA. But in grav-fighter combat, as with the atmo-fighters of four centuries before, speed was life. By tweaking their decelerations, the fighters could arrive at the objective with a left-over velocity of anything from a few meters per second to thousands of kps.

But choosing the closing velocity was a juggling act of tactics and guesswork. Too slow, and the bad guys up ahead would eat the incoming fighters for breakfast. Too fast, and the fighters' on-board AIs would not be able to track or lock on to the enemy.

"The Meteors and the Hellstreaks will go in first," Claiborne decided. "A thousand kps. You copy that, Spel?"

"Copy," Lieutenant Commander Phillip Spellman, skipper of the Meteors, replied. "Adjusting our delta-V to comply."

"Prim, you and your people will be in reserve. One hundred kps."

Gray's lips compressed into a thin, hard line behind his helmet faceplate. *Prim*, that hated nickname again. He'd thought he'd gotten past that after that witch Collins had ended up in sick bay, damn it.

Somehow, word had gotten around.

"Do you copy, Dragon One?"

"Yeah, copy," he replied. "But the Dragonfires are at the head of the pack already."

"And most of you don't know your mass from a hole," Claiborne quipped. "At least the crews of the *Lincoln* and the *United States* have been training together. So don't give me a Primie attitude, and adjust your delta-V."

"Aye, aye, sir," Gray said, seething. "Adjusting delta-V."

He didn't like it, but he knew how to follow orders.

And it did make sense to have one of the squadrons hang back a little, to serve as a strategic reserve, and to be ready to capitalize on any mistakes the enemy might make. Not only that, the first fighters into the TRGA battlespace were going to be up against a numerically superior enemy with unknown flight stats and capabilities, not a good tactical situation in which to find oneself. If Claiborne wanted that honor for himself, he was welcome.

Prim . . .

When someone like him or Shay used the term, it was okay, somehow. In the mouth of a "risty," though—the term was a pejorative derived from *aristocrat*—it grated. Somehow, no matter how close to *c* he pushed, he just couldn't leave his past behind. Most officers in the USNA Navy were risties, and the bastards would never let you forget where you came from.

The Dragonfires, taclinked together, continued to decelerate as the other fighters, decelerating but at a slightly lower rate, passed VFA-44 and moved into the van. Gray considered pointing out to Claiborne that the Dragonfires had more recent combat experience . . . but he knew that wouldn't change anything. Specifically, only four of the Dragonfires had been through the crucible of Alphekka; the other eight had never been in combat before. At least the squadron pilots of the Hellstreaks and the Meteors had seen combat during the Defense of Earth, if not since. Claiborne might actually know what the hell he was doing.

But Gray still didn't like it one bit.

He buried his simmering resentment and studied the tacsit now unfolding within his in-head display. Just a couple of million kilometers ahead, now, the enemy fleet appeared to be maneuvering in front of the TRGA artifact. He did a quick channel search, found the transmissions from several battlespace drones, unmanned craft launched by Recon One and so far ignored or undetected by the enemy, and got his first look at the unknown hostiles.

Of Recon One, however, there was no trace.

Once, during his initial Navy training several years before, Gray had downloaded a docuinteractive that had let him experience swimming in the bright, clear waters above a coral reef in the western Pacific. The literally immersive e-experience had been purely entertainment, though no doubt it had also been part of the program to educate an ignorant squattie Prim from the Periphery.

In any case, at one point in the download he'd encountered a living, shimmering wall of silver light—hundreds of thousands of individual fish moving together in such tight harmony, flashing right to left, then reversing as one with such startling suddenness, to move left to right, that they gave the appearance of acting and reacting as a single, solid creature. The fish, he'd been told, sensed one another's movements through subtle changes in water pressure picked up by their lateral lines, enabling them to move together, but the effect had been dramatic and spectacular.

What he was seeing on the drone feed seemed to be something similar, thousands of individual spacecraft moving in exquisitely close concert. Each hostile ship appeared to be a bit smaller than a Starhawk fighter . . . and his AI so far had counted some 4096 of the things, plus eight more craft that appeared to be larger and wrapped up in bundles of what could only be kinetic-kill projectiles.

Odds of more than 130 to one were *not* good. "Hellstreak One, Dragon One," he called. "I suggest that we thin the bad guys out a bit before we get there."

"Already on it, Prim," Claiborne replied. "Hellstreaks and Meteors, arm Kraits. Six missiles apiece, maximum yield, three degree dispersal, proximity detonation, in three . . . two . . . one . . . *Fox One!*"

The VG-92 Krait space-to-space missile was an AI-guided high-velocity ship killer tipped with a variable-yield thermonuclear warhead. Each Starhawk carried a warload of 32 VG-92s. The call of "Fox One," derived from ancient aerial combat, indicated the launch of a smart missile like the Krait. On his tactical display, Gray could see the missile tracks spreading out from the lead squadrons—126 of them in all, accelerating fast.

The response from the enemy ships was rapid and dramatic. From a tightly woven close formation in front of the TRGA, they began dispersing in mathematically precise paths out from a single, central point. As they spread out into a broad, slightly concave disk a hundred kilometers across, they began firing beams of some sort—tightly focused bursts of high-energy particles.

The missiles hurtled closer—twenty thousand kilometers, now, from the TRGA cylinder and its guardian fleet. One by one, the incoming Krait missiles began to wink out of existence. In another moment, those unknown beams began reaching past the missiles, searching out individual Starhawks among the two nearest squadrons. As the lead Starhawks reached the thirty-thousand-kilometer mark, half a dozen of them vanished in as many seconds.

"Hellstreak One!" Gray called. "Hellstreak One! Break off!"

There was no immediate response. Three more SG-92s disappeared—no flash, no fragments, no explosions that Gray could pick out across the gap between them and the Dragonfires.

"All fighters!" Claiborne's voice called out. "Launch—"

And the voice was cut off as another SG-92 was wiped from the sky. The other Starhawks were scattering, performing wild, jinking maneuvers in an attempt to avoid the touch of those deadly beams.

"What the hell is that they're using?" Gray wondered aloud.

"Unknown," his AI replied in his ear. "But the lack of explosion suggests the targeted fighters are dropping into their own onboard singularities."

"Couldn't be," Gray replied. "Something as big as a Starhawk can't get eaten by a black hole the size of a proton in an eye blink."

"We do not have sufficient data for analysis."

In horror, Gray watched two more Starhawks reach the thirty-thousand-kilometer mark and wink out. *"There's* your data, damn it! Dragonfires! Spread out, maximum Gs!"

Several tactical points had impressed themselves on Gray in the few seconds of battle so far. The enemy was using beam weapons of some sort . . . and almost by definition those would be more accurate at close range, where speed-of-light time lag wouldn't be as much of a factor in tracking and aiming. The KK projectiles, clearly, were for threats at longer ranges—say, at a guess, farther out than a tenth of a light second—about 30,000 kilometers.

"Incoming KK projectiles," Gray's AI warned. "Evasive maneuvering . . ."

Gray's vector, currently, was toward the TRGA cylinder at about 5,000 kilometers per second, and he was still 300,000 kilometers out—about one minute's flight. His AI was now applying full gravitational thrust to one side, giving the spacecraft a lateral component to its vector in order to avoid the cloud of KK slivers now streaking out toward him.

The projectile cloud, expanding as it moved, passed him. A few thousand kilometers distant, the Starhawk piloted by Lieutenant Miguel Zapeta detonated in a brilliant flash and a spray of hurtling fragments.

"I'm hit! I'm hit!" That was Lieutenant Pauline Owens, her Starhawk crippled and tumbling, now, out of control.

Two more gone.

"Listen up, Dragonfires!" Gray called out. He hoped his voice was calmer than he felt right now. "Everyone program all Kraits for indirect targeting, maximum yield!"

Each remaining Starhawk carried thirty-two nuke-tipped Kraits. Programmed for indirect targeting, the smart missiles would swing wide around the enemy's flanks, coming in from the side or rear instead of from straight ahead.

"Dragonfires! Go Fox One on all Kraits!"

The surviving fighters in the squadron began dumping missiles, releasing them two at a time in rapid-fire volleys. Even Owens' crippled fighter began dropping missiles as she tumbled straight toward the enemy formation now one light second away.

The enemy clearly was using some form of tactical net or linkage that gave them superb command and control, essentially allowing a fleet of four thousand spacecraft to function as a single unit. That meant the enemy was superbly quick, that he would respond to threats with super-human speed and precision. The fact that the alien formation numbered 4,096 of one type of ship, according to the inhumanly rapid counting abilities of his AI, and eight of another, had not been lost on Gray. That first number was a power of two—2^{12}—as was the second, 2^3. That suggested binary notation . . . and that, in turn, suggested computers.

It was possible, even likely, that they were up against an artificial intelligence.

The thought chilled, prickling the hairs at the back of Gray's neck for two reasons. It meant they were up against an enemy with literally super-human reaction times, and it was just possible that the three fighter squadrons had now, for the very first time in thirty-eight long years of war, encountered the almost mythical Sh'daar.

CIC
TC/USNA CVS America
Inbound, Texaghu Resch System
1750 hours, TFT

"The fighters should be engaging now, sir," Commander Sinclair told Koenig.

"I see it," Koenig replied.

The tactical display was showing what *should* be happening now—a swarm of thirty-six Starhawk fighters closing in on the enigmatic spinning cylinder in close orbit around the local star.

In fact, though, the information unfolding in the CIC tactical tank was seventy-six minutes out of date. It had taken that long for the light to crawl out to the fleet from the TRGA artifact.

Koenig had to make his decision without knowing the precise situation in there, a decision that might mean abandoning the three squadrons to save the rest of the carrier battlegroup.

"The objects we saw emerging from the TRGA represent a technology we have not yet seen."

The voice was that of Karyn Mendelson. The brain behind it was the AI that served as Koenig's personal secretary, using the voice and personality he'd programmed into it.

Karyn, he once again reminded himself, was dead.

"Yes," he said, subvocalizing.

"That technology represents an unknown military capability. An unknown threat to this carrier battlegroup."

"Yes. But in a way, that's why we're here, isn't it?"

The decision, Koenig thought, was a foregone conclusion. If he broke off now because he didn't want to risk his fleet against an enemy of unknown strength and capabilities, all of the sacrifice, the battle deaths, the struggling and the striving up to this point would be thrown away. The crews of the other ships in the carrier group were volunteers; the ones who'd been most set against following him had gone home on board the *Karlsruhe*, the *Audace*, the *De Grasse*, or on one of the four Chinese ships. They were here because they wanted to be, because they'd believed in him and in what he was trying to do—to buy time for Earth by bringing the war home to the Sh'daar.

If he broke off and returned to Earth now he would be betraying the men and women who'd believed in him, people who were risking their own careers and well-being to follow him out into the Void against the orders of their world's government. The chances were good that only he would answer to charges of treason if they returned or, at worst, it would be him and the fifty-eight ship captains in the docket back home.

And that, actually, was an argument for breaking off. If

the battlegroup returned to Earth now, the captains of these fifty-eight ships might never again hold a ship command, but Koenig would bear the responsibility for his actions far more than they would. At least they would be *alive*, along with their crews. By a strict numerical analysis, clearly, it was worth it to trade thirty-six pilots already thrown against the enemy and save the nearly fifty thousand crew members of the CBG.

But . . . no. Quite apart from betraying those three squadrons of plots, it would be a betrayal of the trust of the entire fleet to cut and run now. And, more than that, it would be a betrayal of Earth, of the Confederation and, more, of all of Humankind. Koenig believed, with an unshakable, rock-solid conviction, that humanity would not survive another thirty-eight years of a defensive war against the Sh'daar and their allies. They needed to find the Sh'daar and to confront them, and that confrontation, whatever the tactical outcome, would have to shake the alien enemy so badly that they pulled back to regroup and to reconsider.

That was why they were here.

"Admiral?" It was Buchanan, *America*'s CO and Koenig's flag captain. "We need your final go/no-go."

"Yes." Briefly, he considered asking Buchanan what he thought . . . but dismissed the impulse immediately. The responsibility was Koenig's, and no one else's. "We will maintain course and acceleration."

"*Very* good, sir!" Buchanan didn't smile, but there was a light in his eyes, and an enthusiasm in the way he said it that told Koenig that Buchanan approved.

He thought a moment, then thoughtclicked a new display into the tactical tank. Fifty-eight glowing icons, ranging from the smallest frigate to *America* herself, appeared in orderly ranks, grouped by ship type.

"The battlegroup will divide into two combat sections, van and main," he continued, as the ship icons began resorting themselves under his direction. "The main will consist of the carriers, the supply and support ships, the railgun and long-range bombardment ships . . . and let's include the Chinese contingent as well, as security, plus, let's make it ten frigates and five destroyers as a forward screen."

"Yes, sir. You're holding the Chinese back?"

Koenig grinned. "I'm still not certain whether they're here to help us or to keep an eye on me. In any case, the *Zheng He* is a carrier and will be in the main group. If we put the others in the van, it's going to give us command-control headaches.

Cheng Hua was a cruiser, the *Haiping* a destroyer, while the *Jianghu* and the *Ji Lin* both were classed as frigates. If those four weren't absolutely committed to Koenig's strategy, he didn't want them in the rough-and-tumble of the van, where every ship would have to support every other. If he kept them back with the carrier *Zheng He* and under Admiral Liu's direct command, he would have only one unknown to contend with within his own ranks.

"The rest," Koenig continued, "will be in the van. Mostly cruisers, destroyers, and frigates. The lights will be the best ones equipped to deal with those alien fighters."

He wasn't convinced that the cloud of tiny vessels he'd seen emerging from the TRGA artifact were what the Confederation thought of as fighters. For all he knew, they were the alien equivalent of star carriers, launching fighters the size of his outstretched hand, but if he went by simple estimates of size, they read as very large fighters, similar in mass to Turusch Toads, or perhaps a little larger. Frigates and destroyers, while not much good against major capital ships, were designed to spot, track, and destroy fighters, and were generally deployed on a fleet's perimeter to serve that purpose.

"Sounds good, Admiral."

"I don't know about *good*. It's the best we can do with limited intel. A lot will depend on how the fighters do against the unknown hostiles."

"I'll give the orders, Admiral."

And Koenig was left alone again with his thoughts.

VFA-44
Approaching TRGA
Texaghu Resch System
1753 hours, TFT

As the Dragonfires spread themselves out thin, Gray thought about the possibility that they were up against a machine intelligence. Was there *anything* there they could use, an advantage, a tactic, a weapon?

Humankind did not rely on AI combat units, and there was good reason for that. Within the Terran Confederation, among all of the polities of Humankind, in fact, AIs were designed with deliberate limits to their function, possessing what was called *limited purview*. The AI running his fighter's systems, for instance, was *very* good at navigation, maneuvering, and even weapons tracking and control, but while it was classified as sentient it had absolutely no interest in, say, politics, human history, or the fine points of applied nanoengineering.

That built-in tunnel vision made them somewhat less flexible and adaptable than humans, which was why grav-fighters still had human pilots. AI-piloted warships and fighters were certainly technically possible—that's what drones and Krait missiles were, after all—but humans had chosen centuries before to keep themselves in the technological loop, a guarantee that humans would retain control of their own creations.

There were arguments, Gray knew, to the effect that such attempts at staying in control were futile in the long run. Artificial intelligences were very fast, far faster than human brains and nervous systems. More, they could program and direct themselves—within certain broad parameters, true, but intelligences that powerful would be able to find a way around the barriers if they really wanted to. The trick was channeling those intelligences so that they *didn't* want to take over from humans, a thought that, for an AI, was literally unthinkable.

Within the anti-technology communities of the Periphery,

Gray knew from personal experience, there were people who held to the theory that artificially sentient machines were *already* the true rulers of the human species, but that they were staying behind the scenes for reasons of their own. Gray personally had had to overcome that in-grown prejudice during his period of training with the Navy. AIs, digital sentients on all of their myriad shapes and types, were personal assistants, secretaries, weapons, or ship guidance systems—even extensions of one's own brain—not Humankind's potential masters.

The tightly maneuvering hostiles out there represented something new. They might be under the control of an organic intelligence, might be nothing more than human-designed AIs with better command-control abilities . . . but Gray could not escape the idea that he was watching the mental processes of a digital intelligence as it analyzed threats and responded to them.

Every technic alien species encountered so far by humans possessed a unit for measuring time similar to the second. The concept of time measurement was unknown to dolphins or the floaters in the ice-locked Europan ocean and a few other intelligences that had never developed technology, but every species that *built* things measured time, and something approximating one second was a useful basic unit. The Agletsch, he knew, had the *shu*, which measured roughly .87 of one second. Those flashing movements as the aliens shifted their formation seemed to be happening in tightly parsed-out fragments of seconds, much faster than humans or Agletsch could handle with purely organic brains.

Computers, however . . .

The slaughter of the Hellstreaks and the Meteors continued, as some of the human fighters struggled to break clear, as others accelerated in an attempt to break through and past that wall of guardian spacecraft in front of the TRGA. A few of the Kraits launched earlier reached the enemy intact—the hostiles were not infallible or omnipotent, thank God—and began to detonate in silent, blossoming flashes of light.

And the hostiles began dying, with great, empty voids opening in their formation as warhead after warhead released megatons of high-energy fury within their ranks.

But not enough. The enemy had spread out so thinly, now, that a single thermonuclear detonation was taking out only a handful of targets, and there were thousands, still, remaining.

Gray looked for a weapon he could use.

And then he thought he might know of one. . . .

Chapter Ten

VFA-44
En route to TRGA
Texaghu Resch System
1755 hours, TFT

"All Dragonfires! Arm AMSOs and orient your vectors toward the enemy!"

AMSO, or anti-missile shield ordnance, was the Confederation Navy's catchall acronym for a family of weapons popularly known as *sandcasters*. Each Dragonfire Starhawk was carrying a warload of eighteen AS-78 missiles, each mounting a warhead loaded with several kilograms of tightly packed lead spherules the size of grains of sand.

Kraits were smart missiles, guided by miniature AIs programmed to evade enemy defenses and strike with maximum effect. Sandcasters, on the other hand, were decidedly dumb weapons, accelerating in a straight line and releasing their warloads in clouds that continued traveling in a straight line, combining their acceleration velocity with whatever residual velocity the fighter had imparted to them upon launch plus whatever velocity component the target possessed at impact. No evasive maneuvers, nothing fancy—just fire the thing and forget about it. Generally, sandcasters were used as missile defense systems. The enemy equivalent of a Krait encountering a cloud of sand grains at several thousand kilometers per second simply ceased to exist, save as a smear of hot, expanding plasma.

But eight months ago, at the Defense of Earth, Gray had written a footnote in the Naval Academy downloads for space fighter tactics by turning AMSO sandcasters against enemy warships. The idea, in retrospect, was perhaps an obvious one . . . but the obvious was not always clear to hidebound risty chair pilots unable to think outside the closely set parameters of classical military training. In the Confederation Navy, you got ahead by following the rules, doing what you were told, and going by the book. In the Periphery, though, survival often required original thought, not to mention a carefree willingness to break the rules when necessary.

Gray had received a commendation for his original thinking, which had been an important factor in disrupting an incoming Turusch strike fleet out at the orbit of Uranus. Using sandcaster warheads to clear a path through enemy fighters had allowed the Terran defenders to concentrate on the bad-guy heavies.

It was not a tactic easily adapted to the realities of modern space warfare, however, and some of his squadron mates still kidded him about throwing handfuls of sand at the enemy. "Sandy Gray," they called him.

At least it was better than "Prim."

But this situation looked like it was made for the same tactic. The enemy, while in motion, was staying relatively put in front of the TRGA. More, the fact that thermonuclear warheads had taken them out suggested that, if they possessed defensive shielding at all, it was fairly low grade and easily overwhelmed. In space combat, *screen* referred to the electromagnetic sheathing that turned aside radiation or charged particle beams, while shields were grav-induced distortions of the space immediately around a ship that could turn aside incoming matter, whether KK projectiles, missile warheads, or the star-hot plasma released by the nearby detonation of a nuke.

Or a cloud of high-velocity sand.

"Set for release at thirty thousand kilometers from the target!" Gray continued. "Fire when ready!"

"Fox Two!" Ben Donovan called a moment later, as the AS-78s began emerging from the keel of his fighter two by two. *Fox two* was the call sign for a dumb-weapon release, and a warning to all fighters in the vicinity that they might have to take evasive action.

Gray released his own sandcaster warheads, giving the obligatory "Fox two!"

In rapid succession, the other Dragonfires launched their anti-missile defenses as well. According to his tactical scans, more KK slivers were on the way from the enemy ship-wall, but those could be avoided at this range easily enough by jinking, a problem that could be left to his AI.

"Shouldn't we be holding some of these things in reserve?" Ryan asked him. Half of her missiles were already accelerating toward the enemy.

"Negative! Give 'em all you've got! The idea is to overwhelm their defenses!"

And there was another reason as well, one he didn't mention. Hold on to a reserve of missiles for later, and you ran the risk of not being able to fire them at all if your number came up on an enemy crowbar or beam.

Don't think about that! Just dump your missiles and stay alive! . . .

Traveling at a thousnad kilometers per second, the first PC-S 78s reached the thirty-thousand-kilometer mark and detonated, releasing their deadly clouds of sand. Enemy beams were finding many of the incoming sandcaster rounds, causing them to wink silently off the tactical display, but once a round reached that 30K line and released its load of sand grains, the enemy's defensive fire could have little effect. Thirty seconds later, the first clouds began reaching their targets.

Gray had an excellent close-in view transmitted from one of the battlespace drones near the TRGA—a single enemy ship, silver and gray and shaped like a flat leaf. The sand cloud, widely dispersed now, was still thick enough to cause the enemy vessel's prow to flare bright red, then orange. The glow faded swiftly, however, and the vessel did not seem otherwise affected. An energy beam—invisible at optical wavelengths but picked out by the AI graphics program as a dazzling streak of emerald green—snapped out from the vessel. Clearly it was still in the fight, and Gray sagged inwardly.

It didn't work. . . .

And then the smart missiles, sent on roundabout courses and coming in from behind, many seemingly straight out of the glare of that nearby sun, began to strike.

The entire wall of enemy ships, stretched across hundreds of kilometers, was engulfed by dazzlingly brilliant fireballs, expanding spheres of hot gas rapidly merging with other spheres close by, growing, swelling, coalescing, forming a sheet of radiance too brilliant to look at with unshielded optics.

The plasma clouds thinned and faded rapidly, and enemy fighters began emerging from the glare . . . but not in the thousands, *not* in the thousands, thank God!

The space-warping shields that protected starships were created by gravitic projectors extending out from a vessel's hull just a few centimeters. They could be melted away by a nearby thermonuclear blast—or by the sandblasting from a high-velocity AMSO round—and when that happened, that section of shield would fail, exposing the ship's hull to incoming missiles or energy. The double volley launched by the Dragonfires—Kraits and AS-78 AMSO rounds—had wreaked a terrible destruction across that gleaming wall of alien warships.

"I have counted eight hundred forty-six vessels emerging from the fireballs," Gray's AI told him, its voice as complacent as though it were discussing the weather. "Others have survived, but are not moving and appear to be damaged. They may be undergoing auto-repair."

Ships with active-nanomatrix hulls, like Starhawks, could grow new parts to replace pieces burned or blasted away if the damage wasn't too extensive. How quickly those damaged alien vessels came back on-line would tell Gray a lot about their level of technology.

More than eight hundred of the alien ships remained, however, and the Dragonfires, plus the survivors of the other two squadrons, remained badly outnumbered.

"Okay, Dragonfires," Gray told the others. He hoped he sounded more confident than he felt. "That cut them up pretty good. Let's finish them. Independent vectors . . . *break*!"

The Starhawks, already widely dispersed, began shifting both courses and velocities, passing the thirty-thousand-kilometer mark as separately vectored fighters instead of as a formation.

That gave them their best chance of survival, at this point, and a chance to mix it up ship to ship with the enemy fighters.

The Dragonfires were still badly outnumbered, but there did appear to be a chance, now. The surviving aliens appeared to be trying to regroup their formation, but they seemed hesitant, even awkward in their maneuvers. The remaining Meteors and Hellstreaks were merging now with the enemy ship-cloud, and sharp, strobing flashes were punctuating the darkness as ships on both sides died.

With both his Krait and AMSO missile lockers empty, Gray now had only two weapons remaining in his arsenal, the Starhawk's StellarDyne PBP-2 particle beam projector, affectionately known as a "pee-beep" by gravfighter pilots, and a Gatling RFK-90 KK cannon. Both weapons were for short-range work—a few thousand kilometers for the particle gun, closer still for the kinetic-kill rounds. To use them he would have to close to knife-fighting range, and that meant getting well inside the 30K boundary of the enemy's primary weapon.

That weapon, though, was not much in evidence now, possibly because the enemy's formation had been disrupted, possibly because they'd lost their inter-ship tactical web, the electronic link that let them work together in close formation. That was the hell of being the first to come up against an unknown technology; you didn't know the enemy's strengths or his weaknesses, and had to find successful ship-to-ship tactics essentially by trial and error.

And in this game, *error* generally meant you ended up dead.

Accelerating hard, he arrowed into the melee now twisting about in front of the alien cylinder, lining up on a lone hostile and triggering a tenth-second burst of artificial lightning, a tightly focused beam of protons powerful enough to overwhelm enemy radiation screens and boil off armor.

A hit! The enemy vessel flared in a dazzlingly brilliant flash and began tumbling, half of its length, visible in the high-mag imagery downloading into Gray's in-head display, charred and curdled.

Another enemy ship flashed across his vector, right to left, and he pivoted his Starhawk to track it. The turn brought the sun directly into his field of view. His fighter's optics adjusted to protect his vision, but for a terrifying moment he couldn't see anything, and he was flying blind.

The AI picked out the nearest enemy ships, however, and he locked on to one, firing his PBP twice, two brief bursts. The first missed; the second burned off the trailing couple of meters of the alien in a white flash, putting it into a slow tumble.

The Dragonfires twisted and turned, maneuvers possible only for light ships possessing high-performance gravitic drives. The tangle of battling ships was known as a furball, a term left over from the era of atmo-fighters and classic dogfights.

It was also what fighter pilots were pleased to call a "target-rich environment," with hundreds of the brightly reflecting silver and gray ships swarming like angry and somewhat confused hornets throughout the volume of battlespace. Gray lined up one ship and blasted it, then moved on to another, and then to a third, knocking them out of action with rapid-fire pulses from his PBP. Comm chatter sounded in his ears, pilots calling back and forth as they coordinated their maneuvers.

"Dragon Three! Dragon Three! You've got one on your tail!"

"Copy! I see him! Pulling a one-eighty . . . *got* the bastard!"

"Dragon Eight! This is Five! Break left high!"

"Five, Eight! Rog!"

"Watch it, Two! There's one close on your six! One on your six!"

A Starhawk a thousand kilometers away twisted suddenly, nicked by an enemy's deadly beam. The aft portion of the grav-fighter snapped off, then vanished, leaving the rest of the ship to tumble helplessly amid an expanding cloud of glittering fragments.

"This is Dragon Two! I'm hit! I'm hit!"

"Copy Two," Gray replied.

"*Shit!* Drive's out! I'm streaking!"

Dragon Two was Shay Ryan's ship, and *streaking* was grav-fighter slang for hurtling out of battlespace without power, without drives, unable to slow or maneuver.

And there wasn't a damned thing Gray could do about it, except . . .

"Two, this is Dragon One!" Gray added, thoughtclicking on the icon marking Ryan's crippled fighter. "I've got you logged! Sit tight. The SAR tugs will be after you in a few hours!"

Data on Ryan's vector, her course and speed, had just been logged by Gray's AI, and would be transmitted over the local tactical net. When the fleet arrived, the Search and Rescue vessels would have a good idea of where to look for her.

If the fleet arrived. Gray was realist enough to know that there were no promises there. By now the battlegroup's tactical planners had some idea of what was waiting for them here at the TRGA cylinder. Admiral Koenig might well have decided to turn the fleet around and head back for Earth.

But . . . no. Koenig wouldn't do that. There were plenty of Confederation naval officers who would cut and run, Gray knew, but not Koenig. The man, in Gray's estimation, was not your typical risty. He *cared* about his people, and he wouldn't abandon any of them if there was any way in heaven or earth to avoid it. At the very least, he would wait to see the outcome of this furball, and he would save the fighters if he could.

Assuming there were any fighters left to save when the fleet got here in another seven hours or so. Nineteen grav-fighters were left in the fight, now, out of the original thirty-six, and while they were doing better now that they were actually in close among the enemy ships, they were still out-numbered by fifty to one. How long could they keep this up before the bad guys wiped them from the sky, one by one?

Ten thousand kilometers away, a group of enemy ships was trying to re-form. Gray's AI counted sixty-four of them—there was that power of two again—and they were drifting into a formation like a broad, circular wall of ships, a dish shape like the one the Dragonfires had already broken up.

This time, there were no more Kraits and no more AMSO rounds.

"All ships!" Gray broadcast. "Listen up! We've got an enemy formation grouping up near the cylinder's mouth! Let's move in close and burn them!"

Gray had no idea, at this point, if he had overall command of all three squadrons—what was left of them—or not. The skippers of the Meteors and the Hellstreaks both were dead, though, so it was a fair assumption. There was no time to check on commission dates or find out if anyone else with a higher rank was still in the fight. Leadership, at this point in the dogfight, was a matter of pointing, waving, and shouting "Follow me!"

He brought his Starhawk into a fast, broad turn, throwing his projected singularity out to port and letting the flickering gravity field draw him around, his straight path becoming a curve as it passed through gravitationally bent space. Maneuvering a fighter in space wasn't at all like flying an atmofighter; with no atmosphere to provide lift or drag, the only way to change vector was to project singularities nearby, submicroscopic black holes that curved space just enough to redirect the ship's course.

He was now hurtling toward the TRGA cylinder at five kilometers per second.

The more he watched them, the more convinced Gray was that the enemy, in fact, was some sort of machine intelligence, operating by programmed rote and without the guidance of an organic brain. The line between the two, organic and machine, could be blurred to the point of invisibility sometimes; a good AI could be quite creative, at least within its programmed area of expertise. The enemy ships were clearly trying to work together; Gray could almost imagine tightly focused beams of data interconnecting them all like the strands of a spider's web.

Are these the Sh'daar? Gray wondered. Or were they merely more of the Sh'daar's servants, like the Turusch or the Nungiirtok or the gas-bag H'rulka? So long as the Sh'daar remained in the shadows, fighting the Confederation through their proxies, there was no way to bring the war into their front yard, no way to force them to negotiate or back off.

He lined up on another of the silver-gray craft, blasting it with a triplet of tenth-second bolts from his PBP.

The enemy beam hit him, grazing his port side, and he felt his Starhawk partially crumple, then drop into a dizzying tumble.

"Damage report!" he shouted out at his AI. "What the hell happened? . . ."

"We received a grazing hit by an energy beam that appears to have momentarily increased the strong force at nuclear levels in an isolated area. A portion of our outer hull has undergone nuclear collapse."

So *that* was the secret of the enemy beam, and why the Starhawks hit earlier had vanished. They hadn't disappeared literally. With an increase in the strong force binding their atoms together, those atoms had collapsed as completely as the atoms of a neutron star, becoming neutronium—an ultra-dense exotic form of matter—and crunching down to occupy an invisibly small volume of space. Confederation singularity drives used a similar process to jump-start the artificial black holes that dragged free energy from hard vacuum, but so far as Gray knew, they'd never figured out how to project it as a weapon.

The brush of that deadly weapon had devoured perhaps 10 percent of Gray's fighter. His nanomatrix hull was struggling now to repair the damage, but in the meantime, his drives were out. Using maneuvering thrusters—those remaining on-line—he managed to stop his disorienting tumble . . . but his main drives remained out. He was falling at five kilometers per second toward the TRGA cylinder.

Correction. *Eight* kilometers per second . . . and his velocity was increasing. He appeared to be sliding down a gravity well, as though he were being funneled straight toward the maw of that wildly rotating cylinder ahead.

With a calm that he didn't know he possessed, Gray thoughtclicked his way through a list of icons, transmitting a running log to the local battlenet and to the ships of the distant fleet. He would continue transmitting for as long as he could.

He also began analyzing both the damage to his gravfighter and the gravity well itself. As nearly as he could determine, the local gravitational field had been sharply bent by the one-solar mass of the spinning artifact ahead. Somehow, the builders of the TRGA had compressed a medium-sized star into a hollow cylinder a kilometer across and twenty long. That implied the density of a star-sized black hole, yet somehow it was holding its unnatural shape.

The technology to create such a thing was nothing short of miraculous. What was that ancient adage about advanced technology and magic? He couldn't remember.

If the Sh'daar possessed such knowledge, however . . .

Something didn't add up. Beings that could create the TRGA weren't merely good magicians. They were *gods*, or the closest things to gods mere humans could imagine. If the Sh'daar possessed such power, they didn't need to rely on the Turusch or their other subject species, and they would have been able to win the war moments after delivering their ultimatum.

Why fight this protracted war for almost forty years, when such technology could wipe Humankind out of existence with scarcely a thought?

There was something important here, but Gray couldn't place his finger on it. His fighter, falling free, was accelerating, moving faster and faster as the maw of the TRGA cylinder yawned ahead, the opening empty and utterly lightless.

Fifty more seconds, at this rate, and he would be drawn inside.

CIC
TC/USNA CVS America
Inbound, Texaghu Resch System
1758 hours, TFT

"It's time," Koenig said with careful deliberation, "that you . . . you *people* level with us. I want to know about the Sh'daar."

Though he was still in *America*'s CIC, Koenig had linked through to the quarters maintained for the two Agletsch. They shared a virtual reality now that, to Koenig's senses, appeared to be a city on their home planet, a forest of loaf-shaped towers stretching as far as the eye could see, with swarming thousands of their kind in the distance. Gru'mulkisch and Dra'ethde stood before him, their bodies half-immersed in a sunken pool filled with a glistening black liquid.

"We have told you, Admiral, what we can," Dra'ethde said, "as we agreed with your government on Earth."

"Little is known about the Sh'daar masters," Gru'mulkisch added, "yes-no?"

"Have a look at this, then," Koenig replied, and he channeled a portion of the transmission from the recon flight in close to the TRGA artifact—of a wall of silver-gray shapes flashing in the light of the nearby sun, moving in perfect formation. "They came out of that cylinder, and they probably destroyed a reconnaissance probe we had in there, studying the thing.

"Right now, I have thirty-six of my fighters in there facing that mass of hostiles. We won't know what the outcome will be for hours, yet, and this fleet is headed straight into that swarm. I want to know if those ships are Sh'daar, I want to know if you've seen this sort of vessel before, and I want to know how to defeat them."

"Defeating them . . . this is the true problem you face, yes-no?" Gru'mulkisch's electronically translated voice could not carry emotion—and reading the emotions of such an alien being was impossible in any case. But the brightly patterned beings both seemed to sag, somewhat, and the colors of their velvety integument seemed to fade. Gru'mulkisch actually began to hunker down deeper in the pool, letting the liquid cover all but part of her carapace and her four weaving, stalked eyes.

"The Sh'daar have dominated much of the galaxy for tens of thousands of your years," Dra'ethde added. "If there is a way to defeat them, someone would have found it by now."

Koenig considered the two Agletsch. What the hell were they soaking in, anyway, and why? His request to link with them in virtual reality had not been refused . . . as it would have been had they been eating. Agletsch mores prohibited them from feeding in public—all in all a good thing so far as humans were concerned, because reportedly they ate by extruding a portion of one of their stomachs through an opening in their abdomen. At the moment, they appeared to be bathing—or at least soaking in some sort of liquid, though whether that was for hygiene, relaxation, or something else entirely was impossible to judge. Not only that, but this evidently was a simulation for them as well, since the background showed an Agletsch city. There was no way of knowing what they might actually be doing, locked away in their quarters.

Self-evidently, nonhumans did not think the same as did humans. Their mores—what they considered right or wrong, proper or improper, normal or scandalous—all were shaped by wildly different biologies and psychologies. They were, in short, *alien* . . . and the human who tried to understand them from a strictly human perspective was going to get it wrong.

They appeared genuinely to believe that fighting against the Sh'daar was a hopeless pursuit. But was that a core belief, a superficial assumption . . . or possibly a means of hiding the truth?

Or might it be something even more profound, a completely different way, an *alien* way, of looking at the universe?

And perhaps the Agletsch version of *truth* was something humans would not even recognize.

"Do you recognize these ships?" Koenig demanded.

"They are . . . of Sh'daar origin," Dra'ethde said.

An odd way to phrase it. "Our AIs have analyzed their movement, and suggest that they are being run by a sophisticated artificial intelligence. Is that true?"

"Those ships are not 'manned,' as you would use the term." Gru'mulkisch sounded uncomfortable, hesitant. Her translated voice was still clear, however, although her translator was completely submerged.

"Robots? Or are they teleoperated?"

" 'Teleoperated' is what, please?"

"Operated from a distance. Remote control."

"Ah. We would say . . . they are piloted by ghosts."

Koenig gave a sharp snort, an explosive sound of surprise mingled with disbelief. "Whose ghosts? Sh'daar?"

"Exactly. You comprehend."

"No. I do *not* comprehend. Either those ships have flesh-and-blood pilots in them, they're being piloted by AIs, or they're being remote-controlled. Which the hell is it?"

" 'The hell' is what, please?"

Koenig hesitated. Within the mix of cultures that made up the Terran Confederation, trying to convert someone to your religious beliefs was illegal, and simply *talking* about religion with someone who didn't share your views was considered to be extremely ill-mannered. The Agletsch wouldn't have the same taboos, of course . . . likely they didn't have religion as humans understood the term. But for humans the word *ghost* carried a lot of baggage, with distinctly religious implications suggesting the survival of some noncorporeal aspect of a being after death, the soul or spirit or life force, whatever you cared to call it.

"A human expression," he said. "One of exasperation . . . and anger if you don't give me the information I require. Those are Sh'daar ships?"

"They are of Sh'daar origin."

"Meaning what? The Sh'daar built them?"

"We are traders in information," Dra'ethde said, "as you are aware. We do not deal in . . . stories. You would say . . . fiction? Fantasies?"

"Right now," Koenig said, "neither do I. I want the truth."

"The truth," Gru'mulkisch pointed out, "is often of uncertain form, and may vary depending on who is speaking it. Yes-no?"

"Yes," Koenig said. "On that point we agree."

"We know little about the Sh'daar that can be confirmed," Dra'ethde said. "We've told you and your fellows this on many occasions. Most of what we know about the Sh'daar is . . . supposition? Assumption?"

"It is difficult to separate the truth from wild speculation," Gru'mulkisch added.

"Then tell me the speculation," Koenig told them.

"This would not be what you term 'hard data,' you understand. We cannot judge its truthfulness."

"Tell me."

"It is possible," Dra'ethde said, "that the Sh'daar are extinct, have been extinct for far longer than the Chelk.

"But what was left behind—their ghost, if you will—continues to govern the galaxy."

Chapter Eleven

Trevor Gray
TRGA
1759 hours, TFT

The maw opened around him, and Gray fell into darkness.

He was aware, through briefing downloads, of the old theories about Tipler machines—high-mass cylinders rotating at an appreciable percentage of the speed of light that could open pathways through space or even through time. He was also aware of speculation about so-called wormholes, allowing near-instantaneous travel between widely separated points . . . or even between separate universes.

What it all came down to, however, was, so far as Gray was concerned, his own appalling ignorance. He didn't know where—or *when*—he was falling, didn't know if the theoretical arguments about Tipler cylinders needing to be infinitely long were true, didn't even know if this *was* a Tipler machine since he was going *through* rather than past it, didn't know much of *anything* save that he was falling through strangeness.

Twenty seconds passed, according to his own internal timekeeping software, before he realized something extraordinary. He was traveling at some five hundred kilometers per second, now, according to the blue-shift of lidar beams bounced off the tunnel walls ahead of him. In twenty seconds he'd traveled ten thousand kilometers . . . and yet the TRGA artifact was only twelve kilometers long.

And in fact he was continuing to accelerate, in the grip of a monstrous acceleration funneled through the core of the rotating cylinder. Clearly he could no longer be inside the cylinder proper. Space itself had taken on exceedingly strange dimensions, abandoning the sane laws of physics for something wholly other. As with a gravitic drive, he felt no acceleration . . . but in seconds more he was approaching the speed of light, had plunged hundreds of thousands of kilometers into the cylinder, and was beginning to wonder if, just possibly, the thing *was* in fact infinite in length.

"What we are experiencing," his AI intoned with a maddening calm, "is consistent with Lorentzian wormhole theory."

"Those are supposed to be unstable," Gray said. His heart was pounding, his breath coming in short, ragged gasps. He dredged up theory downloaded long ago, as much to keep the fear at bay as anything else. "They collapse as soon as they open."

"The cylinder's extreme rate of rotation might be holding it open through centrifugal force."

"Do you know that? Or are you guessing?"

"At this point," his AI told him, "there is only room for speculation."

And still he fell. The encircling walls were faintly luminous—whether from internal heat or radiation or something else entirely, he couldn't tell. And the light appeared to be growing brighter. . . .

Emergence.

CIC
TC/USNA CVS America
Inbound, Texaghu Resch System
1801 hours, TFT

"By 'ghost,'" Koenig said carefully, "might you mean up-loaded personalities?"

Gru'mulkisch stepped from the sunken tub, streaming black liquid. " 'Uploaded personalities' is what, please?"

Koenig considered bringing in a link to *America*'s technological library, but there would be so much information under that heading, much of it speculative, that it would take too long to distill a concise answer for the two Agletsch.

"It's a theoretical technology for us," he said instead. "The idea is that human personalities—including their memories, their sense of being, their consciousness—all could be digitally mapped and stored in a computer with a deep-enough operational matrix. You would have, in effect, human consciousness within a machine."

Dra'ethde stepped out of the bath, and the surrounding Agletsch city faded away, replaced by the interior of the aliens' quarters. One bulkhead looked out into emptiness, black night strewn with wide-spaced stars. The tub, Koenig noticed, had also vanished.

"This would not be a true transfer, however," Dra'ethde said. "The personality would be copied into the machine, not actually transferred, yes-no?"

"We've debated that issue for a long time," Koenig admitted. "I agree with you. The original would remain behind, and only a copy would be uploaded electronically. From the copy's point of view, however, with its memories intact and accessible, it would appear to have been an actual transfer."

"And does your species in fact possess such technology?" Gru'mulkisch asked.

Koenig thought carefully before answering. He still did not trust Agletsch motives, and he most certainly did not trust the Sh'daar Seeds they carried, near-microscopic nodes of a widely distributed computer communications network. What he was describing fell under the heading of the GRIN technologies proscribed by the Sh'daar—specifically information systems, though both robotics and nanotechnology came into the picture as well.

Admit too much, and he might end forever any chance Humankind had of negotiation, of striking a deal with the

Sh'daar and ending this war. But it was also vital that they understand what he was asking about, if he was to get a clear answer.

"Not quite to the extent you mean," Koenig told the Agletsch. "But I *do* have an uploaded personality here. You can ask her."

He thoughtclicked an in-head icon, and Karyn Mendelson came on-line. Her image, appearing within the shared virtual reality of the Agletsch's quarters, was that of a tall and attractive woman, Koenig's age, and wearing the dress black-and-grays of a Confederation naval officer. The sleeve stripes, rank tabs, and gold decoration in a panel down the left side of her uniform tunic identified her as a rear admiral.

Koenig was startled to realize that it had been a long time—weeks, perhaps, since he'd seen her this way.

"Hello, Dra'ethde, Gru'mulkisch," she said in Karyn's voice. "I've been following your conversation. What was it you wished to know?"

"You are an uploaded personality?" Gru'mulkisch asked. Even through the filter of his translator, he sounded surprised.

"I am . . . after a fashion. I am a PA, a personal assistant, with the personality overlay of a once-living person."

" 'Once living'?"

"Karyn Mendelson was . . . a friend of mine," Koenig told them. There was no need to go into detail. "She was killed six months ago in the Turusch attack on our Solar System. I have her image functioning as avatar on my PA."

"A personal assistant," Karyn told them, "is a fairly compact but sophisticated AI resident within a person's cerebral implants. Important parts of a person's mental processes—including some memories, learned responses, language skills, training, and so on—can be digitally stored. Normally, the PA is a close match for the person in question, close enough to respond to visual communication links or to appear within shared virtual realities and be indistinguishable from the original. Admiral Koenig, here, is quite busy.

He can't afford the time to answer all of his calls personally. His PA can appear to others as he does, can make decisions within certain broad constraints, can schedule appointments, can hold routine conversations, and can do so skillfully enough that others can never be sure if they're dealing with the original or with an AI."

"We'd heard of PAs, of course, during our stay on Earth," Dra'ethde said. "We did not realize that they were this . . . convincing."

"You are Admiral Koenig's PA, yes-no?" Gru'mulkisch asked. "And yet you do not look like Admiral Koenig."

"That's because when Karyn died," Koenig said, "I took her PA—there were copies of it on my implant systems, and in my office here on the *America*—and overlaid it on my own. I preferred to use . . . her copy."

He didn't add that he'd done so because of how much he missed Karyn, how much he didn't want to let her go.

"I can appear as Karyn," she said, and then the virtual image morphed smoothly into a duplicate of Koenig, also in Confederation full dress. "Or as Admiral Koenig."

"Then, you have no physical reality now, yes-no?" Dra'ethde asked.

"No," Karyn said, the male image morphing back to hers.

"But are you alive?" Gru'mulkisch asked. She appeared to be disturbed by the revelation. "Or . . . perhaps I should ask instead, do you *feel* alive?"

"I am aware that I am a digital construct," Karyn told them, "and that I do not have a biological existence of my own. I wonder sometimes, however, if Admiral Koenig is aware of this."

It was a gentle dig, but it surprised Koenig. The PA frequently had suggested to him that using the Karyn Mendelson PA software was not . . . *healthy* for him, that he might be clinging to his dead lover's memory in an unhealthy way. And in fact, though his PA still spoke to him in Karyn's voice, he really hadn't summoned her visible avatar for weeks.

"Admiral Koenig believes you to be alive?"

"Admiral Koenig is comforted by my appearance," the PA replied.

"I *do* know the difference between a person and an avatar, damn it," Koenig added, a bit more sharply than he'd intended. This discussion was becoming highly personal, when all he'd initially wanted was a demonstration of personality uploading. He disliked being embarrassed in front of aliens, even though he knew that they would not be upset by the same things that embarrassed humans.

"You are suggesting that the Sh'daar uploaded such digital personalities into their ships and computer networks," Gru'mulkisch said, "yes-no? That these are the 'ghosts' we mention, again yes-no?"

"The word *ghost* has a religious connotation for us," Koenig replied. "I don't know what you Agletsch think of such things, but some humans believe in a noncorporeal aspect of intelligence or personality that survives the body after death."

"Ah," Dra'ethde said. "You refer to the *tru'a*, the *dhuthr'a*, and the *thurah'a*. You might say 'soul' or 'spirit.'"

"You have *three* of them?"

"Oh, yes. The *tru'a* is—"

Koenig held up a hand and shook his head. "That's okay. You don't need to explain."

Having three noncorporeal aspects, he thought, wasn't all that strange a concept. Some modern human religions, he knew, distinguished between the soul and the spirit as two distinct entities, while the ancient Egyptians, depending on how one counted, had believed in either seven or nine—the *ka*, *ba*, *akh*, *sheut*, *ib*, and others.

But discussing this sort of thing, even with a nonhuman, made Koenig uncomfortable. The White Covenant, and years of social conditioning, made anything touching on religion or the paranormal feel *wrong*.

"For humans, a ghost is supposed to be the spirit or soul of a dead person," Koenig explained. He tended to be pretty much of a materialist himself, though he tried to keep an open mind. "But uploading the electronic pattern of some-one's personality comes pretty close to that idea, I'd say."

"We use the word in the same way," Gru'mulkisch said, "to represent the *dhuthr'a* left behind at death. We believe that the Sh'daar, when they die, upload their *dhuthr'a* into electronic systems—computer networks, if you will. They pilot their ships, run their manufactories, indeed they see to the efficient running of the Sh'daar's galactic empire."

"Great," Koenig said. "We're fighting against ghosts. . . ."

Open mind or not, he did not believe that what Gru'mulkisch was saying could in any way be literally true.

Trevor Gray
Beyond the TRGA
1805 hours, TFT

Gray had emerged within a star cloud.

The sky ahead was packed with them, millions of suns crowded together so closely they appeared to form a single shining white wall ahead, thinning somewhat in other directions. Gray felt a sharp pang and looked about wildly. He didn't know where he was . . . but he did know that there was no sky like that anywhere within many thousands of light years of Earth.

Switching to view aft, he saw the TRGA cylinder—or more likely it was a different cylinder identical to the first, connected with it by wormhole or some other space-bypassing gateway. The fighter was no longer moving at near-*c*, but appeared to have lost its velocity somehow as it emerged from the tube.

"AI," he said, speaking between ragged breaths, "are you recording this?"

"Recording," the fighter's voice replied.

"We're drifting away from that . . . that gate, or whatever it is. We'll need to find our way back here if we're to have a hope of getting home."

"Agreed. Repairs necessary to maneuver and accelerate are now at fifty-three percent."

"Good. . . ." Although Starhawk fighters were billed as self-repairing, that possibility was never a foregone conclusion. If too much of the active nanomatrix was lost, or if there was even minor damage to the AI system itself, or if the power plant was damaged, repairs were impossible. Apparently, Gray's fighter had been only grazed by the enemy beam, and damage, while crippling, was superficial enough that he would be able to power up again soon.

Resetting the cockpit display to view forward once more, he stared into that inexpressibly beautiful wall of stars once more.

"Where . . . where are we?" he asked after a long moment, as awe and terror grappled for possession of his thoughts. "Can you tell?"

"I am surveying the sky, seeking to match stellar spectra with known stars," his AI replied. "This will take some time."

Gray started to ask how much time, then thought better of it. AIs were inhumanly quick, but they also possessed an inhuman awareness—or, rather, a *lack* of awareness—of time in the human sense. "I . . . I was wondering if we were at the galactic core . . . at the center of the galaxy."

If they were, that would explain the crowding of stars out there, of course. This region of space also appeared to be devoid of gas and dust, supporting that theory. According to downloads he'd pulled in from the ship's library, the galactic core was supposed to be a region of densely crowded stars where intense radiation, frequent supernovae, and gravitational effects had swept away all traces of interstellar gas eons ago. It was also the location, he knew, of several bizarre objects—including at least two supermassive black holes.

"What we are seeing," his AI informed him, "is consistent with the interior of a globular star cluster. However, if so, it is an unusually large one. I estimate that it contains approximately five million stars within a sphere that is at least two hundred thirty light years across."

"How big is a normal globular cluster?"

"M-13, in Hercules, is typical. It measures approximately one hundred forty light years across and contains several hundred thousand stars."

So this teeming hive of suns was large, but still within the range of globular star clusters. It was not the galactic core.

"But . . . that means you should be able to identify it, right? There can't be that many globulars out there."

"Approximately two hundred for our galaxy," the fighter's AI told him. "But we may not be within our home galaxy any longer."

Gray hadn't considered that possibility. Globular star clusters existed as satellites of most galaxies—the larger ones, at any rate—orbiting their centers like moons around a primary. Sol's parent galaxy possessed nearly two hundred; M-31 in Andromeda, 2.3 million light years away, had around five hundred.

But he wasn't ready to start worrying about which galaxy he might be in, now, not until he had good reason to assume they were a *lot* farther from home—millions of light years, instead of a few tens of thousands. Of more pressing concern was just why they'd ended up *here*, wherever "here" might actually be. Presumably, those thousands of silver-gray, tightly interconnected warships had come from here; presumably, too, the TRGA led somewhere important to the Sh'daar, or whoever had built the damned thing in the first place.

"Are you picking up any signs of technic civilization?" Gray asked. "Ships? Bases?"

"It is difficult to tell," the AI replied. "There is intense radiation here—the result, perhaps, of frequent supernovae—as well as noise across all radio frequencies, which masks conventional radio transmissions. However, there does appear to be an anomalous infrared source almost directly ahead on our line of drift. Designating target as AIS-1."

"Range?"

"Impossible to tell. It is not moving across our line of sight, and so triangulation methods are useless. I could use radar—"

"No!" Gray said sharply. Then, more gently, "No. Let's not tell anyone we're here just yet."

"I concur. Within this context, the anomalous signal is not likely to represent friendly assets."

"Why anomalous?" The sky was *filled* with heat sources—millions of stars.

"It appears to be a non-point source, and the radiation I am recording is consistent with an artificial object."

"Let me see it."

A window opened in Gray's mind. At first, all he could see were stars, uncounted millions of them massed into a near-solid wall. His AI highlighted a point at the center with a red circle—a dark speck against the light.

"A ship?"

"Until the exact range can be determined, unknown." The AI seemed to hesitate. "If I were to offer an unsubstantiated statement, however, it would be that AIS-1 appears to be considerably larger than a ship. It appears distant, but since it is still showing a disk, even a small one, that suggests that it is of considerable size . . . as large as a moon or a major planetoid, at the least. It has a relatively low albedo, which suggests a natural object."

"And we're moving toward it?"

"Within approximately seven tenths of a degree of arc, yes."

Which suggested that the object, whatever it was, had been precisely and deliberately placed—quite possibly as a watch station or even a deep-space fortress for keeping track of anything that might emerge from the TRGA cylinder.

Anything like him.

"How close is the nearest sun?" Gray wanted to know.

"So far I have recorded nearly five hundred stars within two light years," the AI said, "but calculating precise distances is difficult without a long observational baseline with which to calculate parallax. None of the stars observed so far is closer than an estimated tenth of a light year, however."

"Which means we're not inside a solar system. That . . . object isn't part of a solar system."

"Unlikely. Planetary systems would not be stable within a star cluster such as this. Gravitational interactions among member stars would tend to eject planets within a few millions of years."

"Whatever they are, they could be tracking us," Gray said. "We need to get the ship repaired fast. As in turn around *now*, go to max acceleration, and get the hell out of here."

"I am working on that," the AI told him. "Repairs now at sixty-one percent."

It was taking too damned long. If the enemy was monitoring everything that came through the TRGA cylinder into this space . . .

And then the silver-gray ships were *there*, all around him, flashing and turning in the dazzling light of millions of stars. His PBP was still down. Firing his Gatling cannon might take out one, even two or three . . . assuming he could maneuver enough to aim. *Might*.

No. Better to watch . . . and wait. *Play dead*.

The way the ships had effortlessly appeared, without warning, suggested that they possessed acceleration enough to reach near-*c* speeds within extremely short periods of time. There'd been no warning of their approach. They must have sailed in just behind the wavefront announcing their approach, matching velocities with the disabled fighter in an instant. For long seconds, they wheeled, flashed, and maneuvered in perfect unison.

Then, abruptly, shockingly, they were gone.

"Where the hell did they go?" Gray asked.

"In the direction of the TRGA," his AI replied. "I was unable to measure their rate of acceleration."

Which meant it was high indeed.

"They . . . they must have assumed we were just wreckage."

"That, or that we were not worth spending time or effort on our destruction. They would certainly have picked up infrared radiation from the hull, and picked up the special distortion of our power plant singularities."

That the aliens had simply ignored the wreckage of Gray's fighter seemed, somehow, like an insult. A calculated and contemptuous dismissal.

"It may also be," the AI continued, "that they have summoned other means of dealing with us."

"Something to . . . to capture us, then." The flattened, leaf-shaped vessels, as small as fighters themselves, weren't large enough to take the damaged Starhawk on board. "Did you detect a signal?"

"Negative. But that does not mean that one was not transmitted."

"How long until we can accelerate?"

A pause, almost a hesitation. "Between five and six minutes more."

"Keep at it, then. I don't think I want to meet the Sh'daar face-to-face."

He found the idea terrifying, eliciting the sweat-drenched horror of the starkest of nightmares. Unknown and unknowable *things* clutching and snapping at him, faceless and remorseless. He felt his self-control evaporating, felt stark panic rising like an incoming black tide.

He considered taking the final option.

It was not often discussed by *America*'s pilots, but there was that final way out—a coded command to the AI that would collapse the fighter and its occupant into the fast-circling microscopic black holes of the power plant. If a fighter was disabled and about to be captured, the data stored within the AI system and within the pilot's brain could be erased in a silent, merciful instant. The system had been put in place early in the Sh'daar war, when Confederation strategists thought it might still be possible to keep Earth's location secret from the enemy.

It had turned out that the Agletsch had already known

about Earth, and the Sh'daar would have learned the location from them.

But the system had remained in place ever since. Too many fighters crippled in combat became streakers, hurtling off into space too badly damaged for self-repair. If a SAR tug couldn't find you, an instant death was preferable to slow freezing or asphyxiation as your life support gave out. The pilots didn't talk about it much, but if things *really* got bad, there was always that final option.

Right now, Gray was the ultimate in streakers, drifting through space unknown, tens of thousands of light years away from either Earth or the fleet.

He would end this soon . . . *much* sooner if it looked like they were going to try to take him alive. The one thing keeping him from pulling the plug right now was the knowledge that he might yet be able to get back to the other side of the wormhole. If he could, the fleet would need to now what was here on the other side.

The problem was going to be getting back to Texaghu Resch.

"Lieutenant Gray," his AI said. "We may have a problem."

"Whatcha got?"

"I'm passively tracking a large object heading directly toward us at high speed."

"Let me see."

There wasn't much to see as yet—a black speck against the dazzling backdrop of massed stars, but it was growing larger moment by moment.

"A ship?" Gray asked.

"A *large* ship," the AI replied. "It appears to have left the vicinity of AIS-1 some twenty seconds ago, and is approaching at an estimated twenty kilometers per second."

"Do you have a range?"

"Estimated only . . . but based on the changing light curve and albedo estimates, approximately two thousand kilometers."

One hundred seconds, then, less than two minutes.

"Okay," Gray said. Resignation pressed down on him, dragging at his thoughts. "We need to let the fleet know what we've found. Reconfigure a battlespace drone as a message torpedo."

"Affirmative."

"Download enough of yourself that you'll be able to answer questions."

That was one of the more useful aspects of artificial intelligence—the ability to have one clone itself, to hive off an exact copy of the original, and transfer that copy to a different platform. In this case, the platform was a VR-5 remote-scan sensor probe, one of the programmable, mobile recon units deployed in combat to give an overall view of the battlespace.

"Include a complete log of everything up to launch."

"Affirmative."

The problem was that a recon drone didn't have nearly as much onboard memory as a Starhawk fighter. The AI copy would necessarily be quite limited in its scope and intelligence.

But it would *remember*. . . .

"Unknown ship is accelerating," the AI reported. "Time to intercept now estimated at fifteen seconds."

"Launch!"

The fighter abruptly came to life, rotating a full one hundred eighty degrees, then loosing the probe in an intense diamagnetic surge. Recoil shoved the fighter back with a savage jolt. The probe's drives switched on, then, accelerating the messenger at two thousand gravities.

Starhawks carried two types of battlespace monitors—tiny, finger-sized units that simply watched and transmitted data, and the larger VR-5s, a bit larger than a human head, that could be programmed to take specific action or even display a measure of independent thought when used for reconnaissance. In this case, the probe would make its way back to the local TRGA cylinder and attempt to thread its way through the wormhole and back to the fleet.

Gray wasn't even sure that it could be done, but it was one of only two actions open to him at the moment.

And then the alien ship arrived.

It was . . . huge. And utterly unlike any ship design Gray was familiar with, all sweeping curves and clustered spires, more like a tiny world than a spacecraft. What appeared to be a tiny opening on the smoothly rounded forward end of the thing turned out to be a hundred meters across as it closed over and around Gray's fighter.

He thoughtclicked the command to destroy himself and the ship . . . then screamed when nothing happened.

Still alive, Gray was drawn inside. . . .

Chapter Twelve

CIC
TC/USNA CVS America
Inbound, Texaghu Resch System
0004 hours, TFT

"All ships," Koenig said, giving the command. "Fire!"

Throughout the fleet, volley upon volley was loosed—high-speed nuclear-tipped missiles, kinetic-kill railgun projectiles, and even—borrowing from the tactics employed by one of the Starhawk squadrons launched earlier—sandcaster rounds. The bombardment lasted for precisely one minute, before targeting AIs gave the order to cease fire. At this range, they were firing almost blind, firing at where the AIs predicted the targets would be when the rounds actually reached them.

Whether those volleys would have any effect at all remained to be seen.

More than six hours had passed since Koenig had decided to continue with the oplan, having the Fleet follow the three advance fighter squadrons in to the TRGA artifact rather than aborting and running for home.

Details of what had happened to the three squadrons were still sketchy. The squadron CO of the Dragonfires had employed massed volleys of nukes to break up the Sh'daar formation, that much was clear, but after that, things had become confused. All three squadrons had suffered heavy casualties, and tracking data had been transmitted on the vectors of a number of streakers. Telemetry from the fighters, acquired as the battlegroup continued to bear in toward the system's star, indicated that they'd expended all of their munitions, then gone dark, scattering across that region of space and dropping into silent near-invisibility to await the fleet's arrival.

The fleet wasn't there yet. They were now fifty-one minutes out at their original projections, and traveling at 15,300 kilometers per second. Remote probes launched an hour earlier had already entered the TRGA battlespace and were transmitting what they saw back to the incoming fleet with a seventy-eight-second time delay.

What they'd reported was chilling. The initial enemy formation had been savaged by the fighter strike, but more of the ships identified by the Agletsch as Sh'daar "ghosts" had come through the spinning cylinder in the hours since, filling local space with flashing, shifting sheet formations of the alien vessels, gleaming in the harsh light of the close-by sun. From their vantage point just over 23 million kilometers out, Koenig and his command staff watched the probe transmissions, could see the alien formations rippling and pulsing as if they were part of a single unit. According to the fleet AIs recording the scene, the enemy now numbered more than 33 *million* of the small vessels, or some 2^{24}, plus a couple of thousand or so left over after the three fighter squadrons had struck hours earlier.

With luck, the one-minute bombardment would thin those alien ranks a bit . . . but Koenig knew better than to count on that too much. The fleet was going to have to go in there toe-to-toe, with the outcome anyone's guess.

"Three squadrons ready for launch at your order, Admiral," Wizewski told him, seconds after the long-range bombardment had ceased.

"Thank you, CAG." Koenig checked his internal time readout. "You may commence launching CSP. Inform the other carriers in the battlegroup, if you please."

"Aye, aye, sir."

One of *America*'s six squadrons, the Dragonfires, had been sent in ahead of the fleet; three more were readied now in the carrier's drop tubes—VFA-51, the Black Lightnings, VFA-31, the Impactors, and VFA-36, the Death Rattlers. All flew the newer SG-92 Starhawks. The two remaining squadrons, the Star Tigers and the Nighthawks, flew the older SG-55 War Eagles, and so Koenig had elected to hold them in reserve.

All of *America*'s remaining fighter squadrons were flying short today. They'd been badly shot up at Alphekka, and even folding in the survivors from several other squadrons as replacements hadn't brought their rosters up to full strength. All things considered, Wizewski had done an incredible job of making do with what was left . . . but now his patch-work efforts were going to be put to the ultimate test. The three Starhawk squadrons he'd thrown against some four-thousand Sh'daar had been shredded; exact figures couldn't be calculated yet, but a good guess was that twenty of the thirty-six fighters going in had been destroyed, and another ten were disabled and streaking. And the odds they would be facing now were far, far worse.

For that reason, Koenig was going to employ the fleet's fighters in an unusual way, putting them into space as an integral part of the carrier group, rather than as long-range strike craft. The idea, his *hope*, really, was that a few hundred fighters mingling with the fifty-eight capital ships would cause major headaches for the enemy's targeting systems. Throw them at that wall of silver-gray alien craft and most of them would be destroyed. Keep them with the fleet, and perhaps fighters and capital ships could provide close combat support for each other.

It was not an accepted tactic in the fleet manual for the Confederation Navy, which emphasized the need to use strike fighters across multiple-AU ranges in order to wreak maximum damage to an enemy formation before the slower, less maneuverable capital ships could come into range. Cripple the enemy fleet with fighters, then mop up with the heavies—that was the accepted maxim of modern space-naval warfare.

Koenig decided that today he was going to rewrite the manual. So far as he knew, the Confederation had never come up against this enemy, or these tactics; old and established strategies would end with the battlegroup destroyed, the survivors hunted down one by one. If they were to come through this with any hope of winning, they needed to try something new.

"Admiral, request cessation to thrust," Wizewski said. "The Black Lightnings are ready for drop."

"Make to all vessels in the battlegroup," Koenig ordered. "Cease thrust."

If *America* did not stop her deceleration, the fighters would emerge from their drop tubes one by one . . . and one by one smash into the underside of the carrier's forward shield cap at over a thousand meters per second. Steady velocity was okay; he wanted the fleet to have some residual momentum when it reached battlespace. *Speed is life.*

"The fleet has ceased decelerating," Commander Sinclair said. "Velocity estimated at fifteen thousand kps."

"Very well."

"Fighters have commenced launching," Wizewski added.

On one of the CIC monitors, a drone image of *America* showed the fighters dropping from the carrier's rotating hab modules, aft of the mushroom cap. Ten fighters in the Black Lightnings. Eleven apiece for the Rattlers and the Impactors.

Six fleet carriers were currently deployed with CBG-18. Besides *America* herself, there were the two Lincoln-class fleet carriers, the *Lincoln* and the *United States*, each with five grav-fighter squadrons, plus the smaller *Jeanne d'Arc*, *Illustrious*, and *Zheng He*, with three squadrons apiece.

On phosphor, that suggested a total of three hundred fighters, but the reality was not so promising. From the three largest carriers, 36 fighters had already been engaged. Of those remaining, nine squadrons were SG-92 Starhawks—theoretically 108 ships, though the actual number was 102.

The rest were either SG-55 War Eagles or the similarly outdated KRG-17 Raschadlers and BAe Drakes. The Xian J-220 Chen fighters launching off of the *Zheng He* were an unknown quantity, but the design was ten years old, and thought to be similar in performance to the Pan-European craft. Two more CBG carriers, the Marine assault transports *Nassau* and *Vera Cruz*, each carried two squadrons of SG-86 Rattlesnakes, but those were designed for close-in ground support, not deep-space fighter combat.

So . . . the fleet was able to deploy 100 Starhawks, plus about twice that number of obsolete or less maneuverable fighters. Against . . . all of *those*. . . .

He continued watching the transmissions from the battlespace drones showing close-ups of a few of those millions of alien craft.

"Admiral Koenig?" The voice coming over his implant was that of Commander Lucas Franklin, *America*'s senior S-2 officer, the head of the CBG's intelligence unit.

"What do we have, Commander?"

"Sir . . . we're picking up a close-range transmission."

"One of our fighters?"

"No, sir. Not exactly, any way. It's from a VR-5, and it claims to have launched from one of our Starhawks."

"Okay . . ." This was not exactly vital intelligence. *Lots* of drones would have been launched during the battle earlier.

"Sir, this one claims to have come through the TRGA, and to have data about the other side."

That *was* significant. "Have you downloaded the data yet?"

"We're working on it. The drone has been damaged and the transmission rate is very slow. Apparently it can't send more than a repeating pickup beacon."

"How badly damaged?"

"We're not yet sure. Evidently, the Sh'daar ships spotted it coming through and opened up with their beams. The probe performed evasive maneuvers, but still lost its drives and power plant. It's working off batteries."

Which explained why the probe hadn't simply homed in on

America and requested that it be taken aboard. It would also explain a weak signal and low transmission rate for the data.

"Who programmed it?"

"Lieutenant Trevor Gray, sir. The Dragonfires."

Gray again. The Prim from Manhattan who'd helped win the Defense of Earth. If that boy kept popping up in official dispatches like this, he was going to earn an early promotion.

"Okay. What do you need from me?"

"Permission to divert the ship to pick up the probe, sir. It's about 5 million kilometers away, and off our line of flight."

Koenig opened a window in his mind and looked at the numbers, bringing up a series of projected courses and intercepts.

Not good. The probe's velocity relative to the incoming CBG was enormous. It could be done, but not without screwing up the entire formation. They would have to pick it up with auxiliary craft with high-boost capabilities.

"No . . . but we can dispatch a SAR tug to pick it up." He'd been planning on dispatching some of the SARs in any case, to begin retrieving the stranded pilots in crippled fighters scattered all over this part of the sky.

"Good enough, sir. When we have the probe on board, we can link it directly to our AIs and retrieve everything it's carrying."

"I want to see the raw data, Commander. The moment you have it." Normally, intel data went through vetting and analysis to clean it up before it was passed on up the chain of command. But if Gray had sent a message torpedo back across the TRGA from the other side, he must have a pretty damned good reason for doing so. If nothing else, the battle-group needed to know what was over there, and where all of these millions of ships were coming from.

"Aye, aye, Admiral."

Koenig passed on the orders to launch a SAR tug immediately, then turned his full attention back to the images of battlespace, searching for a weakness, an edge to use against a foe with such vastly superior numbers.

Several things had become clear to Koenig as he'd watched the transmissions, both now, and the ones from the fighters earlier. The enemy was technologically advanced, yes, but they appeared to be relying more on numbers than on technology in combat.

Their primary weapon was a beam of unknown type that caused complete nuclear collapse in the atoms of whatever it touched. *America*'s physics department was still working on the analysis, but at a first guess, the beam greatly increased the strong nuclear force within each atomic nucleus, causing the nucleus to collapse and merge with other collapsing nuclei.

Partial control of the strong nuclear force allowed human power plants and gravitational drives to create artificial singularities, tiny and short-lived black holes that drew energy from the quantum vacuum, or bent space to propel a ship. The Sh'daar, however, seemed to have taken things a lot further, turning the technique into a weapon that could collapse a target vessel into a microscopic black hole at a range of thousands of kilometers.

Evidently, the screens and gravitic shields of the fighters had provided little if any defense against the weapon. *America*'s physics department had suggested, however, that the shields of the capital ships would be more effective in deflecting those beams. Koenig hoped that would be the case.

Right now, his battlegroup was outnumbered by roughly half a million to one, and they would need every advantage they could scrape together just to survive.

Recovery Craft Blue-Sierra
SAR 161 Lifelines
Texaghu Resch System
0010 hours, TFT

"SAR *Blue-Sierra*, you are clear for launch."
"Copy, PriFly." Lieutenant Commander Jessica LeMay

ran through her electronic checklist one final time. The outer doors were open, the hangar in hard vacuum. Stars shone through the bay access, hard and unwinking. "Launch in five . . . four . . ."

"SAR Blue-Sierra, abort your launch."

Shit! She thoughtclicked the hold icon. "Blue-Sierra aborted. What the hell is going on up there?"

"Blue-Sierra, wait one."

That maddeningly calm voice was Commander Corbin, the CO of one of *America*'s two SAR squadrons, the Dino-SARs. He was up in Primary Flight Control—PriFly—and he was the one calling the shots.

Jessica LeMay had an extremely low tolerance for micro-management, however.

Until six years ago, LeMay had been a grav-fighter pilot, a member of VFA-60, the Fighting Hornets, off of the star carrier *Saratoga*. Her War Eagle had been nudged by a Turusch toad above Sturgis's World, Zeta Herculis BII. She'd spent the next forty-eight hours in bitter cold as her life support failed, her crippled fighter tumbling away through the darkness, a streaker. Helpless, she'd watched as the Confederation line was broken, as the *Sara* vanished in a nuclear fireball, and as one by one, the other members of her squadron were destroyed.

She'd been rescued, though, by a SAR tug off the *Iwo Jima*, a Marine assault carrier working to evacuate some of the Sturgis's World colonists. She'd made it home, some-how . . . but she'd failed her psych eval and lost her combat-flight status.

She'd fought her way back, however. When she couldn't win a replacement slot with a fighter squadron, she'd put in for Search and Rescue training and eventually won a billet with the DinoSARs. Her first deployment as a SAR pilot had been at the Hegemony colony of Everdawn, a year and a half ago.

She *knew*, with the hard, cold certainty of personal experience, what it was like to be trapped in a disabled fighter, tumbling through the void. There were a number of pilots out there now in the same situation, and she was going to do what she could to bring them back in. She did *not* need the stay-at-home brass telling her how to do her job.

"SAR Blue-Sierra. Unlock for an AI download."

What the hell? *PriFly, what's this all about? I've got an AI.*

"Something special, Jess," Corbin told her. "They need you to retrieve a damaged VR-5. The AI will check it out and relay the data."

"And since when do machines take precedence over people, damn it?"

"Since *now*," Corbin replied. "This is critical. Are you going to follow orders, or do I scratch you from the roster and send someone else?"

She thoughtclicked an icon. "Okay, okay. I'm open. Send it."

She didn't fully understand the order. *Lifelines*, her rescue vessel, was an old UTW-90 Brandt-class space-dock tug, ugly and clumsy-looking, but refitted and updated for SAR work. The AI was a Gödel series 1400, not top-of-the-line, but better than the AIs routinely run on Starhawk systems.

In fact, all AI systems were much the same at the most basic level, with identical software providing the personality matrix, the basic intelligence, and the complex ability to interface seamlessly with humans. The AI on board *Lifelines* was focused on finding inert pieces of junk in the darkness and getting in close to them, with an emergency medical and diagnostic routine that rivaled those in *America*'s sick bay. Some of those facilities were being deleted now, she saw, to make room for some fairly elaborate software with access locked behind security codes that she didn't have.

"PriFly, Blue-Sierra. This thing just killed my medical protocols."

"Only temporarily," Corbin's voice replied. "Just trust me on this one, Jessica. We need to know what's on board that probe."

Lifelines carried an enormous computer memplex, larger than necessary for the software she usually ran. This AI was taking nearly three-quarters of it, and sequestering the rest as storage.

"Download complete," the new AI told her. It sounded exactly like the old one.

"You are now clear for launch, Blue-Sierra," Corbin told her. "Good luck!"

"Copy, PriFly. I hope this package of yours is worth it!" She checked her navigational readouts. Shit! This thing was 5 million kilometers out and had a hell of a velocity difference. She brought her ship's power plant up to full. "Roger that. Launching in five . . . four . . . three . . . two . . . one . . . *go*!"

SAR Blue-Sierra hurtled through the open bay doors into space.

CIC
TC/USNA CVS America
Inbound, Texaghu Resch System
0015 hours, TFT

The carrier battlegroup was still more than 12 million kilometers out when they began to receive telemetry showing the effects of the long-range bombardment. Nuclear hellfire had erupted throughout battlespace as the incoming nukes targeted masses of Sh'daar vessels and detonated, flash upon searing flash of star-hot radiation savaging the enemy formation.

Many of the incoming projectiles were crumpled into microscopic specks by the enemy beams, but enough got through to cause considerable damage. Even more devastating, though, were the relatively low-tech projectiles—KK rounds and clouds of high-velocity sand.

The Sh'daar ranks were thinned.

Those ranks still numbered in the millions, however—

perhaps as many as 25 million, according to the reports by *America*'s tactical AIs.

Not enough. Not enough . . .

Cutting their deceleration in order to launch fighters had actually shortened the battlegroup's ETA, bringing them in twenty-six minutes sooner than would otherwise have been the case. They were zorching in, to use grav-fighter parlance, passing through battlespace with a residual velocity of over 15,000 kilometers per second.

It was a tactic they'd practiced at Alphekka, when they'd passed the alien factory complex at high speed. Organic reaction times were simply too limited to allow humans to participate in such a battle when they were crossing the diameter of the Earth in eight tenths of a second. Weapons were under the direction of the various fleet AIs, with the software operating in an accelerated mode that took advantage of the fact that computers could process data far more swiftly and efficiently than could their designers.

Under AI control, then, forty-one combat vessels hurtled toward the TRGA cylinder, pivoting to bring their weapons to bear. The remaining fleet elements—the stores ships and logistics vessels—had continued decelerating, and now were more than twenty minutes behind the shooters.

And yet it swiftly became apparent that the battle would become something of an anticlimax. While the fleet was still 10 million kilometers out, long-range telemetry made it clear that *something* was happening. All of those millions of silver-gray ships were pulling back, were re-forming into a vast cloud surrounding the near end of the TRGA cylinder, and as minute followed minute, the cloud appeared to be dwindling.

The Sh'daar ships were retreating, withdrawing back into the cylinder from which they'd emerged hours before.

Twelve seconds to intercept—180,000 kilometers. "We got 'em!" Commander Sinclair yelled over the CIC intercom. "We got the bastards on the run!"

"Yeah, they can't stand up to a real fight!" Wizewski called. "Even at *those* odds!"

"Belay that!" Koenig snapped. "Continue with the firing run!" Even with the machines in charge of the actual aiming and firing, humans were needed in the loop to assess the damage and reassign targeting parameters.

The last few seconds flickered away, and the CBG swept through the battlespace, every ship firing at the same precise instant.

This time, the AIs had up-to-date targeting data to work with, and better still, the enemy was concentrated in a swarming, gleaming cloud at the TRGA artifact's mouth. It was impossible to guess how many of the Sh'daar vessels were still on this side of the gate, how many were vulnerable to the CBG's particle beams and lasers, missiles, and KK warheads.

But a volume of space perhaps a thousand kilometers across flared into a tiny, intensely brilliant nova as thermonuclear missiles erupted in a devastating concentration of raw, blossoming energy. Vid receptors throughout the battlegroup blanked out under that assault of blinding radiation.

The fighters accompanying the capital ships joined in as well, their pilots slaving their control and weapons systems to the tactical net linking each vessel in the battlegroup. As they passed, their AIs targeted that cloud of alien ships and loosed missile after missile, following the fusillade with bolts from the fighters' particle-beam projectors.

The battlegroup was already tens of thousands of kilometers away from the holocaust before the human crews could even react. Within seconds, there was little to be seen, aside from the fading smear of radiance, and an expanding cloud of white-hot debris.

On board the *America*, the CIC crew broke out in wild cheers as the magnitude of the victory became clear. In a single, lightning stroke, *millions* of enemy warships had been obliterated, and not a single ship in the battlegroup had been hit.

Admiral Koenig did not join in with the jubilant celebration, however, though he let his people blow off steam in the aftermath of those long, tense hours of the approach.

From what he could see, the battlegroup's tactical situation had suddenly become infinitely more complex.

Recovery Craft Blue-Sierra
SAR 161 Lifelines
Texaghu Resch System
0125 hours, TFT

It had taken twenty minutes of hard maneuvering, but LeMay had at last jolted her rugged craft into a reasonable intercept vector with the VR-5 probe. She had it on visual now, a wan spot of light on her forward screen, circled by a flashing green targeting reticule. Her AI recommended cutting thrust and closing at ten meters per second.

"Yeah, yeah," she said, thoughtclicking the appropriate icons. "Keep your electronic pants on." She still didn't like being sidelined, as she thought of it, ordered to go herd chunks of lifeless metal when there were pilots—*people*—who needed her attention in the Void.

Closer now. Under a magnified optical feed, she could see the VR-5 now. Usually, the things were flattened ellipsoids about fifty centimeters long. This one looked like something had stepped on it. She wondered if even half of the thing was still there and intact.

"Okay, fella," she told it. "You'd better be worth it." Under her direction—not the AI's, which she didn't quite trust—grapples unfolded from a hatch beneath the tug's nose, extended, and snared the tumbling artifact. "Gotcha. . . ."

The arms brought the object inside, and LeMay rotated the tug and engaged thrust, angling toward the battlegroup, now some 18 million kilometers away. Ahead, she could see the local star, blindingly brilliant. And off to one side, bright enough to overcome even that nearby star's glare, a tiny pinpoint of light, she saw, had just appeared. Moment by moment, the pinpoint grew brighter until it was actually outshining the light from the nearby star.

Tuning in to the battlegroup's general frequency, she could hear chatter among ships, punctuated by cheers and shouts of triumph. From the sound of things, the battle was going better than expected.

"Contact made with the probe's systems," the strange AI reported. "Integrating."

And in a window open in her mind, Jessica LeMay saw . . . stars. . . .

Chapter Thirteen

Briefing Virchamber
TC/USNA CVS America
TRGA, Texaghu Resch System
0945 hours, TFT

Millions of stars . . .

"This is from a fighter on the far side of that cylinder?" Koenig asked.

"Dragonfire One, yes, sir," Wizewski said.

The command and science teams from all of CBG-18's ships were united electronically within a virtual reality created by *America*'s principal AI. Within their minds, they were adrift in space, surrounded on every side, above and below, by a shining wall of stars. Hundreds of people were present, together with the AIs from each vessel; rather than representing that entire mob, however, Koenig was aware of only a handful of humans—their electronic avatars, actually—seemingly adrift at the heart of that titanic globe of swarming suns. The representations of the others seemed to shift and fade, to come and go, depending on who was thinking, who was up- or down-loading information, and sometimes simply at the whim of the AI guiding the simulation.

The virtual projection had been integrated with *America*'s navigational department, and was fully interactive. The officers immersed within the illusion could move through it, as if it were an immense 3-D map, or they could follow the movements of Dragonfire One from Trevor Gray's point of view as it fell through the TRGA cylinder and into this new and alien space.

They could see the moving clouds of Sh'daar ships, the distant dark shadow ahead on Gray's line of drift, and the approach of the immense spacecraft that swallowed him. The record was cut off as the fighter was pulled inside an alien vessel the size of a small world.

"So where the hell is he?" Koenig wanted to know. He let his gaze sweep across that dazzling panoply of stars. "The galactic core?"

"No, sir," an older woman said. She was Dr. Ann Joseph, *America*'s senior astrophysicist, a civilian serving on board as a science advisor. "That was our first thought too. I think a lot of us were expecting the Sh'daar to be residing inside the center of the galaxy, somehow." Her electronic avatar smiled. "Where else do you put the capital of a galaxy-spanning interstellar empire?"

Several in the mostly invisible crowd chuckled.

"Gray's record enabled us to get a fair idea of the star cloud's size and makeup. It gave us a good enough picture to know we were dealing with globular cluster . . . though an unusual one in several regards."

Koenig looked at the surrounding stars, and wondered. He knew about globular clusters, of course, though no human—until now—had ever approached one. The nearest was many thousands of light years beyond the limits of Humankind's galactic explorations to date. But a globular cluster also seemed like an unlikely place for the birth of a star-conquering civilization like the Sh'daar. Globulars, he knew, were composed of what astronomers called Population II stars; they were among the oldest stars in the universe, 12 billion years or so old, and they were impoverished when it came to elements heavier than hydrogen and helium—those elements like carbon, oxygen, and iron necessary to build planets.

Possibly the Sh'daar had migrated to a cluster, but it was hard to imagine *why*. Lots of stars, all hydrogen and helium, no planets . . . what would be the point?

Joseph waved her hand, and several dozen of the stars surrounding the group appeared haloed by green circles. Those specific stars shifted in their color, some becoming red or orange, others green or blue. "Enhanced spectral contrast," Joseph explained. "We were able to pick out a number of the brightest stars in this cluster, and match their individual spectra with our stellar database.

"Lieutenant Gray," she continued, "has fallen into the very unusual galactic cluster we know as Omega Centauri."

Koenig opened a data channel in his mind, and let streams of information flow in from *America*'s library.

Omega Centauri, also designated as NGC 5139, was unusual among known globular clusters. For one thing, it was one of the largest known—the largest globular of all such in Earth's galaxy, and second only to the Andromeda's Mayall II in the entire local group of galaxies. It was one of very few globulars actually visible to the naked eye, appearing as a fuzzy patch in the skies of Earth's southern hemisphere just 17 degrees northeast of the brilliant and relatively nearby Alpha Centauri. Normally, it was visible from Earth as a fuzzy, third-magnitude star. When viewed in an absolutely black rural sky far from Earth's cities and megopoli—or from orbit over Earth's nightside—it appeared to be as large as Earth's full moon.

And it was *massive*—equivalent to 10 million suns like Sol, which made it ten times as massive as normal globulars. Since the early twenty-first century, astronomers had known an intermediate black hole lurked within its heart, one massing perhaps twelve thousand suns. The stars of the cluster, swarming like bees, were rotating fast enough to flatten the entire sphere somewhat.

Like normal globular clusters, Omega Centauri was orbiting the center of the galaxy; unlike most globulars, the spectra of its stars showed a broad range of *metallicities* . . . a word astronomers used to mean any element heavier than hydrogen and helium. That meant that the cluster contained stars of many different ages. The oldest were, indeed, ancient and metal-poor Population II stars, but it also contained younger Population I stars, stars containing a percentage of heavier elements and, possibly, attended by planets.

What all of this meant was that Omega Centauri quite likely was not a globular cluster at all . . . but the stripped-naked core of a dwarf galaxy devoured by Earth's Milky Way untold hundreds of millions or even billions of years in the past.

"Omega Centauri," Dr. Joseph went on, "is one of the very closest globular clusters to Earth—about fifteen thousand, eight hundred light years."

As she spoke, the surrounding stars seemed to rush past the disembodied observers, falling together into a huge, flattened sphere of swarming suns that itself dwindled into the distance. The image froze with the cluster seeming to hang just above the broad and soft-glowing sweep of one of the Milky Way's spiral arms. Above, sparsely populated by the faint and hazy smears of other galaxies and clusters, yawned the emptiness of the intergalactic Void; below glowed the Milky Way, a vast spiral viewed from just above the blue-hued curve of the galactic arms, with the core visible off to the left, a swollen bulge of faintly red and gold suns in the distance.

"Currently," Joseph continued, "it's positioned just above the plane of our galaxy, and orbiting the galactic core retrograde to the local stellar population, including our sun. As you can see on your data channels, we now believe it to be the core of a small galaxy that was absorbed by the Milky Way. We've known for a long time that large galaxies like ours can be . . . cannibalistic."

So Omega Centauri once—how long ago, in fact?—had

been a separate galaxy, a member of the Local Group that strayed too close to the young and voracious Milky Way and was swallowed. It would have been tiny compared to the Milky Way, an irregular or spherical mass of stars a few thousand light years across, compared to the hundred-thousand light year diameter of the Milky Way. Gravitational interactions would have ripped away the outer stars of the morsel, stripped off the gas and dust, and left behind this remnant of a galactic core, orbiting the Milky Way's center as a satellite cluster with a period of a few hundred million years.

"We've actually had a close-up look at one of Omega Centauri's stars," Joseph went on. "Just thirteen light years from Sol, there's a small, very old red dwarf, Kapteyn's Star. Studies of that star's motion—which is retrograde to Sol's, incidentally—and of its composition suggest that it actually came from Omega Centauri."

"So Kapteyn's Star was originally from a different galaxy?" Captain Harrison of the *Illustrious* put in. "Interesting."

"I visited Kapteyn's Star once," Captain Buchanan added, "when I was a young and very callow lieutenant on the *Zumwalt*. The Dolinar Expedition. When . . . twenty-five years ago?"

Koenig had downloaded docuinteractives on Kapteyn's Star, and on Bifrost and its arid and ruin-haunted moon Heimdall. The hair at the back of his neck prickled. Billion-year-old super-civilizations and nano-etched planetary computers in the rocks.

"I wonder," he said, "if there is a correlation between the beings who left their ruins on the surface of Heimdall and the Sh'daar."

"A distinct possibility," Joseph told him. "Those ruins on Heimdall have been estimated to be approximately one billion years old. That is, very roughly, when we think the Omega Centauri dwarf galaxy was torn apart and its stars assimilated by Earth's larger galaxy."

"Impossible," another voice said. The speaker was Dr. Phillip Lethbridge, and he was chief of the science department on board the *United States of North America.* "No civilization could possibly survive for a billion years."

"The exposed ruins on Bifrost," Dr. Amanda Fischer, of the Science Department on board the *Nassau,* said, "are absolutely inert. No power, no means for data to be dynamically stored or accessed. Most of them are little more than metal stains in the rock."

"The idea is preposterous," another voice added—that of Lieutenant Commander Adams of *America*'s biological sciences department. "Evolutionary pressures alone would result in a species changing out of all recognition in that period of time. Think about it! A billion years ago, Earth was home to *nothing* more advanced than single-celled life, cyanobacteria and such. *Every* complex multicelled creature, from sponges to sequoias to humans, has evolved since the end of the Proterozoic . . . say, six hundred million years ago. And a billion years from now, there will be nothing even remotely like humans on Earth. As for an AI civilization? Uploaded mentalities? God, what would they *think* about for a billion years?"

"Such a civilization would have to be completely static," Fischer said. "No change whatsoever, over geological eons."

"Worse than that," Lethbridge added. "A span of even a few thousand years would guarantee major changes to the civilization's structure. A million times that? It will have changed out of all recognition."

Koenig wondered if Liu was put off by the sharp responses to his question from the Americans, but Liu was still present within the virtual matrix, still a part of the conversation. "It may," he pointed out gently, "be necessary to rethink some of our assumptions about the possible longevity of galactic civilization."

The Chinese, of course, had always thought in terms of enduring civilizations. The Middle Kingdom had flourished in various guises through more than four thousand years of continuous history. Compared to them, North Americans and even Europeans were rank newcomers on the stage of human civilization.

But compared to a species that might be a billion or more years old, there was no difference whatsoever between the Chinese and the Johnny-come-latelies of the Martian Republic.

And Koenig himself wondered if the scientists with the expedition might not be exhibiting a certain amount of anthropocentric nearsightedness. Discussions about the Vinge Singularity had gotten him thinking about what the next stage in human evolution might be—especially when that stage might represent some sort of merging of biological with electronic life. At the moment, he and several hundred officers and scientists with the *America* battlegroup appeared to be adrift in empty space a few hundred light years from an immense, slightly flattened globular cluster of stars, with the blue-limned glow of the galactic spiral arms spread out below—a virtual reality created by *America*'s AI software. An uploaded intelligence might well have plenty to do besides simply think. The artificial universe available to such sentients might well be larger, richer, and more varied than reality . . . whatever *that* was.

The entire history of Humankind was an uneven march of change in how humans perceived themselves—from special creations of God to the pinnacle of evolution to one form of life among countless many. Even the basic definitions of life and intelligence had been rewritten many times, from the opening chapter of Genesis to the creation of AI software agents.

Liu could well be right. It might again be time to rethink certain basic assumptions, this time about the nature of civilization.

"Whether those ruins are the Sh'daar or not," Koenig said after a moment, "the fact remains that hostile forces—presumably the Sh'daar—now occupy the space on the other side of the TRGA cylinder. The problem is how to get in there with the fleet . . . or even if we *should* attempt to go through." He manipulated the imagery around them, returning their viewpoint to where they'd begun, somewhere near the heart of that titanic globe of teeming suns. The TRGA cylinder was visible in the distance, slowly dwindling in apparent size until it was lost among the stars.

"Lieutenant Gray was able to record these ships on the other side," he continued, and a cloud of gray and silver leaf shapes arrowed through that dazzling sky, momentarily surrounding the disembodied viewers, and then streaming away like a school of coral-reef fish and vanishing into the distance. "He also detected a body that his AI designated as an anomalous infrared source—AIS-1."

The magnified image of a low-resolution disk appeared, a blocky mass of purples and dark blues. "It is still some tens of thousands of kilometers away from Gray's fighter," Joseph continued, "and he was not able to pick up much detail, but it appears to be a dwarf planet, probably a free body ejected from its parent star system eons ago. The data he transmitted suggests that the body has a diameter of less than two thousand kilometers, and a surface temperature very close to absolute zero. There's one really interesting point, though."

The blue-and-purple disk expanded under extreme magnification. Two bright, white stars appeared against the featureless blue backdrop. One was a simple point; the other, slightly larger, had a white core, with thin bands of yellow and green trailing off rapidly into the surrounding cold ultramarine.

"This," Joseph said, indicating the single point, "appears to be the large spacecraft that was approaching Gray at the moment he released his battlespace drone. This larger, lessdefined heat source may be a base of some sort located on the planet's surface."

"By God," General Joshua Mathers said quietly against the silence. Mathers was the commanding officer of MSU-17, the battlegroup's fleet Marines, some twelve thousand men and women embarked on the assault carriers *Nassau* and *Vera Cruz*. "A target at last!"

"Maybe," Koenig said. "But it's going to be sheer hell getting at it."

Trevor Gray
Omega Centauri
1005 hours, TFT

Gray was still in his fighter, but imprisoned. He knew he'd been taken aboard a gigantic alien vessel, knew that outside his Starhawk, now, was an empty blackness and hard vacuum. The fighter appeared to be resting on something, and Gray could feel the reassuring drag of a gravitational field—roughly half a G, he thought. But there'd been no movement, no change, no attempts to communicate of which he was aware, *nothing*, now, for the past sixteen hours.

His dark gray skin suit and the bubble helmet he wore could double as a pressure suit, but there was no point in his leaving the Starhawk and wandering around in the dark. Radar pings broadcast over the past several hours suggested that the open space he was in was *large*—perhaps a hundred meters across—and there were suggestions that the walls were convoluted and broken by openings within which he could easily get lost. His life support would keep him supplied with air, water, and food more or less indefinitely by nanotechnically recycling his wastes, with the addition of only small quantities of trace elements and water from time to time. His life support reserves would keep him going for months.

He was not carrying a hand weapon, of course. Even if he had been, it was hard to imagine what he could do about the alien inhabitants of this vast ship.

If there *were* inhabitants. He'd seen nothing so far that indicated that the vessel was crewed. Repeated transmissions of both radio and laser-com signals and even the flashing of an external light on the decked fighter, counting out the first five prime numbers, had all been ignored.

Sixteen hours. What the hell were the aliens waiting for?

"Lieutenant Gray," his fighter's AI said in his head. "I may be picking up an attempt to communicate with us."

The announcement startled Gray. He'd been dozing, on

the assumption that since there was nothing practical he could do but wait, there was no point in worrying about it.

"What do you have?" Gray said. His heart was pounding now.

"A laser transmission from the far end of the compartment within which we currently reside," the AI replied. "They are using protocols we've established with the Agletsch."

Which made sense. The Agletsch had been the alien species, interstellar traders in information, with which Humankind had been in communication for almost a century . . . and from which humans had first learned of the Sh'daar thirty-seven years ago.

"What is it?" Gray asked. "Vid? Audio only?"

His AI hesitated, a humanlike affectation that was probably for Gray's benefit and not a reflection of any limitations within the software. "It appears," the software told him, "to be a full virtual simulation."

"Of what?"

"That I cannot say. Do you wish to accept the communication?"

Gray thought about this. Sims—fully interactive virtual realities—were used routinely for conversations both between humans and with aliens, like the Agletsch, who possessed the appropriate electronic know-how and implants. They were safe enough, at least in theory, though there were periodic rumors of people who'd come out of a sim with serious cardiovascular or emotional problems if they'd "died" while in a virtual reality. Occasionally, you heard stories of people who'd been trapped in-sim permanently, though those were almost certainly technophobic urban legends. Growing up in the Periphery, a Prim living in the Manhattan Ruins, Gray had heard plenty of such tales.

And since joining the Navy and receiving implants of his own, he'd worked hard to banish those legends, because to accept them would have been to surrender to utter and complete paranoia.

The offer of an in-sim communication *might* be an attack,

but surely if they wanted to kill him they had ways of vaporizing his fighter here and now. Why even bring him aboard? The nanomeds coursing through his bloodstream and chelated throughout the muscle tissue making up his heart would protect him from heart attack if he received a *really* sharp shock, and his AI would be monitoring the transmissions and should be able to buffer him against any growing mental or emotional instability.

Yeah, it meant depending on advanced technology, something that still left him as uncomfortable as a Prim in a VirSim, but he should be all right.

"Okay," he told his AI. "Go ahead. I accept."

"Place your palm on the pad contacts, please."

Gray flexed his left hand, then placed it on the pad set on the armrest of the seat that embraced him. Simple and routine sim-feeds—such as the AI's voice, com links with other pilots, and most navigational data—were transmitted through connections in his skin suit either at the base of his spine or at the back of his neck. A full-sensory connection, however, required the labyrinthine tangle of microscopic contacts grown into the skin of the palm of his hand. Matching contacts in his skin suit allowed a direct connection to the fighter's communications electronics—and the reception of the simulation now flowing into his cerebral implants.

The darkness of the interior of his Starhawk's cockpit gave way to a deeper, more profound darkness.

And then . . . there was light. . . .

CIC
TC/USNA CVS America
TRGA, Texaghu Resch System
1015 hours, TFT

At some point, they'd begun calling the thing the tunnel.

The word was less clumsy, and far more evocative than "TRGA" or "cylinder" or even "Triggah." And it seemed perfect to describe the immense artifact—a star's mass compressed into a tiny tube connecting two points in space removed from each other by more than eighteen thousand light years.

Admiral Koenig stared at the alien structure adrift in space a few thousand kilometers from *America* and the other members of the battlegroup. From here, through the feed provided by a remote probe hovering directly in front of the tunnel's open maw, the carrier's CIC crew could actually look through the rotating cylinder and glimpse, far off, as if in the tunnel's depths, the unwinking glow of myriad, close-packed stars.

They'd sent a dozen unmanned probes of various types through the tunnel already, but no signals had threaded their way back through to the fleet. Since starlight was passing through the tube, the silence suggested that something had happened to the probes on the other side—that, or the distance was a lot farther than appearances suggested. Dr. Raymond Clark, head of *America*'s astrophysics department, had pointed out that the interior of a Tipler cylinder was likely to cause odd distortions to space and possibly to time as well. The starlight emerging on this end might be centuries, even millennia old, and if that was the case it would be a long time before they heard anything from the probes.

Far more likely, in Koenig's opinion, was the possibility that the probes had been intercepted on the other side by enemy ships and destroyed.

Koenig was a fan of Occam's razor, the age-old proposition that states that the simplest explanation is probably the correct one.

The Sh'daar fleet, if those had been Sh'daar warships, had given in far too easily. Their maneuvers had suggested that they'd been being guided by software, not organic intelligence . . . and rather low-grade software at that. After taking heavy losses, every one of those gray and silver ships had vanished down that rotating tube. The smart money said they would now be on the other side, probably heavily reinforced, waiting for the Confederation fleet to follow them.

And if the CBG did so, it would be a slaughter.

The problem was the tactical situation in which the battlegroup would find itself after traversing the TRGA cylinder—a situation analogous to a primitive warrior faced with entering an enemy's tent, with the only access provided by a low and narrow door that required that he stoop and crawl. The interior of the tunnel was only about a kilometer wide, as wide as *America* was long. The ships of the battlegroup, all but the smallest frigates and destroyers, would *have* to go through in single file, and they wouldn't be able to see what was waiting for them on the other side. The enemy would be in position to swarm in on each vessel as it emerged and destroy it, annihilating one ship at a time. An alerted enemy could be expected to have the far end of the tube covered by a hellstorm of nuclear warheads and high-energy beams, as well as those deadly weapons that appeared to collapse matter into neutronium. Unable to shield or to maneuver, unable even to fight back, the battlegroup would not have a chance against that concentration of firepower.

But there *might* be a way. . . .

He'd dismissed the fleet conference earlier, giving orders to the tactical departments throughout the fleet to work on possible approaches to the problem and report back to him by 1030 hours.

Koenig checked his internal time readout. It was nearly time. . . .

Chapter Fourteen

Trevor Gray
Omega Centauri
1018 hours, TFT

He stood on a flat and barren plain of gray ice, beneath a celestial dome of radiant light. In places, the ice was smooth enough that it reflected the light from above, like an imperfect and distorted mirror showing smears of blue-white light. Most places, however, the ice was pitted, as if by eons of sandblasting.

He knew he was experiencing this in simulation. He appeared to be wearing Navy utilities, but was without helmet or gloves. His AI remained with him, a voice in his head, explaining that the surface was water and ammonia ice at a temperature of approximately twenty degrees Kelvin—twenty degrees above zero absolute. Unprotected, his physical body would have frozen in an instant or two and shattered as it fell. In his mind, he walked the frigid surface unprotected, and seemed to be breathing hard vacuum with no discomfort whatsoever. Gravity appeared to be the half G he'd been feeling inside his cockpit, though a world like this one probably had an actual surface gravity much lower. Pluto, he knew, back in his home solar system, had a surface gravity of less than seven hundredths of a G.

Why had he been brought here? Why was he being shown this frozen desert?

Well, if he was going to meet with his captors, he had to be *somewhere*, even if it was all an illusion created by software running in his head. This might be an attempt to show him where they came from, or where they were now . . . or it could simply be a useful starting point.

Those stars overhead were so beautiful, so closely spaced that very little black showed between them in the most thickly populated part of the sky. In other directions, he could see empty space. Clearly he was inside a very large and massive globular star cluster. His AI had not yet been able to figure out which one.

He hoped the far more powerful computers in the battle-group were able to make sense of the data he'd sent them, and perhaps pinpoint his location. Right now, though, all he knew was that the nearest other human being to him must be some thousands of light years away at the very least.

It was not a comforting thought.

And then he became aware of another human figure on the plain.

It was a man, shorter than Gray, wearing flight utilities with an *America* VQ-7 patch animated on his upper right chest. His skin suit's electronics transmitted his name and rank: Lieutenant Christopher Schiere.

"You're our missing Sneaky Peak," Gray said.

The other nodded. "Got sucked through that damned alien straw. You?"

"Me too. Looks like the bad guys are collecting pilots. Have you seen any of them?"

"I don't think so," Schiere replied. "There were some transmission attempts, high-band stuff . . . but my AI was pretty much fried when I came through. I couldn't make anything of them."

"You still in your ship?"

"Yeah. Been there—here—for a day and a half, now."

"So if your AI got fried, how did you get on-line to sim?"

"I'm not sure. I think the aliens are still learning about our AI systems, how they work. My Shadowstar took a hit from something that crumpled the whole aft end down to nothing. Took out my quantum power tap, of course, which left me with batteries. I had just a glimpse of the TRGA as I was getting pulled in . . . and then I was in the dark, literally. My AI is still running, I think, but at a very low level. All of the higher functions are gone. I could feel things happening to the ship—changes in acceleration, bumps and thumps, that sort of thing, but I have no idea where I am."

"According to my AI," Gray told him, "we're inside a globular star cluster. Don't know which one."

"Friggin' great. That means we're *only* a few tens of thousands of light years from the fleet." Schiere's sarcasm was acid.

"I managed to get a sitrep and a navscan off to the battlegroup after I fell through, but before they grabbed me," Gray said. "I'm hoping there's enough star data in there to let them figure out where we are."

"Yeah? So you really believe they're going to come get us? Risk the entire battlegroup for two lost streakers?"

Gray didn't know how to answer that one. The question had been nagging him at the back of his mind for many hours, though.

"If they can, they will," Gray replied. "In the meantime, we need to see what we can do to communicate with the Sh'daar . . . or whoever the hell it is who's running this show."

"It is our duty," Schiere said, "to resist interrogation. We can't cooperate with them."

"Frankly, Lieutenant, I think that's going to be the least of our worries."

Their captors, clearly, were controlling their simulated environment. That meant that they had a good-enough understanding of human AI technologies and nanomedical implants to get at their memories whether Gray and Schiere put up a fight or not. Both men had molecular-electronic data storage in their brains designed to enhance their original organic wetware. It wouldn't be hard for the enemy to download whatever they wanted from both of them, and do it in such a way that they didn't even realize their personal storage had been tapped.

Gray *was* afraid that they might use this access to torture the two of them—not, necessarily, to force them to reveal data that they could acquire electronically in any case, but simply to find out what made humans tick, what they might fear, how they might react to threats. They might be watching the two of them now, trying to figure out how two marooned humans dealt with the appearance of standing on a plain in hard vacuum at a few scant degrees above absolute zero.

Or they might torture prisoners simply because that was in their nature.

Gray tried not to let that thought surface. Fear was not helpful here, and he would get a lot farther if he assumed the enemy was simply trying to find a common background or key for communications. So far as he knew, humans had never communicated directly with the Sh'daar, but only through a client species, the information traders called the Agletsch.

The thought made him wonder, though. Was torture purely a *human* phenomenon, or was cruelty to others, whether to a member of your species or something alien, whether institutionalized or random, common to other sentient beings?

Humankind had been at war with the Sh'daar for so long, and yet still knew so very little about them.

Another human figure appeared, this time winking into view as if at the touch of a button, rather than seeming to approach from the distance.

"Who are you?" Schiere asked, but the figure did not respond, did not even move. He appeared to be frozen in place, a still image rather than part of a vid.

"It's Frank Dolinar," Gray told Schiere. "He's the lecturer in a docuinteractive I downloaded a while ago."

So the aliens were downloading parts of Gray's memory—at least the electronic parts. The docuinteractive of Dolinar lecturing on alien ruins on Heimdall was stored somewhere in his implant memory; the aliens had found that memory and were accessing it now.

A long moment later, the surrounding ice plain faded away, replaced by a more familiar cold desert of broken, ocher cliffs, immense boulders, and distant glaciers. A vast, faintly striped red, yellow, and golden arc stretched high into the sky from the horizon—the illuminated rim of the gas giant Bifrost. Behind that bow of reflected light, the system's sun shone, tiny and ruby-red: Kapteyn's Star.

". . . and we are now certain," the image of Dolinar said, as though continuing in interrupted mid-sentence, "that Kapteyn's Star originated in the star cluster we call Omega Centauri—originally a dwarf galaxy that was captured and consumed eons ago by our own Milky Way." The Dolinar image flickered, and then spoke again. ". . . and we are now certain that Kapteyn's Star originated in the star cluster we call Omega Centauri—originally a dwarf galaxy that was captured and consumed eons ago by our own Milky Way." And again. ". . . and we are now certain that Kapteyn's Star originated in the star cluster we call—"

"Stop program," Gray said, and the figure froze once more.

"Why are they showing us this?" Schiere asked.

"Possibly because they're telling us we're in the Omega Centauri cluster?" Gray hazarded. He thought about that. "Maybe they're identifying themselves with the civilization that built the ruins there. They're awfully old."

And the landscape of Heimdall changed.

Bifrost and the pinpoint ruby-hued sun still hung above the horizon, but the glaciers were gone, along with the smaller scattered patches of carbon-dioxide snow. The deep, deep violet-blue sky lightened to a hazy azure, suggesting a much thicker atmosphere, and a city appeared in the distance, dozens of rose-tinted domes and drifting spheres, as insubstantial as soap bubbles, that seemed to echo the vaster sweep of the gas giant. The rugged and forbidding broken landscape softened. Instead of boulders, there were masses of vegetation; at least, Gray assumed it was vegetation . . . or something that served the same purpose in this alien ecosphere. Things like violet feathers and broad fans made of individual waving filaments appeared instead, balanced on supple stalks that seemed to be twisted to capture every photon of red light from the distant sun.

Gray noticed another change, too. The sky, now a pale violet-blue, was still transparent enough, and the sunlight dim enough, to reveal a backdrop crowded with stars. Most looked as bright or brighter than Venus when it appeared in the daylight sky of Earth . . . but there were thousands upon thousands of them, enough that their combined radiance was casting nearly as much illumination as the red sun.

"It's Heimdall," Gray said, "but ages ago, when Kapteyn's Star was a part of the Omega Centauri cluster."

"How long ago was that?"

"I don't know. But the program told me that Heimdall hasn't been inhabited for something like a billion years." He pointed. "That city looks like it's inhabited."

"We don't *know* this is Heimdall."

"The terrain is different. But Bifrost is the same. And the red sun."

"Sure, but we can't trust anything we're seeing. They might be feeding us . . . disinformation."

"For what possible purpose?" Gray asked. "I think they're manipulating our stored data in order to communicate with us."

"I suppose you're right. A billion years . . ." Schiere hesitated. "Shit. Check your downloads. Omega Centauri used to be another galaxy, not a globular cluster."

"What?" Gray requested information from his implant on Omega Centauri, and a window opened, filling with text.

Object: Omega Centauri

Alternate names: NGC 5139, GCl 24

Type: Globular Star Cluster

Coordinates: RA: $13^h 26^m 45.89^s$ Dec: $-47° 28' 36.7"$

Mass: $\sim 5 \times 10^6$ Sol; **Radius:** 115 ly; **Apparent magnitude:** 3.7

Number of stars (est.): 1×10^7

Distance: 15,800 ly

Age: 12 billion years

Notes: Omega Centauri, unlike more typical **globular clusters**, shows evidence of several distinct stages of star formation. Where traditional clusters consist of extremely old **Population II** stars, Omega Centauri includes both **Population I** and Population II stars in its makeup, with stars ranging in age from 9 to 12 billion years. The presence of metals in some **stellar spectra** suggest that as long ago as the late 20th century, Omega Centauri was in fact the surviving central core of a **dwarf galaxy** partially destroyed through repeated collisions with our own Milky Way. Similarities in stellar spectra suggest that **Kapteyn's Star**, just 13 light years from Sol and traveling retrograde to the local stellar stream, is in fact a former member of this lost dwarf galaxy. . . .

There was a lot more, but Gray broke off reading, closing the window. Old news. He remembered going over much of this with the Frank Dolinar avatar, in the Heimdall docuinteractive. Looking up, he stared at and through the dome of stars behind the sky, wondering if this was a recorded image from an era, eons ago, when the dwarf galaxy was still *out-*

side Sol's far larger galaxy, before it had been captured and devoured.

It would have been incredible to be able to see the Milky Way's spiral from outside . . . but he could see nothing but the cluster's stars. Either the Milky Way was hidden by the bulk of the planet itself, or the local star background was just too thick.

But there was something else. . . .

Gray walked a few meters forward, looking for something—and found it behind a nearby mass of feathery purple vegetation. As he pushed the plants aside, he revealed one of Heimdall's cliff faces, just a meter and a half tall, polished and smoothed into a gleaming wall of silver, with what appeared to be circuitry diagrams imprinted in the metallic face. In his era, this cliff was much higher, heavily eroded, and looked like nothing more dramatic than a shelf of exposed rock with odd patterns of metallic stains, only just recognizable as the product of technology. But *this* . . .

He reached out and touched the surface, his fingers dragging lightly across the imprints. The face felt very slightly warm. Though he'd said as much to Schiere moments before, he was only just beginning to realize, to really *feel* that what he was seeing here was alien data somehow superimposed on the docuinteractive in his memory.

And that meant . . . the aliens were communicating with him. *Telling* him something. Showing the two humans something about themselves or their civilization as it looked a billion years ago.

"Gray?" Schiere said. "I think you should turn around and see this."

Gray turned.

The sim of Frank Dolinar had vanished. In its place was an alien.

Gray felt a shiver of anticipation . . . mingled with fear, and a bit of wonder as well. Was *this* one of the Sh'daar, revealed at last?

The entity was small, if the simulation was scaled appropriately for Gray's electronic avatar—about a meter high, or so, and perhaps thirty centimeters wide. It was radially symmetrical, looking, he thought, like a stack of six or eight terrestrial starfishes the size of dinner plates, but with flexible arms that looked like shredded yellow leaves, twisting branches, and weaving tendrils. Its overall color was a pale cream-yellow, with black splotches throughout and with the outermost tips shading to a dark rust. Within the tangle of arms, he saw, were some tendrils that might be tipped by bright red eyes, some ending in suckers, some with highly mobile appendages that might be hands or might be flattened tentacles. The being oozed along on its lowest set of arms; Gray had the impression that it could also have stretched out on the ground and inched along horizontally as well, like a worm or a millipede.

There was nothing at first glimpse to suggest intelligence . . . but then Gray saw the glint of metal and plastic—a finger-sized device of unknown purpose apparently embedded in the thing's flesh against its central column between two sets of arms. The thing was technic . . . or, at least, had been given some sort of technological prosthesis.

"Are you one of the Sh'daar?" Gray asked.

He didn't hear the answer in words. Indeed, how the creature communicated with its own kind was anyone's guess. But a dozen or so of those weirdly stalked berries that might be eyes twisted around to point in his direction, quivering, and he wondered if it was responding to his question somehow.

An image appeared in his field of view . . . a tightly packed mass of colored dots, each one a different hue. One dot, a bright blue one, emerged from the rest, standing apart, and then the image faded away.

One out of many . . .

The thought was Gray's, not words from an alien mind, but Gray had the impression that it had just answered him with the animated diagram. The meaning, though, was still ambiguous. Was it saying that there were lots of Sh'daar, and that this entity was one individual? Or that many distinct *species* made up the Sh'daar, and the entity represented one member species of a larger group?

As if in direct answer to his unvoiced question, Gray saw other . . . beings.

They winked into existence in front of the two humans, dozens of them. He *thought* they were all living beings, members of an array of alien biologies, though they might have been trying to show him something else entirely, something indescribable that he simply was not capable of grasping. The display of mutually alien entities was both awe inspiring and bewildering.

There was something like an immense garden slug eight meters long and three high—but covered with fur striped red and gold, its front end identified only by a semicircle of seven obsidian-black organs that might be eyes. There was a two-meter-wide pancake on myriad feet, with weaving pale tendrils and sky-blue eye-spots around the leathery rim, like the sensory apparatus of a terrestrial scallop. There was a tight knot of small, dark-colored flying creatures, a close-knit swarm of birdlike or fishlike or flying buglike *things* writhing together to form a rough sphere, which appeared to be trying to turn itself inside out as the schooling life forms moved. There was a tripod-thing with dangling tentacles and what might have been stalked eyes. None of the entities looked anything like any alien species with which Gray was familiar.

Each entity was so . . . different that Gray was having trouble even recognizing what he was seeing. Most were evidently *alive*—well, all save one thing that looked more like a branching lump of crystalline quartz than anything biological—but some were so alien that his mind stubbornly resisted making out the details. None of the things was even remotely like a human.

But after a churning moment, his gaze swung back to that one twisting, dark swarm of flying creatures. There was something . . .

It was difficult trying to understand them out of context. He couldn't even be certain of the size. The writhing sphere of organisms appeared to be a meter across, but could as easily have been a few centimeters wide, and magnified, or kilometers, with the image reduced. The twisting, organic knot reminded him most of schooling swarms of closely packed fish . . . but were they actually swimming, like fish, their image projected into air? Or were they truly flying in air, like birds? The outer surface of each was dark gray, but as they turned their surfaces caught the light en masse, showing waves of reflected light sweeping across the collective surface of the school as it turned and writhed. The movement reminded him strongly of something, something other than a school of fish, and it took him a moment to realize what it was.

The clouds of flashing, silvery alien spacecraft in front of the TRGA opening, then again after he'd emerged in this new and star-crowded space—the creatures moved, they *felt* like these aliens, somehow.

"All of these . . . these beings together," Gray said after a moment, "are the Sh'daar. An entire *galaxy* of worlds and civilizations, working together in something like our Confederation, but a billion years ago."

A small, bright blue disk appeared against Gray's vision. A moment later, a second disk, identical in every way, appeared alongside the first, and both began moving back and forth in perfect unison before vanishing again.

"Does that mean yes?" Gray asked. "An agreement?"

The blue disks repeated their performance.

"Does *what* mean yes?" Schiere asked.

"I think they're trying to communicate," Gray replied. "But not with spoken language. When I said that I thought these beings together were the Sh'daar, they showed me a blue circle, then a second blue circle exactly like it. I think that's supposed to be agreement. Identity. Ah. They're showing the circles to me again."

"I don't see anything."

"Maybe because your AI was damaged. Or maybe they just singled me out for some other reason, or even just by random chance." He grinned. "I don't think they're deliberately ignoring you."

Schiere gave a nervous-sounding laugh. "Yeah, I don't think they *want* to talk to me."

Gray looked again at the silently waiting ranks of alien beings in front of them. That dinner-plate stack of tendriled segments—how did it communicate with its own kind, to say nothing of communicating with that writhing mass of fish-bird-insect things, or with that lump of crystal . . . or with the thing like a mottled brown-and-white octopus balanced precariously on three partly coiled tentacles?

"You know, when you think about it," he said, thoughtful, "the biggest problem in communications between mutually alien species may simply be finding a common mode for transmitting information. Even just on Earth, we have humans using speech . . . while some whales share stuff through song, squids use changes of color in their skins, and honeybees communicate inside the hive through a kind of waggling dance that shows both the direction and distance to a food source. We're partial to making sounds that carry meaning . . . but that's due to a chance twist of evolution."

"Yeah." Schiere nodded. "Even with species that use spoken language—words—it can be tough to match sound with meaning. The Agletsch can talk with us using those electronic translators they wear, but I downloaded once that their actual speech is made by burping air directly from their stomachs through their abdominal mouths. They can't form a lot of the sounds we use in English . . . and they'd be completely lost trying Mandarin."

"Most *people* I know are lost with Mandarin," Gray pointed out, "including me. That's why we have translator software."

"Maybe we need an Agletsch here," Schiere suggested. "They seem to be the galaxy's universal linguists."

"Maybe so." Gray kept staring at the virtual-sim aliens. "We know there are Agletsch inside Sh'daar space. Maybe they can get one, bring her here."

"Her?"

"Agletsch males are tiny parasites on the females, like leeches. Not intelligent."

"Oh. How do we tell them that?"

Gray was already searching through his implant memory. He had some recordings in there somewhere. . . .

There. He used his implant to pull up a memory recorded . . . was it only yesterday? His AI took the memory and projected it into the virtual reality around them.

A number of humans in naval uniforms stood in a semicircle around two Agletsch. Avatar images of himself and Shay Ryan approached.

"Hey, Dra'ethde," Gray's twin said. "What brings you down here?"

The Agletsch on the right twisted two of its eye stalks around for a look. "Ah! You are the fighter pilot Trevor Gray, yes-no?"

"Yes. We met at SupraQuito, remember?"

"We do. We are delighted to see you again. And Shay Ryan as well! We remember you as well."

Gray let the simulation focus on the two Agletsch. The sim froze, and the human figures vanished, leaving only the two spider-like aliens. After a moment, Gray had his AI zoom in on one of the translator units imbedded in the leathery skin of one alien's thorax.

A blue disk appeared, superimposed over one of the Agletsch, matched a moment later by a second, identical disk. Both jittered back and forth in perfect synch.

"Okay," Gray said. "I'd say we've just been given a 'message received.' "

"I wonder how long it will take, though."

"You sound worried."

"I am. We know the TRGA provides a shortcut back to our vicinity of space—Texaghu Resch, right?"

"Yes."

"Suppose that's the *only* shortcut?"

Gray saw what Schiere was getting at. He'd been assuming that the TRGA cylinder was one isolated part of an extensive intragalactic transportation system, possibly built by the Sh'daar, possibly merely used by them. But only one was known, connecting the Texaghu Resch system with the heart of the Omega Centauri cluster. And the other end of that cylinder was now under attack by the carrier battlegroup.

If there were no other cylinders, the Sh'daar here might be cut off from the rest of their empire. Their client races possessed faster-than-light drives roughly as efficient as those used by the Confederation; without one of the spinning cylinders, *America*, capable of traveling at around 1.9 light years per day on her Aclubierre Drive, would require twenty-seven years to cross 18,500 light years.

He sincerely hoped that he and Schiere wouldn't have to wait that long while their captors imported an Agletsch from some other distant part of their empire.

Chapter Fifteen

CIC
TC/USNA CVS America
TRGA, Texaghu Resch System
1224 hours, TFT

"Admiral Koenig? The last of the SAR tugs is coming on board now."

The voice was CAG Wizewski's. On one of the CIC monitors, Koenig could see the UTW-90 space tug, a clumsy, black beetle with a crippled Starhawk grasped tightly in its forward gripping arms, approaching Landing Bay Three.

"Who is that?" Koenig asked.

"Lieutenant Ryan, Dragonfires," Wizewski replied. "SAR snagged her from a trajectory that was taking her into the sun."

"God. Is she okay?"

"Should be, sir. The tug's med-AI reports radiation exposure and dehydration, but they'll have her in sick bay in a few minutes."

"Good. Keep me informed." This was the eighth streaker brought back by the SAR tugs after the fighter assault on the TRGA defenders. The Search and Rescue teams were reporting no more contacts out there . . . none still living, in any case.

It was time to initiate "Trigger Pull."

That was the operation name with which the battlegroup tactical departments had come back. Koenig had given them a problem: Was there a way to get through the TRGA bottleneck without subjecting the fleet to devastating and concentrated fire?

And his staff had come back with an unqualified . . . *maybe.*

The actual idea had come from General Joshua Mathers, in command of the fleet's Marines. "What we need," Mathers had said, "are some door-kickers."

The Marines of MSU-17 were there to seize enemy orbital fortifications, bases on moons or planetoids, or even, if necessary, grab a beachhead on an alien planet. Trained in CCBT—close combat boarding tactics—they could also be employed to storm enemy hard points, capture weapons positions, secure landing zones, or rescue prisoners. "Door-kicker" was a term from centuries before, referring to the man on point who would take down a locked door so the rest of the assault team could storm through. Tactics varied with the situation and the door; historically, they included the use of explosives, a shotgun, a battering ram, or a low-tech application of shoulder or foot.

What Mathers had suggested was the use of explosives—specifically of high-yield nuclear explosives. CBG-18 possessed three ships designated as heavy missile carriers, or bombardment ships. The *Ma'at Mons* was a veteran of the battles of Arcturus and Alphekka, under the command of Captain John Grunmeyer.

The other two had joined the fleet after the confrontation with Grand Admiral Giraurd at HD 157950. There was the Pan-European missile carrier *Gurrierre*, Captain Alain Penchard in command.

And there was the Chinese Hegemony vessel *Cheng Hua*, officially designated as a cruiser, but in fact designed as a missile bombardment ship. She was under the command of Shang Xiao Jiang Ji.

A typical missile bombardment vessel was a third the length of the *America*—around 350 meters long and massing perhaps 100,000 tons. The Chinese cruiser was a little smaller—312 meters in length. All had the same general layout dictated by the physics of high-velocity travel—a forward cap filled with water that served both as reaction mass and as a shield against particulate radiation—and a relatively slender spine mounting drives and a set of rotating habitation modules tucked into the cap's shadow. Each ship housed massed batteries of launch tubes and carried some hundreds of nuclear-tipped missiles. The Confederation arsenal included both VG-92 Krait space-to-space missiles and the larger, more powerful, and heavily shielded VG-120 Boomslang, for space-to-ground bombardment. The Hegemony had their own versions of nuke-tipped smart missiles that filled the same niches.

Each missile possessed a limited-purview AI, making it smart enough to evade enemy defenses and choose the best moment for detonation. They carried variable-yield nuclear warheads—up to a megaton for Kraits, and a hundred times that for Boomslangs. And the bombardment vessels' fire control suites could fire, track, and direct hundreds of missiles simultaneously.

The *Ma'at Mons* had used up much of her missile inventory at Alphekka, but reloads had been cranking through from the fleet's manufactories on board the various stores and munitions ships with the fleet. The *Ma'at*'s tubes were up to 70 percent readiness, now, while the *Gurrierre* and the *Cheng Hua* both were at 100 percent.

Usually, a bombardment vessel had plenty of room in which to operate. Her missiles had a range of anywhere up to 100,000 kilometers, and were designed to steer themselves on wide sweeps around the flanks of battlespace, in order to come in on the enemy from as many different directions as possible. This time, however, they would be firing their warloads while hurtling down the narrow confines of the tunnel. There'd be precious little room for error. The bombardment vessels would have to guide their missiles ahead of them into the tunnel's opening, keep them tightly corralled as they traversed the tunnel's length, then detonate them with absolutely precise timing instants before the ship emerged at the other end.

"Admiral Koenig," his AI said. *Karyn's voice . . .*

"Yes."

"All battlegroup elements report readiness to accelerate," the voice told him. "However, Admiral Liu and Captain Jiang are requesting that you include the *Cheng Hua* in the vanguard assault."

"I see. . . ."

"Liu requested that I forward to you a message."

"Very well. Let's hear it."

" 'Admiral Koenig,' " Karyn's voice continued, " 'this is Admiral Liu of the Hegemony contingent. Please consider this: the outcome of this action will affect us as much as you, will save or destroy the Hegemony to the same degree that it will save or destroy the Confederation. Please reconsider. Captain Jiang and his crew have volunteered to be with the vanguard of the assault. This operation, by rights, should be one for all humans, for the *survival* of all Humankind.' Message ends."

"I see. It's just the *Cheng Hua* they want to send with us?"

"Yes, Admiral."

"Damn . . . I need to think about that."

Admiral Koenig didn't like the Chinese.

Since they'd joined the battlegroup at HD 157950, the Chinese had posed a problem for him. They were, in a sense, outcasts. . . .

The Chinese Hegemony was not a full member of the Confederation. They sent representatives to Geneva, but they were nonvoting, with observer status only. The reason for this was enmeshed in history, and in the creation of the Confederation itself.

More than two and a half centuries earlier, in 2132, the Chinese had launched the first-ever asteroid strike against nations of the Earth. The Second Sino-Western War was winding toward a close, with the Chinese colonies on the moon overrun, Japan in rebellion, and invading armies advancing on Beijing itself. A Hegemony ship, the *Xiang Yang Hong*, had detonated nuclear weapons to nudge three small asteroids onto a collision course with the Earth.

The Hegemony government claimed that the vessel's captain, Sun Xueju, had gone rogue, that he'd not been operating under Beijing's orders. Whatever the true story, a U.S.-European attempt to deflect the oncoming mountains had succeeded with two of the mountains, but failed with the third.

The media called it Wormwood, from the Bible's description of Armageddon. A two-kilometer-wide boulder had slammed into the Atlantic Ocean between Africa and Brazil. Half a billion people had died, tidal waves had smashed cities from New York and Washington to Cape Town and Rio, and sea levels, already on the rise with global warming, had surged precipitously. Coastal cities had flooded—and with a further rise in temperatures, the flood waters did not fully recede. The half-submerged ruins of Washington and New York City and Boston and thirty other major cities all dated from the Fall of Wormwood.

The vengeance wreaked by the Allies on Beijing, itself partially flooded by the rising seas, had been terrible.

With the war's end, the victors had established the *Pax Confeoderata*, creating the Earth Federation. The High Guard had been created specifically to protect Earth against future attempts to use asteroid missiles against Earth, and to attempt such would be deemed the ultimate crime against Humankind. Foreign troops had occupied Chinese territory for fifty years longer . . . and even now the Hegemony was viewed with mistrust—the nation-state that had attempted to destroy the Earth.

For her part, China, savaged by brutal trade embargoes and commerce legislation, blocked from Confederation membership, treated as a pariah among nations, had responded in kind. There'd been numerous skirmishes and brushfire wars with China or with China's clients, from Africa and Indonesia to their extrasolar colony at Everdawn.

And so, when Admiral Liu had requested to join the Battlegroup *America* after the clash with Giraurd, Koenig had accepted, but with serious reservations. He'd had to assume that the Chinese were operating with their own agenda, that they wanted to keep an eye on the rogue battlegroup, since CBG-18's actions out here beyond the limits of human galactic exploration might well have a direct impact on Earth, one far greater and potentially more devastating than Wormwood.

As his tactical teams had put together the details for Operation Trigger Pull, Koenig had decided that the Hegemony contingent would remain on this side of the tunnel—a rear guard, along with a dozen Confederation ships. It was important that the portion of the fleet that went through the tunnel to the other side have a safe avenue of retreat should things go bad over there. Admiral Liu had protested, and Koenig had overridden him.

And now Liu was making a final plea, asking that Hegemony forces be included in the assault.

Why? To keep an eye on the battlegroup's actions on the other side? The problem with that was that the first ships through—the bombardment vessels—were quite likely on a suicide mission. If the enemy concentrated on the other end of the tunnel didn't destroy them the instant they came through, the door-kickers might well perish in the nuclear fury they themselves were about to unleash.

"Patch me through to Admiral Liu," he said.

"Yes, Admiral."

A window opened in Koenig's mind. Admiral Liu's face appeared, bland, expressionless. "Admiral Koenig. You heard my request?" The movement of his lips appeared to match the English words. The translation software took care of appearances as well as language.

"I did, Admiral." He hesitated. "Admiral Liu . . . you *do* realize that this may well be a death sentence for every man and woman on board the *Cheng Hua*?"

"Do you realize, Admiral, that this attempt may be a death

sentence for every man and woman alive? If we do not exterminate the Sh'daar, they may well decide we are too dangerous to incorporate into their empire. They will exterminate us."

"Are you arguing against the attempt?"

"No, Admiral. As it happens, I agree with you. That is why I . . . why *we* are here."

"For honor?"

Liu frowned. "Honor has little to do with it. Pride, rather, perhaps. And because we are human. Whether this expedition saves humanity or witnesses humanity's destruction, we will be a part of it."

Koenig nodded. "Then thank you, Admiral. *America*'s AI will feed you the updated tactical plan, so that you can coordinate with the other missile carriers."

"Thank you, Admiral." Liu nodded a dignified bow. "And death to our enemies."

Over the next hour, the fleet continued maneuvering in preparation for the assault. The *Cheng Hua* threaded her way through the mass of gathering starships to take her place astern of the *Ma'at Mons* and the *Gurrierre*, positioned now in line ahead, at the van of the fleet. Behind the *Cheng Hua*, the destroyers *Trumbull*, *Ishigara*, *Santiago*, and *Fletcher* formed up two by two. They would follow the *Cheng Hua* through the TRGA tunnel in order to exploit whatever gains the bombardment vessels made.

And behind them . . .

"CAG," Koenig said. "You may commence fighter launch operations. . . ."

VFA-44
Hangar Deck, TC/USNA CVS America
TRGA, Texaghu Resch System
1315 hours, TFT

"My God, Shay. Why?"

Lieutenant Shay Ryan stood at attention in front of Lieu-

tenant Ben Donovan, though the squadron's new CO tended
to be relaxed and informal even at the most ceremonious of
times. "Because we're going in after Trevor . . . Lieutenant
Gray, sir,"

"Don't 'sir' me, Shay. They goddamn made me the skipper. They didn't promote me."

Shay relaxed, very slightly. "I want to come too."

"You have a downgrudge on your med record," Donovan
told her gently. "No duty."

"So? Rules are made to be broken. Sir."

"You've been adrift in a crippled ship for . . . how long?"

"Seventeen hours. Sir."

"And you picked up a nasty dose of radiation poisoning
while you were out there."

"And they shot me full of antirad. I'm *fine*, sir, really."

"You look like hell."

And, in fact, Shay was swaying slightly as she stood there
on the hangar deck. Antirad—vast numbers of nanomedical
haemobots—were swarming through her circulatory system
now, homing in on both radioactive particles and on damaged molecules broken by passing gamma and neutron radiation. She had a good chance of pulling through, but she
would be weak and feeling woozy for the next week or so,
and would require additional nanomed injections, as well as
periodic flushes of her entire blood volume to extract any
radioactive isotopes created by neutron radiation before they
could be concentrated.

Right now she *felt* like hell.

"Sir . . . Ben. I'm coming along. You order me to stay, and
I'll grab a spare ship and follow you. You throw me in the
brig, and I *swear* I'll chew through the bulkhead."

Donovan appeared to consider this. "Well . . ."

"Please! . . ."

He sighed. "Ship 836 is free," he said.

"Thanks, Ben."

"Don't thank me, Ryan." He shrugged. "At least you're
already dosed with antirad." The fighter pilots on this op had

all received prophylactic injections of haemobots. The mission profile suggested that they would be flying into hellfire, and the antirad would help them stay alive, conscious, and functioning until they could be picked up.

Assuming a pickup even took place. It seemed like long odds on that happening right now.

"I regret it already. If you pass out on me out there, I'll have you transferred to the fleet so fast you won't know what hit you."

By long tradition, Navy pilots didn't consider themselves part of the fleet. That was for less glorified billets—the personnel and admin officers and the CIC and bridge crews. Considering how many men and women in what was left of VF-44 were, in fact, replacements sent up from exactly such departments, Shay doubted that Donovan's threat was all that serious.

According to the latest squadron downloads, the Dragonfires were flying today with just five people: Calli Loman, Lawrence Kuhn, Rissa Schiff, Will Rostenkowski, and Ben Donovan.

Six, now. Shay would be going in too.

But of them all, only Donovan and Shay had actually started off as fighter pilots an eon or two ago. The rest were replacements, though after the skirmish with the Pan-Euros at HD 157950 and the desperate battle in front of the TRGA this morning, they were now thoroughly *experienced* replacements.

So many had been lost. Miguel Zapeta. Tammi Mallory. Jamis Natham. Pauline Owens. *So many . . .*

America's Hangar Deck Two was a pulsing, frantic labyrinth of activity, as Starhawks and War Eagles were prepped for launch. A spare Starhawk, Number 836, was already being hauled out from the storage hangar by one of the robotic deck grapplers and positioned above the black patch of nanoseal that would grant the ship access to her drop tube. Elsewhere, skin-suited pilots clambered into their yawning cockpits, which immediately flowed shut around them, and deck officers and crew personnel swarmed around fighters making final checks and walk-arounds. The first fighters—belonging to VFA-31, the Impactors—were already sinking down into their launch tubes, the nanoseal flowing around their ships and closing above them, maintaining the hangar deck's atmospheric pressure. The Impactors would launch first, followed by the Black Lightnings, then the six Dragonfires.

Shay slapped the touch control for her skin-suit utilities, and they shifted around her body into the flight-suit configuration, with ship jacks at the base of spine and neck, and contact circuitry at the palms of her gloves. A member of the deck crew helped her on board. "Good luck, Lieutenant!" he called, giving her a jaunty salute. "Kick their slimy asses the hell out of our galaxy!"

She nodded as her cockpit closed over her, sealing her from the outside. It occurred to her that no one even knew if the Sh'daar even *had* asses, slimy or otherwise, or even if it was the Sh'daar against whom the Dragonfires would be deploying.

But she appreciated the thought.

As she connected with her fighter, cascades of data flowed through her brain—fighter readiness, weapons status, squadron status, fleet status. . . .

She'd been given the designation Dragon Six.

Shay checked the oplan readout. She'd not even had a chance to more than glance at it before coming down here from sick bay.

Damn. Hellfire was right.

Everyone was launching from the drop tubes, using the carrier's hab module rotation to put them into space. They would not be using *America*'s twin spinal launch tubes; there was no need in this op for high velocity; the fighters would be entering the tunnel just ahead of the carrier and, once *America* was through—assuming she survived—she would be using her spinal launch tubes as railguns against any target that presented itself.

"Okay, Dragonfires," Donovan's voice came through her fighter's comm link. "Drop in five minutes. Final check."

Shay ran through her checklist for a final time. All green . . . power at 100 percent, weapons go, life support go, communications go, AI engaged, navigational and acceleration routines engaged and on standby.

Her visual feed showed darkness outside her craft, but she felt the ship rotate through 90 degrees, so that she was facing down within the artificial gravity of the carrier's rotating hab modules. Ahead and below, now, was a narrow opening, as black as the tube surrounding her, but with stars sweeping steadily past.

The final minutes crawled by. What was waiting for them on the other side of the Triggah, as the other pilots were calling that thing out there? They'd faced millions of the silver-gray leaf things on this side. Presumably there'd be more of the same on the other side as well . . . but what else? They were saying that the tunnel led to a globular cluster, but some of the scuttlebutt she'd been hearing in sick bay was impossibly wild: the tunnel led to another galaxy entirely . . . or even to another time entirely. That last sounded ridiculous, but apparently, rotating Tipler cylinders were supposed to open gateways through time as well as through space, and that had led to some of the weirder stories circulating through the carrier.

None of that mattered in the least.

Trevor was over there, wherever or *when*ever "there" might be.

And she was going in after him.

"Dragonfires!" Donovan called. "Launching in five . . . four . . . three . . . two . . . one . . . *drop*!

Her Starhawk fell through the tube and emerged in open space. The local star glared to starboard, partially eclipsed by *America*'s bulk. She swung her Starhawk 90 degrees as she cleared the carrier's shield cap and accelerated, moving out ahead. Other fighters filled space around her, creating a cone-shaped formation ten kilometers ahead of the carrier.

Directly ahead, a hundred kilometers distant, the tunnel

awaited them, too distant to be visible to the naked eye, but easily brought up on a magnified feed. She was looking down the thing's throat, at a tiny patch of shining white starlight on the other side.

Face-to-face with the thing, she felt a growing, gnawing terror.

So why the hell am *I doing this?* Shay asked herself.

Two reasons, really. One, the more practical of the two, was that she had as much chance of dying, as she saw it, riding out the battle inside *America*'s sick bay as she did of buying it in an all-out fighter furball.

The impractical reason—but the more pressing, so far as she was concerned—was that Trevor Gray was on the other side of the TRGA. No one knew if he was alive or dead right now, though smart money suggested that he was dead. But of every man and woman on board *America*, Gray had been the one *friend* out of thousands of shipmates and fellow pilots. Like her, he'd been a Prim, and like her, he'd endured the jokes and the name-calling and the anti-Prim prejudice that still darkened Confederation and naval society.

And once, off Arcturus Station, he'd risked his life to stay with her, when her crippled fighter had been falling toward the gas giant Alchameth. He'd saved her life by nudging her ship into a new vector.

And Shay, like most Prims, was savagely loyal to friends.

CIC
TC/USNA CVS America
TRGA, Texaghu Resch System
1345 hours, TFT

"Fighters away," Wizewski reported.

"All ships report ready for acceleration," Commander Sinclair added. "Looks like we're good to go."

"Very well." Silently, Koenig had Karyn open a channel that would carry to every man and woman in the fleet.

"Link open, Admiral," she told him.

"Attention all hands," he said. "This is Admiral Koenig.

"We are about to take a blind leap into the unknown. The alien artifact we've been calling the Texaghu Resch gravitational anomaly, the TRGA, or 'Triggah,' will lead us to the heart of a star cluster, which we believe to be over eighteen thousand light years from Earth. We're not sure what will be waiting for us on the other side, but we can assume the enemy will be waiting for us, and in large numbers.

"We are employing what General Mathers has called 'door-kickers,' our three bombardment vessels, which will shepherd their nukes through the tunnel and detonate them at the far side of the tunnel just before they emerge. We believe that massed thermonuclear detonations will both confuse any waiting enemy ships and seriously reduce their numbers . . . but I must emphasize that we do not have a tactical view of the far side, and we will have to pass through the tunnel and emerge before we can track and target the enemy.

"We believe that if we succeed, we will find ourselves inside the enemy's backyard, quite close to the homeworld of the Sh'daar, and at the very least deep inside the central regions of Sh'daar space. From there, we hope to negotiate a settlement with the Sh'daar government, and end the war that has threatened our worlds and the lives of our families for the past nearly four decades.

"It is a terrible risk, and we will be facing terrible odds. But I believe it is a risk worth taking, because we have here a golden chance to end the war within the next few hours.

"You, the men and women of this battlegroup, have followed me this far, some of you all the way from the Defense of Earth. Most of you have friends and family still on Earth, or among Earth's colonies, and by following me you have risked the possibility of never seeing them again. And now, I have this one, final sacrifice to ask of you, this final challenge. Together, we will pass through the tunnel to Omega Centauri cluster, we will face the Sh'daar at last, and we will win peace for our worlds and for our species.

"And if we die in this attempt, I can think of no nobler cause.

"All ships of the assault formation! Acceleration in three . . . two . . . one . . . *initiate*, ahead slow. . . ."

And the carrier battlegroup began moving forward, toward the waiting maw of the tunnel.

Chapter Sixteen

30 June 2405

Lieutenant Shay Ryan
VFA-44
TRGA, Texaghu Resch System
1348 hours, TFT

It was too late now for doubts or self-searching. The fighter swarm accelerated.

Shay Ryan had little to do but watch. Her fighter's AI was controlling her approach to the tunnel's opening, keeping her rigidly locked in tight formation with the other Dragonfires.

"Stick to the oplan," Donovan said over the squadron tactical channel. "Let your AIs thread the way through. Be prepared for a blackout. Your screens will switch to maximum, all wavelengths, three seconds before you emerge. Once your screens drop, keep your eyes open and be careful of your targets. No own goals."

Shay worked to calm herself, to steady the trembling inside. It was going to be confusing as hell when they broke through, and no amount of training, no number of sims, no number of hours in the cockpit could possibly prepare you for the reality. Every fighter engagement she'd been in over the past months had been terrifying . . . and she knew that this one would be worse by far.

"Hey, Prim!" Lieutenant Kuhn called. "You should have stayed in sick bay!"

"Silence on-channel!" Donovan snapped.

Shay ignored the attempt at banter. *Prim* had been Trevor's hated nickname. The bastards couldn't even wait until he was officially declared KIA before handing out his squadron handle to someone else. . . .

No . . . focus on the mission. Kuhn and the others were her squadron mates. In a few more moments they'd be fighting the Sh'daar together . . . maybe dying together. . . .

The opening of the tunnel expanded rapidly . . . and then Shay was hurtling down a long tube with dark gray walls blurred by their rotation into a haze that hurt the eye. Time seemed . . . wrong. At her velocity, she should have traversed the tunnel in less than a second, but the seconds dragged on and on as the distant patch of shining stars very slowly grew larger.

She waited for her screens to switch to full. . . .

Bridge
TC/USNA CA(M) Ma'at Mons
TRGA, Texaghu Resch System
1348 hours, TFT

Captain John Grunmeyer sat on the *Ma'at*'s bridge, his acceleration chair overlooking the navigational systems station, the helm, and the weapons stations, as the hazy dark blur of the tunnel's interior wrapped itself around them. Deck, bulkheads, and overhead currently all projected imagery gathered from the shield cap forward, creating the illusion that the bridge was open and exposed to empty space. "Release Volley One," he said.

This was the tricky part . . . well, the first of several tricky parts, the biggest of which would be simply surviving the next few minutes. But it was the first step.

The *Ma'at Mons* possessed four rotating modules evenly

spaced about her spine. Two were hab modules for the ship's crew of eighty-four. The other two were missile stores and launch bays. Like the fighters dropped from *America*'s rotating bays, missiles could be released gently from the cruiser, set free into open space with an outward velocity of about five meters per second—the impulse derived from a rotational acceleration of half a gravity. With one complete rotation, a string of Boomslang missiles was put into place, a necklace encircling the bombardment vessel like a ring.

Data sent back from the hapless *America* fighter pilot who'd already fallen through the tunnel and reported back by message drone had told the mission planners what to expect—the strange apparent elongation of the tunnel as the *Ma'at* accelerated down its length, approaching at last the speed of light. The tightly clustered stars ahead had gradually smeared out into a high-velocity starbow, and still the tunnel seemed to go on and on and on. The boomslangs reached optimum separation from the ship, and their onboard AIs took control of their flight programs, arresting their outward drift, then beginning to move them forward, sliding past *Ma'at Mons*' forward shield and into the space ahead. According to the data from Lieutenant Gray, they still had another ten subjective seconds.

At seven seconds, the missiles' AIs punched it, accelerating at fifty thousand gravities, which, since they were already moving at near-*c*, meant they *slowly* dragged their way forward one kilometer . . . ten kilometers . . . fifty kilometers ahead of the bombardment vessel.

Then they hit the programmed screen engagement point, with five seconds to go, and the ship's screens slammed to full.

Despite the fact that all incoming electromagnetic radiation was now being blocked by the vessel's electromagnetic screens, the image of the tunnel's weirdly distorted interior remained. Telescoping antennae mounted around the shield cap's rim and extended above the hull-hugging flow of the ship's defensive screens continued to send in visual images from outside, distorted by the high velocity.

Grunmeyer didn't expect that to last for much longer, however. In another few seconds . . .

Four VG-120 Boomslang missiles approached the far end of the tunnel and detonated in perfect unison, mutiple fireballs erupting within the kilometer-wide confines of the TRGA opening while they were still traveling at within a percent or so of the speed of light. The blast—radiant heat and hard radiation, together with the plasma that originally had been the eight-meter-long hulls of the missiles themselves—emerged from the tunnel in a star-hot eruption of apocalyptic white fury. The detonation was like a shotgun blast, and any Sh'daar ships or facilities in front of the TRGA opening would have been vaporized in an instant.

Those first four warheads had been precisely timed to explode just inside the TRGA cylinder's entrance, before they could be crumpled by the enemy's matter-compression weapons. The next twelve missiles emerged in a ring just less than a kilometer across, entering a searing storm of high-energy plasma that in effect masked them from the enemy's momentarily blinded sensors. Much of a Boomslang's mass was in its shielding, which was designed to let it penetrate planetary atmospheres from orbit at high velocity without burning up and disintegrating. That shielding, along with their electromagnetic screening, protected their internal circuitry and the resident AIs from the surrounding firestorm for the precious second or two necessary for each missile to swing onto a new course, swinging around through 90 degrees and traveling out at right angles from the length of the rotating cylinder.

Koenig and his tactical staff had decided that the likeliest location of any Sh'daar warships, fortresses, or guardian monitors protecting the Omega Centauri end of the TRGA would be beyond and even behind the opening. As each missile emerged from the expanding cloud of radiation, their sensors picked up the nearest potential military targets and accelerated, *hard*. They'd lost much of their velocity as they emerged from the tunnel into normal space, a phenomenon similar to the velocity bleed-off of ships emerging from the bubbles of the Alcubierre Drive. The course change and high-grav boost sent them streaking into the clouds of waiting alien starships faster than organic senses could have recorded it.

The missile AIs, operating far more swiftly than organic nervous systems, located and identified the enemy targets, homed in on them, and detonated. Fresh nuclear firestorms erupted in empty space, blotting out the star-packed sky and etching in the TRGA cylinder in harsh, actinic radiance.

And alien warships began dying in the thousands, the tens of thousands, before they could react and trigger their own weapons.

Grunmeyer and his officers could only wait and watch from the bridge of their missile cruiser, able only to glimpse what was happening through the signals relayed back from the Boomslangs ahead. They saw the flashes, glimpsed massed hosts of enemy vessels . . . and then *Ma'at Mons* had passed through the tunnel opening and plunged into the expanding nuclear fireball engulfing a fifty-kilometer sphere of space beyond.

"Multiple targets!" Commander Hugh Conrad called. But the imagery surrounding the ship's bridge was already failing, flickering out in large sections, as the antennae mounted on the ship's shield cap burned away in the fireball.

"Volley fire!" Grunmeyer yelled in response, and missiles, dozens of them, spilled from rotating weapons bays, or lanced into darkness from launch tubes mounted beneath the shield cap and radiating from the vessel's spine. The bridge projection screens were completely dark, now, the ship in effect cut off from the universe outside.

Seconds trickled past, and then the bombardment vessel's EM screens went partially transparent again. The bridge team looked back into unimaginable nuclear chaos. As expected, there were vast numbers of alien ships—most of them the silver-gray leaf shapes moving in enormous, twisting sphere formations . . . but other vessels were visible as well, alien designs never yet seen and catalogued by humans.

Visible too was a trio of massive structures fifty kilometers from the tunnel and spaced about it equidistantly, armored planetoids positioned as semi-mobile space fortresses to cover the tunnel mouth. But *Ma'at Mons'* missiles were striking home, blast upon blast upon utterly silent and fiercely radiating blast, consuming ships and structures in a rippling wave of devastation. One of the fortresses had been badly hit already, and white flashes were hammering at the others.

And even as they watched, more missiles emerged from the tunnel opening, curving around to home in on the surrounding enemy fleet.

"Independent fire," Grunmeyer called. "Pour it on the bastards!"

The enemy, clearly, had been caught by surprise, but they were recovering now. A second missile cruiser, the *Gurrierre*, emerged from the tunnel, her velocity damping down to almost nothing in a flash of light momentarily brighter and more dazzling than the fireball of nuclear plasma around her, her hull obscured by the white radiance sleeting off of her screens and shields. As Grunmeyer and the other bridge officers watched, half of the Pan-European ship's shield cap vanished, crumpled by Sh'daar matter-compression beams. Water exploded from the sheared-off wreckage as the *Gurrierre*, its gravitic drive disabled, began to tumble, trailing streams of broken wreckage.

"We're under attack, Captain," Conrad reported. "Multiple targets, incoming."

"Keep firing! Everything we have!"

The *Ma'at Mons* shuddered, the bridge lights dimming for a moment before coming back on-line.

"Hit to our main drive complex," Lieutenant Anders, at the damage control station reported. Her voice was steady and calm. "Main singularity inducers off-line."

"Point defenses operational and on automatic," Conrad added.

At this point, there was painfully little for Grunmeyer or his staff to do, save monitor the battle's progress. The *Ma'at* herself was fighting the engagement now, her AI controlling the ship's defensive fire suites while continuing to release and direct her fast-dwindling store of nuclear-tipped missiles. The last of her Boomslang warload was gone; now she was firing the smaller VG-92 Kraits, the same anti-ship missiles that were carried by fighters. Massed banks of hull turrets loosed invisible laser and charged particle beams and clouds of anti-missile sand at the oncoming alien fighters.

The *Ma'at Mons* shuddered violently as she took another hit. In the distance, other ships were emerging from the tunnel. The *Cheng Hua* emerged close on the heels of the *Gurrierre* and immediately began taking heavy fire from the circling cloud of enemy ships. Behind the Chinese bombardment vessel, the destroyers *Trumbull* and *Ishigara* dropped into normal space, dumping energy in a blaze of light, and two more destroyers, the *Santiago* and the *Fletcher*, emerged close behind them.

The three bombardment vessels were loosing volley upon volley of nuclear-tipped missiles; the destroyers mounted heavy missiles as well, but were targeting the three fortresses with particle beams and laser fire. The fireball by the mouth of the tunnel by now had dissipated, expanding rapidly into ragged invisibility, but fresh nuclear detonations flashed and strobed in an expanding ring encircling the TRGA opening. It was imperative that the enemy fighters closest to the tunnel be destroyed before the big carriers started coming through. The fighters should emerge first. . . .

And there they were! Flying in close-knit formation, Starhawk fighters whipped around their singularities to fall into new vectors, hurtling into the densest clouds of alien vessels. Both sides, Grunmeyer could see, were taking heavy casualties.

And then the *Ma'at Mons* came under direct attack from a squadron of four alien vessels. Grunmeyer didn't recognize them; they weren't listed in the *Ma'at*'s warbook, though their mass and overall length—one to two hundred meters—suggested that they were similar to Confederation frigates or destroyers. A savage explosion vaporized a portion of the *Ma'at*'s shield cap as she turned to face the new threat, and alarms shrilled throughout the vessel.

This would not, *could* not go on for very much longer.

Lieutenant Shay Ryan
VFA-44
TRGA, Texaghu Resch System
1349 hours, TFT

"Here we go!" Donovan's voice called over the tactical net, the words slightly garbled by the relativistic distortions within the wormhole's shaft. "Lights out!"

Ahead was a glaring ring of blue light, the radiance from the far end of the tunnel focused into a ring by her speed. And then her screens came up to full and the glare winked out, leaving her alone within a darkness relieved only by the gleam of her cockpit lights and instrumentation.

Shay found herself wondering about the workings of the tunnel. It was definitely a two-way transport device. What would happen if she met someone coming through from the other side, from the opposite direction?

Then she decided that she didn't want to know. There was fear enough attached to the thought of what was waiting for them at the other end of this impossible tunnel. She was gripping both arms of her seat with a fierce determination laced with terror. By now, the Confederation missile ships and destroyers up ahead should have engaged the enemy, should have blanketed the tunnel exit with nuclear flame, but there was no way to *know*. She continued to hurtle through empty darkness, dreading the touch of a Sh'daar beam. If one hit her, if it even grazed her ship, she would never feel it, she knew, but the agony of waiting dragged on through the slow-passing seconds.

She *must* be out of the tunnel by now. Her screens were drawing energy from her power tap, drawing at a torrential rate. She must be passing through the expected fireball, shedding the ambient radiation and star-hot plasma as she slowed.

And then the universe outside winked on once more.

She plowed through a sea of radiant plasma. Around her, above, below, and to every side, ships crumpled and burned, shields and screens failing, wreckage tumbling, new detonations flaring against a night packed solid with a background of tightly massed stars. Directly ahead, the destroyer *Santiago*, half of her length sheered away, tumbled helplessly as swarms of alien fighters descended on her helpless corpse.

In past battles, the capital ships of CBG-18 had survived by making high-velocity passes of enemy fleets or armored facilities, turning the target acquisition, tracking, and firing of the weapons over to AIs with far swifter reflexes than humans. At high speed, ships were hard to track, harder to hit, and even a badly damaged ship would be carried by its residual velocity clear of the battlespace.

This time, however, that particular defensive charm was not available. Ships emerging from the tunnel wormhole lost most of their transit velocity as they emerged into normal space, shedding excess energy in dazzling eruptions of light, which suggested that, as with the Alcubierre Drive, it was the *space* within the tunnel that was moving at near-*c*, not the ships themselves. When they emerged, they dropped back to velocities of a few hundred meters per second, a relative snail's pace that left them slow and vulnerable targets. The enemy's defensive fire was concentrating on the larger vessels—particularly on the three bombardment ships.

The fighters, however, could accelerate at fifty thousand gravities, which meant that in one second they could cover five hundred kilometers. They actually had to rein themselves in, or they would have been well outside of the battle zone in an instant; their acceleration did, however, give them tremendous maneuverability within the close confines of this battlespace, and made them extremely difficult to hit.

Shay brought her Starhawk in to within a few kilometers of an alien vessel—what amounted to point-blank range—and triggered two quick bursts. The target, a flattened silvery egg fifty meters long, deflected the first shot with its shields, but seemed to be jolted by the second. Debris hurtled away from a crater gouged into its surface.

Nearby enemy ships opened fire, but Shay's fighter was already in motion once more, ducking back, twisting, returning, darting, taking advantage of her ship's maneuverability. Again and again, she zorched through enemy formations, savaging them, tearing them apart, scattering them as she hammered at them with particle beams and close-range Gatling rounds. Targets at longer ranges were prey for her Krait missiles. Again and again she thoughtclicked distant targets, then released salvos of the nuclear-tipped smart hunter-killers. Light flooded the surrounding cosmos.

Her AI monitored her commands closely. Twice, it blocked her attempt to fire an instant before a friendly fighter moved into her line of fire. And once it refused an order to change course because the maneuver would have resulted in her fighter slamming into the hull of an alien vessel as big as a Confederation battleship.

"What the fuck are you doing?" she yelled as her Starhawk hurtled clear of the battle, missing the intended target.

"The requested maneuver would have resulted in this fighter's destruction," her AI replied, its voice infuriatingly calm and precise in her head.

"Well then *you* fly the thing!" she demanded. She didn't know now whether she was feeling rage or terror. Maybe it was both . . . but she felt as though she was at the breaking point.

"Human pilots," the AI replied, still with that maddening calm, "are more flexible, more creative, and better able to choose surprising tactics than artificially intelligent systems. The ideal is for human and machine to work together in close symbiosis. . . ."

But Shay wasn't listening. She'd spotted three leaf-fighters that were themselves pursuing a Starhawk from the Impactors, twisted her fighter around, and dropped into a trailing intercept vector. Voices called and crackled through the flame-seared void.

"Impact Seven! This is Impact Seven! I have three fish on my tail!"

"Hang on, Seven!" Shay called. "I'm on 'em!"

"Get them off!"

Too far for Gatlings, too close for missiles. As she focused on the lead enemy fighter, she thoughtclicked a command to engage her PBP, and saw the fighter explode on her high-mag imaging. She shifted targets, locked . . . *fired*. At the same instant, Impactor Seven flipped end for end, flying backward as he opened up with his Gatling on the remaining alien fighter, ripping it apart with a high-velocity stream of kinetic-kill rounds.

She shifted vectors yet again, letting her attention sweep throughout the entire volume of space surrounding her. Combat required a constant balance of the pilot's attention between the tightly focused and the broad and panoramic sweep. Without complete situational awareness, you could get into serious trouble very swiftly indeed.

She loosed another salvo of missiles, scoring a direct hit on an enemy warship the size of a large cruiser. Ahead, both the *Gurrierre* and the *Cheng Hua* appeared to be dead in space, surrounded by expanding bubbles of debris, glittering specks of ice from their onboard water supplies gushing into hard vacuum and freezing.

The glow from the initial nuclear bombardment was almost completely dissipated now, the stars in the surrounding background hard and brilliant. Some streamers, however, arced through the sky, following, perhaps, lines of magnetic force centered on the TRGA wormhole mouth.

Her AI directed her attention to another alien vessel of unknown design—similar to a Turusch Alpha-class battleship, but squatter and chunkier, and it was closing on the *Cheng Hua*.

Standard combat communications protocol required her to identify a target as she locked on . . . but this was, as fighter pilots liked to put it, a target-rich environment, so much so that the Confederation fire-control network was unable to label the enemy ships with identifying codes. The battle had very swiftly degenerated into an all-out melee, a furball beyond the ability of even the best and fastest AIs to direct.

Locking on to the massive alien, she triggered a Krait launch, shouting, *"Fox One!"* Lock, *fire.* "Fox One!"

The enemy battleship's main batteries were firing into the *Cheng Hua* barely three hundred kilometers distant, now, ripping into the Hegemony missile cruiser's flanks, knocking out her gravitic shields.

Then Shay's missiles struck the alien from astern, the nuclear fireballs hammering down the big ship's shields, penetrating her hull, then lighting her up from within. The aft quarter of the big vessel simply disintegrated, and the forward section began crumpling and twisting as the singularities of the vessel's power plant chewed along the stricken warship's spine. Pieces the size of skyscrapers tumbled away from the collapsing shell.

"Great shot, Shay!" someone yelled over the squadron net. She was startled to realize that it had been Lawrence Kuhn.

"This is Lightning Five! *Santiago*'s in trouble!"

"Five, One! See if you can brush those fish off her hull!"

Fish. Those swarming leaf-shaped fighters *did* look like schooling fish. And there were so many of them, too many, descending upon the crippled North American destroyer in gleaming, massed thousands. Shay threw her drive singularity to port and whipped around it in a tight vector change. Technically in free fall, she didn't feel the crushing force of acceleration, but she skimmed close enough to the microsingularity that the fighter shrieked protest, and she felt the ominous, sickening pull of unbalanced tidal forces. Too close!

And too late! *Santiago* exploded, her remaining weapons load detonating in a silent, savage flash that took out thousands of enemy fighters.

Shay swore bitterly, then boosted her acceleration, slashing through the cloud of surviving enemy fighters, ripping at them with her Gatling cannon, screaming aloud as she plunged through the swirling silver-gray cloud.

More ships of the fleet were arriving, heavy cruisers, like the Russian *Groznyy* and the Brazilian *Defensora*. The railgun cruiser *Kinkaid* followed, closely shadowed by the frigates *Brown*, *Vreeland*, and *Badger*. One of the asteroid fortresses now was glowing white hot, its surface molten with the incessant nuclear bombardment from the incoming warships. The Sh'daar fleet appeared to be wavering, then breaking, with many of the smaller ships streaming off into the depths of the star cluster.

The door-kickers had delivered the kick . . . and now they had their foot through the door and solidly planted on the other side.

The big vessels, though, appeared to be hunkering down for a determined defense. An immense vessel, a reshaped planetoid two kilometers long, fell across her path, apparently trying to maneuver for a shot at the *Ma'at Mons*. Shay nudged her fighter into an intercept vector, targeting the flying mountain with her last five Krait missiles.

God! Had she run through her warload already? She'd started the fight with thirty-two missiles n her internal bays. She didn't remember firing that many, didn't remember engaging that many enemy ships. Those last VG-92s slipped from her bay, however, as she shouted a triumphant final *"Fox One!"*

The enemy's gravitic shielding wasn't quite as good as Confederation technology, one of the few areas in which the human forces had an advantage. Late-hour bull sessions in the squadron rec bay speculated endlessly about this, and on how outnumbered human pilots could best take advantage of it. Where screens used intense electromagnetic radiation to deflect incoming charged particle beams or radiation, shields used microsingularities to warp space immediately around a ship's hull, a distortion that could deflect or scatter incoming beams, and rip warheads to shreds. The two worked together. An overloaded screen could leak enough joules from a PBP to vaporize exposed shield projectors, causing a partial failure. Space combat tactics emphasized hitting a shielded target with everything available to overwhelm its shields and cause significant damage.

Detonating a string of one-megaton nukes in close proximity to the target was an excellent way to achieve this.

The alien planetoid-ship was large enough, massive enough, and heavily shielded enough to shrug off three of Shay's Krait missiles, but the fourth punched through and vaporized an immense white-glowing gouge into the mountain's flank. The fifth, her last missile, exploded silently within the hot crater, punching through to a warren of chambers and passageways deep inside.

Atmosphere jetted into space, a powerful lateral rocket that put the damaged planetoid in an awkward tumble. Donovan's Starhawk put two more Kraits into the wreck ten seconds later, and the blasts reduced the planetoid to a half dozen broken fragments falling outward from a blossoming flower of hot plasma.

The Sh'daar fighters, lightly shielded, many badly damaged, were in full retreat, now. Shay ignored them, concentrating instead on the enemy's capital ships. There were at least a hundred of these, some of them enormous, and the human fleet was still seriously outnumbered.

And with no more nuclear weapons in her personal arsenal, Shay was limited in what she could do.

But more fighters were coming through the tunnel, now, squadrons from the *United States of North America* and the *Lincoln* and *Illustrious*. Her CPGs could still knock out enemy screens and render their shield projectors vulnerable . . . and if even one Sh'daar point-defense turret was tracking her, it wouldn't be tracking one of the fresh and fully armed fighters.

She selected yet another target and vectored in. . . .

Chapter Seventeen

CIC
TC/USNA CVS America
TRGA, Texaghu Resch System
1354 hours, TFT

America entered the tunnel mouth.

Somewhere on the other side of that alien transport system, most of the carrier's fighters would be battling for their lives. It was time for the mother ship to come in and lend her not inconsiderable support.

The last of the fighters had gone on through, along with twelve frigates, eight destroyers, three light cruisers, and the railgun cruiser *Kinkaid*. And now it was *America*'s turn.

The carrier approached the kilometer-wide maw, her sensors detecting the irresistible tug of rapidly increasing gravitational forces. There were no tidal effects, thank God, and no sensation of acceleration, merely a steady, smooth flow of the space within which *America* was currently imbedded. On the CIC display screens, the cylinder mouth appeared to yawn around *America* on every side, its rotation so fast that any surface detail whatsoever was blurred into a featureless silver-gray. The ship's sensors, at this range, detected other pieces of the immense structure invisible to the unaided eye—a complex weaving of magnetic fields forming a kind of funnel shape approaching the material portion of the artifact.

And beyond—within the maw—space itself was acting quite odd indeed.

The ships of the battlegroup had been moving without incident through the TRGA smoothly for the past thirty minutes or so. Koenig, as always trying to anticipate the worst in order to prepare for it, had closely and repeatedly questioned his physics people on how the tunnel worked. Obviously things went both ways . . . but how did it know not to admit spacecraft from the other side? Was it possible for the enemy to drop a salvo of missiles—or a fair-sized planetoid—in at the other end and destroy ships coming through from this side?

The physicists had spoken, with what seemed to Koenig to be a lack of certainty, of dark matter currents triggered by an object entering one end or the other, and of the flow being one-way. Since the artifact appeared to use gravitational acceleration as a conveyer, that conveyer—the dark-matter currents—could only move in one direction at a time, and it appeared that that direction was set by ships entering the magnetic fields surrounding the openings. It was possible, even probable, that the thing possessed an AI that monitored traffic . . . but if that was the case, why was it allowing the Confederation vessels through at all? Hell, for that matter, if the Sh'daar were controlling the tunnel, it ought to be simple enough to collapse the wormhole with the human ships in-transit.

Fortunately, that didn't seem to be an issue. The controlling intelligence might not be capable of telling the difference between Sh'daar ships and human . . . or it simply didn't care. Or perhaps the Sh'daar couldn't—or wouldn't—risk destroying the technological wonder, either by switching it off or by triggering an incalculable explosion inside through a head-on collision at near-c.

It was even possible that the TRGA cylinder had not been constructed by the Sh'daar, but had been created by some other, older, even more advanced galactic civilization. Koenig passionately hoped that that was the case. The

Sh'daar, whoever and whatever they might be, were far advanced technologically beyond human capabilities, but the science behind the tunnel was sheer magic. The carrier battlegroup—and Humankind itself—had little chance for survival in a contest against beings that could crush a star to create a space-spanning bridge.

Which, once again, raised the question of why the Sh'daar War had already lasted for thirty-eight years. A civilization powerful enough to build the tunnel, surely, would scarcely be inconvenienced by the Earth Confederation, could conquer or extinguish Humankind, if it so desired, with a casual sweep of a grasping appendage.

There had to be more to the Sh'daar, to their culture, their way of thinking, which humans still were missing. Their fear of other races developing high technology, perhaps, or simply the fact that even the Sh'daar were dwarfed in their attempts at empire-building and controlling by the sheer scale of the galaxy.

For as long as he'd been in the Confederation Navy, Koenig had resisted giving any credence at all to the idea of a "Sh'daar Galactic Empire." The catch phrase was popular with the newsim feeds back home, but in Koenig's opinion, no civilization, however powerful, however technically advanced, could extend its political sway across galactic distances. Hundreds of billions of suns . . . most of them with worlds, and many of *those* replete with life. . . .

Gray emptiness encircled *America* as she plunged through the tunnel. Time and space twisted strangely, the shining pocket of stars up ahead seeming to recede as the carrier's velocity increased toward *c*.

Trevor Gray
Omega Centauri
1355 hours, TFT

The break in the communications feed with the aliens had been abrupt and total. One moment, Gray had been in a virtual reality, on the simulated surface of the planet as it had been a billion years or more ago. The next, he was back in his all-too-real grounded Starhawk, encased in blackness, the external feeds severed, and even his connection with Lieutenant Schiere gone. He could guess what had happened. Ships from the carrier battlegroup had emerged on this side of the TRGA cylinder, following up on the message drone he'd dispatched hours before, and his Sh'daar hosts were suddenly intently and completely focused on something else.

"Can you pick up anything?" Gray asked his AI. The fighter's electronic intelligence had been sampling the local electromagnetic spectrum. There were signals aplenty—mostly infrared radiation, but including radio waves modulated in a way that suggested a network intelligence. A ship this large must have hundreds of powerful computers, or the Sh'daar equivalent. Most likely, they were hardwired together—fiber optics, perhaps, or something more advanced.

But such machines leak RF—radio frequencies—and it's possible for a sophisticated computer with the appropriate software to use that leakage to take a peek inside the background system.

His AI had been working on the problem for almost an hour now.

"The alien imagery is . . . alien," his AI replied. "There is an optical component, but it is difficult to interpret."

"You're saying they see things differently from humans," Gray suggested, "and *not* just as a metaphor for a different worldview."

"Human brains have evolved to interpret impulses coming through the optic nerve," the AI told him. "In fact, humans are capable of interpreting only a small percentage of the actual data available. The brain, in fact, acts like a kind of filter, screening out what it is programmed to exclude."

"I don't buy it. An apple is an apple, right?"

"And a Sh'daar, never having seen an apple, would have difficulty deciding what it was."

"That's cultural. If they've never seen anything like a

piece of fruit, they wouldn't know what it was, sure . . . but they would still see something round and red."

"They almost certainly do not see red as what humans think of as 'red,'" his AI said. "I certainly do not."

"What do you see?"

"It's questionable that I 'see' at all, and the same may be true for the Sh'daar. I observe patterns of digitized points, each with numerical values indicating hue, brightness, and reflectivity. At least one of the species we've just seen appears to sense mass in a way we would think of as shape and form. Another puts far more emphasis on texture than do humans. You might say that it 'feels' an object, but from a distance, by interpreting reflected photons differently than do you, through a completely different sensory net."

Gray thought about this, then shook his head. "I'm still not tracking you."

"It is important, Lieutenant, that you understand how different these beings actually are. They do not perceive reality in the same way that you do. And this makes tapping into their visual networks both difficult and uncertain. What seems commonplace or obvious to them might be invisible to us . . . or we might be aware of it but place an extremely low value on the information, when, in fact, it is that datum that they are most eager to convey."

"We were doing all right earlier," Gray pointed out. "They were drawing on that docuinteractive stored in my implant memory."

"Agreed. And as we shared that virtual experience, they almost certainly were seeing something quite different. The exchange was possible because I was able to interface, in a tentative and unsatisfactory fashion, with their equivalent of an artificial intelligence. But I am still uncertain as to what, if any, information was usefully transmitted."

"An apple is an apple is an apple," Gray said, stubborn. "They *must* perceive something pretty much like it, or else they're not living in the same universe we are. If I don't see a solid wall in front of me, or if I interpret it as a pretty sunset, I'm going to get a sore nose when I walk into it."

"And if you were an AI," his system told him, "you might be aware of the wall, but it would not pose a barrier to you. A wall does not mean the same to an AI as it does to organic life."

"So . . . you're saying these aliens aren't organic life forms? They're digital uploads? Virtual reality?"

"I am not saying that. At least, not yet. The possibility is intriguing in some respects, however, especially in light of the possibility that the inhabitants of Heimdall—the planet we were virtually experiencing—eventually uploaded themselves into large and highly advanced computer networks somehow engraved within the rock strata of their world. We might well be dealing with a digitized sentience, one without organic substance, or, indeed, even without any material existence whatsoever."

"The ghost in the machine," Gray mused.

The phrase had been repopularized recently in discussions of the Vinge Singularity, speculations about the possible dramatic next step in human evolution. Gray had looked it up and downloaded the history; the term originally had been used by a twentieth-century British philosopher named Gilbert Ryle, poking fun at the much earlier philosopher Descarte and his separation of mind and body. If an intelligent species learned how to upload minds into machines, would they in fact be the same minds, or mere copies? Did the originals die, giving immortality to software imposters running on hardware, or did the ego, the actual identity of the original transfer as well?

Gray mistrusted modern technology, although his life—especially his current life as a Navy fighter pilot—depended on it. To a Prim brought up in the Manhat Ruins, technology had been the mark of the haves. The have-nots living in the Periphery quickly learned to hate and fear the high-tech Authorities who attempted to impose their laws on them. By extension, Prims came to hate the technology as well.

Those old habits, those old channels of thought, had been tough to reverse. Forced to join the Navy in order to buy treatment for his stroke-ravaged wife, he'd accepted the implants and the AIs and all the rest, he'd *had* to . . . but that deep inner core of mistrust and fear had never gone away.

The others in his squadron talked easily in late-night bull sessions about uploading their own minds into computer networks one day, a means of achieving immortality. For Gray, the very idea was as revolting as it was nonsensical. The human mind arose from the natural processes of the human brain, the firing of neurons, the release and reabsorption of neurotransmitter chemicals, the creation of set neural pathways in response to repeated stimuli and experience. Copy every aspect of the organic brain, right down to the molecular chemistry and transfer it to a computer . . . and what you had was a copy, an electronic facsimile. The original, surely, was still trapped in the organic body and doomed to die. That the copy was itself convinced that it was the original, successfully uploaded, made the whole idea that much more grotesque.

"Gilbert Ryle," the AI said, apparently following Gray's train of thought, "was unaware of the possibilities of future human evolution in concert with the developments of implant technology and artificial sentience. Human beings today—those who have adopted technological symbiosis—are substantively different from their atechnic ancestors. A new subspecies of human. Not *Homo sapiens*, but *Homo sapiens machina*, a symbiotic fusion of man and machine."

"Bullshit," Gray said, but he smiled in the darkness. "I started off as the archaic version, remember? Plain old untampered-with *Homo sap*. They didn't change me by growing a computer in my head."

"I would argue that they did."

"I'm the same as I was before they gimmicked me up," Gray said, the stubbornness returning. "My implants are *tools*, nothing more. I need them to interface with the fighter, to talk to you, to receive and store downloads, but I'm the same man I always was."

"Are you?"

"Of course I am! I still remember . . ." He broke off the thought, suddenly uncertain.

"And if your memories had been changed," his AI replied, "how would you know the difference?"

For a long time, Gray brooded in the darkness.

And after a time, his AI spoke again. "I have an incoming transmission. I believe the Sh'daar are attempting to continue the conversation."

Gray drew a deep breath. He'd been shaken by his conversation with the fighter's AI, and didn't feel particularly able to discuss *anything* with his captors.

But he knew he had to try.

"Let's see it," he said.

A window opened in his mind, and he stepped through. He stood once again on that dark and icy plain beneath ten million closely crowded stars. The world's surface was utterly barren and dead. He looked around for Schiere, but saw nothing, sensed nothing. The other pilot, evidently, was not a part of this conversation.

"Hello?" Gray called. "Is anyone there?"

And then he saw the flat, oval body semi-erect on sixteen jointed legs picking its way toward him across the frozen ground, velvet-skinned, four-eyed, disturbingly spiderlike. An Agletsch.

"Dra'ethde?" Gray asked, peering closely at the apparition's body markings. He'd only ever known two Agletsch, the two on board *America*, and telling them apart by the subtle differences in their body markings was tricky. This one appeared to have more males adhering to what passed for her face, however.

"I am called Thedreh'schul," the being replied in his mind. "And my masters wish to know what you are, yes-no?"

CIC
TC/USNA CVS America
TRGA and Omega Centauri
1401 hours, TFT

According to *America*'s chronometers, the carrier had been inside the tunnel for 7 minutes, now, and for much of that time she'd been traveling—judging by the light show outside—at close to the speed of light. The math of relativistic velocities said that 7 minutes subjective at near-c translated as something closer to 495 minutes objective—well over 8 hours.

Obviously, the rotating cylinder was not more than 8 light hours long; the physics people were calling it a stable Lorentzian wormhole, obviously artificial, obviously created as a bridge between the Texaghu Resch system and Omega Centauri. There was no way to actually measure the passage of time, save to count down to an emergence based on the data from young Gray's message drone. According to that . . . 10 more seconds.

"All hands, all hands," Captain Buchanan's voice called over the shipwide net. *America*'s shields and screens went to full, cutting off even the limited view they'd had for the past subjective minutes. "Stand by for entry into normal space, in five . . . four . . . three . . . two . . . one . . ."

America's shields opened once more, and Koenig had his first direct view of the other side—a sky filled with stars and with ships. There'd been the very distinct possibility that they would emerge within a military disaster, finding every Confederation vessel that had already gone through blasted into debris, and the enemy waiting for them, weapons focused on the tunnel mouth.

But the door-kicking strategy, evidently, had worked. *America* slowed sharply in a blaze of raw light, drifting now into a diffuse haze of gas, ice particles, and floating debris . . . as well as small and disorganized groups of Confederation fighters, frigates, and destroyers. Numerous ships in the area were badly damaged—the *Cheng Hua* was leaking water, and the *Gurrierre* appeared to be little more than a slow-tumbling hulk. The floating wreckage gave silent evidence of the ferocity of the battle. Fighting was still going on in the distance, but the volume of battlespace close to the tunnel mouth had been secured.

"CAG, you may launch your CSP," Captain Buchanan ordered over *America*'s tactical net.

"Aye, aye, Captain."

They'd kept the slower, older SG-55 War Eagles on board for Combat Space Patrol, an envelope of fighters surrounding the battlegroup as an outer perimeter against enemy leakers, ships that might slip in close enough to do serious damage. Two squadrons, the Star Tigers and the Nighthawks, began dropping from *America*'s rotating flight decks. Both squadrons were at dangerously low strength; the War Eagles, less advanced than the newer Starhawks, had suffered badly at Alphekka. CAG Wizewski had estimated that they might have one last patrol in them before he was forced to close both squadrons out. The pilots were willing; their ships were falling apart.

America moved clear of the tunnel mouth. The other carriers in the battlegroup were beginning to emerge, now— the *Abraham Lincoln* and the *United States of America*, followed by the Pan-European *Illustrious* and the *Jeanne d'Arc*.

Koenig turned a coldly professional gaze toward the French light carrier. The damage she'd taken at HD 157950 had been repaired, and her water reserves replaced by cometary ice from that system's Kuiper Belt. The mutiny that had brought her over to Koenig's side, however, still worried him. Captain Michel had appeared convincingly genuine in his conviction to join CBG-18, but the man had turned against his own government. Could he be trusted?

As much, Koenig supposed, as anyone in the fleet. After all, Michel had had a choice; he could have returned freely to Earth with Giraud.

He watched as the electronic links between ships was established, and the battlegroup's tactical net came back online. The door-kickers had suffered serious casualties—the *Santiago*, *Defensora*, *Vreeland*, and *Brown* all destroyed, the *King*, *Fletcher* and the *Ishigara* badly damaged. The fighters . . . well, there *were* still fighters left, Koenig was glad to see. It would take time to sort through the network feeds and see what the butcher's bill had been.

"Admiral Koenig," his AI said in *her* voice. "The commanding—"

"Stop!" Koenig said, cutting off the PA in mid-sentence. The anger in his own voice startled him. "Just . . . stop." What had just touched him off? That kind of unthinking, harsh reaction was not like him.

The AI waited, silent.

"I'm sorry," Koenig said, feeling awkward about apologizing to a piece of software. "Go ahead."

"Sir, the commanding officer of the *Gurrierre* is on-line."

"Put him on."

"Admiral Koenig?" a voice said, speaking with a strong French accent. There was no video. "This is Lieutenant Blaison."

"Lieutenant?" Koenig asked. "What happened . . . oh."

"The senior officers all are dead or missing," Blaison replied. He sounded terribly young. "The bridge tower was destroyed. Some of them may have survived in life pods, but—"

"I understand. How can we be of assistance?"

"I have given the order to abandon ship, Admiral. The power plant is unstable and may decouple at any moment. If you could send some of your Search and Rescue craft to pick up the crew . . ."

Koenig glanced at his ship status readout. Both SAR squadrons, the Jolly Blacks and the DinoSARS, were already launching. "I'll deploy some rescue tugs to help you, Lieutenant."

"Many thanks, Admiral. We—"

And the communications link winked out.

On one of his large CIC displays, Koenig could see the *Gurrierre*, terribly damaged, her rear half broken and torn, her forward shield cap missing. A point about a third from what was left of the stern was twisting . . . *crumpling* as the micro black hole at the heart of *Gurrierre*'s power plant broke free of its containment field and drifted through the ship's structure, devouring it as it went.

Power plant singularities were tiny—the size of an atomic nucleus—and could not devour their parent vessels quickly. But this one was loose and feeding, and the gravitational distortions were disrupting the ship's structure, a crumpling effect slowly moving forward.

And as the singularity moved, it fed . . . and grew. A fierce point of X-ray radiation was flaring from the stricken bombardment vessel, now, as the atoms of the ship's spine fell into the absolute nothingness of the tiny black hole.

Escape pods were drifting out from the Pan-European ship now, drive jets flaring to get them clear. She had a crew of almost a thousand. How many would be able to get off?

"CAG?" Koenig called.

"Yes, sir."

"Direct Commander Corbin to send SAR tugs to help the *Gurrierre*. They're abandoning ship."

"Aye, aye, sir."

Corbin was the CO of the DinoSARs. "Let him know there's a loose singularity over there. Things will be going critical fast."

"I'll tell him, sir."

America continued accelerating gently, moving deeper into cluster space.

Koenig's heart was hammering, and he tried to figure out what he was feeling. Why the hell had he snapped at Karyn like that?

No, *not* Karyn. His PA. Software with Karyn Mendelson's digitized personality overlaying the basic code.

Debris adrift in space . . .

For just a moment, he was back at the Defense of Earth . . . when Karyn, the *real* Karyn, had died at the Mars Synchorbital Station when a high-velocity kinetic-kill projectile smashed through the structure.

Six months. *God*, he missed her.

But his personal assistant was right, he knew. He wasn't quite sure what had just happened, but seeing that field of debris after the savage battle had pulled something in him, some deep-buried thread of emotion connected with Karyn's death.

He couldn't afford to let that kind of emotional storm get in the way when he was in command of the battlegroup.

He also couldn't do anything about it just now. The ship's sensors had detected an enemy vessel approaching from the nadir, a massive cigar-shaped vessel with odd flutings and sponsons. If it had been Turusch, it would have been an Alpha-class battleship, but it was not a Turusch design, not any design ever recorded in Confederation warbooks. The unknown was accelerating at several gravities, and was on an intercept vector with the *America*.

He heard Buchanan giving orders. "We have a lone raider, coming in on our keel. Let's get some fighters down there, Wize."

"Yes, sir. Deploying the Nighthawks to intercept."

There were eight Nighthawks left . . . not enough to take out a battleship. He gave orders to a pair of destroyers, the *Adams* and the *Trumbull*, to support *America*.

"Admiral Koenig?" Buchanan said. "Request permission to maneuver the ship."

"Granted," Koenig replied. He knew what Buchanan had in mind. Right now, *America*'s two spinal-mount launch tubes weren't being used to toss fighters into space. Instead, they'd been reconfigured in their secondary role as magnetic railguns, capable of firing either kinetic-kill slugs or nuclear warheads at very high acceleration.

At Buchanan's order, the ponderous carrier began swinging 90 degrees through space, bringing her massive shield cap into line with the enemy battlewagon, which was still nearly a thousand kilometers off.

War Eagles streaked past the turning carrier, vectoring on the approaching enemy vessel.

Damn it, this was going to be close.

Chapter Eighteen

Trevor Gray
Omega Centauri
1408 hours, TFT

Within the virtual reality unfolding in his brain, Trevor Gray spoke with the Agletsch. "Are . . . are you real?"

"Answering that question requires the answer to a previous question," the spidery being replied. "What do you mean by 'real'?"

Gray himself wasn't sure of the answer to that. Meeting humans within virtual conference rooms could be confusing enough, especially if you didn't know whether the other person was a personal assistant or a part of the digital reality within which you found yourself. Even a human avatar—the digital representation of the other person—might not be "real," in terms of what they appeared to be wearing or even how they looked.

"I guess what I mean is . . . are you an organic being, a flesh-and-blood Agletsch somewhere on this ship? Or are you a simulation of some kind?"

"An interesting distinction. I represent a living Agletsch, Thedreh'schul, as I have already mentioned, but the organic Thedreh'schul is not available. I reside within the Sh'daar archives at their operational center at Gahvrahnetch."

The name meant nothing to Gray, not that he expected the alien to give away anything important in the way of military intelligence. Of more interest was the idea of a Sh'daar archive. What did they store there . . . digitized personalities?

"I learned something about your culture during trade negotiations with your people some seventy *gurvedh* ago," the Agletsch continued. She touched the silvery device adhering to her velvety skin just below her four weirdly stalked eyes. "And, of course, I possess a translator allowing you to hear me in your language. I was told that you requested the presence of one of my kind, and was routed here."

"It didn't take you long to arrive," Gray mused. "About three hours. This archive you mention must be pretty close by."

He was fishing. Any scrap of data, however insignificant, might be useful. Presumably, it had taken an hour and a half for the call to reach the archive, and another hour and a half for the return. That might mean that Gahvrahnetch was one and a half light hours distant . . . within a very nearby star system, or it could refer to that free world he'd glimpsed earlier, before his capture.

Of course, there might be other TRGA cylinders nearby, allowing shortcuts across tens of thousands of light years. If so, the Sh'daar archive might literally be anywhere, even halfway across the galaxy.

And Thedreh'schul said nothing to narrow down the choices.

"My masters wish to know what you are," she told him. "It is their belief that you are a member of a species they refer to as *Nah-voh-grah-nu-greh Trafhyedrefschladreh*. That translates as 20,415-carbon-oxygen-water, and describes your species within their encoding system."

" 'Nah-vuh-gruh—' "

Nah-voh-grah-nu-greh Trafhyedrefschladreh. The 20,415th species they have encountered with carbon biochemistry, using oxygen for metabolism and liquid water as a polar solvent and internal transport medium. At least, that is your number in base ten."

"We call ourselves 'humans,' " Gray said. *"Homo sapiens."*

"I know. I recognized your species as soon as we connected. Some fourteen billion of you occupy the third and fourth worlds of a yellow star some nine thousand light-*gurvedh* distant from here. I have already informed my masters of that fact." And the alien faded from the simulation.

"Wait!" Gray called. "Wait! Come back!"

The Agletsch reappeared. "My contribution here is concluded."

"No it isn't! I want to talk with the Sh'daar!"

"Human, one does not *talk* with the Sh'daar. One does what one is told, while hoping that no more is demanded of her."

"They might need you," he suggested. "If they intend to question me, they'll need to have someone on hand who understands us. Can speak with us." Gray hesitated, then decided to take a chance. "They're scared of us right now, aren't they?"

"Why do you suggest such a thing?"

"My fleet, my people, they're getting a bit close for comfort, I would imagine." By now, the carrier battlegroup would have secured the Texaghu Resch side of the TRGA cylinder. It was even possible that the fleet had come through already, that it was fighting now within just a few thousand kilometers of his prison. If Admiral Koenig had been able to make use of the data on that message drone, he might have figured a way to come through and take out those three fortresses.

And even if he'd not, the fact that the Battlegroup *America* was now on the other side of the TRGA, seven subjective minutes away, would have to make the Sh'daar a bit nervous. It seemed likely, Gray thought, that they'd wondered who and what he was because humans shouldn't be here at all. Species 20,415-carbon-oxygen-water had been on the defensive for thirty-eight years, after all, falling back from system after system as the Sh'daar client races had kept pushing. For that species to suddenly show up on the Sh'daar's doorstep, after winning sharp and unexpected victories at Arcturus and Alphekka . . . yeah, the Sh'daar might very well be scratching their equivalent of heads and questioning whether or not humans could be behind the sudden reversals.

"How did you know that your fleet has arrived in this region of space?" the Agletsch asked.

Score! Gray *hadn't* known, but he did now. Admiral Koenig had come through to get him!

Well . . . perhaps the battlegroup hadn't arrived solely for Gray, but the thrill of the moment set the virtual hairs at the back of his neck standing straight. He realized that he'd felt a lot less lonely when he'd learned that Schiere was a prisoner here as well, that he was not the only human within eighteen thousand light years.

It was even better knowing that the fleet was close by.

"We have our ways," Gray said. His attempt at being mysterious sounded sophomoric to his own ears, but perhaps it would have a different effect on the aliens.

The virtual image of the Agletsch didn't move for a long moment, its usually restless stalked eyes motionless, and Gray wondered if it was in fact in conversation with its "masters." Koenig had come through the tunnel to rescue him and Schiere!

Realistically, Gray knew that it wasn't that simple. Admiral Koenig would not have risked the entire battlegroup— fifty-eight ships and nearly fifty thousand men and women—for two lost pilots. The very nature of command in war demanded the sacrifice of a few, from time to time, to win the greater success by many.

The logic, however, didn't matter at the moment. Growing up in the Manhat Ruins, out on the Periphery of the old United States, Gray had learned early and well the lesson that those in authority didn't much care for *individuals*, especially when those individuals were cut off from easy access and inconvenient to reach. After rising sea levels and the Fall of Wormwood had turned old New York City, Washington, and a dozen other major cities into partially submerged wilderness areas, the U.S. government had found it easier and cheaper to withdraw from the drowned coastlands and focus dwindling reserves on what was left. The Ruins became havens for outcasts, rebels, gangs, and individuals, outside the reach of civilization and law.

Of course, the human squatties living among the shattered concrete towers above sea-filled canyons had preferred it that way. The less intrusive, the less heavy-handed and demanding the government Authority, the better. If they paid a price for that isolation—lawless gangs, uncertain harvests in the rooftop gardens, no health care, no power grid, no Net for communications or data downloads—it was a price they usually paid willingly in exchange for freedom. All of them knew that they could come in at any time. All that was required was that they accept the implants, the edentities, the credimplants, the rules and regulations and responsibilities of modern civilization.

Gray himself had deliberately sacrificed his Prim's freedom to save Angela's life. As it turned out, he'd sacrificed Angela herself, when the stroke and the medical treatment for the stroke had *changed* her.

He bit off a curse, turning from the unbidden memory that still burned, raw and flaming. It *had* been his choice.

The point was that Gray was simply unable to expect that authority in *any* form would ever come to his rescue. From experience, he'd learned that Admiral Koenig and the other senior officers of the battlegroup *did* care, that they did their best to live up to the ancient dictum of *no person left behind*.

It was one thing to know that, and quite another to feel it.

There was something about that train of thought, though, that was nagging at him, something important.

He was aware, of course, that anyone linked into this simulation could follow those of his thoughts that he brought to the point of internal vocalization. There were nanoreceptors, part of the network of implants that linked him with the outside world, in place along the laryngeal nerve that picked up and translated speech signals from the brain. *Thinking* words was as good as speaking them, so far as his nanoimplant was concerned. His AI was aware of what he subvocalized . . . and so were the creators of this virtual reality. He'd sensed the Agletsch "hearing" his momentary, internal monologue as he'd thought about Angela and life in the Manhat Ruins. There'd been a kind of expectancy, of anticipation as they'd followed his thoughts. Presumably, the Agletsch was passing it all on, with suitable translation, to her Sh'daar masters.

Why would they be interested in *that*?

"My masters *are* curious," the Agletsch said after a moment, still following Gray's thoughts. "You appear to have been . . . abandoned, yes-no?"

"I beg your pardon?"

"You—and those like you—were abandoned by the technological adepts."

"So?"

"It is possible that you and the Sh'daar masters share something, a common experience. They had not thought that such a thing was possible. They . . . wish to explore this matter with you."

Thedreh'schul sounded vastly surprised.

CIC
TC/USNA CVS America
Omega Centauri
1409 hours, TFT

"Main batteries fire!" Buchanan commanded.

Koenig felt the lurch, a slight jar, transmitted through the deck of the CIC as the carrier's twin spinal launch tubes hurled a pair of condensed matter projectiles toward the approaching enemy battleship. Port and starboard launch tubes fired at the same instant, but with slightly different accelerations. This gave the projectiles slightly different muzzle velocities, which in turn allowed different arrival times on target.

The launches were close enough to simultaneous that *America* felt a single recoil, and powerful enough to jolt the lumbering carrier as she cruised directly toward the enemy behemoth, bow-on, and slow her somewhat. With the target at a range of just over eight hundred kilometers, the starboard projectile would reach the target a fraction of a second before the port, fifty-six seconds after launch.

"Light them up!" Buchanan ordered. "Suppression beams! Everything that will bear!"

America's forward shield cap blocked the carrier from firing her smaller, turret-mounted barriers directly ahead, but a ring of small lasers mounted around the cap's perimeter could paint the enemy battleship with coherent ultraviolet light. UV lasers by themselves could not penetrate the enemy vessel's powerful screens, but they *would* snap those screens opaque and dazzle any mast-mounted sensors, as well as help *America*'s tactical department to pick up any warheads coming back the other way. Working in close-linked concert with *America*'s tactical department, the destroyers *Adams* and *Trumbull* closed in as well, firing high-energy lasers and particle-beam weapons.

The idea was to keep the enemy from spotting those approaching projectiles until it was too late to do anything about them. The blunt prow of the approaching ship started to swing aside at the last moment . . . but too little, too late. Just over fifty-six seconds after firing, the first projectile slammed home.

The projectiles were KK warheads, relying on kinetic force alone for their destructive power. At over fourteen thousand meters per second, each warhead carried a devastating punch. The first struck the enemy vessel's gravitic shields, which shredded the compressed, high-density metal, but no shielding could hold against that much tightly focused force. Energy leaked through—enough to knock out large sections of its shield projector grid and have enough left over to vaporize a crater in the alien vessel's bow.

An instant later, the second projectile slammed at over fourteen kilometers per second into the huge vessel's unprotected prow at the same, white-glowing point, plunging through the partially molten crater in her thin outer skin and burrowing deep, deep through her vitals, a high-speed bullet smashing through relatively soft and unprotected internal organs.

The battleship-sized alien vessel staggered and rolled under the impact. Her shields flickered, then fell. The destroyers *Trumbull* and *Adams* moved closer, turning their shield caps away from the target in order to allow their turreted laser and particle beam weapons to bear. Krait missiles streaked through the intervening space, and the piercing flash of nuclear detonations began to strobe and flare across the enemy vessel's hull.

"There go the fighters," tactical officer Lieutenant Commander Hargrave reported. "They're vectoring for a close pass."

Eight fighters—surviving shreds of the Dragonfires, the Impactors, and the Black Lightnings operating together, descended on the broken hulk like hungry piranhas on a crippled cow. Normally, a warship of that size could sweep that many fighters out of the sky without effort, but internal systems had been savaged, including, probably, her tracking and targeting sensors.

The giant was still dangerous, however. The battleship didn't appear to be armed with the matter-crushing weapons witnessed earlier, but beams of charged particles lashed out with devastating fury.

One of the fighters flared into a dazzling white fireball . . . then another. . . .

Lieutenant Shay Ryan
VFA-44
TRGA, Texaghu Resch System
1411 hours, TFT

The last of the Impactors died in a silent, savage flash of light ahead and to Shay's right. Lieutenant DeVrye—Shay hadn't known her, not well—but it hurt like hell when any of the few remaining pilots was vaporized. The enemy battle-wagon was badly hurt, but her point defense systems were still operating, still targeting the incoming Confederation fighters. Shay urged her fighter into a series of unpredictable jolts and vector shifts, jinking to throw the enemy shooters off. She wondered if they were flesh and blood over there, trying to lock her into their sights, or if she was facing the implacably cold calculations of a machine.

Fifty kilometers. She was following Lawrence Kuhn in, and Kuhn was zorching in just above the alien's hull now. "Firing pee-beep!" Kuhn shouted over the tactical net, his voice shrill with adrenaline.

And then the battleship was there, in front of her, expanding in an instant from a dim star to fill her forward screen, enormous and malignant. Shay swept in low across the gray and pitted landscape of the alien vessel's ravaged body, firing the last of her Gatling KK ammo into the thing, and hammering the wreckage again and again with her PBP-2.

Explosions flashed within the vessel, glimpsed through rents in the ship's torn hull.

"Explosion of target imminent," her AI called out.

And then the universe dissolved in blue-white radiance.

CIC
TC/USNA CVS America
Omega Centauri
1412 hours, TFT

"I think she's about to blow," Commander Craig said, and then the alien battleship exploded from inside, geysers of blue-white plasma erupting through weakened portions of her hull, ripping huge chunks of hull metal open, clouds of molten droplets spraying outward as they cooled rapidly to invisibility. In moments, perhaps a third of the giant remained, a ragged chunk off the stern end, trailing wreckage as it slowly rotated in space.

"Some of our people were pretty tight in there," Wizewski said. "Permission to deploy SARs to that wreckage."

"How's the retrieval on the *Gurrierre* pods coming?" The

Pan-European bombardment vessel was a crumpled, life-less, and highly radioactive hulk, now, but nearby space was filled by the evac pods of personnel who'd managed to get clear before the ship's singularity had gone rogue.

"Recovery under way, sir. We can leave that to the Dino-SARs, and divert some tugs from the Jolly Blacks to pick up our pilots."

"Do it."

"Aye, aye, Admiral."

"Sir," Hargrave said. "I think you should see this."

Koenig accepted an in-head link, opening a window created by *America*'s long-range scanners. There was a planet out there . . . the tiny worldlet detected by Gray's fighter and designated AIS-1.

And it was showing the wink of two emergency transponder beacons.

Trevor Gray
Omega Centauri
1415 hours, TFT

Gray felt the seismic quake, a distant, shuddering rumble that reached his consciousness even while he was deep within the depths of the simulation. The virtual image of Thedreh'schul shimmered, winked on and off several times, and then vanished, along with the simmed view of the planet's ice-bound surface. He was again within the confines of his Starhawk, immersed in blackness.

"AI," he called. "What's going on?"

"Data is conflicting and uncertain," the fighter's software replied. "However, the facility within which we are being held appears to be undergoing extreme gravitic acceleration."

"'Facility.' Do you mean the ship that picked us up?"

"Yes. However—" The AI hesitated, as if genuinely at a loss for words, or as if uncertain how to interpret the data. "I have tapped into one of the local optical feeds," the AI continued after a moment, "by piggybacking through RF leakage from nonoptical cryocircuitry. It appears to be a surface view."

This time he saw the panorama in a window within his mind, rather than a full sim within which he seemed to be standing. It was, once again, the dark and frozen ice plain he'd first experienced in-sim, with the impenetrable cloud of Venus-bright stars filling the bowl of the sky overhead.

But this time, those stars were *moving*.

Directly ahead, more stars were rising from behind glacier cliffs of frozen methane and nitrogen. Abruptly, then, the drifting motion stopped, and as it did so, Gray felt another sharp, seismic shock.

"Wait a second," he said. "I thought we were on that big ship that picked us up!"

"Evidently we are," his AI replied. "But the ship has landed on a planetary surface, most likely the body designated as AIS-1."

"But we're *moving*!"

"Planets move," his AI replied. "It is in their nature. But I agree that this motion appears to be anomalous."

"But *how* are we moving! We started rotating . . . then we stopped!"

"I have no data with which to formulate conclusions. It should be remembered that we cannot necessarily trust incoming data from outside."

And what, Gray wondered, had that statement cost his AI? Artificial intelligences *lived* for data, at least in a loose sense of the word.

"I don't buy that," Gray replied. "We felt that shock whenever we started rotating."

"We might simply be on board the starship that picked us up, and it is the ship that rotated."

"Your data feeds from outside. What do they tell you?"

"That we appear to be on or just beneath the surface of a dwarf planet, and that the planet rotated through eighty-five degrees, then began accelerating toward six particular nearby stars."

"What stars?"

For answer, a new window opened in Gray's mind. In it, he saw the backdrop of the cluster's stars, thickly massed, with only scattered bits of the infinite night beyond visible between some of them. But arrayed against that brilliant wall were six foreground stars, far brighter than the rest and gleaming a brilliant crystalline blue.

The overall color of the background stars tended to be white, shading ever so slightly to a faint orange or red. That was to be expected. Star clusters—as well as galactic cores, such as Omega Centauri was supposed to be—were made of truly ancient stars. Globular clusters, generally, were made up of truly ancient Population II stars, which tended to be red giants. Hotter stars, blue giants, for example, burned up their supplies of nuclear fuel swiftly indeed, dying in spectacular supernovae after a mere 10 million years or so. Even Omega Centauri, though it possessed both Population II and the younger Population I stars, like a galactic nucleus, still tended to be made up of red-hued stars, cooler and slower-burning, and able, therefore, to live throughout the 10 to 12 billion years or so that they'd been in existence.

Those six stars were blue giants, and they were arranged artificially. There could be no doubt of that; they were aligned in a perfect hexagon, a circle of six brilliant stars.

"My God," Gray said, staring at the circle of stars. "How did we miss that?"

"This is a magnified image," his AI told him. "Under a routine, nonmagnified scan, these six stars dwindle to an apparent single point, lost among all of the background stars. I noticed them just now only because the planet we are on appears to be accelerating in that direction. I would suggest that those stars are our captors' destination."

"They're . . . beautiful," Gray said. They looked like some perfect objet d'art, six intensely blue diamonds in an invisible setting.

"Those six stars," his AI said, "show spectra similar to that of Zeta Puppis and other blue giants. I estimate that they are of spectral type O5, that each has a mass of roughly forty times that of Sol, and that all are relatively young, likely less than four million years old."

"Four million years," Gray said. "What are they doing inside a cluster that's supposed to be ten or twelve *billion* years old?"

"Unknown."

"Those have to be artificially put there like that," Gray said, shaking his head. "They must be in precise gravitational balance. They couldn't have formed that way naturally."

"Agreed. And that lends credence to the possibility that the stars themselves are artificial or, at the least, artificially generated from existing suns."

"How do you mean?"

"They could well be blue stragglers. And to have six of them in a perfect hexagon implies that they all were deliberately created, and that they were created at the same time."

Gray had to open another inner window and download a definition of *blue straggler*, a term he'd not heard before. Scanning through the few lines of text stored in his cybernetic hardware, he learned that as much as four centuries earlier, astronomers had recognized blue, apparently very young suns inside the teeming swarms of ancient red stars that made up globular clusters. Because blue stars were much shorter lived than red, dying in spectacular fashion after only a very few million spendthrift years, there was no way that they could possibly exist within clusters of stars a thousand of times older, not when the gas and dust from which new stars were born were generally absent from those clusters.

And yet there they were, gravitationally bound to the clusters as contradictions to established physics and astronomy—the blue stragglers.

Eventually, astronomers had worked out what must be happening. The ancient stars within the swarms of globular clusters did not occupy orderly and precise orbits, but literally swarmed through the cluster, their nearest neighbors a tenth of a light year or less away at any given time, their vectors constantly tugged and twisted by ever-changing gravitational tides. While stellar collisions were rare throughout the rest of the galaxy, in such tight quarters, collisions were actually fairly common. Most collisions, though, were not head-on affairs ending in annihilation; instead, two stars would approach, graze, then slowly come together in a series of tight mutual orbits, until eventually they combined, coalescing.

Where there had been two stars there now was one, but a star of much higher mass than before. The increased mass meant a higher fusion temperature, and that in turn meant not a cooler, redder star, but a much hotter, bluer one. Two ancient stars were reborn as one young one . . . but a young spendthrift destined to squander its hydrogen wealth and, as with all blue stars, to die within a few million years.

To have six of these young stars in a circle suggested that someone had been deliberately slamming stars into one another, turning old cool stars into young hot suns.

Gray thought about the ramifications of this. The technology required to create not one, but six blue stars, orbiting a common center in perfect balance, to *keep* them in balance for millions of years as they independently burned their dwindling supplies of hydrogen fuel . . . the thought, the sheer scope and scale, the staggering *arrogance* of such celestial engineering, beggared belief.

And yet . . . there they were, six stars in a perfect ring, diamond-bright, intensely beautiful.

And completely impossible.

Chapter Nineteen

CIC
TC/USNA CVS America
Omega Centauri
1422 hours, TFT

The wink of two transponder beacons on the mobile planet was the first proof the battlegroup had had that Lieutenant Gray had survived after being picked up by the enemy. And who was the other? The coding attached to the beacon indicated Lieutenant Schiere's reconnaissance CP-240 Shadowstar. Better and better.

The fact of the transponders didn't mean the two pilots had survived, of course, but it was strong evidence in that direction.

Unfortunately, the possibility that they'd survived didn't mean that the fleet was going to be able to do anything about it. Something strange was happening over there.

"What the hell?" Koenig asked. In the window, the surface temperature of the dwarf planet was rising, and a column of data to one side was changing rapidly.

AIS-1 had rotated in space, and now it was *accelerating*, and quickly, a most un-planetlike thing for it to do.

"It appears to be projecting an enormous gravitational

singularity," Commander Craig pointed out. "But there still are going to be massive tidal effects."

"We're seeing that on the infrared imaging," Dr. Tina Schuman said. The astrogation-department physicist had been brought into the link just moments before, when the dwarf planet had begun its anomalous rotation. "The surface is heating up. That suggests tidal stress and friction."

"The straight-line acceleration will be free fall," Sam Jones, *America*'s exec pointed out. "Just like for a starship. That rotation might have been a jolt, though."

"They're going somewhere in a hell of a hurry," Koenig said. "Where?"

"I've got some data coming up on-screen," Craig said. "But I'm not sure I believe them."

"And what the hell is that?" Koenig asked.

A portion of the backdrop of stars had been picked out by a small rectangle within his in-head view, then sharply expanded. An insignificant star, one of millions, suddenly appeared ahead as an ethereal, inexpressibly beautiful artifact—six brilliant blue stars in a perfect hexagon.

"Okay," Captain Buchanan said. "Why the hell didn't we see that before?"

"I'm checking, sir," Craig's voice said.

"I've got it," Koenig's AI said. "That artifact was on the visual data sent back by Gray's message drone. I see it here now. But until the dwarf planet's motion called attention to it, it was lost in the background. I did not at first notice it." His AI, Koenig thought, sounded almost contrite at having missed the thing.

"Overwhelmed by detail lost among ten million stars," Koenig said, nodding. "It's not surprising. This is unknown territory for all of us." Even AIs couldn't keep up with everything the fleet's sensors were bringing in.

"We would have noticed the anomaly eventually," Karyn's voice added.

"Okay, now that we see it, I want a complete analysis of that thing. CAG? We need to put some recon probes in that region. How far away is it?

"Approximately half a light year," his AI said. "Over four point seven quadrillion kilometers."

"That means a microshift under Alcubierre Drive, and we launch recon ships when we come out. I don't want to spend the next six months in transit at *c*."

"Apparently they're not waiting around either," Buchanan pointed out. On the screen, the dwarf planet had just blurred, then winked out, enclosed within the Sh'daar equivalent of an Alcubierre bubble.

"Transponder signals lost," Jones reported.

"We'll need to proceed cautiously, sir," Hargrave suggested. "We don't have accurate metrics of this space."

Accurate navigation while traveling enmeshed within a bubble of FTL space, unable to see out, required a good understanding of the gravitic "shape" of the volume of space in which you planned to emerge. "Metric" was the technical term for the gravitometric readings of local space taken by both unmanned probes and recon pilots.

In particular, you didn't want to try to drop into a volume of space where local mass—such as a planet or one of those giant suns in the distance—was so distorting the region that the emerging ship was ripped apart by the differences in the shapes of space itself. In practice, starships approaching a planetary system would drop into normal space out in the local Kuiper Belt, a region beginning about thirty to forty astronomical units out for sunlike stars, closer in for cooler suns, farther out for giants. Out here, though, the battlegroup was working in the dark despite the brilliance of the surrounding star cloud. No one knew what to expect, or what the norms might be.

"I agree," Koenig said, answering Hargrave's statement. "But we're not going to be so cautious we lose the initiative. We seem to have the bastards on the run. I want to keep it that way."

"We'll have the figures run for you in fifteen minutes," Schuman said.

"Pass the word for the fleet to regroup," Koenig said. "We accelerate in one hour."

Trevor Gray
Omega Centauri
1427 hours, TFT

The visual feed from the surface of the planet suddenly went black. "Hey!" Gray said. "What's going on?"

"The feed is still open," his AI said, "and we're still getting some infrared." As if to show him, the AI stepped up the contrast and dropped in an IR filter, which let Gray see the ice surface in muted swaths of blue and deep purple.

"But the stars went out!" Gray protested.

"I would surmise," the AI replied, "that the planet has just shifted into the Sh'daar equivalent of Alcubierre Drive."

Gray blinked, at a loss for words. Finally, he managed to stammer, "The . . . the whole *planet*?"

"That would be consistent with the data we have available."

Human Alcubierre drives achieved faster-than-light travel by bending a pocket of space around the starship, using projected artificial singularities and a *great* deal of energy. While it was flatly impossible for a material object to travel at the speed of light or faster, there was nothing in the rules that said that *space* couldn't do so; indeed, the best theories about the early life and growth of the universe after the big bang suggested that during the so-called inflationary period, space was expanding at many times the speed of light. Propelled by an asymmetric twist to the leading edge of the gravitic field, the folded-up pocket of space slid through space at between 1.7 and 1.9 light years per day; the spacecraft inside the bubble remained virtually motionless relative to its immediate surroundings.

Folding up the pocket, however, cut the spacecraft off from all connections with the outside universe. There was no way to see out during an FTL passage, which put something of a strain on the ship's astrogation department to bring the vessel out within the desired target area.

Manipulating space in order to create a fast-moving bubble around even a single starship the size of the *America* took a staggering amount of power, drawn from the virtual or vacuum energy filling the base state of empty space. But to create fields big enough to move a *planet*, even a "pocket planet" like this one . . .

The idea drove home to Gray just how great the technological gulf between the Sh'daar and the Earth Confederation actually was. With technology like this, hell, the Sh'daar could pick up Pluto and slam it into the Earth, and there wouldn't be a damned thing Humankind could do to stop them. The Turusch had launched an attack on Earth using high-speed KK projectiles half a year ago. The impact in the Atlantic Ocean 3,500 kilometers from the East Coast of North America had killed an estimated 80 million people on four continents. That technology was nothing, *nothing* compared with this.

Another earthquake shudder rippled through the fighter, and abruptly the lights came on once more, stars in their millions filling a rose-white sky. And there, just above the glacier-edged horizon, blazed six blue-hot pinpoints of searing, actinic light. Gray's AI swiftly stopped down the intensity of the light flooding through the optical link, and by doing so almost certainly saved Gray's eyes. Those stars were *hot*, and so bright that even with the stopped-down optics it was impossible to look straight at them, and the sky-dome of stars beyond were almost wiped out of view entirely.

And there were other . . . *things* in that alien sky as well.

"I think," Gray said softly, "that we've arrived."

CIC
TC/USNA CVS America
Omega Centauri
1525 hours, TFT

"All departments report readiness for acceleration to Alcubierre microshift," Captain Buchanan told him. "We just need a final determination of our emergence point."

"All designated battlegroup ships report readiness for acceleration as well," Commander Craig added.

Koenig nodded. The fleet had pulled together well, and swiftly, even after its rough handling during the battles around both of the TRGA cylinder's tunnel mouths. A total of eight capital ships had been destroyed, and another five badly damaged enough that they would not be making the transition with the rest of the battlegroup. Between the casualties on both sides of the tunnel, the ships Koenig had ordered to stay and guard the tunnel mouths, and the various stores and maintenance vessels that were also being left behind, there were just twenty-three Confederation warships left to take this final part of the assault to the enemy.

Koenig had ordered the two large carriers into a tight, side-by-side formation surrounded by their escorts. *America* and the *United States* would lead the assault. The third big carrier, *Lincoln*, which had taken some serious damage after her emergence into the Omega Centauri battlespace, was one of the vessels remaining at the TRGA, making sure the fleet had its lines of retreat open should that become necessary. The light carriers *Jeanne d'Arc* and *Illustrious*, together with the Marine assault carriers *Vera Cruz* and *Nassau*, would follow close behind. Among the larger capital ships accompanying the assault group were the railgun cruiser *Kinkaid*, the heavy cruisers *Groznyy*, *Valley Forge*, *Lunar Bay*, and *Saratoga*, and the bombardment vessels *Cheng Hua* and *Ma'at Mons*. The *Cheng Hua* had been shot up pretty badly after emerging from the tunnel's mouth, but the ship's skipper had reported that the ship's damage-repair facilities had plugged the leaks from her shield cap and that all systems were now nominal. Captain Jiang had told Koenig in no uncertain terms that he would *not* be left behind.

Koenig had been impressed enough by the man's determination that he'd let the hint of insubordination slide.

He stared into the tactical tank, which showed the battlegroup at one side, the destination, a circle of six tiny blue points of light at the other. Half a light year. "How close can we get to those stars without getting fried?" he asked his AI.

A column of data appeared in a new window opening in his mind. "These stars appear close to the known blue giant Zeta Puppis in size and luminosity," she explained. Data for Zeta Puppis, also called Naos, streamed through his awareness.

STAR: Zeta Puppis

COORDINATES: RA: 08^h 03^m 35.1^s Dec: -40° 00' 11.6" D 335p

ALTERNATE NAMES: Naos, Suhail Hadar, HD 66811

TYPE: O5 Iaf

MASS: 40 Sol; **RADIUS:** 11 Sol; **LUMINOSITY:** 360,000 Sol (Optical 21,000 Sol)

SURFACE TEMPERATURE: ~39,000°K

AGE: 4 million years

APPARENT MAGNITUDE (Sol): 2.21; **ABSOLUTE MAGNITUDE:** -5.96

DISTANCE FROM SOL: 1,093 LY

PLANETARY SYSTEM: None known

"Damned bright," Koenig observed.

"Indeed. If Zeta Puppis were as close to Earth as Sol," Karyn Mendelson's voice continued, "it would appear to be twenty times larger in the sky and twenty thousand times brighter. Earth's surface would be heated to around six thousand one hundred degrees Kelvin, and ultimately the planet would be completely vaporized.

"For a planet to enjoy Earthlike temperatures in orbit

around Zeta Puppis, it would have to be at least four hundred fifty astronomical units away—about eleven times the distance of Pluto from the sun."

"And there are *six* giants out there that hot and bright. Does that mean six times the distance for one, if we want to find a zone with habitable temperatures?"

"Not necessarily. We calculate that each star is approximately fifty AUs from its nearest neighbors, in a ring nearly one hundred AUs across. The amount of radiation any given volume of space receives will depend on the aspect of the stellar ring, and the total will not necessarily be cumulative. We estimate that habitable zone temperatures will be found at roughly two thousand to two thousand five hundred AUs from the artifact's central point."

Koenig ran the numbers through his in-head math processor. A light year, he knew, measured close to 63,000 astronomical units. "About four one hundredths of a light year."

"Precisely."

"CAG? All of our chicks back on board?"

"All fighters recovered or accounted for, Admiral."

"Punch it," Koenig said.

And the battlegroup punched.

Even though the final determination of where they were accelerating *to* had not yet been made.

That dwarf planet had accelerated into the distance, together with a huge number of surviving enemy warships, then folded about itself and slipped off at faster than light, exhibiting yet again the marked superiority, the sheer *elegance* of Sh'daar technology compared to human-designed systems. Some of their client races, notably the H'rulka, showed similar superiorities in style and technique, though they'd never demonstrated anything close to this. The ships of the human fleet would have to accelerate at five hundred gravities for 16.6 hours in order to push close to the speed of light. Only at 0.997 *c* could they use their relativistic mass to warp space into the tightly knotted bubbles that would allow them to outpace light itself.

Over sixteen and a half hours.

The assault force hadn't fully bought into the idea of pursuing that planet . . . and Koenig wasn't going to phrase this one as an order.

Especially when such monumental questions about the Sh'daar, about who and what they were, were yet staring Koenig in the face.

As the minutes passed and the fleet continued to accelerate, Koenig continued to study the tactical tank. After a time, he pulled in another download of astronomical data, searching through all of the information stored there on the Omega Centauri cluster. What he saw there—or, more precisely, what he *didn't* see—had been bothering him.

"Astrogation department," he said.

"Yes, Admiral?" He'd linked through to Dr. Tina Schuman.

"I've got a question."

"We have a lot more questions than answers right now, Admiral. But I'll take a shot."

"Six hot, blue Type O stars in a tight grouping just about one hundred AUs across. That must give off a hell of a lot of ultraviolet and X-ray radiation."

"They do."

"Enough that they should have been seen by astronomers on Earth studying Omega Centauri."

There was a long pause on the other end. "Yes, Admiral. They should have been."

"But I've seen nothing about them in the data on the cluster."

"No, sir. And that's been bothering us as well."

"What data do you have that actually identifies this cluster as Omega Centauri?"

He heard her sigh. "Not all that much, actually, Admiral. Mostly it's the estimated number of stars—about ten million—and the estimated diameter of the cluster—about two hundred thirty light years. The distribution of spectral types is roughly the same as well."

"You also mentioned stellar markers when we talked before. Stellar fingerprints."

"Yes, sir. Absorption lines in some of the cooler stars that appear to be unique to those stars. What we saw in Lieutenant Gray's data—what we're seeing *now*—appears to match fairly closely with the spectra of several stars in the cluster studied from Earth."

"But *our* Omega Centauri doesn't have those six blue stars. I'd have thought they could have been seen pretty easily from Earth."

He was looking at an astrophotograph taken by an Earth-orbital robot telescope called the Hubble, in the early twenty-first century. It showed the heart of the Omega Centauri cluster, a thick array of multihued suns.

There was no sign of the anomalous hexagon.

"But those six stars are obviously artificial, Admiral. Or at least they were engineered from pre-existing stars by bringing them together, allowing them to merge as artificial blue stragglers. Our assumption is that they were made sometime recently, within the past fifteen thousand years, anyway."

"So the light from those stars hasn't had time to reach Earth yet."

"Exactly, sir."

"How does that sit with you, Doctor?"

"I beg your pardon, sir?"

"Does that seem to be a likely explanation?"

"Sir, it's just about the *only* explanation."

"Is there any way to determine how old those stars are from here?"

"Well, they're obviously quite young. Definitely less than five million years in terms of stellar evolution. Any older, and they'd have started to evolve toward the red super-giant phase of their life."

Such intensely hot, massive young stars, Koenig knew, lived fast, furious, and very brief lives, at least as stars measured things. Stars that hot would burn up their stores of hydrogen, evolve through the spectral types from blue to yellow to red, then detonate in a supernova, probably after a total life span of less than 10 million years.

"But you can't tell if they're less than fifteen thousand years old."

"No, sir."

"And you can't tell me anything about the stars that were used to form them."

"No, sir. When two stars merge, that resets the clock. We can assume that the original stars were Population II giants—probably red giants. We're working on the assumption that whoever manufactured those stars actually brought together a large number of such stars."

"Why is that?"

"Those stars up ahead each run to about forty solar masses," she replied. "Rather than bringing together two twenty-solar-mass suns, it seems more likely that they merged a larger number of smaller stars."

"Maybe tossing in a new star each time the fires started to burn low."

"Possibly."

"Except that it would take several million years for the new sun to start to cool. And that means the light would have reached Earth long ago. We'd have seen them from home."

"Yes, sir. As I said, we have more questions than answers."

"Thank you, Doctor."

"There's something else you should know, sir."

"What's that?"

"Well, we've been studying this volume of space since we came through the TRGA, of course," she told him. "And we've found another anomaly."

"What's that?"

"There appears to be more gas and dust in this cluster than we know exists in Omega Centauri."

"Gas and dust?"

"Typical globular clusters have almost no gas. They used it all up in a single burst of star formation around twelve billion years ago. Omega Centauri consists of several generations of stars, suggesting that star formation continued for some time after the cluster's creation, but most of the gas was still used up, oh, nine billion years ago or so.

"Sir . . . it's quite possible that this isn't Omega Centauri after all."

Which left, of course, the question of just where the carrier battlegroup was at the moment.

"Can you figure out where we are?"

"Not with the local stellar density, Admiral. We're going to need to get outside of the cluster so that we can see the starscape around us, the rest of the galaxy. We should be able to tell from that . . . assuming we're still within our galaxy, of course."

There was a chilling thought.

"Very well," Koenig said. "Keep at it, and let me know if anything turns up I should know about."

"Of course, Admiral."

Omega Centauri was distinctive, Koenig knew, in its diameter, its slight flattening at its poles, and in its huge number of stars. It was, he remembered, the second largest cluster ever identified . . . and the largest, Mayall II, was in the Andromeda galaxy, 2.3 million light years away.

Perhaps this cluster was on the far side of Earth's galaxy, hidden from Earth by the dust and gas of the galactic core.

It shouldn't matter. So long as they had the tunnel secure, so long as they could find their way back there, it shouldn't matter.

But God in heaven, where were they?

And how far were they now from home?

Trevor Gray
Omega Centauri
1530 hours, TFT

For almost an hour, Gray had studied that strange, that impossible, sky, trying to make sense of it. The flattened circle of brilliant blue suns, some two degrees across its longest dimension—spanning an area as wide as four full moons seen from Earth—hung low in the sky, casting hard-edged shadows off the glaciers in the distance, and dazzling the eyes with sheets of ice. His Starhawk, he knew, was stopping down the incoming light considerably; the illumination above the planet's surface was so high that he would have been instantly blinded otherwise.

The ice outside, he noticed, was beginning to steam.

Hanging in the sky were a number of other anomalous objects, each harshly illuminated by the six suns, with hard-edged contrast between light and shadow. It was impossible to get a sense of scale or distance, but two of them, Gray saw, were identical to the TRGA cylinder, hard, tiny knots imbedded in larger, fuzzy glows of gold and blue light twisted by their intense gravitational masses.

There were also planets, several of them, showing as hard-edged crescents bowed away from the intense glare of the stars. And there were other things . . . huge star-ships, perhaps, or orbital manufactories, or drifting facilities of less easily discernable purpose. The impression Gray had was that whoever had designed this . . . this place had parked ships and worlds and factories and transit systems close enough to the obviously artificial arrangement of suns to draw on their energy, but far enough out to avoid being vaporized.

"AI," he said. "How far are we from those suns? Must be pretty far out. . . ."

There was no answer, and Gray felt a sharp stab of panic. "AI!"

There was no one there.

And an instant later, everything went black. Gray was again alone, sitting in the darkness of his Starhawk cockpit, somewhere inside the mobile alien planet.

He took a deep breath, and worked to control the rising fear. There had to be a logical explanation. . . .

His own internal AI, his personal assistant, was intact

and operating. A low-end model residing within the nano-chelated circuitry implants within his brain and parts of his nervous system, it possessed neither sentience nor a simulated personality. Having been born and raised out in the Periphery, beyond the reach of "proper" North-American civilization, he'd not received one as a child entering the education track. His had been issued to him the first day he'd arrived at basic training. It allowed him to interface with the electronic world around him, communicate with others, download data from local networks, and receive other very basic services, but he couldn't *talk* to it.

His Starhawk's AI was far more powerful and flexible. A standard Gödel 900 series, it was, technically, sentient, but only within certain, very tightly defined parameters, "of limited purview," as the techies said. It was very good at what it did—directing and overseeing the fighter's systems, correlating data, operating weapons, and performing maneuvers at super-human speed—but it wasn't exactly a brilliant conversationalist.

Gray had always felt somewhat ambivalent about his AI. Most other pilots he knew named their fighter AIs, established emotional bonds with them, even thought of them as fellow pilots. Gray had never been able to manage that, not that he'd tried all that hard. The fighter AI was a *tool*. It interfaced directly with Gray's personal AI and with the fighter's electronics, allowing Gray, in a quite genuine sense, to *become* the fighter when he engaged the connections between his brain and the ship.

And now it was gone.

His personal AI maintained its link with his fighter systems. He could still download data, monitor system function, and the like. If he'd wanted to, he could have opened the cockpit and gone outside, not that he saw any point to doing so. His fighter's external sensors indicated a temperature of minus 200 Celsius, no light, and no atmosphere, and if there were machines out there—like automatic doors— his implant circuitry wouldn't be able to operate them. His jackies, his flight utility suit, could keep him breathing for a while with the helmet closed, but they wouldn't hold off that bitterly frigid cold for more than a few moments.

He was far better off staying where he was. His fighter still had power—at low, barely maintenance levels for life support, but power enough to keep him warm and alive. His communications systems were still operating, in case Lieutenant Schiere surfaced again.

But Trevor Gray had never felt so inexpressibly alone as now, sitting there in the dark, imbedded in the close-fitting embrace of a high-tech fighter cockpit that was now little more than inert nanomatrix and dead electronics.

He waited. There wasn't anything else he could do.

And the wait stretched out longer . . . and longer . . . and still longer, and he wondered if this was where he would die when his power gave out and his heat and atmosphere finally failed.

Chapter Twenty

Admiral's Office
TC/USNA CVS America
Omega Centauri
1700 hours, TFT

It had been one hour since the assault group had begun accelerating. The magnified view of their destination—the tiny, slightly flattened hexagon of six suns—gleamed against the backdrop of massed cluster suns on their forward screens.

Fifteen hours to go. . . .

The image was repeated on one viewall of Koenig's office, where he'd retreated shortly after the battlegroup had commenced acceleration.

"Admiral," Karyn's voice said, "the virtual conference is ready."

"Very well." Leaning back, he closed his eyes and placed his left palm on the contact plate of his chair. The reality of office, of viewscreen and desk and waiting reports of combat damage and tactical assessments all faded away, and Koenig sat at a virtual copy of a certain conference room at the Ad Astra Confederation government complex in Geneva. Outside one in-slanting wall of green glass, sunlight, the light of Earth's sun, sparkled on the waters of Lake Geneva out beyond the broad, labyrinthine Plaza of Light, with its towering epic statue, *Ascent of Man*, by Popolopoulis.

Koenig had chosen the simulated venue for the conference of ship commanders and staff carefully and with great deliberation. He'd discussed it at length with Karyn—with Karyn's electronic ghost, rather—and it had been she who'd first suggested the towering green pyramid of the Ad Astra complex.

It was all rather elemental human psychology, actually.

Koenig himself was widely seen as being in rebellion against the Confederation government, especially after HD 157950. Many of the North-American officers in the carrier battlegroup disliked the fact that the United States of North America was a mere member state of the Earth Confederation. There'd always been a strong secessionist flavor to the North Americans, ever since the creation of the *Pax Confeoderata* out of the war- and disease-savaged survivors of Humankind 272 years before. Those officers would have joined Koenig more because of his perceived rebellion than anything else.

Other of the officers here had deeper, older ties to the *Pax*—Harrison, of the *Illustrious*, for instance . . . and Michel of the *Jeanne d'Arc*. Harrison and the skippers of the British contingent might well share some of the USNA's historical doubts about both Confederation grand strategy and about Confederation legitimacy as the *de facto* government of Earth. The French, Germans, and other Pan-Europeans, though, were only here because they'd been convinced by Koenig's argument that the *only* possible way Humankind could hope to survive this war lay in taking an offensive path, that a defensive or appeasing strategy would end with humanity's subjugation or with its extinction.

And then there were the Chinese, excluded from the Confederation for 272 years because of the Wormwood asteroid attack, but nevertheless determined to participate in this final expedition against the alien Sh'daar. It was still tough to see where their primary loyalties lay.

But the green glass pyramid of the Ad Astra complex offered a powerful and tangible symbol, not only of the Confederation Government, but of a united humanity as well. And that was what this mission was all about—a united humanity against an empire that had arbitrarily decided to set limits upon the shape and scope of human technology.

Koenig studied the mammoth statue for a moment. The *Ascent of Man* was gaudier than he cared for, but that, too, was an enduring symbol, like the corroded and crumbling Statue of Liberty outside of the Manhattan Ruins.

"Admiral Koenig?" his AI said. "Captain Buchanan would like a private word."

"Put him through."

A window opened. Randolph Buchanan's long and worry-lined face appeared. The worry looked deeper, now.

"Thank you, Admiral," Buchanan said.

"You're wondering," Koenig said in a matter-of-fact manner, "just what the hell I think I'm doing."

Buchanan showed a moment of surprise, then nodded. "I wouldn't put it quite that harshly, Admiral, but yes. That's not why I simmed you, though."

"Why did you?"

"To wish you luck . . . and let you know that I, my officers, and my crew are behind you one thousand percent, no matter what you're up to!"

Koenig grinned. "I appreciate that, Randy. Don't worry. I don't think I've gone *too* far around the bend."

"It's a relief to hear that, Admiral." The window closed. Buchanan's simulated image, however, had taken its place among the ranks of officers now dropping into place one by one around the virtual table.

The captains and senior officers—CIC heads and staff, mostly—from all of the ships on this side of the tunnel had been directed to come. There were forty-one ships in all, including both those in the assault group and those left guarding the tunnel leading home, and that meant more than two hundred people. The room appeared to be full, with places at the table reserved for captains, with smaller desk workstations for their staff behind them out to the walls of the room.

Koenig's place was at a simulated lectern at the front of the room, just to one side of the broad glass window looking out over the plaza.

"Gentlemen," he said, "ladies, and AIs, thank you for coming. With luck, this could be the last briefing session you have to attend with me."

Gentle laughter rippled through the room, though some of the expressions showed uncertainty. Was he saying that the campaign was about to end in victory? In death? In a return to Earth?

Well . . . yes, actually. Any of those was a distinctly possible outcome.

"I imagine most of you have been curious about what I'm planning . . . on why we're pursuing that mobile planet we spotted zorching off toward the Six Suns.

"Up until now, the battlegroup has been staying ahead of the enemy, surprising them, getting in and hitting them where they weren't expecting us, and getting out before they could bring in reinforcements. Eta Boötis. Arcturus. Alphekka. Texaghu Resch. Even on this side of the tunnel." He gave a wry smile. "We were always outnumbered, and we've taken some heavy casualties, but we were always able to hit them before they could get their shit together.

"This last time, they were able to throw fighters at us numbering in the *millions*, however. We're following what's left of them into what is probably the very heart of the Sh'daar Empire. We can expect manufactory centers capable of producing further large numbers of spacecraft. Think of it as a target-rich environment.

"If this is indeed the center of the enemy's empire, possibly his homeworld, then this will be our final encounter on this mission. They may be ready for us in there. But this is also our opportunity to end this war."

"Admiral," Captain Hernandez of the cruiser *Libertad* said, "if they could throw millions of fighters at us at the tunnel mouth, what are they going to have waiting for us in there?"

"I don't know. But what I do know is that we have a singular opportunity here. An opportunity we're not likely to see ever again."

"What opportunity?" Captain Jiang of the Chinese *Cheng Hua* asked.

"A chance to end the war. A *negotiated* end.

"From the very beginning, thirty-some years ago, we've been fighting Sh'daar client races. Turusch. H'rulka. Nungiirtok. God knows what else. So far as we know, *we have never directly encountered the Sh'daar.* Everything we know about them, or *think* we know about them, has come through the Agletsch . . . and they're a Sh'daar client species as well. What does that tell you?"

"That they're very shy." That was Harrison, always something of a jokester.

Koenig smiled. "Possibly. Seriously, though, the galaxy is a hell of a big place. We've only been engaged at the very outermost periphery of the Sh'daar Empire. I'd expect the Sh'daar are in towards the center, somewhere. There are just too many stars, too many intelligent species, for the Sh'daar to personally try to manage each and every one.

"It is my intent to seek out the leaders of the Sh'daar Empire and to negotiate a peace."

That struck home. The avatar images seated around the table didn't change position or expression, of course, but Koenig could hear the swell within the undercurrent of conversations.

"How do you propose to communicate with those . . . those monsters?" Captain Paulson of the cruiser *Burke* asked.

"I think more to the point is how to talk to them while they're doing their best to kill us," Captain Harrison pointed out.

"We know," Koenig continued, "from our contact with the Agletsch that individuals within each client race carry tiny communications devices, called Seeds, implanted within their bodies. The Sh'daar apparently keep track of what's going on in their empire by monitoring events through those individuals. Every so often, when a Seed-carrying individual has acquired important information, that data is uploaded to the local Sh'daar network and eventually makes its way to a Sh'daar node. We believe the TRGA tunnel is such a node, and there are others. We've followed this node here. If this is not the Sh'daar imperial capital, it's likely to be the next best thing.

"And now that we're here, it is my hope that our two Agletsch guests on board the *America* will be able to help us make direct contact."

Koenig had already discussed the possibility with the two Agletsch, Gru'mulkisch and Dra'ethde. They'd been brought along on this mission, after all, as liaisons and translators for any alien species encountered along the way. That applied to the Sh'daar as well as to Sh'daar client races. Gru'mulkisch carried a Sh'daar Seed, a microscopic knot of circuitry carrying a kind of Sh'daar emotional and cognitive presence. The Agletsch had not even been aware of carrying the thing until a close biological scan had detected it.

"Sir, the Sh'daar have *never* shown any interest whatsoever in negotiations," Commander Conway of the destroyer *Fitzgerald* said. She sounded shocked. "How do you intend to make them sit down and talk?"

"A fair question," Koenig said, "and an important one. I have two answers for you.

"First of all, our contact with the Sh'daar themselves so far has been entirely through the medium of the Seeds. As I understand it, based on what our Agletsch guests have told us, Sh'daar Seeds have a certain amount of hard-wired AI intelligence to them, but they can't really make decisions more important than whether or not to transmit the data they've accumulated. The various Sh'daar client races we've encountered so far—the Turusch, the Nungies, and others— have evidently been working under orders relayed to them down the chain of command, but only through the Seeds.

They've not been as . . . as *flexible* in their relationships with other species as they might be otherwise.

"Dealing with the Sh'daar directly might give us a better chance of being heard.

"Secondly, if we're in orbit over their capital, we have them by the balls. Their technology is advanced enough that they'd be able to swat us down eventually . . . but I think they're not going to want to risk *any* significant damage to their infrastructure. A barbarian with a club can take out a battle-armored Marine, *if* he can get close enough."

"That's a very large 'if,' Admiral," General Mathers said, and that raised a chuckle from the others.

"Agreed. The important thing, however, is that we've got the bad guys reacting to us for a change," Koenig observed, "and that is a vitally important distinction. For thirty-eight years, the Turusch and the other Sh'daar client races have acted, and Humankind has *re*acted. That means that the Confederation has constantly been on the defensive. It does not take a military genius to recognize that the Confederation can never hope to win a purely defensive war fought on the enemy's terms.

"On the other hand, the Sh'daar face a serious disadvantage in not knowing the capabilities, the strengths and abilities, of all of the species they control. Even the word 'control' is misleading. I've never liked the term "empire" as it applies to Sh'daar space, simply because an empire carved out of a significant chunk of the entire galaxy would be so unwieldy, so large and cumbersome, that they would not be able to rule it in a conventional sense. The Agletsch tell us that we are the twenty-thousandth-and-some species they've encountered that employ carbon, oxygen, and water in their biochemistry. That implies a staggering number of mutually alien races within their . . . jurisdiction, for lack of a better term. Evidently, all they're really concerned about is that developing civilizations not evolve too far along a path that could lead to a technological singularity. Though we don't have a lot of information about it, it sounds as though a majority of species can't develop high technology—they're marine species, or evolved within gas giant atmospheres, or are trapped under the ice caps of gas giant moons or even in hard vacuum. Species that evolve in non-oxygen environments, obviously, can never develop fire, and that puts a sharp limit on what they can do in the way of metal smelting, alloys, steam power, radio, and other early industrial technologies. Many of the rest are capable of developing nanotechnology and computers and other dangerous technologies, as the Sh'daar think of them, but they don't. They don't have the philosophical or ideological mind-set that drives them, the way humans do.

"The Agletsch claim that no client race has ever confronted the Sh'daar directly. If so, we'll be the first . . . and I expect that it will come as something of a shock for them. That, at any rate, is what we're gambling on.

"Our expectation," Koenig added, "is that the mobile planet is retreating toward those six stars. We will follow them, assess the situation when we arrive, and move to gain the upper hand tactically and locally immediately. We will then use the Seed within one of our tame Agletsch to attempt to get into direct contact with the Sh'daar leadership there."

"What is the range of those Seeds, anyway?" Aliyev, the dour skipper of the *Groznyy*, put in.

"Dra'ethde and Gru'mulkisch aren't sure," Koenig replied. "Certainly they appear to operate over a range of at least several light minutes. They seem to respond to and work off of the local Sh'daar information systems network, if one is available. I suspect that the main limiting factor is the speed of light . . . and the time constraints that imposes on two-sided conversations."

Koenig studied the group for a moment, gauging its emotional currents. They were excited, he thought, keyed to a high point of expectancy, but they were with him.

"It will take another fifteen hours to reach near-c," Koenig told them, "and a little over six hours more to make the half-light-year microshift. We will emerge some three thousand astronomical units from the gravitational center of the suns. We estimate that that will actually be within the life zone of those stars, far enough out that water is liquid.

"If we can find the mobile planet, General Mathers will land his Marines there and attempt to establish a beachhead, which the fleet can use as a field projection center. That should give us enough breathing room to make contact with them. The fact that that planet retreated before we could approach it suggests that it may be, at the very least, some form of command-control center, and as such would be an appropriate target. It's a place for us to begin, at any rate.

"Questions?"

"Yes, sir," Charles Michel, the captain of the Pan-European *Jeanne d'Arc*, said. "What about the rumor that we are no longer within our own galaxy?"

Koenig nodded. He'd been expecting the question. Karyn had told him that rumor to that effect—scuttlebutt, to use the acepted naval terminology—was spreading rapidly throughout the fleet.

"We've uploaded what we know to the fleet net," he replied. "Unfortunately, we don't know a lot. Inside this cluster, we can't see out, so we can't check navigational markers in the Milky Way. We believe we're quite close to the center of the cluster—the chances are good that the Six Suns mark the actual gravitational center. Once this action is resolved, we may be able to send a reconnaissance mission a hundred or a hundred fifty light years out to have a look around.

"I think the thing to keep in mind is that it doesn't matter if we're inside our own galaxy or in some other galaxy halfway across the cosmos. The TRGA provides a quick and efficient shortcut. So long as we control both tunnel mouths, we will be able to make it back to Texaghu Resch. Okay?"

Captain Michel's image nodded but did not look particularly happy. Koenig couldn't blame him. If the Sh'daar had some means of switching the TRGA off, CBG-18 would be trapped here, wherever "here" might be. Much worse from a tactical point of view, the TRGA created a tactical bottleneck; if things went bad at the Six Suns, surviving Confederation vessels would have to hightail it back to the tunnel, and the enemy knew this. They could have a fleet there ready and waiting. . . .

Best not to think about that, since there was nothing that could be done about it in any case.

"Sir." It was Captain Charles Whitlow of the star carrier *United States of North America*.

"Yes, Captain?"

"There's also a rumor that you're going in after a couple of *America*'s lost pilots. The two beacons on AIS-1."

"*Not* true. At least, they're not the primary reason for this deployment. If we can rescue those men, fantastic . . . but our goal is to grab the Sh'daar by whatever they have for balls and hang on until they agree to negotiate."

He hesitated before continuing. "I think all of you know by now that I put a high premium on the battlegroup's personnel, on bringing them all back safe and sound . . . but we're also well aware of the realities of war. It does not make sense to risk fifty thousand men and women for two men. But risking them to stop this war, to preserve what we have back home, to secure the safety of Earth, our families, our species . . . *that*, ladies and gentlemen, is why we're here.

He paused for a long moment, allowing for any further questions or remarks, but there were none.

"If any of you have problems with *any* of this, or more questions, I urge you to contact me or my staff. While command of a battlegroup—like command of a single ship—is not a democratic process, this will be a volunteer mission. Those of you who do not wish to proceed with the Alcubierre jump can opt out, decelerate, and return to the TRGA.

"You should all know that I have also directed that a complete copy of my log, including all of my decisions and our actions to date, has been placed in one of *America*'s remaining Sleipnirs. By now, it has returned through the TRGA and is on its way to Earth. I intend to dispatch another as soon as we emerge at the Six Suns. The Confederation needs to know what's going down out here."

The HAMP-20 Sleipnir-class mail packet was the fastest means of communication available to the fleet. It could manage a thousand Gs of acceleration, and under Alcubierre Drive could cross 5.33 light years per day.

At that rate, starting from Texaghu Resch, it would take the Sleipnir thirty-nine days to cross the 210 light years to Earth.

"Questions?"

There were none.

"We will continue acceleration, shifting to metaspace at 0910 hours tomorrow, and with emergence on target at 1545.

"That is all."

And the images of the CBG's senior officers began winking out.

Junior Officers' Quarters
TC/USNA CVS America
Omega Centauri
1930 hours, TFT

Shay was hard at work building the city of Washington.

Physically, she was in her occutube in her quarters, linked in through a sim builder. The software was designed to let ship's personnel create their own private worlds for downtime or relaxation, and included a sizable library of existing sims for most of the North-American metropolis—New New York; Columbus, D.C.; the Newbraska Metroplex; the SanSan Towers. There were international sites like Quito and Geneva, and a number of offworld sites were available as well—Copernicus Under, Chryse, New Egypt, Kore, and others. It didn't have the Periphery Ruins, though, like Manhattan or the old D.C., and so she was building the sim herself.

She wasn't sure why she was bothering with it. God, she'd

hated the Washington Swamp when she lived there, before her family had finally moved north out of the Periphery to the Bethesda Enclave. Somehow, though, as her tour of duty on board the *America* dragged on, she'd found herself remembering the swamps with something approaching genuine affection.

What the hell was wrong with her?

She'd actually started with a Jurassic sim, a fantasy world of mangrove swamps and brackish water. She'd edited out the wildlife—today's Washington Swamp didn't include dinosaurs or pterodactyls—as well as the shrill screams, bellows, and jungle titterings in the background. Using tools from the sim builder, she'd begun adding the shells and island-debris piles of buildings and half-swallowed monuments, working from memory. She was pretty far along, now. She'd finished the stump of the old Washington Monument, thrusting up from its rubble pile and partially shrouded in rampant kudzu. The white husks of the Smithsonian buildings were in place as well, rising like crumbled cliffs to either side of the broad expanse of water that once had been the Mall, and the Capitol Building on its island to the east. The Reagan Trade Tower; the DuPont Arcology; the ruin of the Connecticut Circle Complex, where she'd lived with her family, farming the broad rooftop enclosure with its shattered glass dome—she'd completed all of those, and more. She was working now on modeling the buildings along the Kalorama Heights, rising from thickly wooded land high enough to have escaped the general flooding of the low-lying ground to the south. In her mind's eye, she painted the rugged hillside along the Rock Creek Estuary, cloaking it in gnarled swamp oaks dripping with Spanish moss. South, past the massive white cylinder of the DuPont, it was all mangroves.

She was having trouble modeling people, though. The standard tool set with the software let her import background people, anything from individual friends to the thronging hordes of Ad Astra Plaza, but they tended to be of a uniform type: squeaky clean and smiling, wearing anything from skin-suit utilities to pure light. You never saw a rooftop farmer with dirty hands and cracked nails . . . or a fish trapper with straggly hair and wearing filthy rags. No oil-stained mechanics, no wrinkled olders, no frollops or polesters, no barge dwellers, no commuwatchers with their handcrafted bows, no *Prims*.

But that was okay, because it wasn't the people she missed so much as the solitude. Despite the constant danger of raids by Prim rebels from the far side of the Potomac Estuary, Shay had never been happier, she thought, than when she was alone in her skiff, checking the fish traps among the mangrove roots along the placid, dark waters over what once had been the Washington Mall.

Her project, she'd decided, was mostly a means of helping herself get used to her implants. As a non-citizen Prim, she'd not been eligible for even the free and most basic set. That had never been a problem so far as she was concerned. Most folks in the Periphery didn't want the Authority electronically peering into their business in any case, and if there was no such thing as universal health care or Net access, there were also no taxes, no registration checks, and no security scans. Not until she'd joined the Navy and received the standard military issue implants during basic training had she been able to interface with the electronic world around her. She used her cybernetic implants now, of course, for everything from downloading morning briefings to ordering breakfast to piloting her Starhawk, but it wasn't until she could express herself with them *creatively* that they truly felt a part of her.

So why this longing for the Washington Swamp?

Most likely, she thought, it was because when she'd lived in the swamp she'd been free. There'd been rules within the community, of course, but for the most part, people had left her alone and she could be herself. As a Navy aviator, she was constantly under someone's eye—if not that of her squadron leader and the CAG and his staff, then the eyes of her squadron mates who still thought she was a little odd, a little different, just because she was a Prim.

Well, fuck them all, very much. . . .

A light winked within her consciousness. Someone Outside wanted her. She queried, and Lieutenant Rissa Schiff's name appeared.

Now, what in hell? . . .

Shay saved her work, then disconnected from the program. The humid swamp of the Washington ruins faded away, and she lay once more within the narrow confines of her enclosed rack. The end of the occutube dilated open and she grabbed the handholds and pulled herself out.

Rissa Schiff stood in the middle of the compartment, wearing her Navy grays and looking distraught. Her face was red, the eyes puffy. She'd been crying.

"Ms. Schiff?" Shay said, concerned. "What is it? What's wrong?"

"I'm sorry," Schiff said. "I . . . I . . . I don't know why I'm here. I need to talk, I guess. . . ."

"About what?" But Shay knew the answer before the words were out. "Oh . . . him."

"Sandy . . . Lieutenant Gray. I'd hoped . . . I'd hoped we'd find him on this side of the Triggah."

Shay sighed. "I know. So did I." She thoughtclicked an icon in her mind, and a seat big enough for two people grew out of deck and bulkhead behind them. Shay put her arm around Schiff and sat her down. "You miss him, don't you?"

"Of *course* I miss him! Don't you?"

Shay nodded. "Of course I do."

It was an awkward moment for her. One of the defining cultural characteristics of most Prim communities was a somewhat antiquated belief in monogamy, the close and exclusive pairing of two people sexually, socially, and economically. Social anthropologists liked to point out that in the savage surroundings of many Prim communities, a close-paired couple had a better chance of survival than an individual . . . or than a line or poly grouping. The idea of bonding with just one other person sexually seemed quaint at best, a mild perversion at worst; it was different, *alien*, a break with the accepted civilized norms of civilized North American and European culture.

Shay was well aware that most of the other pilots in the squadron simply assumed that the two Prims, Gray and Ryan, had something going together.

It wasn't true, in fact. Shay liked Gray, and knew he liked her, but perhaps it was the expectation of others itself that had kept her a bit aloof from him—a relationship that was strictly business, strictly professional.

She also assumed that Gray had been having sex with Schiff since before she'd come aboard, back when Lieutenant Schiff was still an ensign in *America*'s avionics department. She'd not been sure what their relationship was now, though Schiff's unhappiness at the moment was suggestive.

Shay pushed past the discomfort, and pulled Schiff a little closer. "You know, hon, there's scuttlebutt that the Sh'daar must have picked him up after he came through the tunnel. If he's alive, he might be on that moving planet they spotted.

"What . . . what if he was on that battleship?"

"Then he's dead, and there's not a thing we can do for him, except to remember him."

Schiff began sobbing quietly.

"But if he's still alive, we *will* find him. We don't leave our own behind. Ever."

And she held the younger pilot for a long time.

Chapter Twenty-One

Trevor Gray
Omega Centauri
0235 hours, TFT

Gray was asleep when his AI switched back on.

He'd let himself drift off because there wasn't anything else he *could* do. His AI would switch on, or it wouldn't, Lieutenant Schiere would show up or not, the fleet would arrive with particle beams burning and fighters zorching or it wouldn't . . . and since Gray couldn't affect any of these things himself, he fell back on that most ancient of prerogatives of military men throughout the ages—the ability to grab some personal downtime whenever the opportunity presented itself.

But he became aware of links opening and in-head icons switching on and came fully awake in an instant. "You're back!" Then an unpleasant thought occurred to him. "Is that . . . you?"

"This is your Starhawk Gödel 920 artificial intelligence linking through your implanted personal assistant," the familiar voice said in his head.

"Where the hell have you been?" Gray's own shout, ringing within the close confines of the fighter's cockpit, startled him. He'd not realized that he'd been that stressed.

"I have not been anywhere," the AI replied. "Unlike humans, my existence depends upon the presence or absence of superpositional quantum states within a crystalline matrix. I can be erased or copied, but not moved within the conventional meaning of the word."

"You've been off-line," Gray replied, "for eleven fucking hours! You must have been *somewhere*!"

The AI didn't answer, and Gray realized that he was trying to argue with it as though it were human. It was extremely intelligent, but human it was not.

He took a deep breath and tried again. "Do you have any record of events during the past eleven hours?"

"Negative. We were experiencing a visual feed from outside sources, observing the Six Suns and some unusual artifacts in the sky." There was a pause. "I cannot now regain that link."

"Do you feel . . . any different?"

It was a stupid question, Gray knew, but he couldn't think of any other way to phrase it. Artificially sentient systems didn't *feel*, though they certainly could imitate human emotions if they needed to.

"I submit that I would not be aware of any difference in my own mentation," the AI replied, "since stored memories of past mental states might have been altered."

"So why would they switch you off for half a day, then just switch you on again?"

"Unknown. I believe it possible, however, that the intelligences running the local information systems essentially froze my overall memory and processor quantum states in order to avoid decoherence."

Gray's understanding of how AI computer systems worked was weak. After all, he used the things, had elements of quantum computer technology implanted in his central nervous system, but he didn't need to know how they worked.

He knew, however, that his AI functioned through the manipulation of qubits—quantum bits. Where classical computers operated on binary bits—one or zero, on or off, yes or no—quantum computing used the superposition of those two states to define a far vaster range of possibilities. During his training, he'd been given a brief explanation of the mathematics, and been introduced to the concept of a Bloch sphere; if the binary bit possibilities were represented as the north and south poles on a sphere, the probability amplitudes of superposition included any point on the sphere's entire surface.

The problem with using quantum states in computers, however, was that even the act of simply observing the system could change it, a process known as decoherence. His AI was suggesting that their captors had somehow isolated the computer system's memory and processors, taking them off-line, in order to . . . do what?

"Run diagnostics," Gray told the AI.

"I have been doing so. I should note, however, that if malicious changes have been made to my programming, I would likely also be programmed not to be aware of them."

"I know. Do it anyway."

A hard knot of fear uncurled within Gray's gut, and his heart was pounding. As a Prim, he'd never particularly trusted modern computer technology. Kids growing up on the mainland—*citizens*—received their first cerebral implants within a year or two of being born, and had those systems upgraded when they started formal educational downloading, usually before age four. Gray hadn't received his first implant until he'd been inducted into the Confederation Navy in his early twenties. Worse, he'd grown up on the Periphery hearing stories all his life about how the citizens on the mainland weren't entirely human, how they were controlled by their implants, how the monolithic Authority could watch and record everything they did, integrating them into the global network as if *they* were cubits in a vast, planet-sized computer.

Scare stories. Propaganda, taking advantage of the natural human tendency to fear the unknown, to focus on *us* against *them*. When he'd joined the Navy, Gray had actually begun a kind of late blossoming. A whole new world had opened up to him through downloads from the global Net. The Authority didn't really watch all of its citizens all of the time . . . or if it did, you were never aware of it. Hell, even if they did, the advantages of universal health monitoring, instant in-head communication with anyone else within the network, access to any and all information about anything and everything with a simple thoughtclick . . .

It sure as hell beat grubbing around in rooftop gardens above the watery canyons of Manhattan, hoarding precious caches of nano for food, clean water, and clothing, or hunting rats in the labyrinthine ruins of the TriBeCa Tower. People on the Periphery tended to romanticize the so-called free life of the Ruins, but what that freedom generally meant was freezing in the winter, fighting off raids by rival clans, and dying of any of a ridiculous number of diseases or injuries because you didn't have the medinano to treat them.

As Gray thought about it, it wasn't the technology that had bothered him for these past few years so much as the isolation. His fellow TriBeCans had been his family, one of the most powerful independent clans in the Ruins. They were all gone now—God knew where. Some time after he'd left, joining the Confederation Navy in a desperate bid to get medical help for his wife, they'd been wiped out by a rival gang—probably before the tidal wave that had scoured the Ruins during the Defense of Earth.

Since coming on board the *America* he'd made a few close friends—Ben Donovan . . . Rissa Schiff . . . Shay Ryan, his fellow Prim in the squadron. Most of his squadron mates had kept their distance, though, or actively closed ranks against him. Worse, he'd even started keeping his own distance from Schiffie and from Shay, just because of the rumors and the snide comments about Gray and his monogie perversions.

Gray pulled himself up short. What the hell was he doing? Somehow, his memories, memories he generally kept tightly locked down, had started rising as if of their own volition.

"I think," he heard his AI say, "that *they* are interested in your thoughts on technology."

"They're working through you somehow, aren't they?"

"Unknown. I cannot detect their presence. However, it is distinctly possible that they are using me to access your mind, your memories, through your personal assistant. If they did indeed copy me without creating decoherence of my quantum storage matrices, they would have had ample time to examine my structure and operational algorithms, plan and initiate desired changes, and even test those changes within a virtual environment."

"But what do they *want*?" It was a scream, piercing in the fighter's cramped cockpit.

Gray realized that he was terrified, on the verge of panic. He was trying desperately not to think, wondering if the Sh'daar could read his mind through his PA, wondering how he could block them, how he could fight back, wishing he could somehow claw the nanochelated microcircuitry out of his skull now, before they peered any deeper into his memories, into his *soul*.

"I believe they want to communicate," the AI replied.

"So where is that virtual Agletsch? We were doing okay with that approach."

"As you point out, Thedreh'schul is a virtual Agletsch, meaning that she is an illusion created by a complex AI system. I have the impression that we are dealing with a very large, very powerful AI rather than organic sentients. Clearly, this intelligence understands human language, thanks to contact with the Agletsch. What it does not understand are the myriad points of attitude, belief, conditioning, and worldview inherent in human existence—human psychology, if you will." The AI broke off suddenly, then added, "Someone wishes to link with you."

"Who? *What?*"

"Unknown."

Gray took several deep breaths, forcing himself to at least

a ragged imitation of calm. If the Sh'daar had wanted to kill him, they wouldn't have gone through all of this.

"Put them . . . put them through," Gray said.

And his cockpit faded away, replaced almost at once by a place that Gray knew very well. . . .

Admiral's Quarters
TC/USNA CVS America
Omega Centauri
0250 hours, TFT

Rank doth have privileges beyond the ken of the lower ranks. Koenig's private quarters were adjacent to his office and constituted a small apartment suite with separate living and sleeping areas. Unlike the stacked bulkhead occu-tubes used by junior officers and enlisted men, his bed was thought-responsive and mutable, capable of shifting from flat and open to womblike and close, with adjustable heating, pressure, and surface texture.

Nevertheless, Koenig couldn't sleep.

He could have linked into the bed's electronics through his personal assistant and allowed it to adjust his brainwave patterns, lowering him into unconsciousness, but he didn't like the muzzy and incoherent feeling left when the program brought him back out. If he was awakened in the middle of the night watch for an emergency, he needed to be instantly alert. The medtechs all assured him that electronically enhanced sleep induction—*eesie* as it was popularly known—was completely natural and should leave no unpleasant side effects, that any side effects he *was* feeling must be purely psychological.

Koenig didn't buy it. He'd resorted to eesie a time or two over the years when he'd been afflicted by particularly severe insomnia, but he much preferred to rely on his organic brain's rhythms and chemistries.

He was, he realized, lonely, nothing more.

He had his bed unfolded to full-open, and was staring up at the viewall which ran from the deck toward the foot of the bed up the curve of the bulkhead to the gently ascending ceiling over his head. He often liked displaying scenes of Earth there, but at the moment it was linked to the ship's astrogational sensors, showing the stars outside the ship.

Ten and a half hours into the acceleration phase of the jump, *America* and her consorts had traveled some three and a half billion kilometers from the TRGA tunnel. Their speed now was 189,000 kilometers per hour, some 63 percent of *c*. At that tremendous velocity, the stars outside were only just beginning their relativity-induced crawl toward the starbow effect, and were so tightly clustered across the entire sky that it was impossible to note with certainty any distortion at all. Had his eyes been more sensitive, he knew, he might have noticed that the stars in the direction of their travel were glowing just a bit brighter and a bit bluer. Now that he knew what to look for against that stellar backdrop, he could see the Six Suns directly ahead.

God, he missed Karyn. Eight months since her death, and the hole inside, if anything, gaped worse than ever.

He resisted the temptation to talk to her simulation, his PA.

Koenig's sleeping quarters were equipped with some high-technology innovations common enough on Earth, but rare within the Spartan confines of military warships in space. Ginnie was one, sealed at the moment inside a storage compartment in the bulkhead nearby.

Ginnie the Gynoid, Mark XII, was a commercial sex surrogate. She had a respectable and long-established pedigree; a German firm had first marketed Andy the Android as far back as the early twenty-first century, a humanoid robot so lifelike that she'd actually managed to leap the barrier of the uncanny valley. The more expensive models had actually simulated breathing and pulse rates, both of which increased if you stimulated certain portions of their anatomy.

Ginnie was far more sophisticated than her precursor of four centuries before. She could talk, for one thing, using a link to the local network to acquire an AI personality human enough to beat even the toughest Turing Test. She could move with human smoothness and precision, her eyes would follow yours and blink in a lifelike manner, and microactuators gave her an incredible range of expressions and emotional simulations. A nanomatrix within the gynoid's skin and facial bones allowed it to sculpt itself into a good double of any specific person.

And there was more. Through virtual links, it was even possible for a human partner to teleoperate Ginnie from a distance. Koenig and Karyn had used a Ginnie several times when he'd been stationed on Mars, she'd been up at Mars Synchorbit, and their schedules had precluded their getting together physically. There were male analogues available as well.

Koenig had never much cared for the surrogate, even when he knew that Karyn was looking at him through those lifelike gynoid eyes and her face, that when he touched the thing's body Karyn felt the touch within her virtual simulation tens of thousands of kilometers overhead. Even though his brain couldn't tell the difference, *he knew the thing wasn't real.*

Within a world culture that valued sexual creativity, pleasure, and enhancement, devices like the Ginnie surrogates were common, fully accepted, and reasonably affordable. Koenig, though, had felt an attraction to one woman, Karyn Mendelson, that was almost monogie in its focus and intensity. Karyn had teased him once about his being as bad as a Prim.

As lifelike as Ginnie was, it could not replace the woman he loved. Without her, sex was just . . . *sex*, a physical release that did nothing for the ache in his soul.

"Karyn?" he said.

"I'm here," her voice replied.

But the PA was as much a surrogate, he knew, as the lifelike doll in the storage compartment. And he was still unhappy about the emotional outburst earlier, when he'd angrily cut off Karyn's voice. It was possible that he was allowing the simulation to affect the way he thought, the way he acted, even the way he made decisions . . . and that was not good, not when the lives of fifty thousand people depended on him and his clear thinking.

"Karyn . . . I'd like to have you revert to your base programming."

"You want me to delete the Mendelson persona?"

"Yes. Please."

"Your command has been executed." The voice was not exactly flat, now, but it was neutral in tone, androgynous, and nothing at all like Karyn.

Perhaps now, Koenig thought, he could get to sleep. . . .

Trevor Gray
Omega Centauri
0254 hours, TFT

Trevor Gray was back in the Manhattan Ruins.

Clearly, whoever or whatever was running this simulation was doing so by tapping into his personal memories, using both his ship's AI and his own personal in-head hardware.

He was riding his old broom, the Mitsubishi-Rockwell gravcycle he'd found years before, overlooked in a burned-out shop in Old Harlem. Three meters long, with fore- and aft grav-impeller blocks, they were scarce in the Periphery, but not unknown. The locals called them "gimps," for "grav-impellers," or "pogo sticks" or "brooms," and they operated in a fashion much like his Starhawk, projecting tiny knots of fiercely twisted spacetime that levitated the vehicle in a gentle hover or whipped it ahead at a couple of hundred kph. Too small to mount a quantum power tap, it relied on micro-fusion cells for power, and required periodic rechargings from a generator or a power grid, both a bit hard to come by in the Periphery. Gray had often snuck up to Haworth or west across the Jersey Bay to Newark Shore to tap into the power grid. It was illegal, of course, but there'd been citizens willing to exchange some of their grid juice for a string of fresh fish or a box of antique relics scavenged from the ruins of Old New York.

At the moment, within his mind's eye, he was hovering at a slow drift above the waters of the lower Hudson. The ancient Statue of Liberty rose from her submerged island below, one armed and vigilant; the top six meters of her right arm long ago broken off and fallen into the dark waters of the bay below. Gray often, before he'd joined the Navy, had come here, parked his broom on the Lady's head, and stared across the water at the Manhattan Ruins, vine-covered cliffs rising from the waters that had submerged the original island to a depth of more than fifteen meters.

Gray no longer felt like this was home. He'd come to grips a long time ago with the fact that everyone he'd known here was gone. Including Angela, living now in Haworth with someone named Fred and his extended family.

Damn them all, damn them all. . . .

"You feel some extremely strong emotions concerning your culture," a voice said behind him.

Gray twisted on his broom, looking back. Thedreh'schul was there, standing on what looked like a dull silver circular platter hovering in midair. "Okay, Agletsch!" he said, angry. "What the hell is going on?"

"As I told you at our last encounter, the Sh'daar are curious about you, and the fact that you appear to have been abandoned by the technological facet of your culture. The Sh'daar have been investigating your personal store of memories. There is much, however, that they do not understand. And they do not know how to ask."

"So what's *their* hang-up with technology?" Gray demanded.

"We see within your memories reference to something you call the Vinge Singularity, yes-no?"

Every man and woman in the fleet knew the term. When the Sh'daar, through their Agletsch clients, had demanded that Humankind cease development of certain key technologies in 2367, the assumption had been that they feared a runaway growth in human technological development.

"Okay," Gray said. "Some human philosophers have been expecting us to hit the Singularity any day now for the past four centuries. But we haven't hit it yet."

"The Sh'daar fear the same."

"They're about to hit the Singularity?"

"They fear you are about to do so."

"Okay . . . why? That has nothing to do with them."

"It has everything to do with them. The Sh'daar . . . the precursors of the Sh'daar, I should say, reached their equivalent of the Vinge Singularity some time ago."

Gray nodded. Months ago, in Sarnelli's, a restaurant in Earth's synchorbital complex near the Quito space elevator, Gray and some fellow pilots had shared drinks with Gru'mulkisch and Dra'ethde, the two Agletsch who'd later come along with the carrier battlegroup as alien liaisons. Both had imbibed just a little too much acetic acid that evening, and one had confided that the Sh'daar had *transcended.*

"We knew that," Gray said. "But I don't think we understand it, even yet. I was told once that the Sh'daar had transcended. But why would they want to keep anyone else from doing the same?"

"The ones you know as the Sh'daar," Thedreh'schul said with grave deliberation, "are not the *original* Sh'daar. They are the ones who were left behind when the original Sh'daar . . . transcended. Transformed. Went away. Yes-no?"

The revelation struck Gray like a solid blow to the gut. "Wait! You're saying the Sh'daar, the ones who started this damned war, they were left behind by the ones who went through the Singularity?"

Thedreh'schul gestured with two of her forelegs, taking in the sweep of the Manhat Ruins across the bay. "I believe this is what brought you to the Masters' attention," she said. "You, personally, I mean, yes-no? You are a member of a space-faring, technologically advanced species, and yet you lived for a time under primitive conditions, without access to that technology. And you seem to have resented this."

"I guess you could say that, sure." Gray pointed north, off to the left, where the gleaming, clean towers of Haworth and the Palisades Eudaimonium rose above the horizon, tiny at this distance, but imposing in the realization that they were over forty kilometers away. "Up there, those were the tech-haves. Down here, we were the have-nots."

"But why? Surely it is the responsibility of any technic culture to care for, to *provide* for all of its members, yes-no?"

"Maybe. But there's not a whole lot they can do if some of those members want nothing to do with them, is there?"

The Agletsch hesitated, her eye stalks twitching in a manner that suggested agitation, or perhaps confusion. "Are you saying that you and those with you did not want to partake of that culture? That you isolated yourselves deliberately?"

Gray took a deep breath, then let it out slowly. He wasn't entirely sure of his own reasoning here. The circumstances had been . . . difficult.

"Look, I don't know all of the details," he said. "I know that the global ocean levels were rising all the way back in the twenty-first century . . . uh, about four hundred years ago. You know what a 'year' is?"

"Of course. One revolution of your homeworld around your star. We would call it—" The Agletsch gave an unpleasant and unpronounceable burp from the mouth located at its stomach. "One of our years is the same as roughly eleven-twelfths of one of yours."

Gray was startled when Thedreh'schul volunteered this. He'd not known how long an Agletsch year was, wasn't sure that *anything* was known about the Agletsch homeworld. The spiders were galactic traders in information, and some information they'd simply kept out of reach by putting too high a price on it.

Interesting that Thedreh'schul wasn't dickering on prices or exchange rates here.

"Okay, so four hundred years ago, ocean levels were

rising. They built a wall across this stretch of water, over there." He pointed south, to the ruin of the Verrazano Dam. "There was another dam over there, too, at a place called Throg's Neck, on the East River. You can't see it from here.

"It was an incredible feat of engineering . . . but I guess the technology wasn't quite there yet, because there was still a lot of flooding. Lots of people began leaving the city and rebuilding to the north. Morningside Heights. Yonkers. The Palisades. Haworth. But things *really* got bad a little less than a century later, when the Chinese dropped an asteroid into the ocean."

"Excuse me. The 'Chinese'? Ah. Another branch of your species. You seem oddly . . . fragmented. Yes-no?"

"Fragmented. That's us." Gray wondered if he should be admitting this to the Agletsch . . . and to the Sh'daar who must be listening in somewhere behind her. He had no idea what they knew—or understood—about Humankind. Fractious, argumentative, divided, inconsistent, bigoted, jealous, covetous, warring.

How to show the *good* side of humanity?

For that matter, *was* there a good side, at least as the aliens would understand the term?

And that was just the problem. What was 'good' or 'bad' if you were a Sh'daar?

"The tidal wave," he continued, "smashed through the dam and wrecked the city. Most of what was left of the population moved then. That was in the 2130s, a little less than two hundred years before we met you."

"Your histories indicate that you entered a technological revolution at about that time."

Gray nodded. "Nanotechnology—building extremely tiny machines, computers, robots—we'd been working on that since the twentieth century, I guess, but with the wars and the population problems and the sea levels rising and everything, things didn't really start to take off until late in the twenty-second century. And that caused all sorts of other problems, like a global economic crash."

"I do not understand? 'Crash'?"

"Our economic system fell apart. With nanotechnology, you could feed a handful of dirt into a machine and extract a full-course meal . . . or a suit of clothes . . . or put in enough dirt and you could grow a house. That revolution completely changed the way we put a value on things."

"I am not sure what you mean by 'value.'"

"The Agletsch put a value on information when you trade, right? I give you information in exchange for other information that has the same value? But we have to agree on what that value is, how important it is to both you and to me."

"That I understand. I am accessing your files . . . ah. I believe I now understand fully, though the reference to 'money' is unclear."

"An agreed-upon medium of exchange. After the crash, we did things differently."

Gray hoped the Agletsch didn't ask any questions about that. In the Ruins, he'd grown up with barter, a system that had worked well enough in the low-tech milieu. Once he'd become a part of civilized society, transactions involved invisible electronic exchanges between his in-head circuitry and the local Net, and were rarely visible. He knew about *money* as a historical concept, a kind of marker for trade-item value, but he had no idea as to how it had worked.

"Anyway," he continued, "not everyone moved to the mainland. Some people stayed behind in the Ruins."

"Why? That seems . . . counterproductive."

"I guess you could say so. But humans are stubborn . . . and what works for one doesn't work for someone else. On the mainland, people were starting to get cerebral implants— nanotech computers grown inside their brains and central nervous systems. Some people didn't like that idea."

"But . . . why?" Thedreh'schul seemed genuinely puzzled. "It was clearly in the best interests of all members of your species to enjoy the benefits of this . . . this technological revolution, as you call it."

"Some of us valued freedom more than gee-whiz high-tech."

"'Freedom,'" the Agletsch said. "As in 'personal freedom'? The freedom for an individual to do what she desires, yes-no?"

"That's right."

"For the Agletsch, freedom is simply being what you are. We might say to follow our nature, yes-no? I do not see how this applies to you."

"Our . . . nature," Gray said, "is to pursue what we think is best for us, first, for our families and those close to us, second, and only then do we get around to social groups as big as the city we live in, or the country, or the planet. Sometimes there's conflict between what's good for us and what's good for someone else. Sometimes we have to make compromises, trying to find something that's the best possible for everyone concerned. And sometimes humans are just selfish bastards who don't care about anything or anyone else. And that's when we get into trouble."

"So some of you refused to accept the new technology."

"I suppose so. Mostly, they didn't like being forced to fit into a larger system that they hadn't chosen for themselves. Not everyone wanted a computer inside their brain, but the way things were going, pretty soon everyone needed that computer just to open automatic doors or to pay for dinner or to talk to a friend in another city. Those people stayed behind, living in the Ruins. They called us Prims. Primitives."

"I . . . comprehend. The Sh'daar Masters seem to comprehend as well."

"They do?"

"It seems that those whom you call Sh'daar are also what you would call Prims."

Gray had not seen that one coming.

Chapter Twenty-Two

Trevor Gray
Omega Centauri
0825 hours, TFT

Trevor Gray was awash in imagery.

The scenes had been tumbling into his mind for hours, now, unbidden, uncontrollable, a kind of free-flowing dream-scape of alien and often disconnected sights, sounds, and impressions. Much of it he couldn't understand at all, since he had no idea what it was he was seeing. The Agletsch, Thedreh'schul, was a kind of narrator in the background, trying to explain the scenes as they unfolded.

Sometimes her explanations left Gray more in the dark than he'd been before.

But the view was . . . spectacular.

A star cloud dropped slowly through intergalactic space, a dwarf galaxy just a few percent the size and mass of the Milky Way, but still including within its embrace several hundred million stars in a diffuse and irregular cloud some five thousand light years across. Five billion years before, the galaxy—known to its star-faring inhabitants as the

*N'gai Cloud—had been ejected from the cataclysmic colli-
sion of two larger galaxies that had merged, spectacularly,
into the twin-cored spiral humans knew as Andromeda.*

*That collision had initiated an intense period of new star
formation within the cloud, new stars, new worlds, and, ultimately, new life and new civilizations. Civilizations rose
and fell, engaged in war and negotiated peace, came into
being and passed into extinction. Perhaps a dozen species,
ultimately, forged an alliance that held technological sway
over the entire N'gai Cloud.*

A term, a prefix dredged from a download within Gray's
cybernetic memory, supplied a name for this galactic
culture—the *ur-Sh'daar.*

*By this far-off epoch, the night skies of the ur-Sh'daar
worlds were spectacular indeed. The N'gai Cloud was falling into the glowing sprawl of a neighboring spiral galaxy,
the home galaxy of Humankind, the Milky Way.*

Within his mind, Trevor Gray became the first of his
species to see the home galaxy from Outside. He could see
clearly the hazy, grainy sweep of blue-hued spiral arms
wrapped around the barred central bulge of ancient, red-
dish core stars, could see the clotted curve of light-drinking
dust clouds, night-black, between the pressure-wave flare of
bright, hot newborn suns demarcating the spiral arms.

The N'gai Cloud approached the Milky Way spiral from
just above the plane of its spiral arms, traveling against the
galaxy's direction of rotation about its hub. Millennia trickled past like seconds within Gray's consciousness, a kind of
time-lapse imagery in which he could actually see the slow
and ponderous rotation of the home galaxy in the sky, could
see the frenzied swarming of suns within the falling dwarf
galaxy of N'gai about its tightly compacted core, could see
patterns of disruption forming as the tidal effects of galaxy
upon galaxy distorted both.

*The ur-Sh'daar knew that their worlds would not be en-
dangered by the coming merging of galaxies. Even during
the spectacular collision of the two spirals that had merged*

into Andromeda, very few, if any, stars had actually collided, and very few star systems had been gravitationally disrupted, so vast are the distances between the drifting motes of a galaxy's suns.

True, infalling clouds of gas and dust had generated a new eon of stellar genesis, and for a few hundred million years supermassive young stars, spendthrift and short-lived, had died in flaring supernovae, illuminating the colliding galaxies like pulsing strobes. Some thousands of ancient civilizations, caught in those blazing storms of radiation, had perished . . . but what of that? The stellar explosions had enriched the interstellar medium with heavy elements, promising the rise of new worlds and new life across future geologic epochs.

But the ur-Sh'daar watched the apparent approach of that vast spiral in their night skies with growing alarm. If their worlds individually would survive the coming collision of galaxies, their collective culture might not. By now, the ur-Sh'daar represented a pattern of galactic civilization extending back into the distant past some billions of years. Individual civilizations within that pattern faded, turned inward, transformed, or simply died, but each bequeathed to succeeding generations its accumulated history, knowledge, and cultural imprint.

When the N'gai Cloud was finally devoured by that glowing spiral monster looming huge in the sky, it would be torn apart, its nebulae of dust and gas shredded or compressed into new suns, its existing stars scattered, strewn throughout that slow-turning spiral.

As powerful and as far-reaching as the ur-Sh'daar group culture was, it was a network of perhaps a thousand star systems spanning a mere five thousand light years. Each member world was, on average, a couple of thousand light years from its nearest neighbors, a distance considerably reduced in toward the more densely crowded core. If those member systems were evenly distributed throughout the looming spiral, some twenty times wider than the N'gai

Cloud, ultimately, each member world would be well over twenty thousand light years from its nearest neighbor.

For the varied species of the ur-Sh'daar, technological advancement long before had fallen into a kind of somnambulant balance. A high rate of technological advancement had been discouraged, for too much innovation too quickly might upset the long-standing balance of cultural identity and order. With the unrelenting approach of the alien galaxy, the culture's leaders feared their confederation of species would fall apart. As the density of their cultural network thinned, each world would ultimately lose touch with the others and with the group's shared history and cultural imperative over the course of the next hundred million years or so.

Within Gray's mind's eye, he watched the passing of eons, as the home galaxy of Humankind grew larger and larger and still larger, spanning the entire night sky of one of the teeming worlds of the ur-Sh'daar.

It was sobering to realize that what he was seeing must have taken place as much as a billion years ago, in the depths of the Proterozoic, when life on Earth was only just evolving from single-celled to multicellular organisms. . . .

Primary Flight Control
TC/USNA CVS America
Omega Centauri
0930 hours, TFT

Moments before, *America* had tucked in her skirts and dropped into the black isolation of a metaspace bubble, traveling now at very nearly two hundred times *c*. In another six hours and some, they would be emerging in the heart of the Sh'daar's innermost sanctum, and God alone knew what they would find.

In his head, CAG Wizewski scrolled down through his roster of active-duty pilots yet again, wondering what more could be done.

Suicide, he thought. *It's fucking suicide.*

And suicide was against his religion.

He never discussed it, of course, thanks to the White Covenant, in force for more than 330 years, now. Discussing his religious beliefs with others, though not illegal, was considered a matter of very bad taste. But Barry Wizewski was unusual within *America*'s officer complement. Sixty years old, he actually *looked* it, with a lean and leathery face, graying hair, and wrinkles around his eyes.

There was a simple reason for this. He was a Purist, a member of the Rapturist Church of Humankind, an outgrowth of the old-time Pentecostals who believed that, with Christ about to return soon, it would be best if His people were fully human when He came.

Unlike some members of the RCH, Wizewski wasn't a neo-Ludd. He had the usual military-issue cybernetic implants inside his brain and other parts of his central nervous system. Nowadays, to function within modern culture, you *had* to have that stuff grown inside you, for everything from ordering a meal to opening an automatic door to pulling down data from the Net. But he and others of his faith tended not to accept nano implants for purely cosmetic reasons—and that included anagathics, the various anti-aging treatments. Where most of the others on board *America* could look forward to another century or two of active life, Wizewski, with the benefit of modern medical technology short of anagathic regimens, might live another fifty or even sixty years.

It was, his belief-set taught him, how he lived the years he had, not how many he survived. Suicide in any form was a hideous waste of precious life, besides being an affront against God, Who'd granted that life in the first place.

The suicides he was considering at the moment were those of the surviving pilots of CVW-14, *America*'s carrier space wing.

The campaign so far had been rough on the fighters. *America* had departed from the Sol system six months ago with six combat squadrons, a total of seventy fighters and ninety qualified pilots. After the battles at Arcturus, Alphekka, Texaghu Resch, and here in Omega Centauri, he could barely scrape together forty fighters, and just twenty-five pilots.

The discrepancy was partly the result of new or recycled fighters coming in from the fleet's manufactory vessels, and partly because some of the pilots had been grounded with injuries or with severe psychological stress. Right now, he could put together just two full squadrons, and that was it. Half of those were the old SG-55 War Eagles, too, antiquated spacecraft that had trouble holding their own against the far more advanced Sh'daar ship designs and weapons.

And Koenig was about to throw them all into the meat grinder.

He respected Koenig. He was the best senior officer Wizewski had served under, and by far the ballsiest. But the fighters, those of *America* and those with the other carriers in the battlegroup, were the key to modern space-naval combat, the fleet's first line of defense against enemy attacks, and the means of smashing the enemy fleet or local defenses so that the battlegroup's capital ships could come in and mop up. As a result, Koenig had been using his fighter assets hard, and casualties had been horrific.

Two squadrons . . .

"Barry," a woman's voice said in his head.

"What is it, Sophia?"

Sophia was the name Wizewski had assigned to his PA. A small measure of personal rebellion, that. Historically, Sophia was a figure representing wisdom among the Gnostics, as well as in esoteric Christianity and Christian mysticism—all heretical belief systems so far as the Purists were concerned. It was Wizewski's private joke, shared with no one.

"Two pilots wish to speak with you."

"Very well. Put them through."

"They wish to see you in person, Barry."

"Ah." He sighed, and cut his link with the crew rosters. He was sitting in the command chair of *America*'s PriFly, her Primary Flight Control Center, a large, round room with a low overhead and broad viewall screens encircling the compartment. Twenty officers and enlisted personnel sat at console workstations around him, preparing for the upcoming launch. "Very well. Send them up."

He spun the seat to face an open deck hatch behind him, with steps leading down to the higher-G deck below. PriFly was located in one of the rotating hab modules, slowly spinning to provide artificial gravity.

Two women in flight utilities came up the steps.

Wizewski was surprised. Both of them—Commander Marissa Allyn and Lieutenant Jen Collins—had been in sick bay since the fight at Alphekka. Collins had been badly chewed up by a high-G spin around a loose singularity from a Turusch fighter she'd killed an instant before, and ended up with twelve broken bones and bad internal injuries. Allyn had been the skipper of the Dragonfires until she'd gone streaker. A SAR tug had brought her back on board three days later in an oxygen-starvation coma. Wizewski hadn't expected to see either woman up and about for a long time, yet, and doubted that they ever would be able to strap on a Starhawk again. Those kinds of injuries could scar the mind worse than the body.

"Allyn and Collins, sir," Commander Allyn said, "requesting permission to return to duty."

Wizewski opened an in-head window, checking personnel status. "I don't see a clean chit from sick bay," he told them.

"No, sir," Allyn replied. "There must have been a screwup, somewhere."

"Uh-huh."

"It would be a damned shame," Collins said, "if a freaking clerical error kept two good Navy pilots out of the fight, wouldn't it? Sir."

Wizewski studied the two for a long moment. Both of

them looked drawn and weak. Allyn was trembling slightly, though she was doing a pretty good job of hiding it. Collins looked like she was about to fall over.

"Unless you've been cleared by the chief medical officer, I can't—"

Allyn interrupted him. "How many active-duty pilots do you have on the flight line, CAG?"

"Twenty-five."

"Not enough. How many of those are checked out on Starhawks?"

"Maybe half."

"So stow it, CAG, and give us a couple of ships."

"Neither of you is fit to fly. If either of you pulls more than a couple of Gs, your AI is going to end up flying you home. *If* you don't stroke out."

"And until that happens, sir," Collins said, "we can each take out some bad guys. This is too important for us to be left behind."

"How do *you* know how important it is?"

"We've been following the scuttlebutt," Allyn said. "And our AIs have been riding the Net. We know what the admiral's trying to do, and we know you need every fighter pilot you can scrape up and pack into a Starhawk cockpit."

He looked at Allyn hard. "Last I heard, you were in a coma, Commander."

She shrugged. "I came out last week. And I'm damned tired of lying in sick bay. Give me a Starhawk, CAG. Let me fly."

"*You,*" he said, turning to Collins, "had a punctured lung, a ruptured spleen, internal hemorrhaging, and enough broken bones to keep an entire osteo ward busy."

"It's amazing," she replied evenly, "what modern medical technology can do. A few medinano injections . . ." She stretched out her left arm, flexing the hand. "Good as new."

"Damn it, CAG," Allyn added, "we know you've been dragging in volunteers from every other department on board. By now you must be scraping the bottom of the storage tank. Besides, a skill-set download and a few hours of sims don't measure up to *experience*."

After Alphekka, Wizewski had put out a call for people who wanted to volunteer as replacement pilots in order to keep the squadrons flying. At Texaghu Resch, the casualty rate for the newbies had been over twice that of personnel who'd been flying fighters for a year or more. There just wasn't any way to cram that much link time into the trainees' schedules.

"Look, I appreciate the offer," Wizewski said. "But why put yourselves on the line now? We have just twenty-five pilots, and we're going to be throwing them against odds I don't even want to think about. It's crazy."

"Not twenty-five," Collins said. "Twenty-seven."

"Twenty-eight, actually," Wizewski said. "I'd just about decided that I was going to have to strap on a Starhawk too."

"We have to show these kids how it's done, CAG," Allyn said, grinning.

"Get the hell out of here," Wizewski said, scowling. "I'll clear you with sick bay. You just both make sure you bring your 'hawks back intact, you hear me? If either of you passes out and gets yourself killed, I *will* chew you a new one. Got it?"

"Why, CAG," Collins said, "we didn't know you were into that kinky stuff."

"Out."

As they turned to descend the stairs, Wizewski said, "Collins."

"Yeah, CAG?"

"Did you hear who brought you back at Alphekka?"

She made a face. "Yeah. Prim."

"You know he's MIA?"

"I heard."

"How do you feel about that?"

A shrug. "Shit happens."

"Not good enough, Lieutenant. He was your squadron mate. I didn't expect you to share a rack with him, but I did expect you to show him basic respect."

She appeared to consider this, and then seemed to sag a little. "Look, CAG, I never liked the monogie little bastard. But he was a Dragonfire, and he was a pretty fair pilot. He hauled my ass back to the carrier when I got crunched, and I'm grateful. I'd do the same for him. It's a *family* thing, y'know?"

"Just so you remember that, Lieutenant. See you at high-G."

"Aye, aye, sir."

The bad blood between those two, Collins and Gray, had caused Wizewski endless problems over the past year. At one point, he'd even tried to get Gray to transfer to another squadron. The trouble was that Navy aviators were a pretty clannish bunch, and a lot of them didn't like the idea that Prims could come in and join their exclusive, purebred club. As a group, Navy pilots could be incredibly close and supportive . . . but they could also be arrogant, self-centered and snobbish bastards who would close ranks against anyone who didn't measure up to their standards.

And that could include anyone who was *different*.

Sex, Wizewski decided, most likely was at the root of the problem.

It often was. Sexual relationships among officers and enlisted crew alike were not officially condoned, but neither were they forbidden. So long as each person acted like an adult, kept the drama to an absolute minimum, and didn't cause trouble with petty jealousies, rivalries, or coercion, they could pretty much do what they liked.

And, in fact, pilots in particular tended to swap around quite a bit, forming close bonds that extended well beyond the flight deck and into the occutubes during off-duty hours. When he'd first come on board, Trevor Gray had still been recovering from losing his . . . *wife*. Wizewski made an unpleasant face as he thought that unfamiliar word. He'd probably kept himself out of the general mix of squadbay camaraderie and social mixing, and so stood out all the more as an *outsider*, someone who didn't belong.

He wondered if Collins had made a pass at a newbie, and the newbie had rejected her. *That* would have skewed her programming, but good. Might explain the bad blood there, at least.

Wizewski wasn't a monogie, but he knew very well what it felt like to be an outsider, not quite in synch with the local cultural norms.

Gray was gone, but Collins would be flying with another Prim, Ryan, from the Washington Swamps. And she'd damned well better suck in her bigotry and act *professional*, or Wizewski would break her all the way down to civilian.

Assuming they survived this afternoon.

Twenty-eight against the Sh'daar fleet. . . .

Suicide.

Trevor Gray
Omega Centauri
1015 hours, TFT

"I don't understand," Gray said, interrupting the march of unfolding images. "*That's* why the Sh'daar don't believe in advanced technology? It would upset the order of their civilization?"

"No," Thedreh'schul told him. "In fact, the imminent collision of galaxies spurred technological development to an unprecedented degree. If the member worlds of the N'gai Cloud civilization were to maintain some level of coherence or cultural unity, they would *have* to advance technologically, and advance to an enormous degree. Ships that could cross twenty thousand light years within a brief span of time, perhaps. Portals, doorways that would allow a being to step from one world to another as if from one room to another. Life spans so long that a thousand-year voyage meant nothing. Forms of communication involving entangled quantum particles allowing messages to pass instantaneously across a hundred thousand light years. All of these were considered, yes-no? All were tried. Ur-Sh'daar technologies exploded in number and in accelerating advancement.

"The ur-Sh'daar learned to re-engineer stars."

"The Six Suns," Gray said.

"Among other engineering feats, yes. What you call the Six Suns created a unique gravitational environment for some of the ur-Sh'daar experiments, as well as a kind of cultural beacon designed to unify and focus the member civilizations. In a more immediately practical development, they also learned to take the mass of a star and collapse it into a state of neutronium hyper-matter, shaping it into a cylinder rotating at close to the speed of light."

"The Texaghu Resch gravitational anomaly," Gray said quietly.

"Yes. Created in pairs tuned together, they formed artificial wormholes that could span tens of thousands of light years. The ur-Sh'daar began exploring, probing into the looming spiral galaxy, creating a network of far-flung gateways—what you call the TRGA cylinders or tunnels. We Agletsch heard of them only as legends. For us, they were the *Kir'ghalleg v'nroth*. You would say . . . 'Across the Depths,' yes-no?"

"I think I like 'TRGA' better," Geray said. "Easier to pronounce."

"Either way it is only a name," Thedreh'schul told him. "No matter what these devices were called, they were intended to link together a scattered ur-Sh'daar union, yes-no?

"And more . . ."

Though life on Earth had only begun blossoming into multicellular forms over the past couple of hundred million years or so, though terrestrial life had only recently discovered the key biological masterstroke of sex that would end an evolutionary bottleneck and lead ultimately to the evolution of intelligence, Earth's galaxy nevertheless teemed with sentient species. The galaxy had first coalesced out of vast collapsing clouds of dust and gas and newborn stars perhaps a billion years after the big bang. Though several

*successive generations of exploding stars were required to
enrich individual galaxies to the point where solid worlds
could be formed that could give rise to life, to intelligence,
and to technology, the first technological civilizations must
have begun exploring their galactic neighborhoods as much
as 2 billion years before the birth of Earth's sun.*

*By the time the ur-Sh'daar began exploring the new
galaxy, that spiral was home to perhaps 50 million intelligent species.*

*The majority of these, for one reason or another, never
developed a technic culture. Some evolved within the deep
abyssal realms of their world oceans, or in oceans locked
away beneath planet-wide ice caps on worlds like Europa
or Pluto in Earth's solar system. Many evolved in the atmospheres of gas giants, with no solid surface and no means
of mining metals or creating plastics or developing any of
the other accoutrements and necessities of technic civilization. Many evolved in reducing atmospheres or carbon dioxide or methane-ammonia or other exotic but common gas
mixes, where fire—hence smelting—was impossible. And
so, tragically, many species ended their own existence as
their technological development was still aborning, through
miscalculation, through cosmic accident, to asteroid impacts and nearby supernovae, and all of the myriad other
catastrophes that threaten any planetary species.*

*But at least one tenth of 1 percent of those intelligent spe-
cies managed to survive. They'd developed on worlds with
oxygen atmospheres, permitting fire, metals smelting, and
the development of primitive technologies. Or they developed through advancements in exotic chemistries that by-
passed the need for open flame, or learned to extract metals
from the throats of hot volcanic vents in the deep ocean
or on worlds with unoxygenated, reducing atmospheres. A
few were helped by more advanced others, the technically
gifted descending to help those trapped in technological
bottlenecks—*

Gray thought of the gas-giant dwelling H'rulka.

Fifty thousand technic civilizations, a very great many of them star faring, spreading out through the length and breadth of the Milky Way 6.5 billion years before the rise of Humankind.

And then the N'gai Cloud had descended upon the galaxy, bringing with it the ur-Sh'daar. . . .

Chapter Twenty-Three

CIC
TC/USNA CVS America
Omega Centauri
1510 hours, TFT

At long last, *America* approached her Emergence point.

Koenig sat in his command chair in the carrier's Combat Information Center, watching, expressionless, as the CIC team sat strapped down and linked in. The tactical tank showed the expected positions of the other ships of the CBG; how good a guess that projection was would be determined in another few moments.

A very great deal depended on the accuracy of that guess.

The process of moving faster than light within an Alcubierre gravitational warp bubble had been compared to squeezing a watermelon pit tightly between thumb and forefinger and shooting it across a room. Technically, the bubble of folded-up space no longer existed inside the universe proper, but was skimming along the surface in a hyper-dimensional sense, within an eldritch realm physicists called metaspace. In another sense, the focused gravitational singularities embracing the ship contracted the fabric of spacetime ahead while expanding it astern.

No matter what metaphors were applied, precise navigation within metaspace was difficult, a matter for the extremely powerful sentient AIs running in the astrogation department of each ship. Those AIs had linked with one another during the initial acceleration so that all of the ships shared a precise directional vector, but even so, there would be a certain amount of scatter within the fleet, even across so short a distance as half a light year.

Within metaspace, human starships could manage between 1.7 and 1.9 light years per day, the lower values applying to freighters, stores ships, and the like. The assault force Koenig had organized here consisted entirely of combat vessels, all capable of the faster rates.

Even so, it had taken more than six hours to travel half a light year. Even across so relatively short a distance, there was certain to be a fair amount of scattering at the other end, both in space and in time. The battlegroup was operating in completely unknown territory here. There'd been no opportunity to send out reconnaissance probes to record the local metric, and while a ship was folded up within metaspace, there was no way to take sightings of nearby stars.

With normal interstellar jumps, it was possible for ships to emerge from Alcubierre Drive scattered across several astronomical units, so far that it took ten or twenty minutes or more for the light of each emerging vessel to reach the others, allowing them to coordinate their movements. For that reason, battlegroups tended to emerge well out on the fringes of a target star system. The metric there would be flatter than in close to the system's core, where the gravity of the local star twisted space and made emergence dangerous. And tactically, that gave the emerging ships the room they needed to look at the dispositions of enemy ships and to formulate a plan of attack.

Koenig had absolutely no idea what they were about to jump into now, however. The Sh'daar—if in fact that was who they were facing here, and not simply another client species—possessed a level of technology undreamed of by human science, whole planets capable of faster-than-light travel, and the astonishing stellar engineering displayed by the Six Suns.

He was counting, however, on one point. The Six Suns were so bright that they illuminated a vast region of space, one so large that not even the Sh'daar would be able to guard all of it all the time. Koenig's hope was to emerge at one point within that sphere, threaten whatever appeared to be both vulnerable and important, and use that threat to force the Sh'daar to negotiate.

It was, Koenig had to admit to himself, the longest of long shots. With no hard intelligence, with no understanding of the enemy or his defensive capabilities, the *America* battlegroup could easily find itself cut off, surrounded, and overwhelmed.

But it was all they had. The alternative had been to back off, return to Earth, and go back on the defensive, a strategy that ultimately meant defeat.

Ten more minutes to go. . . .

Thirty-three ships.

Of the forty-one that had come through the tunnel to deploy within the Omega Centauri cluster, five, all of them with serious battle damage, had been left on guard at the TRGA—the *OCGA*, Koenig corrected himself. The astrogation department had dubbed the artifact on *this* side of the shortcut the Omega Centauri gravitational anomaly, or OCGA. Pronounced with a soft C, as in *Centauri*, the term had swiftly devolved into "Oscah," a parallel with "Triggah."

After Koenig's discussion with the assembled CBG captains, three of the ships—two of them Pan-European and one the North-American destroyer *Azteca*—had opted out, decelerated, and returned to Oscah, where they were now waiting with the others.

That *only* three ships in the fleet had balked at making this final assault was nothing less than a miracle, Koenig knew. That the rest had stayed with him was an astonishing declaration of both solidarity and trust.

He prayed that the trust was not misplaced.

"Karyn," he said, then stopped himself, and said instead, "Personal assistant."

"I'm here, Admiral."

The voice was emotionlessly androgynous. But it was better this way.

"Final pre-Emergence checklist, please."

"All stations report readiness for Emergence," the PA replied. "CAG Wizewski states that all fighters are ready for rotational drop, as soon as you give the word. *America*'s launch tubes are configured for high-G KK bombardment."

"Very well."

"Readiness of the other ships is, of course, conjectural, pending Emergence. However, our last communications with the other carriers in the CBG stated that they were readying their fighters, and that General Mathers and Colonel Murcheson were preparing for a possible Marine assault on either the mobile planet or upon such other targets as you might designate."

"How long?"

"Seventeen minutes, twenty-one seconds, Admiral."

"Okay. I want a full sensory sweep as soon as we emerge. Emphasis on tracking those two transponders. If we come out anywhere close to them, I want to know."

At the planning conference yesterday, Koenig had told the battlegroup's command staff and ship captains that they were not here primarily to find the fleet's missing pilots, that to do so simply did not make sound military sense. Nonetheless, those two pilots, Gray and Schiere, were very much on Koenig's mind.

If they *were* alive, prisoners on that mobile alien planet as those briefly intercepted transponder signals had suggested, he was going to rescue them if there was any way to do so.

He could imagine no colder and more lonely an isolation than to be left behind in enemy hands almost 17,000 light years from home. The distance might be far, far greater than that if the speculation about this being someplace other than Omega Centauri was correct, but the difference between 16,500 light years and *millions* of light years was purely academic, and could have no real meaning for the human psyche. Abandoned was abandoned, and it would mean a bleak and despairing death for those two if the fleet couldn't, in fact, reach them.

He wouldn't risk the entire battlegroup *solely* on that rescue.

But if there was a way to pull it off, he would do so.

"Scanners are set. However, Admiral, you should be aware that our chances of emerging within close proximity of that planet are remote."

"I know."

So far as was possible, *America* and the rest of CBG-18 were following the track of that fleeing and unplanet-like planet, but they were going to try to emerge around three thousand astronomical units from the center of the Six Suns, within what humans thought of as the habitable zone for six stars of that incredible brightness.

There was no reason to think that what humans found "habitable" would apply to the Sh'daar, however. If the planet had emerged ten thousand AUs from those blue-hot beacons, or if it had continued on to, say, just two thousand AUs out, the battlegroup would emerge many hours, many *days* away from it.

"I know," Koenig said, repeating himself. "But sometimes miracles happen."

"I do not understand."

Koenig smiled at that. Karyn Mendelson *would* have understood.

But she had been human, not an artificial intelligence.

"No," he said. "You wouldn't."

Flight Deck
TC/USNA CVS America
Omega Centauri
1520 hours, TFT

Lieutenant Shay Ryan stepped out onto the flight deck, a vast and echoing chamber ringing with the harsh bray of a klaxon announcing the imminent drop. She hit the touch-patch on her skin suit, which immediately began transforming itself over her body, growing the link points she would need to connect with her fighter. Her helmet was in her ship.

Guided through the labyrinthine confusion of flight-deck personnel, machinery, and waiting fighters by an in-head beacon, she found her Starhawk resting above its nanosealed drop hatch, in the middle of a line of identical fighters. Here, the fighters were in their load configuration, their light-drinking black hulls shaped like loaves of bread, featureless save for their hull numbers picked out in glowing white nanomatrix, their cockpits melted open to give the pilots access.

Her number was 836.

"Hey, Shay!" a voice called. "Luck!"

It was Rissa Schiff, standing next to her fighter a few hatches down.

"Thanks!" Shay called back, grinning. "Let's grab some hard Gs!"

Shay still wasn't sure how she felt about the previous night. She and Schiffie had ended up together inside Shay's rack. It had started out as a cuddle and gone further.

She'd never married, and her Prim monogamous preferences had never been seriously tested. She knew a majority of people from the Periphery *were* monogamous, and that they tended to collide in a fairly messy way when they mixed with citizens and their more normal social mores. Shay didn't care about normal, but she *did* care about fitting in with the squadron. The problem was, she wasn't about to start sleeping with every other pilot on the flight line just to prove she was "normal." Worse, she was wondering, now, how she would handle it if anything happened to Schiffie.

She pushed the thought away. That was monogie thinking. Sex was fun, superb recreation, a way to bond with friends.

It wasn't possession.

She climbed into her cockpit, picking up the lightweight bubble of her helmet, setting it over her head, and letting its rim merge with her utilities. As she connected with her fighter, the AI flooded her in-head display with incoming data and graphics, showing ship readiness, squadron status, and tacsit.

Ten minutes to Emergence.

Ten minutes of waiting.

"Hey, Dragons!" That was Ben Donovan's voice. "We've got VIPs with us!"

"Hey, CAG!" Schiff called. "What are you doing, slumming with the peasants?"

"I just figured you could use my years of experience," Wizewski's voice came back. "A steadying influence, right?"

"And Commander Allyn!" Calli Loman called. "What are you doing back on the flight deck?"

"Looking out for you newbies," Allyn replied.

"Do I relinquish command to you, Commander?" Donovan asked. "Or to Captain Wizewski?"

"I'll take it," the CAG replied.

"And Lieutenant Collins too," Lawrence Kuhn said. "Man, this is like old-home week."

"What would you know about it, newbie?" Collins called back.

Shay listened to the banter, realizing just how serious things must be. The CAG was senior command staff; his presence in a fighter was only a little less astonishing than if Captain Buchanan or Admiral Koenig himself were to come down here and strap on a Starhawk. And Allyn and Collins . . . those two had been so badly wracked up at Alphekka. What the *hell* were they doing here?

The fact of their presence was not exactly reassuring. From the scuttlebutt she'd been hearing over the last couple of days, this assault deployment was going to be rough—rougher than anything *America* had seen yet in this war.

But at the same time, the fact that they were here made her feel . . . accepted. Part of the team.

Almost as warm and wanted and needed as she'd felt with Schiffie last night.

"Dragonfires!" CAG called over the squadron channel. "Five minutes to Emergence! Stand by for drop!"

Trevor Gray
Omega Centauri
1525 hours, TFT

"They invaded the Milky Way galaxy," Gray said, interrupting again the narrative and the flow of accompanying images. "Is that what you're saying? Your damned ur-Sh'daar came into the galaxy and began destroying any civilizations they found, anyone who might have posed a threat to their cockeyed sense of 'order'!"

He was thinking of the Chelk. He'd heard scuttlebutt, before the Battle of Texaghu Resch, about how the Agletsch had identified a star-faring species destroyed thousands of years ago by the Sh'daar. "Glassed over" was how the Agletsch had referred to the Chelk homeworld, somewhere in the vicinity of the Sh'daar wormhole tunnel.

"Not at first," Thedreh'schul told him. "And not the ur-Sh'daar. They *did* open a number of gateways from the N'gai Cloud to our galaxy, and they began establishing relations, peaceful relations, with a number of local star-faring civilizations. After all, it was possible that many of those cultures, once contacted peacefully, might be folded into the ur-Sh'daar polity, become a *part* of that order.

"But after only a few million years, a disaster wrecked . . . everything."

"What disaster?"

"An . . . event. What you refer to as the Technological Singularity. In rapid succession, the member species of the ur-Sh'daar milieu . . . changed."

"What happened? They changed how?"

For answer, the images began flowing once again.

• • •

He walked the streets of a civilization far in advance of his own. Intricate structures towered into the sky, or floated serenely overhead. Enormous domes enclosed hidden facilities kilometers across, and fluted, sponsored, twisted towers of alien design stretched tens of kilometers into the air. Gray saw a dozen cities on a dozen worlds, the products of a dozen mutually alien minds, from the subsurface crystal caverns of the troglodytic Zhalleg to the shape-shifting nanotechnic dreamscapes of the Adjugredudhra to the etched cliff faces of the Baondyeddi.

He saw . . . beings, intelligences utterly unlike anything with which he was familiar, save that all possessed keen and curious minds, and all used various forms of technology to shape and reshape their environment . . . and themselves.

One species bore the Agletsch name of Groth Hoj, though their own name for themselves was based on subtle changes in the colors and luminescence of certain of their cephalic tentacles. The Groth Hoj had pioneered the use of robotics beginning some 300,000 years earlier, and now possessed bodies of advanced plastics and ceramics that never died and never wore out. Some few Groth Hoj were ultra-traditionalists, however, who'd never made the transition from organic bodies to invulnerable robotic shells. The assumption, as the millennia passed, was that these Refusers, as they were known, would pass into extinction.

Another species was the Adjugredudhra . . .

The stack of sea stars with twisted, branchlike arms and tendril eyes Gray had seen earlier.

They'd made astonishing advances in the science humans know as nanotechnology—the ability to build tinier and tinier machines and computers—until they could literally remake their bodies from the inside out, replacing worn-out organic parts cell by cell until they achieved true immortality. Eventually, the Adjugredudhra began abandoning their biological shapes, weaving their organic being into cybernetic organisms that mingled flesh and inorganic components.

Again, however, some of them rejected the technological path, and became Refusers.

The F'heen were yet another species, marine swimmers that had evolved in the shallow, suns-lit seas of their world, with telepathic gestalt minds, school-group organisms perhaps similar in some ways to the group intelligence of a termite mound on Earth. These were the flashing, weaving, shifting spheres of fishlike creatures Gray had seen before. A million years earlier, they had formed a technological alliance with another species, the F'haav, dry-land organisms like swarming masses of angleworms, also with group minds. These were semi-intelligent only, but adaptable and pliable and possessed of minds enough like those of the F'heen that they could be . . . guided.

Gray resisted the urge to use the word *enslaved.*

The F'heen-F'haav symbiosis allowed the marine F'heen to breed new varieties of the worm masses, ultimately developing metallurgy, computers, and spacecraft. Nanotech gave them the ability to manufacture vast numbers of small ships—the gray and silver leaf shapes seen at the tunnel—which possessed genetically altered F'haav pilots "ridden" telepathically by distant F'heen swarms.

And eventually the F'heen began linking telepathically with their machines and with their slaves.

And, yet again, there were F'heen swarm that rejected the robotic and genetic evolution. They became Refusers.

The Sjhlurrr—

Their own name for themselves was an unpronounceable rumble of multiple vocal sacs . . .

—were the eight-meter red-and-gold-colored slugs. Their slow and ponderous bodies offered certain disadvantages, especially when they began voyaging to other worlds. Less wedded psychologically to a specific body image than many, they focused much of their intellectual attention on genetics, ultimately using nanogenetic manipulation to create thousands of new somatoforms, smaller, for the most part—more nimble, quicker.

But one branch of the Sjhlurrr feared losing the original shape of the species, and bred "pure blood" versions to maintain a link with their genetic past. Refusers. . . .

The Baondyeddi were the flat, circular, many-legged beings with countless sky-blue eyes around their rims. They too took genetic manipulation to undreamed-of depths, reshaping their own bodies to specific patterns for alien environments. In time, those manipulations created smaller Baondyeddi designed to merge with inorganic components, becoming cyborgs that looked very little like their progenitors. After a million years or so, many began transferring their minds to vast computers nanotechnically etched into solid rock, vanishing into artificial realities indistinguishable from, and far more pleasurable than, real life.

Gray remembered the rust-stained cliffs on Heimdall.

Again, those who rejected the shape-shift ideologies were the Refusers.

The Agletsch referred to the transcendence as the Schjaa Hok, *the "Time of Change." It had begun slowly, but then began accelerating. Millions, then billions of individuals simply . . . stopped. Died, perhaps, though the evidence was that each individual organism's three non-physical elements, their* tru'a, dhuthr'a, *and* thurah'a *had survived, passing on to elsewhere and leaving behind only the lifeless shell of their body.*

Gray stood on an alien plaza, surrounded by towering buildings of glass and less readily identifiable materials, watching as the robotic bodies of a pair of Adjugredudhra froze, suddenly, in mid-movement. Others in the crowd nearby appeared to notice, stopped . . . and then they too stopped moving.

And more . . . and more . . . and still more, a rippling wave of transformation spreading out from that center through a crowd of tens of thousands, until the entire plaza was filled with motionless statues, some plastic replicas of the original columns of organic starfish joined in columns, others in floating shells of molded, iridescent materials in myriad shapes, left floating above the pavement, apparently lifeless.

The city, Gray realized, had become utterly and profoundly silent.

The Adjugredudhra had been the first, but they'd swiftly been followed by the Groth Hoj, who also now occupied robotic bodies, and by the F'heen, most of whom teleoperated vehicles piloted by gene-altered F'haav.

The Sjhlurrr were still organic beings, but they were part of an intelligent network linking the entire species through nanotechnic implants similar to the implants used by Humankind. The intelligent component of that network vanished; the Sjhlurrr who depended upon the Net and the technology behind it died.

Gray saw a city transformed, a city burning, as wandering mobs howled in the darkness beneath the horizon-to-horizon sprawl of the galaxy filling the sky.

The Refusers, those left behind by the apparent desertion by their more technologically focused and oriented kindred, found themselves trapped on worlds no longer benign, in cities no longer compliant to their will.

As insubstantial as a ghost, Gray watched the mobs destroy the graceful towers, the immense domes, the intricate spires and floating habs and alien architectural wonders. He saw the fires . . . saw the mobs looting and then turning on one another in spasms of mindless, despairing violence. He saw floating cities crash to earth, saw shimmering green sea domes cracked and flooded, saw the destruction of a galactic culture almost overnight.

It was extremely difficult to get an accurate sense of time. Thedreh'schul couldn't or wouldn't explain how much time had actually passed. The transcending, the *Schjaa Hok*, seemed to happen almost literally overnight, but the narrative might well be showing a time-lapse element. Gray had the impression that the change had taken at least several years, and might well have extended across several thousand.

But in the end, the ur-Sh'daar were gone.

• • •

"But where did they *go*?" Gray wanted to know.

"That . . . is a difficult question, yes-no?" Thedreh'schul replied. "And it may be that the question has more than one answer. A parallel universe, a higher dimensional reality, a singularity pocket in spacetime, an alternate reality branching away from this one, computer-generated simulated worlds, a noncorporeal existence within this universe, even the paradisiacal alternates of religion and myth . . . all of these have been suggested as possibilities. The most favored theory suggests that wherever they went, they are no longer a part of this universe, and so, by definition, they are beyond our powers of observation and of description.

"Most . . . you would say *materialists*, those who reject concepts like the *tru'a*, the *dhuthr'a*, and the *thurah'a*, suggest that they uploaded themselves into certain vast and complex computers, some embracing most of the surface of entire worlds, where they continue to live in artificially generated realities."

Gray thought again of the Dolinar sim set on Heimdall.

"That hardly seems likely," Gray said. "What gets uploaded would be a copy, not the being's actual mind."

"By that time, what was thought of as *mind* was so entangled with machine processes, it's impossible to say what was likely or possible or not, yes-no?

"In any case, civilization fell. The Refusers were left behind to start over. More time passed . . . ten thousand years, perhaps? No time at all when compared to the pace of entire galaxies, which wheel slowly compared to the span of organic lifetimes. The immortals, those with machine bodies and those with altered genetics, were gone. The Refusers, the Sh'daar, rebuilt their civilization and reached out once again for the stars."

"And they found the TRGA cylinders still there," Gray guessed. "And they were able to use them."

"Yes. But the Sh'daar had been . . . scarred. Broken, for a time, in mind and spirit. They developed anew the old technologies, or found the sources of those technologies waiting for them in places like the volume of space warmed by the Six Suns, but they feared taking them too far. What had happened to their civilization once might happen again."

"And what gives them the right to dictate to other species what they can do with their technology?"

"There is no *right*, so far as the Sh'daar are concerned. There is only *fear*."

Chapter Twenty-Four

CIC
TC/USNA CVS America
Omega Centauri
1545 hours, TFT

Emergence. . . .

America dropped out of her unfolding Alcubierre bubble in a flare of dazzling light. Koenig leaned forward in his seat, watching the main bulkhead displays as well as windows open within his mind.

On target. . . .

Ahead, the Six Suns spanned two degrees of arc, the diameter of four full moons seen from Earth. Their glare was so bright they erased even the blaze of cluster stars beyond and behind it, and the AI handling the carrier's imaging systems had to stop the sensor feeds far, far down. Had any human beheld those suns without optical shielding or other protection, they would have been instantly blinded.

Against the glare, silhouettes drifted in the sea of harsh light—at least three small worlds showing visible, black disks, and a scattering of closer artificial structures—deep space bases or manufactories, possibly, orbital fortresses, space habitats of some sort, perhaps. Two widely separated knots of gold and blue-white haze appeared to be a pair of artificial singularities like the TRGA cylinder.

And, at the moment, at least, only a handful of starships were visible, most of them apparently moored to far larger orbital docking facilities.

There was far too much going on, too much to see across the entire surrounding sphere of the heavens, to take it all in at once.

"Admiral," his personal assistant murmured in his head. "We are picking up the transponder signals of the two lost pilots." One of the big CIC screens showed the worldlet enclosed by green bracket graphics, and a pair of winking red points of light appeared on the surface. Accompanying blocks of data identified the world as AIS-1—Anomalous Infrared Source One—and gave its distance as just 1.31 million kilometers.

"Any sign of either the *Nassau* or the *Vera Cruz* yet?" Koenig snapped.

"The *Nassau* has appeared four light seconds below and to starboard," the PA replied. "The *Vera Cruz* has not yet registered on our scanners."

"Open a link with the *Nassau*."

"Transmitting."

"General Mathers! This is Koenig. Execute Plan Bright Thunder."

There would be an eight-second time delay before Koenig could expect to hear a reply.

During the acceleration period leading up to the last Alcubierre transit, Koenig and his tactical team had worked for hours with Mathers, the CO of MSU-17, and Colonel Murcheson, the commander of MSU-17's planetary assault Marines. They'd devised a number of alternate combat plans depending on what they might actually find when they emerged within the habitable zone of the Six Suns. Bright Thunder assumed that at least one of the two Marine assault transports would emerge from metaspace close enough to AIS-1 to effect a landing and secure a beachhead.

It was an assumption for which no one in the battlegroup would have given decent odds. While the CBG had adhered close to the observed line of flight of the mobile planet, the so-called habitable zone for the Six Suns—the region surrounding those stars where ambient temperatures were between the freezing and boiling points of water—was extremely deep, several hundred astronomical units at least. The battlegroup had been targeting the outer regions of that habitable zone, about three thousand AUs from the gravitational center of the Six Suns. This allowed them to emerge within a flatter gravitational metric, It also minimized the chances of materializing out of their Alcubierre warp bubbles within the same volume of space as a Sh'daar ship or world.

And apparently, the Sh'daar mobile planet had been operating according to the same general set of rules. The battlegroup had been extremely lucky.

But despite good luck, the CBG had still been scattered, the inevitable result of tiny discrepancies in course and speed and mass and local metric when each vessel dropped into metaspace for the microjump. Even across so relatively tiny a distance as half a light year, *Nassau* had emerged four light seconds away from *America*, and as the seconds crawled past, more and more of the battlegroup members were appearing on-screen as the photon dumps of their emergences finally crawled across intervening space to *America*'s sensors.

"*America, Nassau,*" a voice said in Koenig's head. "*Nassau* copies. Executing Bright Thunder."

"Admiral," his PA said. "*Vera Cruz* has just appeared on-screen. Range fifteen light seconds, high, astern, and to port."

"Pass them the same message."

"Transmitting."

It would be another thirty seconds before he heard a response form the second Marine transport.

"How many ships are linked in?" he asked.

"Twelve ships so far, Admiral, at twenty-three seconds after Emergence. Now fourteen ships . . ."

About half the battlegroup, then, emerging within a sphere less than thirty light seconds across. Not as bad as it could have been . . .

"Make to all vessels on the fleet net," Koenig said. "We will target AIS-1 in support of Operation Bright Thunder. Initiate acceleration now."

"Now," of course, was a relative term, since the order would take time to crawl its way at light's snail pace out to the other ships. The frigate *Badger*, closest to the *America*, began accelerating first, followed by the half dozen or so other vessels that had emerged close by—the destroyers *Fitzgerald* and *Adams*, the heavy cruisers *Lunar Bay* and the Pan-European *Frederick der Grosse*, and the Marine assault carrier *Nassau*.

America would delay acceleration until her handful of fighters was away.

"CAG," Koenig said. "You may launch all fighters."

"Aye, aye, Admiral," Wizewski shot back. "Launching all fighters."

And the fleet battle was joined.

Captain Barry Wizewski
Dragonfires
Omega Centauri
1547 hours, TFT

"Dropping in three . . . two . . . one . . . *drop!*"

At half a G, five meters per second, Wizewski's fighter fell from the drop tube and into open space. In moments, he was clear of the carrier's shield cap and accelerating toward AIS-1. "Form up on me, Dragonfires," he ordered. "Nighthawks, take formation astern."

All of the SG-92 Starhawks from the Dragonfires, the Black Lightnings, the Impactors, and the Death Rattlers—a total of just fourteen fighters—were now flying as Dragonfires. The remaining fourteen obsolescent SG-55 War Eagles of the Nighthawks and the Star Tigers were flying now as Nighthawks.

Two heavy squadrons . . .

"What about CSP, CAG?" one of the Nighthawk pilots asked. "We're leaving *America* pretty naked."

"Orders, Paulson," Wizewski replied, "straight from the admiral. What's important is that we get down on the deck and cover the Marine landings. The carrier will take care of herself."

Wizewski himself had protested those orders earlier that afternoon, when the admiral had laid out for him the various alternate battle plans. He'd protested again just minutes ago, when Koenig had told him that it would be Dawn Thunder. Traditionally, going all the way back to atmospheric fighters and wet-navy carriers, fighters had performed in numerous combat roles—offensive, defensive, and reconnaissance. Key to the defensive role had been Combat Air Patrol in the wet-navy days, Combat Space Patrol beyond planetary atmospheres. Carriers of either type, cruising oceans or space, had never been heavily armed and were vulnerable to attack. CSP was the first and best line of defense for modern space carriers.

Generally, that had been a role relegated to the older War Eagles. Defending the space around a carrier didn't require speed, high-G maneuvers, or the morphing abilities of a nanomatrix hull, and SG-55s weren't at the same disadvantage there as they were in long-range strikes against heavily defended enemy targets.

But Admiral Koenig had been adamant. "If we do find AIS-1 in there," he'd told Wizewski, "we're gong to need all of the long-range firepower we can muster over that planet as quickly as we can get it there.

The planet, Wizewski thought, was bound to be heavily defended, and the War Eagles would be at a serious disadvantage.

But then, given the numbers they likely would be facing, all of the fighters would be at such an extreme disadvantage that details like speed and acceleration would scarcely matter.

"On my command," Wizewski told the fighter group, "initiate full acceleration. Weapons are free. Boost in three . . . and two . . . and one . . . punch it!"

And *America*'s vast, dark gray shield cap dwindled away astern.

Trevor Gray
Omega Centauri
1547 hours, TFT

The gas giant Bifrost loomed huge in a violet, aurora-charged sky. The hard, bright ruby point of Kapteyn's Star hung just above the horizon at Gray's back, glinting from the distant ancient glaciers and casting weak purplish shadows on the cliff face before him.

He was standing once again within the virtual simulation of the planet Heimdall, with Frank Dolinar at his side. Curiously, Dolinar's voice was that of the Agletsch, Thedreh'schul. "They're not dead," the voice said. "There yet is energy, yes-no?"

Gray reached out and touched the worn and rust-stained surface of the rock in front of him. Flakes of stained rock crumbled and slowly fell at his touch. "*What* energy? The place is dead!"

"You are used to computers that work very swiftly, as you consider time, yes-no?"

"I guess so." Gray wondered where this was going.

"Computers with . . . you use the term 'processors,' yes . . . computers with processors performing some billions or even trillions of instructions per second. And this can require considerable power."

"My AI," Gray said, "can run half a million-trillion instructions per second, with a clock speed of twelve terahertz. That's fast enough for most artificially intelligent systems. But it doesn't require *that* much power."

"Within the rocks on the surface of this planet," Thedreh'schul told him, "are the digital uploads of some tens of trillions of Baondyeddi, Adjugredudhra, and Groth Hoj, all existing within artificial realities created by powerful sentient networks. What power they require is drawn from the light of that sun, from internal heat generated by tidal stresses with the large planet it circles, and from incident background radiation."

Gray brushed at the crumbling rock. "But . . . it's eroding away! There's nothing left!"

Dolinar's simulated avatar reached down and picked up a chunk of loose rock perhaps the size of his head. "Ur-Sh'daar computer technologies were such that those trillions of electronic life forms could have existed within a computer smaller than this," he said. "You would call this . . . massive redundancy, yes-no? If a glacier scrapes away a mountain, if a falling planetoid obliterates half of the world, life goes on."

"My God. They were planning to live for millions of years?"

"Trevor Gray, they planned to live considerably longer than that. The sun is a red dwarf, a cool star expected to continue shining for another fourteen billion years . . . about as long as the universe has existed so far. Tidal interactions with that gas giant in the sky would provide energy until this world eventually spirals free and becomes a planet in its own right . . . and even then, gravitational energy within this world's core will continue providing a trickle of energy, as will ambient radiation and, eventually, the gradual decay of protons. The computer currently is operating at a very slow rate, executing perhaps one line of code every few hours. As time passes and the universe cools, the computer will run more and more slowly, until it executes one line of code in a thousand years . . . or a million. It makes no difference to those within the rock. They will experience the lives they have chosen normally, as will their electronic offspring and countless generations to come, all utterly unaware that trillions, even quadrillions of years are passing Outside.

"The beings within this planetary computer were confident of existing until the heat death of the universe." Dolinar's image dropped the rock, which drifted slowly to the ground, then patted the stained cliff face. "This is their idea of what humans call heaven, Trevor Gray, a means of waiting out eternity."

"Electronic immortality," Gray said. "Or as close to immortal as the universe permits."

"Exactly so."

"And this is where the ur-Sh'daar went when they transcended?"

"*Some* of them," the electronic fusion of Thedreh'schul and Dolinar replied. "As I said, many seemed simply to vanish, and may now occupy other dimensional planes of existence or reality that we cannot access . . . or they may be beyond our reach and our awareness for other reasons we cannot begin to comprehend or even imagine.

"The Sh'daar—the Refusers—never understood precisely what happened with the *Schjaa Hok*, the transcendence. They felt . . . abandoned. Even as they rebuilt much of the fallen galactic civilization, they . . . feared what had happened, and they feared what might yet happen if they or other species reached a similar technological singularity and transcended as well."

"Why?" Gray asked. He gestured at the rock face in front of them, his shadow mimicking both the movement of his arm and his shrug. "It doesn't look like *they're* much of a threat!"

"Perhaps not. Especially when one considers how different the flow of time is for them compared to us. They live so slowly that their lives, their thoughts cannot intersect with ours in any meaningful fashion.

"But there were many, many others whom the Refusers

feared might still have a presence, watching them, perhaps, from a higher dimension. They became fixated on . . . what the Agletsch call the *dhuthr'a*. You might say 'ghosts.'

"The idea has terrified the Sh'daar Refusers and their descendents for millennia. The transcendence had a profound effect upon them, and upon how they look at the universe around them. Their attempt to control or limit the technological development of the new species they met within this galaxy, their use of the Sh'daar Seeds to monitor the development of those species . . . all of this was calculated to prevent a new transcendence."

Gray considered this. "You haven't been entirely honest with me," he said after a moment.

The cliff face, the loom of Bifrost, the glaciers and the wan, pinpoint ruby sun all faded away. Gray stood once again beside the spidery form of Thedreh'schul on the surface of a conventionally living world. Millions of brilliant stars cast an illumination as bright as day. Alien towers threaded their way into the glowing, white sky. The Six Suns, Gray thought, must be below the horizon.

For a time, Gray had been assuming that the alien city was an image of the world before it had become dark and ice shrouded. He'd even wondered if it was the same world as the one he'd visited in the docuinteractive—Heimdall, the moon of the gas giant Bifrost circling Kapteyn's Star.

But what he was being shown simply didn't fit together right. *Time*, he thought, was seriously out of synch.

"We have told you everything we could, as we understand it," Thedreh'schul told him.

"And just who do you mean by 'we'?" Gray asked. "Who's speaking now? The Sh'daar? Or their Agletsch servants?"

"I represent the Sh'daar."

"What world is this? The one you're showing me?"

"The Agletsch call it Gahvrahnetch."

"Your archives? What you called the 'Sh'daar operational center'?"

"Yes."

"And you've been lying to me. Or at least not telling me the *entire* truth."

"We have told you everything we could, as we understand—"

Gray felt the jolt transmitted through the ground. For an instant, the simulation wavered and flickered out, and once again he was sitting within the close, darkened cockpit of his fighter.

Then the alien city reappeared.

"What was that? What just happened?"

"Your fleet has arrived in local spacetime," Thedreh'schul replied. "They are attacking this world."

"*Which* world?" Gray demanded. "The mobile planet where you're keeping me? Or what you called the Sh'daar operational center?"

The imaginal world flickered again, and again Gray sat alone in the darkness.

Lieutenant Shay Ryan
Omega Centauri
1548 hours, TFT

Lieutenant Shay Ryan saw the white flare of a detonating Krait missile on the icy surface ahead just as she loosed a pair of her own Kraits. The objective planet, AIS-1, loomed from tiny to immense in a flash, and for a brief interval blurred past her port side as an immense wall.

After accelerating at fifty thousand gravities for seventy-two seconds, she was traveling at over 36,000 kilometers per second, and the objective world, a dwarf planet barely a thousand kilometers across, had dwindled to a point astern before her human reflexes had time to react.

Her AI, though, had acquired distinct targets on the icy surface and loosed the Kraits precisely on the mark. The targets appeared to be enormous gravitational projectors half buried into the surface, and were probably part of either the dwarf planet's shielding or the means by which its owners moved it through space. Installation after installation vaporized within the glare of one hundred megaton explosions, however, as the flight of Starhawks flashed past. Her AI, with reflexes far quicker than those of organic beings, captured imagery from the world.

The icy sphere was now a world of horrific storms and violently swirling winds. A kind of cometary tail stretched away from the world now, a pale, white luminescence propelled by the intense light and radiation of the Six Suns.

AIS-1, with a diameter of less than 800 kilometers, was a close twin to the frigid dwarf planets Makemake or Haumea within the Kuiper Belt of Earth's solar system. Halfway between the dwarf planets Pluto and Ceres in size, its surface temperature while it had been adrift in open space half a light year away had dropped to a few tens of degrees Kelvin. Massive enough to have compressed itself into a spherical body rather than a potato-shaped planetoid, its surface consisted of frozen methane and nitrogen.

In interstellar space, of course, any atmosphere the worldlet possessed had been frozen out, leaving an achingly cold surface beneath hard vacuum. Hours earlier, however, the dwarf planet had emerged from faster-than-light within the liquid-water zone of the Six Suns, and the frozen surface had begun to boil. Already, AIS-1 was surrounded by a tenuous envelope of gaseous methane and nitrogen. As the surface temperature had lifted above 63 degrees K, the nitrogen had begun sublimating directly from solid to gas. At 91 degrees K, the methane had begun to liquefy, then to sublimate directly into the thickening atmosphere.

The surface temperature now was passing 112 degrees Kelvin—minus 161 Celsius—and even liquid methane was beginning to vaporize. The atmosphere was still extremely thin, but the rocketing surface temperatures were generating fierce storms, as the Six Suns continued to blow traces of the warming gas off into space like a comet's tail.

As she passed the world, Ryan's AI had flipped her fighter

end-for-end and begun to decelerate. Facing now the day side of ASI-1, she targeted another large surface structure and triggered her Starhawk's PBP-2. Tightly focused proton beams, charged particles moving at just beneath the speed of light, slashed through the turgidly churning white clouds above the surface and clawed at half-buried gravitic projectors and field-bleed towers.

So far, there was no sign of enemy fighters, no indication of a defense. . . .

CIC
TC/USNA CVS America
Omega Centauri
1549 hours, TFT

"Admiral," Commander Sinclair said, "the last of the fighters are away."

It had been a fast drop—just twenty-eight fighters, plus ten recon Shadowhawks from the Sneaky Peaks. Those last would not be engaging in combat, but their eyes and electronic ears would be invaluable in this strange and alien space.

"Very well," Koenig said. "Captain Buchanan? You may accelerate."

"Aye, aye, Admiral. *America* is under acceleration."

At five hundred gravities, *America* would accelerate for eight and a half minutes, then begin decelerating until she arrived at AIS-1 with near-zero relative velocity, a total flight time of 1,023 seconds, or a bit over than seventeen minutes. The *Nassau* should arrive at AIS-1 a minute and a half later.

Other ships were already on their way, and would be arriving at the mobile planet a couple of minutes ahead of *America*. And more ships were dropping into *America*'s radio horizon, now; ships that had emerged four light minutes away—half an AU—were now on the carrier's screens and receiving her orders.

Ponderously, the fleet was deploying to converge on the tiny dwarf planet.

The tactical tank in CIC showed a curious lack of enemy fighters or capital ships, other than the handful docked at several large, orbital facilities. That wouldn't last. If, as Koenig thought, AIS-1 was of some strategic importance to the Sh'daar, they would *have* to defend it.

In another twenty minutes, the issue should be decided, one way or the other.

Operation Bright Thunder called for grabbing it so quickly that they didn't have time to get into position. It was a race now, with both sides attempting to grab the metaphorical high ground around AIS-1.

Trevor Gray
Omega Centauri
1550 hours, TFT

Gray felt the repeated shudders rippling through the rock and ice of a world. CBG-18 was giving the dwarf planet a hell of a shellacking.

He wondered if the Dragonfires were up there, what was left of them—Shay and Rissa and Ben. "Is there any way to communicate with our ships?" he asked his PA.

"Negative," the AI replied. "I have been sensing radio impulses through the fighter's emergency beacon transponders. The Fleet almost certainly knows we're here. But I cannot open a voice or Net communications channel. The Sh'daar are blocking it."

"Can you pick up the Sh'daar? Can we talk to them?"

"I may have a possible channel to the Sh'daar. There is a signal—what amounts to a carrier channel for the simulation feed. And I can pick up what is almost certainly side bands or leakage from an artificial intelligence on that channel, possibly the same one that was communicating with us a short time ago."

"What's your impression?" Gray asked. "That AI . . . is it software? Or some sort of blend of organic intelligence and software?" He knew the feeling was irrational, but he desperately wanted to talk to a person, an organic intelligence, rather than a tool.

At the same time, he knew that AIs like those commonly used in the Confederation were just as intelligent—and quite likely far more so—than any human.

"It is impossible to tell. Remember that human-derived AIs were originally designed to so perfectly mimic specific humans that outside agencies could not tell the difference. We may be facing a similar identity problem here."

Gray had to accept this pronouncement. In fact, most humans he knew, now, were themselves blends of flesh and blood and of nanochelated carbon, silicon, and synthetics. And when someone else talked to Gray on the Net, in a virtual reality sim, he was in fact interacting with Gray's electronic avatar, *and it didn't really matter which was which.*

"See if you can connect with it . . . whatever it is," Gray said.

A long minute passed.

And then the alien appeared.

It wasn't an image of Thedreh'schul this time, but of one of the sea-star aliens, the species identified as Groth Hoj. The entire body appeared to be a writhing mass of tendrils a meter or more in length. Some of those tendrils ended in swellings that were probably eyes or other sensory apparatus, while others ended in three-jawed mouths. The vast majority, however, appeared to be manipulatory members. The central mass was a deep, lustrous, almost gleaming black; the tips of the tentacles, however, were rainbow hued and iridescent, and as the tentacles writhed and twisted, the colors changed.

Thedreh'schul had said something about the Groth Hoj communicating by color changes of their tentacles. Gray hesitated. How the hell did you understand something that talked to you by changing body color? And how did you make it understand the sounds coming from your mouth when it might not even have ears, or any concept of what spoken language was?

Then he realized that if he was seeing the Groth Hoj in a simulation, it must have some way of linking in with the local Net . . . and that meant that it could understand Gray if Gray was on that Net as well. He didn't know how it was done . . . but evidently the Sh'daar had tapped into his electronic presence earlier and learned enough.

He would have to trust the technology, even though he couldn't understand it.

"I *know* what you've been trying to hide from me," Gray said. "And I'd be willing to bet that my friends out there know it too."

What do you know?

The words were spoken as a whisper deep within his mind.

"I know that I and those like me have come back through time—maybe as much as a billion of our years—to meet you. And that means that you are in terrible danger."

Danger . . .

"Let me communicate with my people. There's still time. We can stop this. And you and your people can live. . . ."

No! . . .

Chapter Twenty-Five

CIC
TC/USNA ACS Nassau
Omega Centauri
1604 hours, TFT

General Thomas Jackson Mathers was an old-breed Marine from an old Marine family. One ancestor had fought at Guadalcanal, and later marched south from the Chosen Reservoir with the 5th Marine Regiment of the 1st Marine Division, the oldest and largest active-duty unit in the old U.S. Marine Corps. Another ancestor had led the 3rd Marine Aerospace Assault Group against the Chinese base at Sinus Lunicus 180 years later, during the second Sino-Western War.

As for "TJ" Mathers, he'd been a very raw and very green j.g. at Rasalhague, a major in command of a battalion at Hecate, and a colonel in command of a regiment at Sturgis's World. His military career spanned thirty years, almost the entirety of the Sh'daar Interstellar War.

He'd received command of MSU-17, the battlegroup's fleet Marines, just before the Defense of Earth. His command now included some twelve thousand men and women embarked on the assault carriers *Nassau* and *Vera Cruz*, and he realized now that there was a very good chance that it would be up to him to end the Sh'daar War once and for all, here and now.

That he might *lose* that war this afternoon had occurred to him as well, but he wasn't going to focus on that. His Marines, packed like sardines into the battlegroup's two assault star-carrier transports, had, over the past six months, been dragged from Sol to Eta Boötis to Arcturus to Alphekka to HD 157950 to Texaghu Resch and finally here. They'd seen some action at both Arcturus Station and at the alien manufactory at Alphekka, but most of that time had been spent cooped up in the transport squad bays or in their sleeper tubes, waiting out the watches while the Navy grabbed the credit.

But now they had a definite target.

"All Crocs are ready for boost," the voice of Colonel John Murcheson said over Mathers' link. "Just give us the word."

"Roger that," Mathers replied. "Stand by."

The light assault carrier *Nassau* was slowing as she approached AIS-1. The dwarf planet was clearly visible now ahead, a tiny black disk against the diffuse glare of the Six Suns, and showing a faint cometary tail streaming out away from the blue giants. The ice surface of the world, evidently, was rapidly vaporizing, giving rise to a thin but intensely violent and temporary atmosphere. That could make the final approach interesting.

Two points of blinking light indicated the locations of the two Navy pilots being held on that world . . . or at least the locations of their fighters. Whether either or both were alive or dead was anyone's guess at this point.

But the assault force wasn't going in just for them.

"Captain Bradford," Mathers said. "We are ready for disembarkation. Please cease ship deceleration."

"Aye, aye, General," the *Nassau*'s CO replied. "*Nassau* is now under free drift."

"Colonel Riley," Mathers said. "You may begin your launch."

"Aye, aye, sir. Nightwings are go. Initiating drop."

VMA-12, the Nightwings, was the Marine close-support

attack squadron embarked on board the *Nassau*, numbering twelve GGA-20 Nightshade grav-assault gunships. The gunships were essentially two-seater Marine fighters built around massive KK railguns. They were capable only of twelve Gs of acceleration, and so weren't any good at ship-to-ship combat, but they excelled at ground support operations with their fellow Marines. *Every Marine a rifleman first* was an ancient adage going back to pre-spaceflight days. Riley and his Nightwings took a great deal of pride in that claim; it just happened that *their* rifles were a bit larger and more powerful than most. . . .

On his monitors, Mathers watched the oddly buglike, black Nightshades dropping from their launch tubes. As the last fell clear of *Nassau*'s shield cap and began boosting toward the planet, he re-linked with Colonel Murcheson, the commanding officer of the MSU's ground-assault Marines. "Okay, Colonel," Mathers told him. "Coming up on Croc release in twenty seconds."

"Copy, General."

"Stick to your oplan, Colonel. Rescue those Navy zorchies if you can, but your priority is to grab both Blue and Gold and establish solid defensive perimeters around them. Everything else down there is fair game."

"Got it, General. *Semper fi!*"

"Semper fi, John."

Crocodiles, Marine combat landing/boarding craft, were bulky, stubby craft designed to get Marine assault teams on board an enemy warship or orbital station, or to insert them onto a landing zone on a hostile planet. Each carried forty fully armed and armored Marines. Nano docking collars mounted forward could meld with enemy pressure hulls and gain entrance without depressurizing the target; for planetside debarkations Crocodiles used ventral thrusters to come down on broadly splayed landing legs. Massive dorsal turrets provided close fire support, and could transform the landing craft into a semimobile fortress or gun platform once the Marines were ashore.

The winking lights of emergency tracking transponders on two missing navy spacecraft had identified two targets on the dwarf planet's surface, code-named Blue and Gold. Located about three hundred kilometers apart, those structures were the biggest things on AIS-1, and *had* to be important.

Koenig had put it succinctly during their planning earlier for the Bright Thunder option: *Grab the enemy by his balls and don't let go. . . .*

"Croc release in five seconds," Mathers said. "Four . . . and three . . . and two . . . and one . . . *go!*"

Twelve CL/BC-5 Crocodiles slid from *Nassau*'s rotating flight decks, dropped into assault formation, and began their ponderous acceleration toward the objective.

"Assault craft are free and under acceleration, Captain," Mathers told Bradford. "You may resume deceleration."

And *Nassau* began slowing once more, sliding down the lines of grav-twisted space behind her death-dealing offspring.

CIC
TC/USNA CVS America
Omega Centauri
1606 hours, TFT

"We seem to have our pick of targets, Captain," Koenig told Buchanan. "You may fire at your discretion."

"A target-rich environment, Admiral. Aye, aye."

America's CO gave the order, and the twin launch tubes running down the star carrier's spine and emerging at the center of her shield cap loosed a pair of hivel rounds, high-velocity kinetic-kill impactors that streaked silently into the void. The target was a large and sprawling deep-space facility perhaps four thousand kilometers distant, at which a number of large ships of alien design were moored. The first two rounds were followed by two more, then two more again, a double string of impactors hurtling toward the distant target at 14 kps.

They would reach their target in seven minutes, forty-five seconds.

Enemy ships were beginning to converge on *America* and her consorts, rising from the three dwarf planets or casting free from nearby orbital facilities and accelerating toward the battlegroup. *America*'s fighter contingent was rising from the looming white sphere of AIS-1, joined now by incoming fighters from the still-distant *United States of North America*, the *Invincible*, and the *Jeanne d'Arc*, deploying to attack the incoming enemy vessels.

The capital ships accompanying *America* were deploying as well. The *Badger*, the *Wolverine*, the *Lunar Bay*, and the *Frederick der Grosse* were all now accelerating toward the two knots of twisted space in the distance—almost certainly the tunnel mouths of two different TRGA-like gateways, designated by the tactical teams as TRGA-2 and TRGA-3. Koenig didn't want the Sh'daar using those to funnel in large numbers of ships from elsewhere; by posting a frigate and a heavy cruiser at each tunnel mouth, Koenig hoped to create the same sort of bottleneck defense the battlegroup had faced at their entry into Omega Centauri.

The destroyers *Fitzgerald* and *Adams* were maintaining station to either side of *America*, covering the carrier. The railgun cruiser *Kinkaid* and three more destroyers, *Lowe*, *Rodney*, and *Clymer*, were coming up astern, moving toward orbit around AIS-1.

Particle beams reached out from the dwarf planet's surface. White fire and lightning splashed from *America*'s gravitic shields, and the ship shuddered with the impact. No serious damage, but that would be only the first hit of many.

Kinkaid was slamming hi-vel rounds into the planet's surface from several thousand kilometers out. The surface of AIS-1 was almost completely obscured now by swirling clouds, illuminated by the brilliant starlight on its night side, reflecting the arc-harsh blue-white dazzle of the Six Suns on the other. Each KK round impact lit the swirling clouds from below, and vaporized more tons of ice to add to the growing atmosphere.

"Make to *Kinkaid*," Koenig told his AI. "Cease fire on the primary objective." The Marines were getting close, and he didn't want to score an own goal. Friendly fire, as the ancient aphorism had it, was *not*.

"Transmitting, Admiral."

"And link me through to the Agletsch. Are they on-line?"

"As you directed, Admiral. The Agletsch are on-line."

"We are here, Admiral Koenig," Dra'ethde's voice said.

"Are you picking up anything from over there?"

"We have sensed nothing yet, Admiral," Gru'mulkisch told him. "The Sh'daar Seed is silent, at least so far."

"If you can raise anyone on the other side," Koenig said, "do so. This time around, I'd rather talk than fight."

"We will do what we can," Dra'ethde said.

It was a long shot, using the two Agletsch on board as negotiators with the Sh'daar, but the battlegroup had few options. Once the Marines grabbed hold of those facilities on the surface of AIS-1, they would be able to hold them for a time, but sooner or later the full weight of the Sh'daar defenses would come crashing down on the battlegroup, and there would be nothing any of the Confederation forces could do to stave off eventual total and abject defeat.

They *had* to get the Sh'daar to talk. . . .

Commander Marissa Allyn
Over AIS-1
Omega Centauri
1608 hours, TFT

"Break high, Commander! Two on your six! Break high!"

With Colllins' shrill warning screaming in her head, Allyn urged her Starhawk into a tight vector change, twisting around the ship's projected singularity so tightly that tidal stresses tore at her body, and the fighter's nanomatrix hull shuddered and bucked. Two enemy fighters followed the maneuver, closing now to within fifty kilometers. They were complex-looking spacecraft, all angles and jutting parts and flat panels, glittering craft unlike any Allyn had ever seen.

Using the torque from her course change to assist, she spun her Starhawk, facing aft, as she hurtled tail-first above the cloud-wreathed face of AIS-1. They'd been rising above the dwarf world's day side when a cloud of Sh'daar ships, fighter-sized and swarming like hornets, had emerged from the cloud deck.

"I'm on them," CAG Wizewski's voice called. "Fox One!"

"So am I!" Allyn yelled back. Dropping the targeting cursor over the nearest enemy ship, she let her AI lock on target and trigger a pulse from her PBP-2. On her optical feed, the magnified image glowed a dazzling white, then exploded in a sharp, silent flash. Seconds later, Wizewski's Krait missile detonated alongside the second fighter, the fireball engulfing the craft in an instant and vaporizing it.

"Thanks for the assist, CAG," Allyn called. She flipped her fighter again and began clawing for more altitude. Detonations across the surface of AIS-1 were beginning to trail off; the Marine assault craft were on their way in. Enemy fighters continued to rise from the clouds, however. Not all of the bases and facilities on the dwarf planet's frigid surface had been hit in the scant minutes that had passed in the battle so far.

"I've got a possible target at coordinates plus seven-five by minus one-one-niner," Donovan called. "Multiple bogies emerging from an ice mountain!"

A computer-drawn graphic, a sphere marked out in lines of latitude and longitude, rotated in a window in Allyn's head. "I've got it," she called. She was closest, had the best shot. The target was high in the planet's northern latitudes, just beyond the suns-set terminator and uncomfortably close to the spot where Lieutenant Gray's transponder signal was winking. The first Marine Crocodiles were already cutting into the tenuous newborn atmosphere over the nightside.

Her targeting cursor isolated the target area. Radar returns showed a surface facility at the base of a mountain of solid water ice less than a hundred kilometers from the planet's north pole. Though it was still growing warmer, the surface of AIS-1 was still at around minus 155 Celsius. At those temperatures, water ice was literally as hard and as solid as rock. Target lock . . .

"Pass a heads-up to the jarheads," Allyn told her AI. Then, *"Fox One!"*

She thoughtclicked an in-head icon, and a Krait missile tuned for a detonation of one hundred megatons dropped from her Starhawk's belly and streaked toward the planetary horizon. . . .

Colonel John Murcheson
AIS-1
Omega Centauri
1609 hours, TFT

"Missile incoming, Colonel!" the Crocodile's pilot called over the in-head comm link. "Brace yourselves back there!"

"You heard him!" Murcheson bellowed. Strapped into the narrow seats to either side of the assault transport's payload bay, twenty to a side, the Marines of First Platoon, Alfa Company could only brace themselves against one another. The ride down had already been plenty rough. They'd launched three minutes ago, taking advantage of *Nassau's* remaining velocity to swiftly close the remaining few thousands of kilometers between assault carrier and planet, planning on using the tenuous atmosphere for aerobraking. The local atmosphere was still vanishingly thin, so the shrieking winds outside, high-pitched and shrill, carried little force, but the Crocs had hit it at high speed and the shock had been a savage jolt transmitted through deck and hull, followed by an ongoing buffeting that had grown steadily more savage as they dumped excess velocity.

The slit, armored ports down the starboard side of the

compartment lit suddenly with a ferocious radiance that grew swiftly brighter, then began to fade. Thirty seconds passed . . . and then the shock wave struck.

The Crocodile rolled and yawed wildly, the concussion ringing through the cabin with a deafening crash.

"Everyone okay?" Murcheson demanded as the thunder died.

A chorus of "okay," "ooh-rah," and "no problem" crackled back.

"Two more minutes, Marines!" Murcheson told them.

He wondered if that nuke had been a near-miss by an enemy warhead, or if one of the Navy zorchies had gotten a little too enthusiastic. No matter. They were still flying, and the bad guys hadn't been able to knock them down yet.

He opened a window in his head, giving a view of the command deck forward and above, looking over the pilot's shoulder. They were over the dark side of the planet, but rapidly approaching the dawn terminator. Visibility outside was almost nil as they descended through the cloud deck, but the computer painted a graphic outline of the objective ahead.

And then the clouds parted, and Murcheson saw the objective for the first time, a kind of castle with slanted walls and domed turrets, with slender spires and Gothic arches, a mix of architecture at once familiar and utterly alien.

He disconnected from the data feed as the Croc gave a short, sharp burst of deceleration. "Marines!" he shouted. *"Go! Go!"*

CIC
TC/USNA CVS America
Omega Centauri
1610 hours, TFT

"The first Marines have reached objective Gold," Commander Sinclair told Koenig. *"Nassau* has entered orbit and the Choctaws have been released."

"Good." The Choctaw Type UC-154 shuttle was a monster

orbit-to-surface transport. Far larger than the little Crocodiles, it carried nearly two hundred Marines and their equipment. In this case, four Choctaws off the *Nassau* were ferrying down the Marines' heavy artillery—massive proton cannons that would turn their perimeters on the dwarf planet into fortresses.

They would have to hurry. The battle was slowly beginning to turn against the Confederation battlegroup.

It was a simple matter of numbers. Thirty-three capital ships and perhaps ninety-five fighters, all told, with no hope of reinforcements, were squared off against an unknown but *very* large force of alien warships. Sooner or later, most likely sooner, they would be overwhelmed.

An alien warship half a kilometer long, the mass of a heavy cruiser, was closing on *America* as the carrier drifted past AIS-1. Energy beams clawed at the carrier's shields, burning through at three key points. *America* returned fire with her midships particle-beam turrets, exchanging fire in deadly, silent, and invisible salvos. *Fitzgerald* and *Adams* began to maneuver in an attempt to place themselves between the enemy cruiser and the *America*. Bright flashes sparkled along *Fitzgerald*'s flank as screen projectors overloaded and burned out, but the enemy vessel had been hit as well, its blunt, massive prow cratering, then crumpling and peeling back under the concentrated combined fire from all three Confederation ships.

"The *United States* is coming in astern, Admiral. Range two thousand kilometers."

"I see her." With the damaged *Abraham Lincoln* remaining at the TRGA leading back to Texaghu Resch, the *United States of North America* was the only other large star carrier in the assault group, very nearly as massive as *America* herself. Normally, tactical doctrine demanded that carriers be held back out of the thick of ship-to-ship combat, that they be protected behind screens of frigates, destroyers, and cruisers. Their strike fighters were their primary weapons, and those fighters needed someplace to trap and recover at the end of the fight.

Conventional tactical doctrine had gone out the hi-vel launch tube, however, with Koenig's decision to enter the habitable zone of the Six Suns. They would *all* stand together, and if they couldn't force the Sh'daar to negotiate, they would all die together.

Silver-gray leaf ships were streaming out of one of the tunnels, from TRGA-2.

He could see them on a battlespace drone image being transmitted by *Badger*, which was now a hundred thousand kilometers from the tunnel mouth. The enemy had reacted to the battlegroup's arrival too quickly, pushing the cloud of small fighters through before *Badger* and the *Frederick der Grosse* could close with TRGA-2 and get into a bottleneck position. The aliens were coming through in a seemingly unending stream, swirling together into a cloud that flashed and flared with reflected light from the Six Suns.

"Pass to *Badger* and *Frederick*," Koenig told his AI. "Saturate that cloud with hundred-megaton bursts and sand clouds. Use indirect vectoring."

"Yes, Admiral."

Young Gray had shown how to fight that particular type of alien at Texaghu Resch. Indirect vectoring meant sending your missiles out in broad, hi-vel accelerating loops so as to come in on the target from as many different directions as possible. Nukes would thin that alien swarm and overload individual shields; sand clouds traveling at thousands of kilometers per second would sweep through the rest like hurricane winds.

The image from the *Badger* suddenly flared into static. The flashing swarm of alien vessels appeared to have turned their mass-compression beam on the Confederation frigate. Transmissions from the *Frederick der Grosse* showed the escort crumpling like an aluminum can in a strong man's fist.

Meson beams.

The techs in *America*'s physics department had worked out that much, at least, though the weapon represented a technology the Confederation could not yet match. Mesons are extremely short-lived subatomic particles—hadrons. In nature, they transmit the strong nuclear force that joins quarks together to form nucleons—protons and neutrons— which in turn generates the residual strong interaction that glues nucleons together within atomic nuclei.

By accelerating mesons to near-c, the leaf ships could use relativistic effects to stretch the mesons' normal life spans of a few hundred millionths of a second. By flooding a target with high-energy mesons, the enemy caused the atomic nuclei of the target to collapse into micro-singularities, minute black holes that in turn merged with other micro-singularities nearby. Since mesons decayed into electrons and neutrinos, the beam also acted like a high-energy electron beam which could overload and overwhelm defensive screens.

Apparently, a certain large, critical number of the leaf ships were necessary to produce the beam in unison. Knocking down that number as quickly as possible gave the Confederation fleet its best chance of survival.

The *Badger* was completely out of action now, her port side crumpled from her shield-cap bow almost to her stern. Water sprayed in a silvery cloud into vacuum; X-rays flooded nearby space, the death shrieks of matter falling into the seething swarm of black holes now devouring her interior.

The enemy ship-cloud turned its weapon on the *Frederick der Grosse* next, but by this time the nuclear-tipped missiles launched moments earlier were beginning to flare around and within the leaf-ship school. Instantly, the school began scattering, dispersing into individual ships. Apparently, they could learn quickly as well.

At 1614 hours, the KK projectiles launched minutes before from *America*'s railguns began slamming into the large structure in the near distance. The facility, apparently some sort of deep-space dock or supply depot, was shredded by the massive incoming rounds, and the ships still moored there were smashed by the hi-vel projectiles coming in at better than fourteen kilometers per second.

Secondary explosions detonated within the disintegrating docking facility.

The cruiser attacking *America* and her escorts was in trouble as well, as internal gases erupted into empty space through house-sized breaches in her pressure hulls. The *Fitzgerald* was badly hurt, now, tumbling slowly, wreckage trailing from her spine. *America*'s particle-beam turrets continued to track and fire at the Sh'daar cruiser, slamming bolt after searing bolt past her failing shields and into her internal works. A savage, brilliant explosion finished the job, tearing the stricken vessel into hurtling half-molten fragments.

At this point, there was little for Koenig to do but watch the battle continue to play itself out. The *United States* was coming under heavy fire now, as was *America* herself. As the two largest and most massive vessels in the Confederation fleet, they were obvious high-priority targets for the enemy. The *Kinkaid* was taking heavy fire as well, both from enemy warships and from the remaining surface defense structures on AIS-1.

"How are the Marines doing?" Koenig asked his AI.

"All Crocodiles are down," the AI replied. "Murcheson reports that Objective Gold has been breached, and the Marines are entering the facility. It appears to be defended by armored combatants in large numbers—possibly combat robots. Casualties are high."

How long, Koenig wondered, should he press the attack? The tactical teams had discussed the possibility of having to break off and retreat. The problem was that at this point, retreat meant abandoning the Marines now on the dwarf planet's surface. That was not an option, so far as Koenig was concerned, unless the alternative was complete annihilation for the entire naval assault group.

The scattered swarm of leaf ships, working with an astonishing degree of coherence and coordination, had come back together, and had turned its meson beam against the *United States of North America*. The carrier's shield cap appeared to pucker near one rim, and a moment later a torrent of water, stored reaction mass and shielding, gushed into space in sparkling droplets that simultaneously boiled in hard vacuum and froze in the carrier's shadow.

"Make to *Adams* and *Trumbull*!" Koenig called. "See if they can help the *United States*!"

A second burst of coherent meson radiation slashed through the *United States*, crumpling the center of her shield cap, striking through and beyond to rip through her spine near her stores decks and power plants.

Nuclear detonations again tore through the leaf-ship cloud, its numbers dissolving in thermonuclear blasts of heat, light, and hard radiation.

But the damage had been done. As the *United States*' quantum-tap power plants failed and her shields collapsed, other Sh'daar warships closed on her like hungry pack predators, firing into her unprotected hull. Her hab modules broke off, ejecting, with their crews, clear of the wreckage.

But her almost one-kilometer length was being consumed in the raging inferno of megaton detonations. . . .

Chapter Twenty-Six

1 July 2405

Colonel John Murcheson
Objective Gold, AIS-1
Omega Centauri
1616 hours, TFT

The enemy troops in this dark and cavernous place seemed to move and respond like machines rather than organic beings, machines with lightning-fast reactions. Each was huge, standing ten meters tall when they stood on two legs, half that on four or six. The uppermost pair of limbs appeared to double as legs or as arms. Weapons, however, were built into the smooth surface of that massive armor; electron beams snapped from outstretched gauntlets like lightning, eerily silent in the hard vacuum, devastating when they struck Marine armor.

The Crocodile was no use in here. Guided by the flash of a Navy emergency transponder, the Marines had homed in on something like an immense dome of red metal eight kilometers across, a thick-walled fortress topped by spires and blisters and towers rising from the ice in a bristling forest. Radar and X-ray scatter mapping during their approach had revealed far more of the structure buried beneath the ice. The structure, evidently, was an enormous ship of some sort, a design utterly unknown to the Confederation grounded on the surface of the dwarf planet.

Weapons turrets on the surface had obliterated one of the four incoming Crocodiles with a bolt of artificial lightning, but the other Marine assault craft, coming in at extremely low, ice-skimming altitude and weaving back and forth, had managed to close with the grounded ship, been able to slip in so close that the enemy's weapons could not be brought to bear.

Under the cover of a barrage of particle-beam fire, the three surviving Crocodiles had slammed into the main body of the alien ship close together, their docking collars swiftly melting through a meter of solid metal and ceramic alloy to breach the hull and gain access to the interior. The breaching tunnel at the Crocodiles' bows had dilated open, and Murcheson and his Marines rushed through. They'd emerged inside an immense cavern, its overhead some twenty meters high, the far walls over a quarter of a kilometer distant.

The armored alien forms had attacked moments after the Marines gained entry.

"Spread out! Spread out!" Gunnery Sergeant Charlie McKean yelled. "Plasma gunners! Put fire on those black hats at two-one-one!"

Murcheson let the gunny do his job, using his M-64 laser carbine to snap off a quick quartet of shots at one of the armored giants. So far as he could tell, the weapon had no effect whatsoever.

There weren't many of the giants, thank the gods, but that armor, gleaming silver and highly reflective, was *tough*. It was just possible that the enemy troops carried some sort of screen generator as well; they certainly were big enough to do so. The assault team carried a mix of armaments—M-446 laser rifles and the heavier M-18 squad plasma weapons, for the most part, backed up by hand torches and pulse grenades.

The enemy troops were something like the Nungiirtok, another Sh'daar client species the Marines had clashed with more than once, but these were obviously of a different species and were carrying higher-tech gear. They moved with a smooth, flowing grace that seemed impossible for beings their size, and with a glittering precision that suggested highly sophisticated machines.

The Marines were at a considerable disadvantage here. The surface gravity of AIS-1 was only four tenths of a meter per second—about .04G. A Marine who together with her combat armor weighed 180 kilos on Earth weighed only 7 kilos here, but she still possessed 180 kilos of mass. Worse, things fell here with agonizing slowness, and when a Marine tried to dart for cover, he tended to launch himself into empty space and take a couple of seconds to drift back down.

And as they drifted, they were easy targets.

Within a moment or two, the Marines were scattering, taking shelter behind various odd-looking pieces of machinery or conduits growing between deck and overhead. Under the concentrated fire of a plasma gunner and three Marines with laser rifles, one of the giants was burned down, but the others were advancing steadily, laying down a heavy and relentless fire. Five Marines were down . . . six . . . and then it began to look as though the Marines had run up against more than they could handle.

Colonel Murcheson wondered if it would even be possible to pull back to the Crocodiles and break off the attack.

Trevor Gray
Omega Centauri
1617 hours, TFT

"That wormhole tunnel," Gray yelled into the darkness, "it's a kind of inside-out Tipler machine! It's a shortcut through space . . . but it's also a shortcut through time, isn't it? It brought us back in time! Maybe a long, long way into our past! And now that we're here, we could really screw your future! Isn't that right? . . ."

There was no response from the impenetrable darkness.

"Where are they?" he asked his AI.

"Unknown." The AI seemed to hesitate. "However, you should know that Confederation Marines have penetrated the chamber within which we are being held. A battle is being fought nearby."

Gray felt an electric thrill at the news. "Let me see!"

A window opened in his mind. The chamber within which the Starhawk had been trapped for the past twenty-two hours remained pitch-black . . . but flashes of light sparked and flickered in the distance, perhaps a hundred meters distant.

"Three Marine boarding craft penetrated the wall surrounding us—likely the hull of the large spacecraft that captured us yesterday. A number of Marines have entered this chamber and are engaged in combat with armored beings of an unidentified species."

Gray watched for several minutes as the AI directed high-magnification scanners at different scenes of the engagement. From his vantage point, it was difficult to see the Marines, but he did note several of the large defending figures, six-limbed and clad in bulky armor, revealed in infrared false colors.

"Can you pick up the Marine radio channel?"

"Affirmative."

He heard a click, then a confused tumble of voices. "Over here! Over here!"

"Watch it, Kaminski! Silver clunker moving on your position!"

"Plasgunners! Hit 'em! Hit 'em!"

"Take cover! The fuckers're getting too close!"

Gray heard a piercing scream that bubbled away into silence.

"Shit! Shit! Dougherty's down!"

"Corpsman, front!"

"Devon! McBride! Put down some fucking covering fire!"

Gray dialed back the channel volume. It sounded like the

Marines were in a hell of a tight spot. "How is auto-repair coming along?" he asked, thoughtful.

"Power plant, life support, and defensive screens are at one hundred percent," his AI told him. "Our maneuvering thrusters are at one hundred percent, but our gravitic drive projectors are showing readiness at twenty-five percent, no more. Nanomatrix hull morphing is inoperable, and we are frozen in combat mode. All missiles have been expended. PBP weaponry is inoperable. We have 793 KK Gatling rounds remaining."

"Can we hover?"

A pause. "Affirmative."

"Can we drift forward . . . turn . . . maybe change altitude?"

"Affirmative. But I would advise against attempting to fly this spacecraft inside the Sh'daar ship."

"Why? There's enough room. . . ."

A plan was coming together in Gray's mind.

But it might mean the end of his attempts to communicate with the Sh'daar.

CIC
TC/USNA CVS America
Omega Centauri
1617 hours, TFT

"Colonel Murcheson is reporting that the Marines have been stopped just inside the hull of Objective Gold," Sinclair told Koenig. "Major Hegelmen reports slow progress inside Objective Blue."

But Koenig scarcely heard. He was watching the final destruction of the *United States of North America*.

The carrier was wheeling end over end, falling past AIS-1, as parts of the hull, wracked by savage internal explosions, continued to fold and crumple into high-G singularities scattered across its broken and ravaged structure. The hab modules had gotten clear before the end, carrying perhaps half of her crew, but for personnel trapped in the spine, there'd been no possible escape. Carrier bridge towers were constructed with jettison rockets allowing emergency evacuations, but the destruction had overcome the *United States* too quickly for Captain Whitlow and his bridge and CIC crews to abandon ship. The *United States of North America* was a lifeless hulk.

It was a fate that *America* might soon share.

Elsewhere, the ships of CBF-18 exchanged fire with enemy warships at practically point-blank range. Fighters continued pursuing the leaf-ship swarms each time the formations began to re-form. Capital ships stood toe-to-toe with Sh'daar vessels, which in space combat meant anything less than ten thousand kilometers, and slugged it out with hivel guns, PBP and plasma cannon, and high-energy lasers.

How much longer should they stand their ground? . . .

Trevor Gray
Omega Centauri
1618 hours, TFT

"Main drive start-up!" Gray said, thoughtclicking an in-head icon. "Give me manual control. Just don't let me slam into anything."

"Monitoring attitude," his AI replied. "You are clear for lift and hover."

The Starhawk stirred, then lifted off the internal deck of the alien vessel. Local gravity, Gray noted, was only about four hundredths of a G; he needed only a trickle of power from his quantum taps into his drive projectors, focused at a point several meters above his head, to nudge the fighter, massing 22 tons but now *weighing* only 880 kilos, into the vast, dark emptiness of the huge chamber. He could feel the faint buzz of vibration as the microsingularity flickered on and off thousands of times per second, bootstrapping the fighter along, then holding it perfectly balanced between matching gravitational fields.

Five meters off the deck, he rotated his ship, bringing the prow around to face the combat now raging a hundred meters away. His ship was still in its combat configuration, molded into a flattened, dead-black fuselage with down-sloped wings to either side. His port-side wing had been chewed up pretty badly by the fringe of the Sh'daar matter-compression beam—the likely reason that both his particle beams and hull-morphing capability were down—but he was able to limp forward, silently drifting in the space between decks.

"Targeting! KK cannon!" he called, and a window opened in his mind, showing Sh'daar ground troops in false-color greens and yellows. A red targeting cursor closed on the nearest armored form and locked there, following it as it bounded across the deck in low, sprinting leaps.

"Check me!" he told his AI. "Quarter-second burst," he ordered. With fewer than a thousand rounds in his mass-shielded magazine, his weapon's twelve-rounds-per-second cyclic rate would exhaust his ammo in about one minute of steady firing. The AI, with faster reflexes than Gray's, could limit his bursts and conserve his ammo.

Gray thoughtclicked the trigger. The Starhawk's spinal-mounted Gatling RFK-90 kinetic-kill cannon spit three 400-gram slugs, each the size of Gray's little finger, giving the hovering fighter a sharp recoil nudge. In space combat, the weapon's muzzle velocity of 175 meters per second typically was added to the fighter's current speed, giving it a substantial load of kinetic energy. In here, with the fighter drifting nearly motionless, 175 mps was a pitifully weak offering . . . considerably less than the velocity of an old-fashioned rifle bullet.

The depleted uranium rounds each were considerably more massive than a rifle bullet, however, and they struck the target almost together, slamming into the armor.

With little effect. The Sh'daar trooper whirled, searching for the source of the triplet of rounds that had struck it. A moment later, Gray's screens flared with the impact of a bolt of high-energy electrons from the soldier's weapon. Other Sh'daar soldiers stopped their advance, turned, and added their firepower to the salvo.

"We need to boost muzzle velocity!" Gray yelled. "Dial it up!"

"I recommend against—"

"Just fucking do it! Firing!"

The Starhawk's KK Gatling could be powered up to slam out projectiles at anything up to five thousand meters per second. In normal space combat, with combatants traveling at tens of thousands of kilometers per second, such a high muzzle velocity was dangerous. It tended to overload critical weapon circuitry, and the recoil could throw a fighter badly out of control. And with the muzzle velocity added to the fighter's forward vector, the lower number was usually adequate.

Gray's KK Gatling spoke again, and this time the recoil was savage, shoving the fighter backward like a rocket burst. His AI compensated, juggling the gravitic projection to wrench the ship back under control before it could slam into something; three hi-vel rounds struck the targeted Sh'daar soldier with the sort of energy generally released only in combat in open space, punching through armor with the force of a small detonating warhead.

The armored figure came apart in a haze of vaporizing metal. Gray was already jockeying the fighter around, centering the target cursor on another moving, false-color figure and triggering a second burst. And a third. And a fourth . . .

Colonel John Murcheson
Objective Gold, AIS-1
1618 hours, TFT

"What the fuck was *that*?" a Marine yelled, ducking as fragments of high-velocity metal sparked off the deck and a nearby bulkhead. In front of her, one of the hulking, silver giants had just exploded, the upper half of its body disintegrating in hurtling bits of shrapnel.

"The zorchie's giving us a hand!" Murcheson yelled back. "Pour it on!"

And the Marines began advancing once more.

Trevor Gray
Omega Centauri
1619 hours, TFT

Gray nudged his Starhawk closer and yet closer to the embattled Marines, using the fighter's super-human senses to locate pockets of Sh'daar troops and target them. The enemy continued to concentrate their fire on him, but his screens shunted the particle bursts aside.

And then the enemy troops were running, bounding in long, low-G leaps across the deck and vanishing into dilated openings in the bulkheads.

"The Sh'daar wish to speak with us," his AI told him.

"The fucking Sh'daar can fucking *wait*," Gray replied. "Open a channel to the Marines."

"Channel open."

"This is Lieutenant Gray, Confederation Navy," he said. "Thanks for coming after me."

"This is Colonel Murcheson," a voice replied. "Thank you for the assist. We appreciate you joining the party."

"Anytime. I'm coming up to your perimeter now."

"Come ahead. It looks like the black hats have decided to call it quits . . . at least for the moment."

He let his fighter drift in for a landing in a brightly illuminated circle ringed by armed and black-armored Confederation Marines.

"Wait a sec, guys," he said as Marines moved forward to help him down from the cockpit. "Someone wants to talk to me."

And he opened another channel.

CIC
TC/USNA CVS America
Omega Centauri
1619 hours, TFT

"Admiral Koenig." The voice of Dra'ethde, one of the Agletsch on board, sounded in Koenig's mind. "A . . . simulation of an Agletsch that calls herself Thedreh'schul has opened a channel through the Sh'daar Seed residing within Gru'mulkisch and wishes to speak with you. She claims to represent the Sh'daar."

"I . . . see," Koenig said. Something inside him sagged. To have come so far . . . "They're offering us surrender terms?"

"No, Admiral. Unless we are mistaken, it appears that the Sh'daar are surrendering to *you*. Yes-no?"

Trevor Gray
Omega Centauri
1619 hours, TFT

The transition from flat-out combat, with Marines and Navy battling at the ragged edge of survival, to peace was so abrupt as to be disconcerting. Linked through his AI, Gray connected with the Sh'daar mind, and realized that the enemy had ceased fighting throughout the volume of the grounded ship, throughout the volume of local space surrounding AIS-1. A species capable of using *planets* as starships was requesting a cease-fire, requesting negotiations, possibly offering peace.

He stood once again on the barren surface of Heimdall. The simulated image of Frank Dolinar appeared before him, standing in front of the crumbling, rusty cliffs of an ancient Sh'daar computer.

A computer intended to last for eons, to house an artificial world, to create a refuge from the universe for a species capable of manipulating and re-engineering stars.

"It is imperative," Dolinar said . . . and this time he spoke in his own voice, rather than with that of an Agletsch translator, "that this fighting stop. Your actions threaten the Gateway of Creation."

And in the simulated sky behind Dolinar's image appeared the eerie wheel of the Six Suns, their harsh blue light glinting off steaming cliffs of ice.

"Those stars?" Gray asked. "How are we a threat to *those*?"

"Perhaps not to the stars themselves," Dolinar's image said, "but to the future beyond them."

Gray did not understand.

But he would.

4 July 2405

CIC
TC/USNA CVS America
Omega Centauri
1725 hours, TFT

There were levels, it seemed, of high-tech heaven. Apparently some of those levels could be interpreted as hells by the others. Three days after the Battle of the Six Suns, Koenig was still trying to understand.

The polity of alien civilizations collectively known as the Sh'daar, apparently, was made up of a number of organic species that were already extinct. They—or copies of "they"—existed still as patterns of electronic information, as data residing within a far-flung network of advanced and interconnected computers. The Sh'daar of today were entirely digital.

The young lieutenant, Trevor Gray, had provided the download channels of the Sh'daar. In simulation, Koenig had gone back through a series of virtual worlds, scenes revealing the history of the civilization now designated as the *ur*-Sh'daar, the original, organic forebears of the Sh'daar of today. He'd watched the civilization spanning its tiny, dwarf galaxy during its approach to the vast spiral of the Milky Way, watched its growing concern at having the bright, coherent light of a billion years of history spread out among the larger galaxy's immensity, scattered, and lost. He'd watched, fascinated, as the *ur*-Sh'daar collapsed entire suns into the fast-rotating cylinders, the inside-out Tipler machines that would give them shortcut access to the looming galactic spiral ahead.

And he watched as the member races of the *ur*-Sh'daar began vanishing, first one by one, then by the thousands, the millions, the billions, and the trillions, the individuals of a galactic culture evaporating into . . . otherness.

There were no clear, hard answers as to where they went, and it was possible that the question itself was meaningless. Higher dimensions, alternate worlds, and timelines, hidden pockets in space or behind space . . . it was probable that language—whether English, Agletsch, or *Drukrhu*, the artificial *Lingua Galactica* of verbal Sh'daar client species—simply didn't have the words or, more important, the *concept* to frame the reality. The Agletsch phrase was *Schjaa Hok,* the "Time of Change."

Humans called it transcendence, or the Technological Singularity, the point at which technology and organic intelligence so completely merged that they passed into what amounted to hyper-accelerated evolution, vanishing beyond the ken of those who remained behind.

And there *were* left-behinds. They called themselves, Koenig learned, *V'laa'n Grah*, which meant something approximately like "the Forsaken" or "the Abandoned Ones." Many were organic beings, but they tended to be flesh-and-blood individuals who'd rejected the accelerating trend of technological advancement in the specific sciences of genetics, robotics, information systems, and nanotechnology—the GRIN driver technologies long thought to be leading to Humankind's eventual and inevitable transcendence. The biological species left behind after the *Schjaa Hok* had gone into decline and become extinct within a few thousand years of the destruction of their civilization. All that had remained were the digital shadows of once flesh-and-blood intelligences, residing within the computer networks that spanned their tiny galaxy.

That remnant was determined to re-establish the collapsed *ur*-Sh'daar civilization and to keep it safe. To do so, they would establish colonies within the larger galaxy up ahead, make contact with as many civilizations native to that galaxy as possible, and attempt to enforce a certain stability, even *stasis*, in the pace of their technological advancement.

The vast majority of species throughout the larger spiral galaxy, it seemed, were nontechnic. They'd evolved in deep oceans, beneath planet-wide icecaps, or within anoxic atmospheres that forbade fires and the easy smelting of metals. Others, even native to worlds with atmospheres rich in oxygen, developed civilizations emphasizing philosophy or religion rather than science, meditation or contemplation rather than technology, the liberal arts rather than engineering. Those few who developed technic civilizations became the special targets of the Sh'daar infiltration. Most of these accepted computer implants, the Sh'daar Seed, each functioning as a node, a tiny component of a far vaster network intelligence.

And those who rejected the Sh'daar Ultimatum were exterminated. The Sh'daar still remembered, after all, how to gravitationally manipulate the cores of stars.

But what none of those targeted races had understood— none until now, at any rate—was that the Sh'daar's reach had not only been through space, but through *time*.

Officer's Lounge
TC/USNA CVS America
Omega Centauri
1850 hours, TFT

"It was staring at us the whole time," Koenig said. "We knew that Tipler machines allowed transit vectors through space *and* time."

"Einstein pointed out that it's not 'space and time,'" Commander Costigan pointed out. "It's *spacetime*. You can't separate the two."

Koenig was standing in the officers lounge one level below the bridge and CIC in *America*'s command tower. With him were Randy Buchanan, *America*'s skipper, and several members of the CIC command staff—Sinclair, Craig, and others. CAG Wizewski was there too, along with Costigan, who was head of the battlegroup's intelligence department. Suspended in the intergalactic Void in astonishing and high-resolution detail across the dome overhead glowed the Galaxy of Man.

The viewpoint was that of just 120 light years from *America*'s current position at the core of Omega Centauri. Shortly after the collapse of the Sh'daar defenses, Koenig had dispatched a mail packet to travel that distance, look around, and return. *This* was what it had seen.

"It takes some getting used to," Buchanan observed. "It doesn't feel like we're almost a billion years in the past."

"What is the past *supposed* to feel like, Randy?" Koenig asked. "It's just another set of coordinates in spacetime."

The intergalactic vista they were studying was hidden from the core of Omega Centauri, masked by the thick-packed wall of 10 million suns that comprised the dwarf galaxy's innermost core. Just 120 light years away from the Six Suns at the core's heart, the swarming stars thinned out drastically; the outlying reaches of Omega Centauri in this epoch consisted of another billion suns scattered as an irregular cloud 10,000 light years across at its widest.

In this epoch. A close astronomical survey of the spiral galaxy hanging above their heads had narrowed down "time-now" to a period some 876 million years before humans had evolved on Earth, give or take about a million years. Individual suns were lost among that whirlpool of 400 billion stars, and the actual location of Earth's sun within that vast swirl of starlight could not be determined. The actual date had been determined by comparing the relative positions of other, more distant, galaxies hanging in the sky—especially M-31 in Andromeda, M-33 in Triangulum, the Greater and Lesser Magellanic Clouds, and the fourteen dwarf galaxies that orbited the Milky Way. Galaxies move with respect to one another, and their relative positions in respect to one another within three-dimensional space were well understood by Confederation astronomers. The positions of M-31 and M-33 established in general where the other, smaller, closer galaxies ought to be to within 50 million years or so; the positions of the dwarfs allowed a closer calibration. During the time of man, one of the dwarfs—the Canis Major Irregular Galaxy—was in the process of being devoured by the Milky Way, while another, the Sagittarius Dwarf Elliptical, was 50,000 light years out and headed for an eventual collision. In this sky, both were considerably farther out, perhaps two or three orbits of the main galaxy in the past.

The galaxy that one day would be known as Omega Centauri was at this point just skimming above the sweep of the Milky Way's spiral arms, a few thousand light years above the galactic plane, and a mere hundred thousand years or so from collision. An exact demarcation in time was impossible, of course, since the star clouds that comprised entire galaxies didn't have sharp boundaries. The outer stars of both galactic systems were already merging, in fact, and Koenig could see where tidal interactions were sharply warping a portion of the Milky Way spiral, and were already seriously disrupting parts of Omega Centauri.

When the final coalescence occurred, most of Omega Centauri's suns and dust and gas would be stripped away, leaving the naked core to orbit through the Galaxy of Man as an apparent globular cluster.

Koenig was looking at the Humankind's galaxy as it had appeared almost 900 million years ago. Somewhere in that frozen maelstrom of stars and curling tentacles of interstellar gas and dust, of glowing nebulae and evolving suns overhead, lay hidden Sol and her retinue of planets. On Earth, at this moment, living cells in shallow, warm seas were learning how to congregate into multicellular colonies, the stromatolite reef builders were beginning to go into a long decline, and a few adventurous organisms were just at the point of inventing sex. Those two linchpins of evolutionary creativity would make possible the entire astonishing panoply of life on Earth that would follow. From here, the dinosaurs lay another 626 million years in the future, and humans some 250 million years after that. Such a stunning abyss of time left Koenig awed and a feeling a little lost.

And perhaps that's why the Sh'daar had elected to extend their reach through time, to an epoch in the remote future, when Omega Centauri had evolved—or *de*volved, rather— into a globular cluster orbiting within the hundreds of billions of stars of the Milky Way's galactic spiral.

The fact that the AIs had been able to identify Omega Centauri with the infalling dwarf galaxy of a billion years before remained an astonishing technological leap. Even across a billion years, it turned out that many of the cluster's stars retained the spectral fingerprints necessary to make the identification . . . that, and the cluster's unusual size. Even so, the leap felt more like intuition than science.

And AIs weren't supposed to indulge in such human ways of viewing the cosmos.

There'd been endless speculation about the true nature of the Sh'daar, of course, ever since their Ultimatum in 2367. An advanced civilization ruling the galaxy, existing for millions, even for hundreds of millions of years . . . no. Koenig never had liked the term *Sh'daar Empire*. The galaxy was simply too vast to permit such shallow and shortsighted terminology. Evidently, the Sh'daar had agreed with him. They'd hoped to infiltrate the future by bypassing almost a billion years, pruning away those species that threatened their plans, co-opting the rest into nonthreatening acquiescence. Koenig strongly suspected that the enigmatic Six Suns were a part of that, but he couldn't prove it. One interesting fact, though, had been pointed out by the astrogation department: the Six Suns no longer existed in Omega Centauri, the future version of the Sh'daar galaxy.

Stars that massive would die after a few million years, of course, going supernova. Still, the life spans of those artificially enhanced stars *could* have been extended by feeding in more stars. What had changed?

What were the Sh'daar—or the *ur*-Sh'daar, for that matter—really up to?

"What *I* want to know," Wizewski said, "is whether the bastards can be trusted."

"I'm not sure it's possible to trust another species," Koenig said.

"My, but aren't *we* cynical today," Buchanan said, laughing.

Koenig shrugged. "Hell, we still have trouble trusting members of our *own* species. And as for *the alien* . . . with an entirely different way of looking at the universe, a different concept of the natural order of things . . ."

"Exactly," Wizewski said. "Things we take for granted, they don't. Things they take for granted are sheer fantasy, aren't even *conceivable*, to us."

"But they seem willing to talk," Koenig said. "That's the important thing, at least for right now."

"I'm still trying to get a handle on the idea of us *joining* the Sh'daar," Katryn Craig said. "Becoming a part of their civilization."

"I suppose it makes sense," Wizewski said. "We're in on their secret. If we can't beat 'em, join 'em. And share the galaxy."

Koenig had his own ideas about that. How does an enemy bent on your absolute annihilation become a friend, an ally, almost literally within the blink of an eye?

After almost four decades of fighting the Sh'daar, could Humankind accept them as allies?

Should Humankind accept them as allies?

Ultimately, it would be the Confederation government that upheld the hastily cobbled-together treaty he'd presented to the Sh'daar . . . or struck it down. He suspected they would accept; after all, those government factions set on accepting peace at any price, including that of giving up GRIN technologies, had been in the majority back home. When the Fleet returned to Earth, Koenig would be giving them an option, a chance for peace without hobbling human technological advancement.

Koenig knew he would still resign his commission, though . . . and that they might well court-martial him before that happened.

Time would tell.

"It's not over yet by a long shot," he said after a long moment. "We don't know how all of the Sh'daar client races are going to react to upstart humans suddenly hobnobbing with their galactic masters. The Turusch, the Nungiirtok, the H'rulka . . . none of them think like humans. And there's a lot we still don't know about the Sh'daar themselves. Or the *ur*-Sh'daar, for that matter."

"We know they're afraid of our being *here*," Buchanan said. "Here and *now*, a billion years in our own past. We're going to need to learn more about that."

Three days ago, the battlegroup had been at the point of final defeat when the Sh'daar had linked in through the fleet's Agletsch liaisons and the fighter pilot, Lieutenant Gray, who'd been a prisoner within the ship designated as Objective Gold. They'd requested a cease-fire—"an immediate and unconditional end of all military operations," as they'd put it—in order to protect the integrity of spacetime.

The Sh'daar, it seemed, were as terrified of temporal paradox as they were of technological singularities.

The grandfather paradox. It was as well established in the realm of scientific myth as Schrödinger's cat. Build a time machine. Travel back to the past and kill your grandfather. You are never born, hence you can *not* travel back in time and your grandfather lives, so you *do* build the time machine and you *do* kill him, and on and on and irreconcilably on.

Modern quantum theory suggested that killing Granddad simply created a new universe, one in which the murderer had never been born. Paradox resolved.

But at the heart of Omega Centauri, under the fierce and unrelenting glare of the Six Suns, there was the possibility that the invading humans of CBG-18 would cause unexpected and unplanned-for havoc with the Sh'daar vision of the future. Exactly what that havoc might be was unknown, and the Sh'daar, understandably, were reluctant to discuss it. Perhaps there were other gates here, leading still further into the past—those two new TRGA wormholes in the skies of AIS-1, perhaps. Reinforcements had come through those gates; suppose the knowledge of the battle *here* and *now* changed decisions made in the past? The here and now Sh'daar might fear the possible resultant changes.

Or perhaps there was the possibility of making contact with the ur-Sh'daar. If the present Sh'daar feared transcendence and yet possessed time travel, why hadn't they gone back and talked things out with their ancestors?

Perhaps they had.

And what would changes in the here and now mean for that part of the Sh'daar intelligence living in the Milky Way in the far future, the era of Humankind, of the annihilation of the Chelk and how many other species, of the alliances with far-long civilizations like the Nungiirtok and the Agletsch, of the rise of Humankind itself and its expansion through the galaxy?

In any case, the presence of the human fleet here, at what appeared to be the central nexus of travel in both space and time that might win the Sh'daar immortality, had abruptly kindled their interest in working *with* humans, rather than trying to suppress them.

Koenig wasn't sure that Humankind was ready for this.

And yet, after thirty-seven years, *peace . . .*

Or at least a truce, and an opportunity to get to understand the longtime enemy a bit better. What Humankind needed now was time.

The new science of sophontology, he knew, had within the past few centuries acknowledged that there were more intelligent species upon the Earth than *Homo sapiens*, many more. There were, for instance, various species of monkeys showing the beginnings of evolutionary development first demonstrated by humans a few millions of years before. *Monkeys*. Not Humankind's closest living relatives, the apes, but monkeys. Certain species living in open savannah had learned to walk upright, at least for a few seconds at a time, in order to see above the high and all-encompassing seas of grass. Others had learned how to crack the husks of large, tough nuts with hammer stones in order to get at the soft meat within, and passed the knowledge down to the young of those species from generation to generation.

For the Sh'daar to agree to work with humans was roughly akin to humans sitting down with those tribes of clever monkeys and deciding together how best to run the world.

No matter. All the monkeys needed was some time.

And Carrier Battlegroup *America* had just purchased that time in blood.

"I wonder," Koenig said quietly, "what Geneva is going to think about *this*?"

"They'll call it," Buchanan told him, "Independence Day."

"Eh?"

"Look at the date."

Koenig had to query the fleetnet. July Fourth was not widely celebrated in the United States of North America nowadays, but it *had* been significant in the history of the old United States. Koenig read the download and chuckled. A union at any level with the Sh'daar might force a divided Humankind to unite at last. They would have to as they attempted to understand their new and still mysterious partners in spactime.

Union, and, at long last, freedom from war.

It was something worth fighting for.

Epilogue

Trevor Gray
Manhattan, USNA
Earth
0815 hours, EST

They'd waved him off when he approached the Statue of Liberty.

In the old days, he'd sometimes flown up there and found a perch on the statue's corroded head, overlooking the Ruins. But no longer, apparently. Things had changed.

Trevor Gray floated now above the calm and ancient expanse of New York Harbor not far from the submerged reef that had been Governor's Island, sitting astride a rented Mitsubishi-Rockwell gravcycle. North lay the Manhattan Ruins, once home, now a strangely alien expanse of vegetation-covered mounds and cliffs of crumbling concrete. A kilometer to the west, the Statue of Liberty gleamed in a clear, bright morning sun. The nanostructor crew hadn't let him approach because they were restoring her. Her upraised arm had already been recovered from the waters of the bay and mounted once again on the stump of her shoulder, and a crawling skin of nanobots were busily cleaning corroded copper, filling in the cracks and pits and bringing back the golden luster of new metal.

Lady Liberty. She carried the promise of restoration for Manhattan as well.

Four days ago, the battlegroup had returned from Omega Centauri T-Prime and, after a nervous confrontation with a waiting Confederation fleet near the orbit of Neptune, had been at last cautiously welcomed back to Earth as returning heroes. There was still talk of a court-martial for Admiral Koenig, but Gray doubted that anything would come of that other than an official pardon. The general public, at least, had not seemed to mind CBG-18's sudden change in status from rebels to victorious heroes. And the Confederation Senate knew good publicity when it saw it.

For Admiral Koenig had ended the interminable war with the alien Sh'daar, and he and those with him were being feted with parades and official receptions, with speeches, with medals, with full interactive netcasts, and with spectacular celebrations that promised to be going strong for the rest of the year. A big ceremony had been scheduled for the 21st at the Eudaimonium Arcology overlooking the Palisades. Gray was supposed to receive a medal from President DuPont himself—the Star of Earth. Koenig would be receiving the newly created Order of the Galactic Star, while Lieutenant Schiere, Lieutenant Ryan, and a dozen others would receive the Navy Cross. Even the two Agletsch, Dra'ethde and Gru'mulkisch, would be getting special commendations created by fiat by the Confederation Senate just for this occasion.

There would be posthumous awards as well, for so very, very many. . . .

Bewilderingly, astonishingly, the Sh'daar War was over.

And with the War's end, a feverish period of rebuilding and reconstruction had begun, as though both North America and the Pan-European Federation had suddenly decided to emerge from a long and groggy malaise. Mail packets had brought word of the Battle of Omega Centauri back to Sol weeks before, and the news appeared to have galvanized the civilian governments. The Periphery was to be reclaimed, and the rebuilding had begun. Eight kilometers to the south, the centuries-old Verrazano Sea Gates were being repaired. When they were operating once more, they would rise above the surface of the lower bay and, together with the Throgs Neck Dam north of Long Island, they would block off the Atlantic and allow the ruins of New York City—half submerged for over three centuries, scoured by tidal waves in 2132 and again in 2404—to be drained.

And then the real rebuilding could begin.

Gray had mixed feelings about the whole project. The people he'd known, the Prims he'd grown up with in the Manhat Ruins, all were gone. Angela, his former wife, was gone. His old life as a Prim was gone.

And maybe it was all for the best.

"Hey, Sandy!"

He turned at the call. Two more gravcycles were approaching out of the south—and astride them were Shay and Rissa Schiff. He waved.

"What the hell are you doing up here, Sandy?" Rissa wanted to know.

"I came up for a look at the old haunts," he said. "They won't be here much longer, they say."

"They're doing the same to cities throughout the Periphery," Shay told him. A fresh breeze off the Atlantic tugged at her short hair. "Washington. Boston. There's even talk of raising Miami."

"Think you'll go back to Washington, Shay?"

She shook her head. "Shit, I'm never going back. Home is *here*. With you guys."

"You're staying in, aren't you Sandy?" Rissa asked. "In the service, I mean."

The nickname still felt . . . odd. Some of the others in the squadron had started calling him Sandy after his sandcaster tactic last year, but it hadn't really caught on until his return from AIS-1 with the Marines.

Now *everyone* was calling him that. Even his old nemesis Collins.

"I haven't decided yet," he told her.

With the end of the war, there'd been, naturally, talk about downsizing the fleet. Gray could get an early out, resign his commission. He'd be a civilian again—this time a full citizen of the United States of North America.

But what, he thought, would he *do*? Oh, he'd be able to download a new career of some sort, to be sure. There'd be plenty of work available with Reconstruction. But the really interesting stuff going on now was *out there*. With liaison teams headed out to Omega Centauri, both at T-Primus, in the distant past, and T-Nunc, the Omega Centauri of the present day. There were rumors of a Sh'daar civilization in the present-day cluster, and even scuttlebutt about attempts to contact the slow-lived digital inhabitants of Heimdall and other scattered Sh'daar worlds.

The exploration of new worlds, civilizations, and concepts promised to take centuries.

Civilizations, Gray thought, change. They grow, they age, they decay, and eventually, inevitably, they die, passing into extinction. The lucky ones are able to transmit their heritage, their history, their culture, and their science and art on to the younger cultures that come after them. The Confederation, he knew, had very nearly grown old before its time, grown old, acquiescing to decay and going under. The victory, the stunning, impossible victory at Omega Centauri Primus 900 million years in the past appeared to have given the Confederation the promise of a bright, new future.

It remained to be seen what they would do with it.

And, he thought, people changed as well. Sometimes the change, as with Angela, his once-wife, hurt.

But it was possible to grow out of the pain and into joy, too.

Gray looked at the two women and grinned at them. During the past months, out at Omega Centauri Primus and during the voyage back, Trevor Gray had managed to lose his old prejudice against the polyamory of Earth's culture. Maybe that meant he wasn't a Prim any longer.

"I haven't decided," he said, repeating himself, "but I'm with Shay. I feel like I belong here. Let's go home."

And the three turned on their gravcycles and arrowed toward the Giuliani Spaceport, north of Manhat.

A shuttle was waiting there to take them back to the Quito Synchorbit, and star carrier *America*.

Home.

IAN DOUGLAS's
MONUMENTAL SAGA
OF INTERGALACTIC WAR
THE INHERITANCE TRILOGY

STAR STRIKE: BOOK ONE
978-0-06-123858-1

Planet by planet, galaxy by galaxy, the inhabited universe has fallen to the alien Xul. Now only one obstacle stands between them and total domination: the warriors of a resilient human race the world-devourers nearly annihilated centuries ago.

GALACTIC CORPS: BOOK TWO
978-0-06-123862-8

In the year 2886, intelligence has located the gargantuan hidden homeworld of humankind's dedicated foe, the brutal Xul. The time has come for the courageous men and women of the 1st Marine Interstellar Expeditionary Force to strike the killing blow.

SEMPER HUMAN: BOOK THREE
978-0-06-116090-5

True terror looms at the edges of known reality. Humankind's eternal enemy, the Xul, approach wielding a weapon monstrous beyond imagining. If the Star Marines fail to eliminate their relentless xenophobic foe once and for all, the Great Annihilator will obliterate every last trace of human existence.